Ania was very young, and Jean Paul that summer was already almost forty. An artist, a creator of puppets and puppet shows, Jean Paul was amusing, imaginative, kind. But to him she was only a child. He never knew that she would remember these months forever as the summer of first love.

"The subject of my novel," Marguerite Dorian once wrote, "is the story of the voyage from childhood into adulthood, its accidents and discoveries on the way. Yet it is also about death and love and foreign cities, about the change of seasons and about a necessary sadness."

Acclaimed for its depth of insight and lyrical power, *A Ride on the Milky Way* has been compared by critics to the works of Elizabeth Bowen, Anais Nin and John Updike. Most recently, film rights to the novel have been sold to the producer of "The Umbrellas of Cherbourg," and the motion picture is scheduled for release in 1970.

Recent Ballantine Books
You Will Enjoy

A RIDE
ON THE MILKY WAY

Marguerite Dorian

BALLANTINE BOOKS • NEW YORK

The author wishes to thank Arthur Fields, the editor who came along for this ride and lent her his knowledge of steering by the stars.

This edition published by arrangement with
Crown Publishers, Inc.

First Printing: February, 1969

Printed in the United States of America.

BALLANTINE BOOKS, INC.
101 Fifth Avenue, New York, N.Y. 10003

To my father

PART I *

Nous sommes écartelés entre l'avidité de connaître et le désespoir d'avoir connu. (We are torn between a craving to know and the despair of having known.)

—RENÉ CHAR, *Feuillets d'Hypnos*

* * * *

JEAN PAUL CAME TO BUCHAREST at the beginning of summer; Ania was nine that year. But before he made his appearance in town on their very street, before his first visit to the house, he was preceded by that lovely disorder, that warm confusion, which was so often to make Mother frown. (Mother was the only one who could argue with Jean Paul. She could even lecture him. He would tilt his head back and look at her teasingly under his short, straight eyelashes; but she was not intimidated.)

He did not come until the beginning of June, yet all through that long, warm spring, their house—an old and dignified one with four tall windows on the street and an old-fashioned, stained-glass fanlight over the entrance door— had radiated a strange impatience. But this restlessness, you understood much later, must have been the anticipation of his laughter in the rooms, the sort of laughter that was to startle draperies and make the silver dishes shiver on the glass shelves. A premonition of his presence was in the air. The fingertips of the fringed tablecloths quivered; a capricious shadow played on the Venetian blinds during the afternoon siesta; and even the wet cherries left over from lunch in the green dish on the serving table, even the cherries would wink mischievously at Ania whenever she crossed the dark dining room, would invite her complicity in an unknown secret.

The summer before that and the one before, all the summers Ania could remember, had always come in furtively. The new season would insinuate itself into the old one, infusing it with summer noises and summer colors, slanting the shadows to a summer angle, until, vanquished by

9

that soft persuasion, spring would lie down spent, wasted. The lilac bloomed, but that was not quite it, quite summer. The garden looked adolescent, its shrubbery a hesitant green. The plums on the plum tree were still unripe, and to eat them Ania had to hide behind the lilac bush with Sonica, her friend next door.

"If I catch you eating green plums once more, I'll tell Madam! D'you want to get sick? That's why you're so small and green!" Tatiana, the red-haired maid they had that year, always managed to find the evidence—a wet plum pit—lost in the gravel, and she was not noted for tact. Hurt, Ania consulted the bathroom mirror: she wasn't green; she was only a bit skinny—her socks wouldn't stay up on her thin legs. But the plums had an acid, cold taste which puckered the lining of her mouth, a green taste of unachieved season. She couldn't give up the vice.

The lilac dried; spent, its pale silken glory hung on cobwebbed branches, and summer felt close. The first watermelon carts crossed the town, and the farmer praised his melons aloud at the back door, hugged them close to his open shirt, checked their ripeness, bending to listen to their green squeak like a fastidious musician bent over his violin. Patiently his horse waited in the sun, shook a hairy ear to chase away the sticky, green summer flies. At noon the light hung from the sky—a giant chandelier with glass beads swaying over the city—making the high noon gleam and sparkle, intensifying it on myriad cut-glass surfaces. Guests came to dinner, and the table was set outside in the garden under Ania's window. The canna flowers planted around the table, which Father had brought home early in spring swathed in newspapers and looking forlorn, now opened the green sheaths of their huge buds and nodded red feathers. Crazy moths circled the white tablecloth, hit the tall glasses with a velvety noise, died in grand style, drowned in wine. At dessert, Tatiana appeared out of the darkness, carrying the first melon of the season, a fat king on a copper plate, to be sliced by Father. And it was this, year after year—the familiar motion of Father's hand skillfully carving two little lids at the ends of the watermelon; the knife plunging deep, splitting the green house open; the red of the pulp like a great laughter exploding through the black teeth of seeds— this was what made the real summer begin.

BUT the summer Jean Paul came to their house started differently. All sorts of signs predicted an upheaval. The late spring nights were intent and heavy, like real summer nights, and a swollen, knowledgeable-looking moon eyed Ania through the embroidered pattern on her curtains. The season swelled brusquely, disturbingly. That year something new and unsettling hid under the usual little domestic miracles, under the yearly routine of buds opening and leaves unfurling.

Strangely enough, confirmation of this came from Tatiana. For quite a while before Jean Paul came to the house, Ania had begun to feel she was undependable. Once her plump person had radiated a feeling of security, but starting that summer it became less sure. You had to be alert. To look out for accidents. And even the innocent routine of combing Ania's hair became full of complications.

Tatiana did Ania's hair every morning. One ribbon she held between her teeth while adroitly tying the other around the tip of a thin, sun-bleached pigtail. (It was too tight; tears came to Ania's eyes.) Then she would contemplate her achievement and plant, in conclusion, two bobby pins on either side of the curly head.

In summer the operation took place in the kitchen doorway on the steps, and all through it there rose from Tatiana's blouse the smell of laundry soap mixed with a strange larder odor. The smell was familiar but somehow indelicate. Ania was almost certain you were not supposed to talk about it. But what was it? What was it? She would assist Tatiana, gravely holding the brush and comb, while her nostrils quivered and followed the high and low tide of the smell. And then one day she knew. Mountain cheese! That was what Tatiana smelled of. Mountain cheese! Yet the discovery only reinforced Ania's embarrassment, and although the smell wasn't completely unpleasant she rejected it, and with it the burden of obscure and embarrassing thoughts it could bring.

But it was too late to discard them. As she stood there submissively and the comb ran a straight part in her hair, the memory filled her mind. She once saw Tatiana through the

11

window of her room washing herself at the washstand. Who would have thought that under her old dress Tatiana was ivory-like, the sweet color of mountain cheese? Only the parts touched by the sun, her arms and her neck, were red and freckled. Then she lifted one of the heavy ivory breasts in her hand. Like an animal, the breast put a pink snout out on her palm. She weighed it thoughtfully, cautiously put it back, with the same careful gesture with which she bought honey melons in the market. Then she pulled the straps of her chemise up on her shoulders and became the everyday Tatiana with red neck and red arms. In the chipped mirror over the washstand she discovered Ania watching her; undisturbed, she smiled at her with red eyebrows and red eyelashes, like a glowing tomato.

Tatiana was the queen of their street. Whenever she stepped out of doors the street surrounded her with a curious sort of homage. It was expressed a bit roughly and impetuously, yet it was homage just the same, Ania felt, trotting at Tatiana's side toward the grocer's shop, her pigtails braided tightly. (Tatiana had a strong, authoritative walk which shook her blouse, her cheeks and her hair bun. The occasional hesitation in her step was due only to the shoes she wore when she went out, an old pair of white brocade dancing shoes Mother had given her. The heels were too high for Tatiana so she sawed them off with the big saw in the cellar. "They look so good on you," Ania would say with admiration—only sometimes Tatiana would lose her balance, and lean precariously backward, trying to retain her dignity. The bare wood of the amputation showed up badly under the white and gold brocade, but Tatiana loved them and wouldn't go to the grocery in her old slippers.)

Had other people seen Tatiana washing herself in her room? Because everyone seemed to know how she was under her blouse stained at the armpits with two dark half-moons. And whenever Tatiana went out the whole street grew hands to reach for the treasures she hid inside her blouse. In the grocery, especially if the grocer was there, she had to walk around holding a protective arm over her breasts (she looked like a hen with a fractured wing). Mr. Totis, the grocer, would wait patiently, his solemn belly wrapped in a white apron. His heavy, opaque ears must have been made in a hurry out of some rubbery, unpleasant material and their seams left unfinished; they would always get very red, revealing his intentions. When Tatiana stood at the counter, her arms loaded, the expression on his face changed from solemn concentration to a cunning shrewdness, his ears flared up and his hand jumped to the unguarded treasure. Tatiana would jump back, her buttocks quivering, and she would give a deep, indignant coachman's shout: "Well now! You ... Miss Ania's looking!" Yet the last part always ended on a note of satisfaction.

Miss Ania stood outside on the sidewalk frowning severely, rubbing one of her ankles with her sandal. Taking a deep breath, she retreated inside her body until she felt lifeless, sexless, like a cardboard form under her cotton dress. She refused Tatiana's zestful shout. When leaving, Ania was always presented with a handful of cherries by Mr. Totis. She accepted them, but she couldn't eat them—she sensed an invitation to complicity; they were still warm from his hand.

Once she gathered all her courage and asked Tatiana without looking at her, "Why do you let him pinch you?"

"Who, me?" Tatiana was sincerely surprised. "An old goat, that's what he is!" she added, pulling her blouse down over her breasts with dignity.

How did Tatiana look from the waist down?

"Be quiet now or your part'll be crooked," Tatiana's voice would say from somewhere up above when Ania shifted from foot to foot trying to evade the inquisitive question; and to ensure the success of the operation, Tatiana would draw Ania's head against her calico-wrapped belly. Ania tried pressing it with her forehead. It answered elastic and hot, like a rubber ball warmed by the sun. A little lower, where her chin rested, Ania felt something like a rustle of dry grass, a hot dampness radiating out of a calyx sticky with summer light and buzzing bees. Tatiana went without panties in summer. Mother gave her two large pairs—they looked like bear underwear. Tatiana admired them spread out on the kitchen table but declared she was going to wear then only on Sundays.

The young boy who helped in the grocery, and the milkman, and the mailman who brought her a bunch of lilac, all, all of them seemed to know how Tatiana was under her dress. If a new delivery man appeared at their kitchen door looking busy and indifferent to Tatiana's treasures, as soon as Tatiana got close to him he would seem quite eager to find out about them. That was why you had to be alert. To watch out for accidents.

Ania never would have thought this could happen to Ion, the vegetable man. He was so tall and slender, like a girl, under the yoke he carried on one shoulder. The coarse peasant shirt he wore was open down the front, and when he bent over the baskets she could look inside and wonder at how white and polished his chest was, far into the deep-blue shadow where his belt ran. He put such sober passion into the way he sang the praises of his vegetables, such eagerness into fishing out of the mysterious depths of his belt that soiled cloth bag with a long, flabby neck like a hen's and counting the change, that he was too busy to notice Tatiana. He had no time for social amenities, and his manner was businesslike; he kept his pointed fur hat on even on the hottest summer days. Besides Tatiana always looked sleepy at that early hour and yawned lustily, displaying a complete lack of interest in her morning visitor. Until the day Mother had to stay in bed with the flu.

Tatiana looked particularly busy that morning, running in and out of Mother's bedroom, her forehead puckered by the added responsibilities. She combed Ania's hair hurriedly in the kitchen. The pots were already boiling on the stove, hissing in horror, their lids making little frightened jumps, calling Tatiana for help. And the cat, its breakfast forgotten in the middle of the domestic upheaval, was trying to rub itself against Tatiana's feet. A slipper shoved the animal away, lifting it under the belly and dropping it at a distance, where it made a soft noise like a tossed ball of wool.

Ion good-naturedly carried the vegetables into the kitchen while Tatiana struggled with the list Mother had made for her. She scratched her bun with a pencil and was suddenly struck by doubt. "What about eggplants? Does Madam want any today? Miss Ania, run inside and ask her." And happy to be entrusted with the mission, Ania ran in through the living room. Disturbed by her eagerness, the mirrors frowned, rippled their waters, and through the door she had banged open, the summer morning burst in, made the sleepy house rock back and forth, rinsed the rooms with sun.

She returned with the answer by the front door, circling the house, because she liked the noise her sandals made on the gravel. And then she saw them. Through the kitchen window. Ion was kissing Tatiana.

She had not seen people kissing like that before and at first she thought they were fighting. But Tatiana didn't look as if she was going to scream. She had her back turned to the window. Ion held her head in his right palm the way one holds the head of a new-born baby, as if Tatiana's red head with the disheveled bun suddenly had become too heavy for her neck. His other hand moved slowly in circles on her buttocks in a sweet, cautious rhythm. It was as if Tatiana had grown another head at her mouth, another head, with blond, close-cropped hair—his fur hat was on the table. It was as if she had grown another head and two more hands—a two-headed monster, a monster quivering, muttering, panting. The monster rocked on its four feet, something stirred inside it, and its two halves split apart. Tatiana, still holding a potato in her hand, stood there gulping air through her mouth. Ion took back his head and his hands and put his fur hat on.

Ania didn't have the courage to talk to them. Running back into the house, she shouted at Tatiana through the open door of the dining room, "No eggplants today," and then ran outside, her pigtails whipping her neck, out, out, far out to the end of the yard, behind the hen house. Panting, she leaned her back against the rotten wood and waited for something to happen. But she couldn't cry. Her legs were trembling. The hen house looked out at her with hen eyes ringed by red flesh. Scrawny violet necks throbbed softly.

At the end of the garden, in that hot wave smelling of hen droppings, it was suddenly summer. Under her closed eyelids, she felt the season growing, swelling, reaching up into the sky. The world was steamy with idleness, ripe, indifferent to the mysteries of the future. The earth turned lazily, carried along the garden, the house, the morning. . . . The trees turned too in the hot silence, their crowns full of sticky, hairy caterpillars. Drowsy with summer, the caterpillars fell thudding on the earth. This is how the real summer started that year, and shortly after that Jean Paul came.

HE MUST HAVE MOVED INTO THE OLD HOUSE late one evening, because nobody—not even Mr. Totis, who stood at the door of his grocery to keep an eye on events, his belly sticking out into the summer light—not even Mr. Totis knew when it happened. The boards closing the fence were still nailed on, but the gate was half open now, the old padlock had been removed and the place where it had hung for such a long time showed a scar of rust. One day at noon Jean Paul was seen in the grocery. He looked rather like a foreigner, wore a leather pouch hanging from one shoulder and was followed closely by Picu, Sonica's mongrel. He stopped and talked to Picu in French—he always reverted to French when he talked to animals—bent, and scratched the dog's ears until Picu, whose rough life was devoid of tenderness, collapsed on his back, his shaggy paws up, and fell in love with him at once.

He didn't wear a coat, didn't have a wedding band and was a late riser. This was all the information the neighborhood could gather during his first week there. Why should a man who spoke French rent that old, run-down house, too large for a bachelor to live in? Mr. Totis now spent all his time out on the sidewalk, looking like a penguin in shirt sleeves—a penguin who had forgotten to put his black tailcoat on; he would stand between the basket of tomatoes and the one of carrots and celery and look expectantly up the street.

Ania knew the old house. She used to climb halfway up the fence and hang there, smelling the garden. (Later, Tatiana would search patiently for the splinters in Ania's palms, fishing them out delicately with the tip of a needle. "Now spit on it!" Tatiana would advise professionally; she did not believe in disinfectants.) The house was hidden by a chaotic garden stirred into green waves by the special sort of wind it seemed to harbor. Toward the middle of the garden, where the bushes became thicker, the green changed to violet and gave off a strange smell of medicine in restless, quivery ripples. It smelled of tree holes; of bitter, damp forest; of earth freshly dug up; of mold; of wet bricks. "What is that smell, Sonica?" Ania would ask when Sonica agreed to come along and smell the garden. "I don't smell anything." "Now, Sonica! Now! Do you feel it? It's like medicine!" "Maybe there's someone sick in the house," Sonica shrugged. But the house seemed abandoned; the gate was always locked. In the weeds the darkness winced as blue lizards swished through, and once a fat rat, grave and slow like a boyar in a fur coat, crossed the garden and disappeared inside a bush. He left his pink, naked tail notched with rings outside, and then remembered it and pulled it inside the bush with a nervous tug.

"That house is going to collapse one day!" Mr. Totis commented, as he pressed down the lever of the bottle of *sifon* with a virile gesture to make sure it worked, before selling it to Tatiana. The bottle snarled, then coughed, spitting carbonated water on the sidewalk. "No one in his right mind would rent such a place!" He was burning with curiosity. He would have liked the roof of the house to fall down (gently, of course) and reveal the stranger in his bed, stripped of all his mysteries.

"Don't you go near that place again, Miss Ania!" instructed Tatiana, alarmed by the news she gathered in the grocery.

"I am not going," Ania protested, but toward mid-morning she always felt a pang of longing for the old garden, like an intoxicating desire for a journey abroad, for another landscape, and she ran there, her heart pounding with terror at the breach of Tatiana's strict discipline.

Tatiana had been supervising Ania's education even more intently than usual during the summer vacation. Swinging back and forth on the iron gate, Ania could see everything that happened on their street, and Tatiana, with considerable experience in neighborhood matters, felt her responsibilities keenly. Lately she seemed especially determined to protect Ania from a row of sweet secrets in which she herself obviously delighted. The hasty way she drew a curtain between Ania and the grownups' world was embarrassing. "This is not for children!" Or addressing the other party, "Hey, you ... Miss Ania's looking!" What happened when Miss Ania wasn't looking was left to your imagination.

Tatiana even seemed to know certain things about Sonica. In the afternoon Baba, Sonica's fat cook, would sometimes leave her kitchen and visit Tatiana, bringing along the box of coffee beans and the coffee mill. She would sit in the shadow of the dark cupboard, the coffee mill planted in the valley of her blue apron between her heavy thighs. The monotonous circle her plump hand made with the handle was reflected in the big copper kettle, the propped-up copper tray and the mortar on the shelf. It amplified her presence in the kitchen. Baba seemed to be made out of many soft, ripe pumpkins under her cotton dress. She said to Tatiana, "Our Miss Sonica, she knows she's a beauty. . . . She's got such ... You should see her how she looks at men! ... Oh, what a ... she is going to be!" Tatiana's happy tomato face took on a great air of complicity. "Miss Ania," she would say indignantly, discovering her in the kitchen doorway, "do you have to play right here? Isn't the yard big enough for you?" The mystery was unsolved. What was Sonica going to be? Baba looked huge, obscene, as she sat there in the somnolent kitchen, her thighs spread lazily apart. Her shadow moved over the shined bottoms of the pans hung on the wall; she laughed, and Sonica's future was obscured. A golden tooth shone inside her black, bottomless mouth.

But in fact there was no need for alarm. The latest news Tatiana brought from the grocery didn't tell much about the new neighbor.

"What do you think a man like that does for a living?" Tatiana shrugged. She was in a hurry that morning. But Mr. Totis kept twirling the toothpick between his front teeth. He was lost in thought. His old mother, who kept house for him in the small rooms at the back of the store, shouted through the open door over the sizzling of the food she was frying that the man must have moved in without any furniture and that was why they didn't see the moving van. The old house must have been rented furnished.

This piece of evidence startled everyone and gave their

speculations new life. But what sort of a man was he, without furniture, moving in just like that, hands in pockets? At ten o'clock, the information was promptly delivered to Baba's kitchen door, together with her groceries. "Is he young?" Baba wanted to know, meditatively holding the bag of sugar against her soft belly. But the conversation was cut short by Fräulein Cuna, Sonica's German governess and Baba's great enemy, who checked personally on every delivery, insisting that the food be properly wrapped. (The way Mr. Totis had of throwing a lump of cheese on the scales and sucking his fingers while he read the weight with narrowed eyes gave Fräulein Cuna indigestion.) "Is he young?" Baba asked again, regretfully parting with the subject. "I think so," the delivery boy said, lifting the empty crate onto his shoulder, yet his hesitation put Baba in a reflecting mood and the sauce for the roast came out much too thick that morning. Why wasn't the boy sure? Either you're young or you aren't.

"You stay away from that place until we know what sort of man he is!" Tatiana concluded upon her last trip to the grocery, and after that Ania couldn't tell Tatiana she knew what sort of man he was. He had an attic room with a glass ceiling, and that very morning she and Sonica had sat there on two small chairs and eaten green plums, which he had passed around in a glass dish openly, not like some forbidden, smuggled treasure. His name was Jean Paul.

"You stay away from that place until we find out what sort of man he is!" And it was impossible to reach past Tatiana's severity and explain to her you'd been there. Her heart heavy, Ania retired to the hen house; chewing at a tendril of grape vine, she had an imaginary but comforting conversation with Tatiana. She knew what Tatiana would have asked her.

How did you get inside his house?—Invited.—What do you mean, "invited"? Did he invite you over the telephone? (Here Tatiana's mouth would have stretched into a scornful smile.) —No, we were in his garden when he came in—Aha! Didn't I tell you to keep away? Isn't Miss Sonica forbidden to play on the street?—Yes, she is, but Fräulein Cuna spent the whole morning in the attic putting mothballs in things and so we

19

thought we'd just run to the old house and back.—You're the one who starts trouble, Miss Ania! So how did you get in?—The gate was open; it felt as if nobody was home. Sonica was scared to go in. (She was five years older than Ania, five years and three days, yet she was scared of the silence under the trees. Twice Ania had to hush her when her dress got caught in the thistle's teeth. They ducked under the bushes and found themselves under a big walnut tree. That's what made the smell of iodine: green walnuts rotting on the damp earth. The house came out from behind the tree suddenly, as if to scare Sonica, dressed up in ivy like a dragon covered with green scales. The front door had a broken window, and a white curtain waved to them like the sleeve of a friendly ghost.)—But when did he invite you, if nobody was home?—He came back just when we were about to leave. We saw him coming in from the street and we didn't have time to get away.—Well, what's he like? Is he young?—Young? I don't really know. Maybe he is.—What *is* he like then?—He had a leather pouch hanging from one of his shoulders and there were groceries inside it. He had velvet pants on.—Velvet? (Again Tatiana's scornful smile.) Come now! Is he a king or something? How did you know it was velvet in the first place?—It was! Ask Sonica. Brown velvet.—Wasn't he angry to find you in his garden?—No, he was glad; he really was. He said his name was Jean Paul and asked us where we lived and if we'd come to look at the sundial.—What sundial?—There's a sundial up under the roof. It has little things painted on it in gold and blue where the hours should be. He told us how it worked. Then I said, "Is that a cuckoo-clock window over there?" Because I thought it looked like one. I expected a real cuckoo, a live one, to push the shutters open and announce the time. (Jean Paul looked at her for a second, his eyes like two dry black jumping raisins, and she noticed his short, perfectly straight eyelashes. Then he had burst into a big laugh, a size too big for such a small man.) "Oh, that's my attic window," he said. "Come and have a look at it." So you see, we *were* invited.—Well, what sort of man is he?—Oh, he's a very nice sort of man.

(Ania kicked a stone with the tip of her sandal, and with it a memory that had come back to her. It wasn't much, a little asperity, something like a funny spot felt as you ran your finger over the flawless surface of their visit. Sonica had smiled at him. Well, everybody knew Sonica was beautiful. Ania herself used to tell Mother, "Sonica is like a big, shiny chestnut, isn't she?" "She is beautiful!" Mother would answer seriously, as if Sonica's beauty were something to be careful with, like a pair of scissors or a thin, sharp, trembling blade. There was a dark, downy dimple in Sonica's left cheek and she could make it come and go at will. But this time her smile had been different. Her lips had parted and under them her white teeth had opened too, as if she meant purposely to show him everything, the soft lining of her mouth and the intimate sight of a pointed young canine to which a bubble of clear saliva clung. Jean Paul had looked surprised for a second, and then enchanted and satisfied as if—as if that smile had been his personal achievement.)

He went through all his pockets with the short, quick motions of a forgetful squirrel, looking for the front-door key. "I haven't got it," he said, and looked amused by this, and they had to walk round the house, crushing weeds under their feet, and go in through the back door. They stepped down into the dark kitchen, and green summer flies, disturbed from their meal on piled-up dishes in the dirty sink, protested and flew away. The bottom of a copper pan rose on the sooty wall like a southern moon before they plunged into the dark corridor smelling of mold and dust and pine wood. The house was somnolent; old furniture spied at them through open doors as they passed by, and in the living room the chairs and sofa wore white shrouds, like ghosts of furniture. "I haven't had time to clean this place," he said. "Come, I want to show you something in the attic."

He wore sandals, Ania noticed climbing the stairs behind him, he wore sandals and no socks. And his ankles were slim, the bones protruding at the sides; his energy seemed to be stored there, like a spring ready to jump; it made him look taller than he really was. A flag of ivy flapped in through a narrow window and there was a patch of sun on each stair. Dust danced obliquely through the air when he opened the door on the top landing.

Halt! Who goes there? Like a faithful old watchdog, a coal stove, blind and cold, wearing a tea kettle on its head, straightened up in the middle of the room. Down, down! Friends! The stove sank back into its cold summer slumber. The ceiling of the attic room was made of glass, of little squares of green-blue glass, and the light coming through it filled the room with a green-blue substance, as if you were at the bottom of an aquarium. The sounds were padded with the same blue-green, liquid silence, and you felt lazy and languid after a little while, like a fat fish trailing a veil-like tail behind it. They took turns to lean out of the cuckoo-clock window and finger the little figures on the sundial. Underneath, the top of the garden swayed this way and that, filled with the sticky torpor of summer.

"Are you an artist?" Sonica asked, inspecting his table loaded with paints and brushes, with boxes of buttons and pieces of fabric lying among empty bottles and old newspapers. A strange smell of molded paper came out of his disorder. "Yes, I am, but you'll never guess what sort!" He wouldn't tell them, and he smiled his peculiar smile with little throbbings around the nostrils. They'd have to come and visit three more times before he would tell them the secret. He had to prepare them for it. "Ania's father is a writer," Sonica informed him, and he said, "Ah," and his small jumpy eyes looked Ania over a second time.

They put the wet plum pits down on the plate, regretfully parting with that acrid bitterness, that green holiday forbidden to the tongue; they had to leave, they really had to, and they dashed down the stairs while he stood at the attic door. The flag of ivy flashed blues and greens at them through the window, and the staircase groaned, its old joints complained.

"Ania! Ania! Sonica!" he called down to them through the trees, leaning over the sundial in his white shirt. "When will you come again? Remember! Three more times," he said, raising three fingers. "I don't know," Sonica said, lifting an arm fatalistically. He laughed, and knocked his pipe on the windowsill. Two sparrows flew away in panic. That's the sort of man he was!

The hoped-for conversation with Tatiana never took place. First of all, Tatiana didn't ask any questions that morning, although Ania lingered at the kitchen door, secretly wishing

to be questioned, to confess and be done with it. But Tatiana
had burned a pot of milk and was busy trying to cover up the
culinary disaster before Mother noticed the smell. Mother
returned late, at noon, exhausted and loaded with parcels.
Ania waited for her at the front door. (Tatiana's inaccessibility
had put her on edge. She had to confess.) But Mother seemed
irritable; it was clear she wasn't in a forgiving mood. "Visiting
with strangers?" she would say. "Whoever gave you permission to go there?" The affair would move immediately into
the dining room, where all serious domestic infractions were
tried. On such solemn occasions Mother would sit like Justice
in her high chair while the culprit stood facing her, holding
onto one of the tablecloth fringes. The embroidery of the
tablecloth, seen through swelling tears, would dance, ripple
and bend sideways until the tears rolled down your nose and
blotted the front of your dress. Tatiana, transformed into a
bailiff, would have brought the culprit in from the garden, but
she could not stand the sight of tears, and after the trial was
over she would call Ania out of her room and tenderly and
secretly take her to the kitchen for spiritual comfort. But this
time, what with the burned milk and the busy morning, Ania
couldn't rely on Tatiana's sympathy. ("I *told* you to stay
away from that place!") Ania resolved to postpone
confession, and for two days she walked around looking
guilty and preoccupied. But Sunday, Jean Paul came to the
house.

UNCLE ERIC WAS COMING TO DINNER that evening and he
was Tatiana's favorite guest (that is, of course, before Jean
Paul came to the house). The relationship Tatiana had with
each visitor was a complicated and subtle one. For one thing,
Tatiana wasn't moved by artists' reputations. Some of their
most famous guests left Tatiana cold. Mother always coached
her before a dinner party, and the briefing usually included a

23

short biography of the guest, a popular version for Tatiana's special benefit. Tatiana would shrug. This proof of total independence pained and at the same time fascinated Ania, who during such dinners suffered under the radiations of fame the celebrated guest seemed to emit at her. Tatiana's classification of their guests was a very personal one, mysterious, indecipherable, and the results were expressed only tacitly, in Tatiana's appearance. For some guests she would put on an apron to cover the stains on her skirts; for others she would change from her old slippers into her shiny brocade shoes; and for still another category she would dress properly, even if it were only to serve coffee and preserves.

Everybody knew of Tatiana's dislike of the skinny little German poet whose work Father had translated last summer. The poet came to work with Father every day and late in the afternoon they would emerge from Father's room to have coffee in the garden. But from his first visit Tatiana wrote him off. Not only was he small and skinny but he wouldn't drink Turkish coffee or touch her famous cheese strudel. Tatiana was hurt.

"He is on a diet," Mother explained.

"That's what makes him small and skinny and—" Obviously the rest of the sentence expressed Tatiana's doubts of his being a man. She ignored him. She didn't bother to change her apron for him and appeared in her worst slippers, the ones the cat used to chew under the kitchen stove. Mother was embarrassed as they came shuffling down the garden path, but Tatiana would plant the cup of weak tea in front of him with lofty severity.

"He is a great poet," Mother said to Ania later in a loud voice so that Tatiana should hear her too. Mother wished to show Ania the distinction between being skinny, and pale-eyed and picking at your teeth and writing beautiful poetry. But Tatiana was unmoved.

Uncle Eric's great appetite and enthusiasm for her cooking won Tatiana's devotion. But also he had once told Mother between two bursts of laughter, which shook the buttons on his fancy vest and made Ania think his rib cage was lined with copper, that Tatiana was "a hell of a good-looking girl," and Tatiana overheard him. Of course, she didn't take this entirely personally, as she had strong feeling about class differences. Personal compliments, Tatiana felt, were to be taken seriously only when coming from Totis or Ion or the mailman. And she understood that for Uncle Eric her personal charm merged with her delicious meals and celebrated strudel. Yet the compliment flattered her just the same and brought out an orange glow on her face and powerful neck.

Uncle Eric's reputation—he was a well-known painter and lived half the year in Paris; his letters looked as if he wrote them with his brush—his reputation would not impress Tatiana. Obviously she was not a snob. She had looked over the painting he gave Father for his birthday, which now hung in the living room. "Miss Ania, why does this man have one hand yellow and the other green?" she asked. Ania didn't know why. "It's an expensive painting," she answered, hoping to impress Tatiana. "Is that so?" Tatiana said thoughtfully, scratching her hair bun with her comb, and then she dusted it with a specially soft rag.

Nobody knew what happened to Tatiana's classification of the guests that summer or when, in the shifting and rearranging of values, Jean Paul became the favorite. Certainly there was nothing that hot summer Sunday to predict such an upheaval. Tatiana dedicated her afternoon to the strudel. Deaf to all interruptions, her upper lip pearled with sweat, her sleeves rolled up, she put passion and fervor into her performance. At dusk the table was set out in the garden and the strudel lay ready on a plate trimmed with paper lace like a beauty queen resting before a contest. And when the taxi stopped in front of the gate, the door banged and Uncle Eric's laughter came around the lilac bush, Tatiana, elaborately dressed, her white apron starched to an unimaginable degree, and wearing her brocade shoes, appeared at the kitchen door.

ANIA WAS SLEEPY TOWARD THE END OF THE MEAL. But she sat very straight in her chair, forcing her eyes to stay open. Her head was heavy, dangling like a Japanese lantern hung on a soft twig. The china dishes were enveloped in a haze; when her eyelids dropped, milky color blurred over their outlines. The shine on the white damask tablecloth made her blink; blinking brought on a new load of sleep. Tatiana, walking back and forth on the gravel, sometimes seemed only a starched white apron floating into the dark distance. Closer, under the light, her face appeared flushed, her hair slightly ruffled. She was serving the dessert, and her glory was now at its peak. Uncle Eric congratulated her as the blond and ruffled cheese strudel, generously powdered with sugar, wearing the beauty marks of dark raisins like a French royal favorite, was slowly lowered onto the table. She was overwhelmed by his enthusiasm.

"You see, Eric," Mother said, "you were not half as lonesome for us as you were for Tatiana's strudel."

"Ah, I long for you, but my longing takes this form."

"What form?" Father inquired.

"The form of the strudel!" His great laugh burst out and his small quick hand with the short fat fingers thrust a paper bill into Tatiana's apron pocket. His nostrils quivered when he accidentally touched one of her treasures modestly hidden under her blue Sunday dress.

Just then they realized someone was standing in the darkness beyond the lamplight.

"There's somebody at the door," Ania said, as if the cage of light around their table had a door; and Uncle Eric stopped laughing and turned on his chair like a big bear, Father lifted a questioning face to the darkness.

A light breeze rocked the garden lamp, the cage of light swayed lazily once, the visitor's shoulders and head emerged from the night and Ania's heart leaped. Why had he come? Why hadn't he waited for her and Sonica to return? Why was he so impatient? A tear of butter dropped silently from the silver cake-spoon Mother halted in mid-air. He moved out of the darkness, the white of his shirt made him look real only down to his waist, the dark velvet of his trousers melted into the velvet of the night. He paused. (Later on they got used to his pauses, which drew all eyes to him, the silence before a show, before the curtain goes up. It made you sit absolutely still, hear your heart pound, wait with trepidation for his voice.) The voice came out calm and surprisingly rich for his stature: "I am sorry to interrupt your dinner." He paused again and looked from Uncle Eric to Father as if trying to decide who was the host. "My name is Jean Paul," he addressed Father. "I am your neighbor—"

Mother smiled and looked up with pleasure, visibly surprised. To Uncle Eric's disappointment, she forgot what she had been about to do and unloaded the piece of strudel back on the big plate. Father got up and threw his napkin on his chair. It landed in the shape of a twisted tower. "Anything we can do for you?"

"May I use your phone? Mine seems out of order all of a sudden and the grocery is closed."

"Go right ahead," Father said. "I'll show you the way." And then they both stepped out of the light and retreated along the gravel.

"Who is that fellow?" Uncle Eric said, eying the strudel with alarm. Was it getting cold? "He has a French accent."

"You don't like him?" Ania asked. Her head was heavy with sleep, which aggravated her irritation.

Uncle Eric looked up at her in surprise, his bloodshot blue eyes blinked, and stretching out his short arm he pinched her cheek. She looked like an apple ripe on only one side.

"You're angry, skinny! Do you like him?"

"Yes."

"Do you know him?"

"No."

"You're sleepy!"

"I am not," she blinked. But her eyelashes kept getting in the way.

At last Mother remembered the strudel. "Yes, he has a

French accent," she said, lifting Tatiana's masterpiece out of its bed of sugar with the silver spoon. The cake traveled swiftly toward Uncle Eric's plate, and he didn't mind very much when after that Mother turned on her chair and called softly into the night behind her, "Tatiana, we have another guest. Please bring another cup. And you can put the coffee on."

"Yes, Madam," answered the night far away.

FATHER LIKED JEAN PAUL. This was important. An outsider might have thought Mother made the rules in the house, steered new friendships in or politely pushed them back to sea. Most of the time Father seemed to be behind his closed door where, if you came in uninvited, you looked at his head behind the monumental inkstand and listened to the screech of his pen (it had a special blunt tip, which he claimed was indispensable to him) until he asked impatiently without looking up, "What *is* it, Ania?" (Sometimes the unexpected visitor would be Tatiana, who, frozen by the cold reception— Father was usually so kind to her—and intimidated by the walls lined with books, would completely forget her request.) In fact, Father was the supreme authority, but he was consulted only at moments of great domestic crisis. Mother was merely a traffic cop standing in the middle of the household, tactfully directing domestic traffic away from Father's door with soft motions of the hands, postponing all important decisions until he came out.

Father was the one who brought people home; he discovered people all the time and triumphantly ushered them to the table in the garden at coffee time or brought them in for dinner without warning. They would stay up late debating around the garden table long after Tatiana had gone to bed leaving Mother in charge of the last round of coffee.

Father must have liked Jean Paul then and there, Jean

Paul still with one hand on the receiver—"They'll send someone tomorrow morning"—and Father, his soft brown eyes enlarged by his glasses, inspecting his guest with unconcealed curiosity and pleasure. He looked funny and apologetic explaining something about his telephone, Father told Mother later that night, a bit like an actor but genuine at the same time. "You can't help talking to him. And he is forgetful too," Father added, delighted, "he doesn't finish his gestures, because he can't remember why he started them." He left the leather pouch on the armchair in the living room and it hung there all night until Mother discovered it after his departure.

But they must have talked a while, Father and Jean Paul, because the strudel got cold. "At long last," Uncle Eric said, when the front door shut with a bang and the gravel made crunchy noises. The lilac bush touched by Jean Paul as he walked by shivered with silent joy. They stood in the light again next to the table, and Ania knew at once: Father liked Jean Paul.

"Have you had dinner?" So Mother too knew that Father liked him. "Then would you have dessert with us?" And then he was sitting at their table and Ania could look at him between the wine bottle and the water pitcher and see how he took the dessert plate out of Mother's hand with a little nod of delight, looking at the strudel with admiration. He was a guest of the grownups now. A little tendril of regret climbed into Ania's throat.

Was his telephone going to be taken care of, Mother wanted to know. Yes, tomorrow morning, but something else was sure to break down again. It happened every day in that old barn. Either a pipe burst or the roof leaked or a window fell out altogether. "Well," Mother said, "we're only next door. You can always come and tell us and we'll help as much as we can." Uncle Eric looked at her, amazed: Mother, who was usually so reserved, her politeness so queenly, all smiles and forbidding blue eyes!

How did he ever find that old house, Father wanted to know. Father was always asking questions, and then he would listen, looking away from the speaker with one elbow on the table, as if the object of his attention was really the rose embroidered on the tablecloth. But it was Mother who, with a little sharp start inside her, as if a word had settled like a bird on the shivery antenna of her intuition, it was Mother who after such talks often knew more about their guests than Father.

"How did you come to rent that old house?"

He didn't, Jean Paul said. He had inherited it two years ago from his old aunt. His mother's sister. He didn't really remember the state the house was in, he hadn't been back to Bucharest for such a long time. "Do you live in Paris?" Uncle Eric asked. Yes, in Paris. "Your accent is unmistakably Parisian." But he was only half French, Jean Paul explained; his maternal family had lived in Bucharest. At one time he used to come here quite often for his summer vacations. He loved the city. "The house has been empty for quite a while, hasn't it?" Father said. Yes, that's how it had deteriorated. He should have come two years ago and tried to sell the house—but, at that time he was—well, he couldn't come. A memory sparkled in his eyes for a second; he smiled and his nostrils throbbed. (Mother looked up at him. "A woman," she thought.) But he was getting used to it now, he said. It was probably the very thing for him. He needed a big workshop and the attic was just right.

"What sort of work do you do?"

A short silence followed, a little pause he manipulated "like an actor," Uncle Eric noticed. Jean Paul tested the silence; it sprang back taut, like a plucked string, the effect was good, the public ready—"I am a puppeteer," he said, looking at Ania. "Ah," Mother exclaimed; the exclamation flew out of her mouth and left her lips parted.

Did he have a regular theatre? Regular shows? In Paris?

Yes, a portable theatre. Yes, regular shows. "I had a contract for an educational program; I was connected with the schools for a while—" For a second he looked irritated and his jaw advanced a bit. "It didn't work out the way I thought it would."

And the shows?

He laughed. "Oh, that was a great financial success! I had mountains of small change. The children paid for their tickets in centimes, you know—"

"You passed the hat," Uncle Eric said.

He looked up at Uncle Eric, his straight eyelashes blinked, the little dark raisins of his eyes lit up, the expression seemed to please him no end. "That's exactly what I did. My pockets were so heavy, I used to exchange the money at a newspaper stand every Friday after the show until one day the lady at the stand asked me impatiently, 'But Monsieur, what do you do for a living?' I think she suspected I was a beggar—come to think of it, I even had a little cloth bag to carry the change." He chuckled.

Was he going to give shows here in town?

He nodded, "Yes," but he was preoccupied with something else. His eyes darted from one object to the other on the table and stopped at the bread basket Mother had pushed out of the way. He reached for the end slice, held it in his left hand while his right one wrapped the white napkin around it. "Watch this, Ania," he said, and he tied a knot, pulled out a corner, twisted something, tucked it in again; a dry, little old woman with a rye-bread complexion suddenly stood up in his left hand. They held their breath.

He kept her standing on the table next to his wine glass. "Martine," he said in a reproachful voice, "I told you to stay home tonight! Why do you follow me around?"

"Mnah!" said the little woman in a sour voice which came straight out of her white scarf, "don't I know you! Someone's got to drag you home before dawn! Last night you—"

"Please, Martine," he said unhappily, "not here!"

"Mnah!" she grunted again, jerking a shoulder with the ferocious tyranny old servants exercise over their bachelor masters, and she walked away and climbed down the table-cloth. Before disappearing she took a long sniff at Father's plate. "Strudel!" she said reverently and then, straightening up with a groan, she turned her little old back to the company and was gone.

They sat in awe for a while, still looking at the side of the table where she had disappeared. With a pang Ania watched how Martine was taken apart, the napkin unrolled, the piece of bread returned to the basket.

"How did you do that?" Mother said. For a second she looked like Ania, her blue eyes enlarged.

"Everything can be turned into a puppet." A silver cake-spoon powdered with sugar lay face down on the strudel plate. He leaned forward and drew a face on it with eyes and nose and a grinning smile; a delicate, silver-looking old lady lay on the plate, her head surrounded with white curls of strudel chips. Then he sat resisting the temptation to lick his sugary finger until Mother passed him a paper napkin.

Later, when he tasted the wine, an intent and silent dialogue took place between him and his drink. He lifted his glass, swallowed slowly, the big Adam's apple moving up and down inside his open collar. With tightly shut eyes and creased eyelids, sealing the wine aroma inside himself, he said, "I was lonesome for you." Uncle Eric didn't seem to like the laughter this earned. "You are being unfaithful to your country," he said. "Or at least to its wine!" And Jean Paul dabbed at his wet lips with the corner of his napkin—he had an aristocratic mouth, thin-lipped and beautifully arched. "Faithfulness," he said, "is such a complicated thing. I can't quite understand why this—this desire for a new taste, for a new shade, for a—Why should it be so reprehensible?" And for the first time Mother put her fork down and looked at him reproachfully. (Later on that look in Mother's eyes was the signal for an argument that would go on for a good part of the night with great gestures of the hands. But that first evening Mother let it go.)

"Ania! Ania!" The night called softly behind the bushes, and Uncle Eric turned on his chair. Another intruder? But he liked Sonica and he liked to tell her she was beautiful. Whenever his laugh was heard over the fence, Sonica would come to visit for a few minutes and stand next to Mother's chair, composed, showing him her liquid smile and her dimple.

"Come, let me look at you, Sonica. How much have you grown this summer?" And Sonica advanced slowly out of the dark until her straight black hair shone in the light like a lacquered helmet.

"Will you have dessert with us, Sonica?" Mother asked.

"Thank you, I don't think I can. I just want to tell Ania something."

Ania climbed off her chair and left the table. They went under the lilac bush.

"Why did he come over?"

"His telephone doesn't work."

"Did he say anything about us?"

"What should he say?"

"That we went over?"

"He wouldn't," Ania defended him. "Sonica, do you know what he is?" She couldn't keep the news any longer. "He is a puppeteer and—"

"Oh, come," Sonica said.

"He is. And he kept his money in a bag like a beggar—"

"Ania, please come back. You haven't finished your dessert."

"I am coming, Mother."

"He made a puppet out of bread for us and then he—"

"Are you coming, Ania?"

Sonica brought Ania back to the table and stood for a second next to Uncle Eric's chair.

"You get more beautiful every time I see you, Sonica," he said, and she smiled, her dimple came out again. Her dark head looked darker the way she carried it on the white plate or her big organza collar. The grownup manners she displayed were awkward for her age and touching. For a second her lustrous black look darted at Jean Paul and then, as if it had been a whim, she took it back and said goodnight. They heard her run along the gravel path and then across her garden.

"A beautiful girl," Jean Paul said. Mother, who was busy folding the napkin, looked up at him.

"Isn't she? Poor Sonica! She doesn't have it easy."

"Ania thinks Sonica looks like a shiny chestnut," Father said, and Uncle Eric stretched out his hand and pinched Ania's cheek again.

"Is your daughter going to be a poet also?" Jean Paul asked Father. Then he looked at Ania as if he had just then discovered her; yet all the while he had been sitting across from her she knew that between them there was another sort of friendship, an earlier one, to which the others weren't yet admitted.

"She wants to be a painter," Mother said. "She paints."

Embarrassed at being suddenly the center of attention, Ania kicked her legs under the table, the tall glasses shivered, the level of the wine danced inside.

"Is that what you want to be?" Jean Paul asked her between the water pitcher and the wine bottle.

"I am going to go to Paris," she said, twisting her fork unhappily, feeling she was blushing, "and study art."

Uncle Eric looked very satisfied and rounder.

"That's the right place to go to study art," Jean Paul said seriously.

"Where did she get this idea from?" Father asked Mother.

"Ask Eric," Mother said.

"You can't be an artist," Uncle Eric waved his napkin. "You're too skinny. Look at me!"

She shrugged, and the strap of her dress slipped off her shoulder.

"If the artists won't take you," Jean Paul said, "I would, Ania. You could become a puppeteer. They are usually skinny."

"Is it a requirement?" Father asked.

"More or less. It would be hard to move a great belly behind the puppet stage. You don't have much space there."

"Nothing personal," Uncle Eric said after he had decided to help himself to another piece of strudel, shaking with slight ostentation the cake-spoon on which Jean Paul had drawn the old lady's face, "but I am inclined to believe that a great belly is a sign of a generous art."

Father put his hand flat on his shirt. He was lean and tall. "Then what does that make my art?" he asked worriedly.

"Ah," Mother seized the opportunity of unburdening herself to someone new, "how do you send someone away to school who can't even eat a whole breakfast? Look at her! Do you know how much she weighs?"

"Nora," Uncle Eric said, "you really are getting provincial! Do you want to go along with her and make sure she eats her meals? If you want her to study, let her go! If not, find her a husband and keep her here!"

"It isn't something we have to decide today, you know," Father said looking at Mother across the table. "Not for ten years at least."

"I know," Mother said, "I know, but—" Her face was flushed.

She didn't finish the sentence. Tatiana's white apron, accompanied by the sound of her brocade shoes, advanced rhythmically along the path. She carried the tray high, and the aroma of the coffee floated behind her like a banner of sweet promise unfolded in the night. They were all silent while she poured.

Through her drowsiness Ania felt that Tatiana had made a spectacular entrance: she moved her buttocks solemnly, slowly and rhythmically under her Sunday dress like a goddess of fecundity. Tacitly Jean Paul acknowledged Tatiana's hidden treasures. The silent homage—a faint quiver of a nostril lit up by the oblique light of the garden lamp—made Tatiana's cheeks burn. She passed his chair twice just to hand him a spoon. Her blue Sunday dress radiated heat, especially the back of it, that lower part where a vertical line of shadow divided it into two triumphant parts.

"Ania, do you know the time?" Mother's right eyebrow gave a secret signal. "Please put the lights on for her, Tatiana."

Tatiana was in an excellent mood. She turned down the bed covers in Ania's room, then sat on the bed listening to the talk outside under the window.

"Who is that man, Miss Ania?"

Drunk with sleep, holding Tatiana's warm knee, Ania lifted one foot, then the other, as Tatiana unbuckled her sandals.

"He is the man in the old house," Ania said, emerging from the nightgown Tatiana was pulling over her head.

"I'll be darned!" Tatiana marveled, bending to collect the slip and pants from the floor. "I'll be darned! I thought it might be him! What's he doing here?"

". . . Invited," said Ania. It sounded to her like a repetition of a conversation she had once had with Tatiana, but through her sleep as thick as syrup she couldn't remember. She felt vaguely it was the right moment to secure a good spot for Jean Paul in Tatiana's guest list, but she didn't have time. Tatiana pulled up the summer blanket, the milky smell of washed flannel mixed with the one of Tatiana's sweat, and sleep came violently, like a torrent.

As Martine predicted, Jean Paul stayed long after midnight. Father led him a few steps out of the cage of light, and then Tatiana was sent with him to the garden gate, which had to be locked from the inside. She stayed there for quite a while and returned panting, her hair bun ruffled, her face glowing with a victorious air that lingered while she cleared

35

the table, straightened the chairs and put the light out. And then the last night moths went to bed too.

JULY nights in Bucharest are hot, and even in the quietest neighborhoods sleep comes long after the lights are out. The gardens are restless; dogs bark sleepily at the moving shaddows; the pavement exhales the heat of the day; the odor of linden trees drifts like a sleepwalker; a streetlamp suspended at a crossing transforms the familiar street into a strange theatrical set with large slices of darkness leaning against fences; a garden faucet drips into a forgotten pail; crickets saw the darkness; lacquered leaves shiver.

Where would Tatiana be going at this late hour? Holding her brocade shoes under her arm, she steps carefully along by the house wall, avoiding the gravel. Her bare feet on the warm pavement make the sensuous noise of lips smacked in happy anticipation. The gate is locked and the key is inside, on the little table in the hall, where it should be. Tatiana hesitates, then puts down her brocade shoes, gathers her skirts and climbs the fence with an agility surprising in someone so plump. On the other side of the fence she pulls her shoes through the bars, puts them on and starts running toward the old house. A white stain is moving toward her outside the gate. The man who has been waiting for her is smaller than Tatiana but he puts a firm arm around her waist. "I haven't got much time," she says, but she walks with him deep inside the dark night under the trees until her throaty laugh and his white shirt are swallowed by the wild garden.

And then, slowly, the darkness becomes thinner, the blue of the morning penetrates the night, chases away the violet. Sleep is full of small, sonorous accidents (the sound of a step in the garden, a door closing softly). Then a rooster takes it upon himself to let the world know that a uniquely splendid morning is about to start. Then sparrows jabber; the milkman's cart rolls in; tin milk buckets rattle; shades roll up; morning glories yawn on trellises. But—won't Tatiana be late?

Tatiana is in the kitchen. She yawns, stretches, scratches one foot with the heel of the other slipper, then proceeds to light the fire in the stove. She watches the small flame reflected in the big-bellied coffee pot, and all of a sudden she start humming.

THE SHADE LIFTED BY MOTHER'S HAND traveled up smoothly, uncovering a bouncy-blue sky; the white curtains twisted, danced in place impatiently. Mother brought news.

"You're invited to see Jean Paul's puppets. Ask Tatiana to iron the blue dress for you to put on."

"Sonica too?"

"Sonica? No, I don't think so."

"Couldn't you ask Fräulein Cuna, Mother?"

"I don't think Fräulein Cuna would like that. Can't you do some things on your own, without Sonica?" Mother said, securing the curtains with their lilac ribbons.

"Well, well," Tatiana received Ania in the kitchen with unusual joviality for that early hour. "Already on your way out? Is there a parade in town?" She was in an excellent mood today, Tatiana. "Shall I put marmalade on both sides?" She buttered Ania's roll, wiping the knife on it skillfully. Her face, still puffy from a hurried sleep, smiled mysteriously when Ania informed her she was invited to the old house. Tatiana's doubts about that place seemed to be forgotten.

"Do you know he is a puppeteer?" Ania tried to stir Tatiana's interest, her last chance to delay breakfast. But morning had never been a good time to lecture Tatiana on art.

"Drink your cocoa, Miss Ania, or there'll be no visits at all this morning."

The cocoa was, as always, too greasy. When Tatiana went into the laundry to look for the blue dress, Ania poured her cocoa into the sink, shortening the breakfast torture, and was innocently rinsing her cup when Tatiana came back into the kitchen and gave her a suspicious look. At long last—and the front of her freshly ironed dress heaved with a big sigh of relief—she was free to leave the house. But—"Wait a minute now!" Tatiana called her back. Half of the buttered roll had been discovered on the table. "Do you want to stay green and small? Or do you want me to serve you green plums for breakfast?" The bargain they finally made was that Ania would take the roll along and finish it on the way, but as soon as she was out on the street she dropped it in the gutter and cautiously pushed it out of sight. (She knew Tatiana's vigilance only too well.) She cleaned her buttery fingers by rubbing them on the fence of the old house and then pushed the gate open reverently.

Jean Paul's voice came down to her from the attic, where she found him moving cardboard boxes around and tearing up wrapping paper. "I am unpacking the puppets," he said. He seemed different today from the way she remembered him last night.

"What is the matter?"

"Nothing."

"You didn't bring Sonica."

"I haven't seen her today."

"Now you know what I am."

"Yes—"

"Yes-yes," he mocked her. "What do you think about it?"

She shrugged. "I've never seen any puppets before."

"Puppets are very serious things," he said gravely.

She nodded. "I know."

He paused. They looked at each other and heard the wooden floor creak.

"Come over here," he said. "Sit on that box. Now watch."

She sat on the cardboard box, quiet and submissive, and watched as he brought out the dark-blue screen and unfolded it in front of her. His hands and white shirt reflected in the lacquered surface made her suddenly think of water at night. "It's not a real show," he said. "This isn't my usual stage. I'll just show my friends to you and you'll see what they can do. You'll see the real Martine too. She's our housekeeper."

There was a short, complicated silence behind the folding screen, a rustle of fabric—or a step?—the air vibrated as if someone were dessing in there and then quietly, without Ania's noticing when it happened, Martine was seated on the top of the folding screen, over to the left, with flowered scarf and big skirts and red felt hands, and was looking down at Ania with two tiny shoe-button eyes, inquisitive and suspicious. She was a favorite puppet, and she must have known it, spoiled and difficult, irascible and absurd and tyrannical and moody; her head made a little rebellious tremor which caused the tip of her scarf to dance nervously in the air. She talked with a lisp, mostly about Jean Paul, complaining bitterly, bent and lifted the corner of her apron to wipe her eyes, and then went on to wipe the top of the screen, the whole length of it, stopping abruptly from time to time to search Ania's eyes as if checking on her own magnetic powers. Then, brusquely resuming her complaint, transformed into a master of ceremonies, she consented to bring out the other puppets, marched ahead of them imitating each one: a princess, a fat mailman, a drummer from a fairy-tale army with all his golden tassels dancing. She checked them gravely, dusted them, inspected their buttons, talked to them, rushed out at them, knocking them down in her zeal, making a loud lovable nuisance of herself.

The puppets walked back and forth along the top of the folding screen, performed sensitive arpeggios, their heads bent, carefully listening to something that was happening inside them where Jean Paul's hands must have been. The morning sun lit their fur hair, their wool curls, made the silk and velvet breathe and quiver.

She had expected to recognize Jean Paul's voice coming from behind the screen, but he wasn't there any more. His voice had untwisted, separated into several different ones, like a string made out of many colored threads. The lid of the cardboard box had printed a painful pattern on her buttocks but she didn't feel it. But when the last puppet had bowed and left and Jean Paul called her from behind the screen in his own voice, her eyes suddenly felt like two suction cups that she had to unfasten—and it hurt—from the sight.

And it was unbelievable after this to see the puppets lying face upward in their boxes. Martine on her side, her skirts limp, her scarf lifeless, her volubility gone; their frozen eyes ignoring you, looking past toward the ceiling.

"They'll need some repair after the trip," Jean Paul said, and with a worried, paternal air one wouldn't have suspected him of, he lifted the puppets out of their boxes one by one, caressed their clothes, blew the dust off their curls like Martine, brushed away the lint with the back of his hand.

She was late for lunch. The twelve o'clock siren on the roof of the Fire Department had mooed over the houses and had fallen asleep again, but they didn't hear it. Jean Paul did say once, "I think you'd better go now," but then he forgot time again. ("But you were there over three hours," Mother said indignantly later. "Do you want me to come and lead you away by the hand? If you ever want to go there again, be home when I tell you to be." But how could you, in that house, in that room on the top of the world, floating through the aquarium light, how could you remember to go home in time?) Jean Paul looked at Ania with intent curiosity, watching her closely, and said, readjusting the ruffle on her shoulder, she could come back as often as she wished. When they leaned out to look at the blue and gold sundial under the window, the line of shadow was past twelve, and they decided she should go home. Hot and sleepy, the garden greenery heaved a long sigh—iodine and mint—and the top of the trees swayed this way and that.

There were too many things to see on the way out. They stopped at the open door of the attic room and listened to the house, to the soft noises of its secret life, to the old curtains swaying and the floors creaking, to the sigh of the worn-out mattresses crowded with pillows covered in worn-out velvet, to the little dance of the tarnished gold tassels. They walked in and out of the shadows on the stairs, crossed the square islands of light on the landing to the old rooms he wanted to show her. A silent moth rose, shimmered in the light, fled into a lilac drapery. "It smells moldy," he said. "These windows haven't been opened for years." But she loved the smell, was getting drunk on it, puffed out her nostrils, and inhaled all the stale dusty air until she was dizzy.

Was he going to live here now, she asked, lifting her eyebrows in hope.

To answer this question seriously he had to sit down on the bed—an old bed with an ornate headboard and little elephant legs—and wonder aloud. It was difficult to live too long away from Paris. But why? What sort of a place was it, she asked, standing in front of him, her hands clasped on her skirt. He nodded gravely. She'd see why when she got there, he said.

There were a number of things he had to do before starting a regular show here, a place to find, and contacts too—. But he forgot to finish his sentence. He suddenly became interested in the velvet bedspread he was sitting on and had been fingering while he talked. Inspired, he took it off the bed, throwing the fat pillows onto the floor, and brought it to the window. Wasn't this the most wonderful velvet she had ever seen! It must have belonged to the last king of France! He wrapped it around his shoulders, gathering the top in a lofty collar, and paced up and down in front of the mirror. "We need a puppet just like this," he said, using the plural for no reason at all, making her heart bounce with obscure hopes as he included her in the mysterious future. He seemed smaller now, all wrapped in velvet, and the beginnings of baldness shone against the high collar, but he was preoccupied with the fold of an imaginary cuff he was moving up and down his arm.

The velvet spread was still across one of his shoulders, trailing on the stairs like a train, when he brought her to the door. He stood like this in the doorway, under the ivy, waving.

THE NEW FRIENDSHIP was like an acute epidemic, and all the members of the household seemed to be infected. Mother tried to be reasonable about it, but there was little she could do except insist on keeping strict hours for meals and sleep. Yet if Father was sitting at the piano with Jean Paul bent over his shoulder, both humming, trying out a French song he had brought them, discipline went by the board. Ania would be sent to the living room twice to tell them supper was ready, but the second time she didn't return to the dining table. She would stand there at Father's side listening—*"Il y avait une chèvre de grand tempérament, qui revenait d'Espagne et parlait allemand"*—until Tatiana appeared in person and announced with a mournful air that the macaroni had got cold.

For several days after that first visit to Jean Paul's house, the official one, Ania seemed to be running a fever. She wasn't really; her forehead and hands felt feverish, but the thermometer she had to hold in her mouth—while she tried, cross-eyed, to read her fate on it—showed nothing abnormal. Yet Mother was worried (the child was too thin!), and as a measure of precaution, a large glass of milk with disgusting yellow stars swimming in it appeared on the kitchen table at four o'clock every afternoon. Ania was summoned to the kitchen by Tatiana, who supervised the long ordeal of milk drinking while doing her ironing on the kitchen table. Tatiana, enjoying this new aspect of her executive power, encouraged conversation during this cozy hour, and Ania took advantage of her receptivity. Wearing a mustache of cream, she unfolded her future for Tatiana's benefit. Did Tatiana know what puppets were? Because she was going to be a puppeteer and have her own theatre. Of course, for that she would first have to go to Paris to study. Jean Paul said so.

"What?" Tatiana would say, a queer smile hovering round her lips whenever Jean Paul's name was mentioned, "What? Leave your own mother and father and go among strangers, just like that?"

Tatiana's merciless way of presenting this dilemma put a dry knot in Ania's throat. Ania sighed, wiped her mouth clean, and with her head between her hands appraised the situation bravely. It wasn't going to be now, she explained; in ten years maybe. But you had to, if you wanted to study.

"What for?" Tatiana asked skeptically. "Aren't the schools here good enough for you? Do you have to go all the way to Paris?" On Tatiana's tongue, the *s* became a rasping *z*, and the city she talked about was always called Pariz. It sounded irreverent. It gave away Tatiana's opinion of the whole matter: she laughed at it. "Wouldn't you rather be a lady like your mother?" Tatiana went on, spraying the linen. The operation was a fascinating one, and Ania had to put her glass down and give her full attention to Tatiana's way of dipping her hand into the bowl of water and then shaking her red fingers in the air with a professional motion of the wrist, like a pianist warming up over the keyboard before a concert. The blue sheet became freckled with damp spots and breathed out a blissful smell of sun and wind.

"That's what you should be when you grow up," Tatiana advised, and the old iron grinning with burning charcoal slid across the sheet and miraculously gave it back its youth. Tatiana was an artist who didn't know the dimensions of her powers. She would guide the nose of the iron inside the tired, wilted folds of a ruffle, and the ruffle would immediately come alive, strong, tremulous and beautiful. Father's pajamas, which had hung upside down in the back yard on the clothes line like sad, limp, striped acrobats, would revive under Tatiana's iron, which put the discipline of pleats into their body and re-established the dignity of starched lapels. Tatiana's art had a way of putting suspense into the ironing of even the most uninteresting pieces of laundry, like handkerchiefs. Flat, square surfaces were attacked first along the margins, which were smoothed out and polished; then the wrinkled area in the middle would be systematically reduced by the nosy tip of the iron, until finally everything shone like a snow-covered garden. Then the white garden would be folded and the iron would give it a last authoritative pat. Yet there was no sign of transfiguration on the artist's face, redder than usual, high above her work. Even this matter-of-fact attitude was fascinating.

"Mh? Wouldn't you rather be a lady like your mother?"

It was a complicated question, as Tatiana couldn't exactly explain what sort of a career that would be, nor how you got there. But if she obviously disapproved of Ania's plans, she seemed to be very fond of Jean Paul. Even if her conclusion was, "He shouldn't put such ideas into your head," Jean Paul had been promoted right away into the highest category of visitors: Tatiana put on her blue dress and brocade shoes whenever he came to dinner.

But soon enough this meant that Tatiana had to wear her best shoes every day. Jean Paul was always there. He would sit and drink Turkish coffee with Mother in the garden, waiting for Father to come out of his study for his mid-afternoon break. Jean Paul's leather pouch hung on the back of the garden chair, proof of his repeated apologies: he wasn't going to stay, he was on his way out shopping for groceries. Yet an hour later when, sprinkled and cooling off, the garden sent up little whiffs of petunia scent, Uncle Eric would drop in and find Jean Paul still there, talking with Mother, laughing with Ania and Sonica. Once he found all of them, their heads bent together over Jean Paul's coffee cup in which he was reading their fortune. At a respectful distance, holding her tray under her arm, Tatiana also was listening, completely absorbed in the game, and she even seemed annoyed that she had to go back to the kitchen and make more coffee for the new guest.

"I don't know why you find him so exciting," Uncle Eric would say. "Maybe it's only that you haven't been abroad for these last years and you're only lonesome for Paris."

"You don't like him, do you Eric?"

"I don't dislike him, but there's something—I don't know."

"Ask Ania to tell you about his puppets," Mother would say then, as if this were an excuse for the surprisingly intent friendship, the spirited, bouncy intoxication that was rising to everyone's head. Uncle Eric would shrug. He wasn't interested in puppets, he wouldn't take them seriously, and only the sight of Tatiana coming down the garden path carrying his steaming cup of coffee could divert him and cheer him up.

Yet Jean Paul knew very well how to stage his absences too. After visiting with them several days in succession he suddenly disappeared. A jar of strawberry preserve, his favorite, waited outside on the garden table at coffee time until the last ray of the afternoon sun reached it, then crossed it, lit the strawberries in three shades of red. He didn't come. Tatiana brought out a third cup; full of hope, she had put her brocade shoes on right after lunch. He didn't come. Guests arrived for the evening, and he didn't come. "Why don't you call him? Maybe he isn't well?" Mother urged Father. Father wouldn't call but dispatched Ania with a note written in verse. Was he coming? Yes, he was, Ania reported, panting in the living room doorway. He did. He arrived in his brown velvet trousers and white shirt, tieless, paused at the edge of the circle of light made by the garden lamp, and everybody stopped talking, they looked up at him expectantly. His eyes jumped with curiosity from one guest to the other. "But where have you been?" Mother said reproachfully, and to her guests, "Meet Jean Paul, he is a puppeteer," and the evening burst into flame.

Laughter and voices could be heard very late at night in their garden that summer; great gestures made by talkative hands ran Chinese shadows over the wall opposite, and Tatiana's generous silhouette moved among them from left to right and back while she collected the dishes. And if Father read to his guests from his poems, her shadow would be seen suddenly motionless at the far corner of the wall and Tatiana herself, as instructed by Mother, would stand still, tray under arm, not daring to take another step, until Father discovered her there and said, "It's late, you can go to bed Tatiana, we'll take care of the table." "It's all right, I'll be up anyway," Tatiana would say with a discreet smile, avoiding looking at Jean Paul, but she would use the interruption to leave, careful not to make a noise on the gravel or let her buttocks bounce under her blue Sunday dress. The summer nights that year had new shapes, new depths, a different lining. And even the bushes at the end of the garden, which absorbed the roaring laughter, even the bushes, veiled in rustling darkness, seemed to recognize his voice.

IT WAS A BIT STRANGE that Fräulein Cuna should not have learned of Jean Paul's existence, but she didn't: to the end of that extraordinary summer nobody told her what was happening in the old house.

"I see *he*'s coming every single day to the house now," Mr. Totis said to Tatiana, a shade of reproach in his voice, as if the family's sudden and intent friendship with that foreigner had robbed him of some rights. But Tatiana was loyal to the house she served and had her own reasons for being discreet.

"Yes, he does come over sometimes," she said, and changed the subject. Lately she had kept out of the grocer's reach and he hadn't had one good chance to pinch her.

"Wait until *Frailai* Cuna finds out Miss Sonica's visiting with him. I see the girls running there every morning."

"Why should she find out?" Tatiana asked, rummaging through the basket of tomatoes to match them for size. "Who's going to tell the *Frailai*? Isn't that child unhappy enough, don't do this and don't do that and not a mother to go to?"

Mr. Totis was thus subtly invited to join the conspiracy against Fräulein Cuna; he was touched, his dark eyes following Tatiana's hips around the shop glittered like the Greek olives swimming in oil in the glass jar on his counter.

"Hey, will you stop squeezing my tomatoes or I'll give you a good squeeze!"

"You wouldn't dare!" Tatiana said, circling the basket to put a safe distance between them.

"Good Lord, what a life that child has!" Baba complained to Tatiana on one of her kitchen visits, taking up the same theme in her own voice, a tobacco contralto. The *Frailai* had had a fit again, she had found flies in the kitchen. "She says everybody has germs! Nothing is ever clean enough for her!" Baba lifted a corner of her apron to wipe her nose. "How can I have germs? I take a little bit of brandy from time to time and I keep clean inside. It disinfects you, doesn't it?" Tatiana smiled knowingly. She knew Baba kept her special medicine on the top shelf of the kitchen cupboard and visited it, like a fountain of youth, several times during the day. On the days Fräulein Cuna nagged too much the number of visits to the shrine of serenity increased.

"I never see her going out," Tatiana commented. "What's the matter with her?"

"Where should she go? She hasn't got a soul she cares for. I bet you she's still—" Baba chuckled, covered the wicked gold tooth with her hand, and Ania couldn't hear what Fräulein Cuna seemed to be still; but it must have been pretty sad, judging from Tatiana's compassionate expression.

Sonica's household had no mother, and Ania was instructed not to talk about it to Sonica. That was why she tried to approach Baba on the subject. But Baba happened to be mincing onions just then. She had put down her knife and turned to Ania a swollen face with tiny red eyes full of tears. Drying them on her arm, she sighed and muffled a groan in her sleeve: "Ah my God, ah my God, was she beautiful!" Shocked by Baba's tears, unable to sense how much of her pain was the sting of onions and how much tragedy, Ania didn't dare ask any more questions.

"But why don't you tell your father?" Ania asked when Fräulein Cuna's rules became unbearable. Sonica shrugged. Fräulein Cuna lived her exile indoors; the house was the only island of civilization she accepted, and anything happening outside it put her in a state of agitation and alarm: the way Ion sent a thick spit of satisfaction onto the curb; the unwrapped bread in the grocery; the buzzing of flies, her personal enemies. A huge bottle of eau de cologne stood on the bathroom shelf and every few minutes she used it to clean her hands of contact with infected Rumania. Her skirts breathed a strong antiseptic smell, and sometimes her upper lip, instead of sliding down over her front teeth, would catch halfway on their dry, perfectly brushed surface. "Have you seen her when she sneers like a wolf?" Baba would say, nudging Tatiana.

"Why don't you tell your father?" Ania asked, her heart aching for her friend. "Do you want my mother to tell him? Do you?" Sonica shook her head. Her dark, gleaming look carried a lucidity Ania mistook for sadness. Sonica knew it was much simpler to learn how to lie skillfully, without blinking. Her father left the house early in the morning with straw hat and silver-topped cane. His office limousine waited for him at the gate, and the sharp smell of his after-shaving lotion lingered behind long after the car had taken him away. You couldn't count on him. Sonica learned to hide a cold by burying her head deeply in her skirts when she coughed or sneezed. She knew how to take care of cut knees all by herself, squeezing the skin between her fingers, then sucking it until the blood stopped. She wasn't brave, she held Ania's hand when they crossed the garden at night, but she was secretive and strong: she did not rely on anyone. She already knew how Time softened the intensity of guilt and bleached remorse if you were only strong enough to be silent, not to confess. And she never lost her head when faced with evidence of her lies; she improvised an alibi at the last minute, used the smallest ripple of compassion and awe stirred by her black, burning beauty.

"God Almighty!" Baba crossed her fat hands over her aproned belly, looking at a wet, panting Sonica standing at the door of the kitchen, back from a secret visit with Jean Paul. "God Almighty! Where have you been? *Frailai* is looking for you!"

"At Ania's." But Baba knew too well what was going on. She accepted the answer without comment.

"Sit down here! You're all wet! I'll tell her you've been here for quite a while. And how is the Frenchman?" she asked, casually turning to her pots.

"I don't know," said Sonica, but the dimple came out in her cheek.

"Lord, is she beautiful! Just like her mother," Baba muttered to the pot; helpless, burning with a visceral compassion aggravated by her last visit to the brandy bottle, she fished a mushroom out of the gravy and handed it to Sonica on the tip of the kitchen knife, becoming her closest accomplice.

Obviously the street reciprocated Fräulein Cuna's attitude, and she was left out of that small and bouncy world where news was exchanged in doorways, love was made over fences, eyes caressed swaying buttocks in the sweet air of summer mornings. A wave of lusty exuberance rose early in the day, rocked the morning glories on their trellis; Mr. Totis took up his strategic position on the sidewalk, a toothpick between his front teeth; the milkman collected the news in one kitchen and rolled it away to the next one.

"A-ha-ha! Did you see the Frenchman has painted his windows? Is he getting married or something?"

"Mm!" Baba commented, handing him the pot for the milk, "why don't you ask Tatiana," and her eyes creased with laughter.

"How would I know?" Tatiana shrugged when her turn came to present the milkman with her milk pot.

"Who's getting married?" Ania wanted to know. "Miss Ania," Tatiana said, her neck and face ablaze, "would you mind keeping out of my way this morning?"

Surely Fräulein Cuna must have seen Jean Paul when he started to come to the house every day. From her terrace, protected by her awning, she must have seen him walk across to the garden table where Mother was waiting for him. Once in a while she must have heard a word, a sentence, caught a chord of his contagious laughter over the drowsy summer silence; but she thought he was just another of her neighbors' guests, and not even when he cut Sonica's hair—Mother was really angry with him!—did Fräulein Cuna learn of his existence. Sonica said she had cut it all by herself, and the governess' blue, hawklike eye did not notice the lovely curve Sonica's hair now had at the nape of her neck—the touch of an artist's hand.

But on Father's birthday? On that unforgettable evening? Didn't she come out on the balcony to watch Jean Paul's puppet show? Yes, she did, but after a while she went back in. She didn't understand what the puppets were talking about and she hated mosquitoes. The event aroused no curiosity in her, and certainly no suspicion.

A wind of silliness had blown through her neighbors' house all that day. Gifts were delivered early in the morning at the front door. The telephone could be heard ringing insistently through the open bedroom windows and then Mother's voice answering, "Oh, do come. You have to meet Jean Paul, we are having a puppet show!" It was going to be a surprise for Father, but Ania couldn't include Tatiana in the secret. It was impossible to approach her, to reach her through the fever of culinary creation that seized her before big dinners. To Father who came sniffing to the kitchen door in the morning to inquire about the menu she gave a grunting answer and banged a saucepan lid like an exclamation mark. (Father helped himself to the raisins put to soak in wine and retreated to his writing grotto.)

Thinking that Miss Ania was still asleep, Tatiana had hurried to kill the chickens in the back yard behind the lilac bushes. But Ania was up; she had come to the door barefoot and clutching the front of her wrinkled pajamas and watched how Tatiana held each chicken in turn between her knees, stretched its neck, made the knife dance swiftly on it— rrrshshsh, how the head, its crest turned suddenly pale, was thrown into the bucket. Blood spurted from the necks; the headless bodies danced in the dust for a long time; and Tatiana, with blood on her face and on one slipper, discovered Ania and shouted at her to go indoors at once. But Ania couldn't tear herself away from the horrible sight; and even when the chickens lay plucked on the table, looking naked in their rosy skin, they still seemed to quiver, a spasm still jerked a wrinkled yellow foot, as if they couldn't forget the horror of what had happened to them.

Then Mother herself came into the kitchen. Like a magician, she made a nest of flour on the pastry board and put three egg yolks in it. Wrapped in white, her hands raised, Tatiana waited like a surgeon to start operating. The mystery of birth rose in the kitchen, blew powder into the creators' eyelashes.

At a given signal Tatiana threw herself at the nest of flour, her hands broke the yellow mirrors of the yolks, let them drip through her fingers, tortured them with zest until the dough was soft as the cheek of a new-born baby. But after that tender interlude Tatiana's mood became positively dangerous, like a dormant volcano. The precautions with which she always surrounded the birth of a cake—you were not to sneeze, or make a draft with the door, or talk about the cake and bewitch it—made you think there must be a god of cakes somewhere, perfumed with cinnamon, wearing a paper doily on his head with a halo of silver foil around it, supervising the ritual. And sometimes he was merciless: the cake didn't come out right, and Tatiana, cheek propped on hand at the kitchen table, mused over something intended to be a culinary victory but which was now paleontological remains. Where was the mistake? Called into the dining room for constructive criticism, Tatiana would listen with a pained face, the wooden tray under her arm, moving her toes inside her slippers helplessly. She would then pick up the relic and leave the room depressed. She could be found still brooding over it late into the evening, and would come to suspect the elements, the water, the air, the fire and the earth, suspect a shift in their relationship, a change of angle, in a moment adverse to baking.

But the birthday cake came out in a blaze of glory, and everything else was ready in time. The chickens, tanned, their wings folded in resignation against their lacquered breasts, reclined in wine, a bay leaf on their chests, a supreme homage offered to heroes. Jean Paul came early with a mysterious box under his arm, and he and Ania stretched a blanket between the two poplar trees. And sure enough, after dinner the guests left the damask-covered table—it looked like a battleground, crumbs and empty glasses and unfolded napkins—and turned their chairs to face the poplars. Ania was on the program too. The audience could hear the stool being dragged over the gravel on which she stood to reach over the blanket, and then her thin voice came with importance, with fervor from the puppet bowing to them. Martine got a standing ovation when she handed Father a red-velvet heart at the end of the play, calling him up to the blanket to get it. A lamp hung in the poplar at the left, lit up the puppets' hair, made them look inspired, aware of the miracle that had brought them alive. Father's beautiful hand stretched up to receive the velvet love token looked gigantic, coming out of a world of flesh and reaching over the blanket into the one of miracles. Martine bent from her rheumatic waist, took Father's hand in both her small red-felt ones, and looking trustfully at him gave him her good wishes, while the audience applauded deliriously.

Because of the hour Sonica hadn't been allowed to come and watched unhappily from her balcony with Fräulein Cuna standing behind her. But Baba, fascinated by what was going on in the neighbors' garden, had come around the fence and was leaning on it, her bushy white eyebrows lifted in surprise. And Tatiana stood behind the last row of guests in her brocade shoes—they were already unbuttoned, for the work entailed by the dinner party had swollen her feet—no less entranced.

An unbelievable night it was too, without stars or moon (a threat of rain had hung over their heads all day long), with a low plushlike sky, dark and passionate. Alarmed by the prospective storm, the poplar trees fretted, showing the silver lining of their leaves, all through the play.

"Is he a gypsy?" Baba asked Tatiana at the first coffee-grinding session that followed that unforgettable night. Tatiana put her head back and had a good fat laugh. The curve of her neck was particularly pleasing when she laughed like that. With a patronizing air, for Baba wasn't used to living among artists, Tatiana reported this to Mother. A thunder of laughter shook the dining-room chandelier when Jean Paul was told about it; the glass beads shivered and tinkled. Next day at the Turkish coffee hour, Mother was startled by a gypsy walking in through the garden gate, an operetta gypsy with a large hat and a wild mustache. He wore Jean Paul's familiar velvet trousers and was just fastening a red belt over them. Through the shrieks and laughter—Tatiana almost dropped the tray of coffee cups—the gypsy explained, as he took off his hat and became a small and slightly bald Jean Paul, that he couldn't cross the street in daylight dressed like that and had carried his hat in a bag. But the mustache was hard to attach, and he had had to put it on at home and cover it with his hand while passing the grocery. Mr. Totis had spotted him: "Hurts like hell, doesn't it, Mr. Paul?" he had yelled sympathetically from his door, putting his small fat hand to an imaginary tooth. Jean Paul had nodded and rushed past. "But don't you think my mother could well have been a gypsy?" he asked, pushing his chest out, caressing his mustache. The mustache didn't fit inside the brim of the small coffee cup and he had to take it off and put it on his napkin. To Jean Paul's noticeable enjoyment, Tatiana put her head back and, arching her neck, abandoned herself to another fit of laughter.

PUPPETS! PUPPETS! PUPPETS!" Tatiana muttered, kneeling by the bed in Ania's room and trying blindly to reach a pile of objects with her mop. Tatiana was the only one who had kept her head above the great wave of puppetry that swept through the house.

"Miss Ania, what is all that rubbish you've piled up under your bed?"

"Don't touch it! I need it for the puppets!"

"But I have to clean the floor. Look at this." Tatiana fished out a red woolen sock, two ping-pong balls, a straw hat with a broken brim and a box full of rattling noises. The box opened, the lid rolled away and a collection of buttons spread all over the floor. It made Tatiana angry. "What the—"

"Jean Paul needs them!"

"Needs this?" With her slipper Tatiana pushed away the red sock. "Is he opening a flea market?"

How could you explain all the hidden possibilities in a discarded red woolen sock—that it might become a red fox, a red bonnet, or a marvelous little vest for an old fisherman with a pipe and a face like a dry apple?

"Wait until tonight, Tatiana. He'll have a look at them. He might want to use some!"

" 'Course," Tatiana said, planting her dusting rag and mop in the middle of the room, leaning on the mop handle like a shepherd in a Nativity painting, "I'll stand right here and wait for him. I haven't anything else to do." The idea appealed to her and suddenly her laugh filled the room, ruffled the organza curtains. The treasure under the bed was moved to the cellar.

"Mother, do you think I still need this old scarf?"

"Which one? It isn't old."

"But do I need it?"

"Why?"

"Jean Paul is looking for a piece of silk just like this, yellow and orange, for his—"

"Ania! It's the scarf Uncle Eric brought you from Hamburg! Please put it back, will you!"

"Do you know yesterday she cut a sleeve off her green sweater?" Mother informed Father.

"What for?" he asked absently.

"Jean Paul needed green jersey for his alligator!"

"Real dedication!" Father said, avoiding involvement in the domestic storm. But it wasn't easy to remain neutral.

"Now she's plucked all the straw from my new broom!" Tatiana erupted into Father's room brandishing the evidence.

"What is the matter?" Father asked, lifting his head from his papers in alarm.

"My best broom," Tatiana complained, holding her favorite instrument under Father's eyes. Father prudently passed the executive powers to Mother and the affair was moved to the dining room. At the afternoon coffee hour Jean Paul listened to Mother's complaint with a delight he was unable to conceal.

"I am serious," Mother said, "this bedlam's got to stop."

But he didn't seem convinced and looked at Mother full of laughter, blinking his short, straight eyelashes.

"I know what I'll do," he said, "we're going to be very serious about it and we'll work every day systematically. I'll make her my assistant. I really need help." And that is how at the beginning of August Ania became an apprentice puppeteer.

An old shirt of Jean Paul's worn like an apron, its sleeves tied round her waist ("Hey, Ania, from here it looks as if my shirt is hugging you!"), she cleaned his dry brushes and sorted all the jars of paint.

"Why do you keep smelling them? Do you sort them with your nose?" He had caught her furtively unscrewing the lids and taking deep, voluptuous sniffs. Her nose was stained with paint and looked as busy as her hands. The old house was full of the putrid smell of newspapers Jean Paul had boiled down in the kitchen to make papier-mâché. They waited for the paste to cool off and, rolling up their sleeves, squeezed the gray mud in the pail until it became creamy and soft and under the pressure of a testing thumb acquired a stable dimple. And then, tying the sleeves of the old shirt securely behind her, she made her first puppet, a clown with blue button eyes. Jean Paul put it in the attic window so that she could see it immediately she came running in next morning. It dried much too slowly. It stood there for three days, ash-colored, blue-eyed, its big nose still wet as if afflicted with a cold. But finally it dried and at long last, dipping her brush in the syrupy red paint which already contained, dissolved in it, a puppet's smile, she could put a vermilion happiness in his grin.

Kneeling on a chair barefoot, she cut the clown's robe out of yellow silk, carefully following the pattern Jean Paul laid before her. The scissors were too big, and she needed both hands to work them. She threaded the needle solemnly, holding it high in the air. The old house was drowsy with morning sleep, and down in the kitchen Jean Paul was getting his breakfast, banging lids and silver. He was usually grouchy early in the morning but that particular day he was singing, and soon bits of song came up the stairs toward her with the shuffling of his velvet mules and the smell of coffee: "*Il y avait une chè-vre-tum-tum ... de grand ta-ra-tum-tum."* He was carrying his breakfast upstairs.

"A puppeteer has to learn how to sew," he said, examining her big crooked stitches critically. "Is there a real school for puppeteers in Paris, Jean Paul? Can you learn everything there?" "Of course you don't learn everything in one place," he said severely. She would have to learn different things from different people. He'd make a program for her in time. You learned costume making and stage setting and this and that—and then you had to forget everything you had learned and put things together all by yourself. She nodded and sighed. It was complicated.

Then the yellow clown, his robe now attached to his neck with strings, his face half buried in a big ruffled collar, stood gloved on Ania's hand looking shy and sad.

"What is he saying?" Jean Paul asked her seriously.

"I don't know yet."

"You've got to know," Jean Paul said sternly. "No puppet ever comes into this world without knowing from the beginning what it wants to be and what it has to say. You made him because you wanted him to say something, didn't you?"

The clown looked up at Jean Paul, intimidated, then put a felt hand on his heart; his silk robe rippled, and he said in Ania's voice, "Oh, Ania, why didn't you finish me sooner? Now I've lost the beginning of summer again!"

"Really? Did she really say that?" Father asked Jean Paul the same evening in the garden after Ania had gone to bed. Jean Paul nodded. "But what did she mean? What did she mean by 'again'?" And behind his glasses Father's amber eyes were suddenly full of shadow. They'd talked about this before, Jean Paul said; it was an old wish of hers to find out about the beginning or the end of a season. To catch it, to smell it, to feel it—the very moment of it. She was always set to watch it and it always eluded her. How did summer come? It wasn't there, not yet, you watched for it every day, and suddenly it was in and out of the city like a wave, and what was left behind was called summer. "Did she say all that?" Jean Paul nodded: "A clown dressed in yellow silk, sad-eyed because he had missed the beginning of summer again. She said she was going to write a part for him in which he asks everyone how summer came this year? She is trying without hesitation for what no mature puppeteer would dare, a poem instead of a puppet play!" And he looked touched.

"What are we going to do?" Mother said, looking so alarmed that both men burst out laughing.

"Now, now," Jean Paul said, putting his hand over Mother's across the table, "no one's taking her from you yet. This is only a game."

But it was not, it was not a game! It was a passion that suffused your blood. It not only changed the color and pace of your dreams at night; it also made you sleep quicker as if you were pursuing a strange happiness, which floated in front of you forever changing, like a kaleidoscope, and which when you awoke became the very day ahead, the apprentice's day in the old house. Had it been only a game, summer wouldn't have ended that way, with all its glorious gold melting in tears. Had it been a game, Sonica would have played it too. But lately she had started to stay out of it, she appeared changed and mysterious.

In August Fräulein Cuna had let down the hem of all Sonica's summer dresses, and suddenly the back of Sonica's knee, a very familiar sight to Ania, was now covered; when occasionally exposed it looked coy, displayed a newly acquired dimple with a tiny blue shadow in it. With intent curiosity and vague alarm Ania watched her friend putting on her father's after-shaving lotion taken from the bathroom shelf. Sonica would run the cold glass stopper gently across her skin at the nape of her neck shivering, closing her eyes under the black bangs. "You're so *beautiful*, Sonica!" And Sonica turned around, watched herself in the mirror over her shoulder, and sighed.

Because her visits to Jean Paul had to stay illegal—she would not ask Fräulein Cuna for permission, she had never mentioned Jean Paul to her—Sonica would arrive at the old house breathless, pleading, interrupting whatever Jean Paul and Ania were doing. "I can't stay long, finish that later, come on outside!" They couldn't work when Sonica was there. Ania had tried to show her how to brush the puppets holding them respectfully at arm's length (she secretly feared that if tickled they might come alive and feel offended), but Sonica was not interested. She didn't like to play with dolls, she said, and Jean Paul managed to hide his smile. "Sonica has other talents," he told them when Ania urged her to become a puppeteer. But he never explained what they were.

A taste of guilt lagged behind after Sonica had left, a threat hung in the air: what if Fräulein Cuna found out Sonica was coming there? And once, to prevent domestic disaster, Baba rushed into Tatiana's kitchen, panting, groaning, dragging her rheumatic leg, and asked Tatiana, her face twitching with complicity, to "run over to the Frenchman and tell Miss Sonica the *Frailai* is looking for her."

But sometimes they talked, the three of them, sitting on the couch in the attic. Sonica's laugh sounded soft and rich under the glass ceiling, felt like the white, sticky, sweet juice of a young plant. In her dark eyes was a call, a plea, which Jean Paul tried not to notice. He patted her cheek and said, "Pretty girl!" and Sonica raised a shoulder, rubbed her face against it—her gesture of disappointment—and sighed. They couldn't do any work when she was there.

"And what did you do today?" Father asked Ania at dinner time. He followed her progress in puppetry closely.

"Today? Nothing. We didn't do anything."

"What did you talk about?"

"We—didn't talk." Ania struggled to put into words that late afternoon with the treetops swaying drowsily left and right. It was true. They didn't talk. They sat at the window and looked down into the garden. Jean Paul had one arm around Sonica's shoulders and the other around Ania.

"Oh, look," Ania had said, "look at my pigtails, how they've grown! When I bend they make shadows on the sundial! Jean Paul! Watch this!" She made funny Chinese shadows on the blue and gold tiles, moving the tips of her pigtails with her hands. But Jean Paul and Sonica didn't answer, something was happening to them.

"You've got to go now," he had said suddenly, urging them to leave. "You'll be late again." And then there was a strange agitated silence behind Ania's back. Skipping home along the wooden fence, playing at jumping the sidewalk stones one at a time, Ania didn't notice Sonica's flushed face, her pouting lip, her reluctant step. Sonica lagged behind moodily, munching the stem of a geranium leaf.

AH, IT WAS A GLORIOUS AUGUST! A canopy of gold tightly stretched over the city; tall days, all alike, steel blue and pure, and the cry of the watermelon man piercing the morning air; hot evenings lined with the city noises in the distance, the dark sky wearing an aurora borealis of neon lights. At night patterns of black leaves ran across your bedroom wall, and the top sheet slipped onto the floor and lay coiled into a white linen animal faithfully watching over you as, intoxicated with laughter, you talked into the pillow in your sleep.

Summer had reached its full stature now. Like a ride through the stars that time was. Carefree, effortless, you soared higher and higher, over the city, over the world until, dipping into the Milky Way, you felt its icy-blue milk splash around your ankles, heard it spill across the dark summer sky. Sometimes, at dessert, Father would search the sky and point out the Dipper or the Giant Bear to Mother and Jean Paul, and they both looked up, silent and bewitched, as if they too were taking off for that galaxy of longings. But you didn't need to read the stars to know the season was now immovable, securely in position, strong and everlasting.

Who first talked of other kinds of trips? Of parting? Of other cities? Of being homesick? No one in particular. But on and off Jean Paul's city came into their talk over dinner, and maybe this finally eroded the stability of summer. When he talked like this about Paris, he put blue bridges across the tablecloth; a dark cathedral stood suddenly where the wine bottle was; the teapot became a marble monument and the silver handle of the fruit basket a glorious Arc de Triomphe which, unaware of the city being created in front of her, Tatiana removed with a deft hand.

It was the very core of summer—yet somewhere deep inside it something must have altered. Subtly, imperceptibly, it started to match the sadness in Father's favorite poem:

I heard the apples jumping to their death
their suicide was fragrant.

Maybe the apples were not ready yet, but the green plums certainly were, plump and bursting out of their tight black jackets, exploding with juice when they fell to the ground. "Does Jean Paul really want to return to Paris?" "I don't know," Father would answer, "ask him." But when you asked him, he didn't give a straight answer. He hesitated. "Some people are like migratory birds," Mother would say, looking up from her book, and in a way Ania felt there was a vague disapproval in her remark: swallows migrated, and gypsies too. If Tatiana happened to be in the dining room, busy stacking dishes at the side table, she would stop work for a second, her elbows at her sides, and her tense back would seem to listen to the conversation.

And there were other signs audible to the expert. The green, acid cry with which Ion the vegetable man advertised his salad altered toward the end of August. It was no more that quick, spiral ascent into the morning air, "buy-fresh-sa-lad," the last a trembling, pure and sharp like a steel aigrette. It became a dramatic "young-young-young-sa-lad-for-sale"; made the salad sound like a tender king's daughter in ruffled green-silk skirts put up for sale in the market place. An inexplicable desolation crept into the summer mornings the days he sold salad.

A gypsy came to the back door to ask if there was any copperware to be cleaned. Yes, they had some. They had to get the big kettle ready for the plum povidla. Mother told Tatiana to give it to the man and bargain about the price. Tatiana had had a busy morning and for a few days now had looked preoccupied. But she put down her knife next to the carp on its bed of newspapers and, postponing the execution, went out with the kettle.

The dark, lanky man squatted in the yard and started to work in ruminating silence. Tatiana went out again to call in his woman, who was sitting on the sidewalk outside, her bare feet in the gutter. She came in, balancing her long skirts caked with mud at the hem. A sleepy, wrinkled baby like an eyeless kitten hung at one of the flabby breasts she had let out of her blouse. The baby munched at it in his sleep. She sat down on the kitchen steps and in a rasping alto voice asked Tatiana for a piece of bread.

Familiar with poverty and condescending in her compassion, Tatiana settled next to the woman and watched. The man had built a small fire on the yard stones and was warming the kettle over it. He dropped a little ball of pewter into the big-bellied pot and rolled it sideways with his tongs while the pewter melted inside, gently spreading a glittering lining. Slowly the big kettle was losing the memories of all the preserves it had cooked the previous summer and was becoming rejuvenated and shiny.

On the kitchen steps the gypsy's yellow scarf and Tatiana's head were drawn close together. Tatiana held up her hand. She was having a consultation about her future. "A trip?" she asked. Her face darkened. "Who's taking it?" Ania drew a bit closer.

"And how should I take it?" Tatiana was just asking. "In water?" So she wasn't referring to the trip now.

The woman let Tatiana's hand go and said with a wide grin, "In wine. Add some crushed sharp pepper and drink it quickly before you go to sleep. It'll make you bleed the next day——"

"What do you want, Miss Ania?" Tatiana had suddenly noticed her. Ania was frightened. She had always been told to stay away from the gypsies because they stole things and weren't clean. Now this one wanted to make Tatiana bleed. "Wait a minute, I'll bring you some bread," Tatiana said to the gypsy, and got up to go inside.

"Let me see your hand, pretty miss." The gypsy spoke with authority and because Ania didn't know how you talked to a gypsy and because anything unfamiliar and ugly made her cringe, she took two timid steps forward and put out her hand unwillingly.

"Hey, you! Leave her alone," Tatiana said, coming out with the bread. "Her mother doesn't like that!" But the gypsy had already taken a look at the small palm and her burning eyes had darted once at Ania's face, leaving two hot marks somewhere inside her being. "Great Lord!" said the gypsy aloud, covering her black lips with one hand. Then she whispered something in Tatiana's ear. "What's she saying?" Ania asked.

"Not the child?" said Tatiana in alarm, tearing herself from the woman's hot whisper and pushing her away. "That's enough now. Don't be silly. Here's your bread. Go wait out in the street." The coin fell into the woman's blackened hand; she gathered her skirts and carried them away.

Tatiana inspected the shiny kettle with an absent, guilty air. Her hair bun hung disheveled at the side of her neck, a sign she was greatly disturbed. She became irritable when the man asked for bread and then for a jug to drink water from. She ushered him out of the yard at last and stayed there at the open gate as if to make sure they left the street too. But preoccupation with something else showed in everything she did that morning. Unusually permissive, she let Ania climb onto the corner of the table to assist at the execution of the fish.

The silver armor the fish wore was torn apart, and scales were sent flying around under the indifferent, viscous eye of their owner. Then Tatiana's expert finger searched the open belly of the carp, pulled out intact the little balloon pearled and veined in red, and presented it to Ania.

"Miss Ania," she said suddenly, "don't tell Madam about the gypsy." She avoided Ania's look and went on searching under the pearly lids the fish had on both sides of its head, pulling out small ribbons of wet red velvet. And suddenly, before Ania could reassure her, Tatiana put down her big knife, her eyes swimming with water, and hugged Ania tightly. Moved by that fit of tenderness, which made her feel frail and precious as if passing through some terrible danger—like when she had whooping cough—Ania, still holding the fish bladder, hugged Tatiana round the hips, put her head on the warm rubber ball that was Tatiana's belly and, with a feeling of infinite security, recognized through the odor of raw fish Tatiana's special smell of mountain cheese.

No one knew about the other Jean Paul, the Jean Paul before ten o'clock in the morning. Not even Mother, and certainly not Tatiana, who never sat down before lunchtime and whose only break was to rub one tired ankle against the other for a second. And Ania wasn't going to talk about it.

But if she went to visit him before ten o'clock in the morning she would find an unknown Jean Paul sitting on the front steps under the arch of ivy, sleepy, unshaven, his shirt crumpled, a few white hairs on his chin (she tried not to look at them), unhappily wiggling his toes in his sandals. He wouldn't answer her greeting; he continued to draw in the smoke of his cigarette resentfully and to blow it out like a grunting volcano. With one eye tightly closed, he looked up at her standing against the sun, then at the black walnut tree, and threatened both of them that he would give up this damned run-down house and go back to Paris. Only in a barbarian country like this did you have to make your own breakfast. At home, a fellow could go down to the bistro at the corner and be served with a decent coffee. Stiffening at being called a barbarian, not understanding what had happened to him, Ania sat silently on the step and didn't dare move. Her hair hurt, too tightly braided by Tatiana, who was always in a hurry in the morning, and the stone felt chilly through her summer panties. And she didn't know what a bistro was. Furious at her silence, he would throw his cigarette butt at the pilgrimage of diligent ants advancing toward his sandal and suddenly go inside. For a while he would move about the kitchen, throw silver in the sink, bang lids, and talk to the coffee pot. Then he would emerge with a steaming cup in his hand and, blissfully closing his eyes in the sun like a big cat, he would become reconciled to the world.

"He doesn't want to stay and he can't make up his mind to return. That's what troubles him," Father said.

"I don't know if he should stay," Mother answered. "What has he done so far for his fall show? Nothing at all. He just talks about it!"

"But first he has to know if he is going to stay or not. What's the use of making all those contacts if you don't know where you're going to work?"

Lately Mother had argued with Jean Paul. "Discipline is the only answer." Jean Paul put his head back and looked at her under his straight eyelashes. "The answer to what, Nora?" But she dismissed his irony. "If you're a serious artist, you've got to learn how to curb your passion, or it will consume you like a fever. And only discipline—"

"Such a frail woman," Jean Paul said, turning to Father,

"and she talks like Savonarola!" And to her, "Art is pleasure! Who says I have to torture myself? Why should I run a fever? The things women dream up!"

"Mother—"

"Yes."

"Who is Savonarola?"

Mother looked at Father for help.

"A French soap manufacturer," Jean Paul said seriously. "They called him after his soap, *Le savon Arola*."

A thunder of laughter chased the night moths away.

"Why do you tell her such things?"

"Very well, then. You explain to her who he was."

"Well, he was—"

"He was a monk. An Italian monk," Father said seriously, "and he—how *do* you explain fanaticism to a child?"

"Don't ask me. I've given her an explanation."

But Mother was not to be diverted. "Maybe—I don't know, maybe it's the fault of our Balkan summers, the linden trees and the siestas and the plump women—is all this very stimulating for you?"

"Oh, I like the women," Jean Paul said.

"I know," Mother smiled. "I am not worried about that!"

"Is it true your Frenchman is leaving?" Baba asked Tatiana. The possessive pronoun referred not to Tatiana but to Ania's household. Jean Paul had been part of it for quite a while. Yet the knowing wink that accompanied the question irritated Tatiana. "How would I know?" Then she asked after a while. "Who told you he was?" Baba couldn't remember. It was just in the air.

But summer was stagnant for a while. It shook itself once when, panting, her straw hat hanging down her back, Sonica ran over to the old house to say good-bye to Jean Paul and Ania. She was going to the seashore for two weeks. Desolate, she looked at Jean Paul imploringly but he only patted her cheek and said, "Good-bye, pretty girl," and after that summer seemed even more lazy and somnolent.

A summer storm broke out one day when Ania was in the attic working at a new puppet, making a sad-eyed, silk-ruffled wife for the yellow clown. The old house shook and creaked, and the walnut tree went mad in the wind, bending and howling like the sea. The house was a big ship out in the storm, and downstairs in the belly of the ship the empty rooms smelled of wet bricks. The rain came in, and Jean Paul rushed downstairs to close the windows. But up in the attic, on the deck, you were safe even if the sound of hail on the glass roof was deafening and the rain made foam on the windows. They just had to sail carefully through the storm with all their sails furled. "Ahoy! Jean Paaauul! Did you close the veranda door too?" "Ahoy! I did. I am coming!" The captain of the ship climbed the stairs; she could hear his sandals on the wooden floor; they were safe. He had brought a basket of green-gages, which smelled of the kitchen cupboard. They ate them standing at the window watching the walnut tree wrestling with the storm. Who was going to win?

And then the black crust of the sky cracked open, the storm stopped and it was daylight again; the old ship still danced on the waters. They looked down and saw Father's big umbrella advancing toward the front door. Under it, walking cautiously around the puddles, was Tatiana. Mother had sent her over with Ania's red sweater. Tatiana seemed to know the garden well, walked with a certain intimate assurance, circled the house and disappeared through the kitchen door. Jean Paul went downstairs for her. But they didn't come up, and after a while Ania went down to them. In the kitchen, startled by Ania's sudden appearance, Tatiana busied herself with her blouse, which had come out of her skirt, and checked the hairpins hanging from her disheveled bun. Jean Paul picked up the umbrella from the floor.

"Tatiana," Ania shouted passionately, "come upstairs and see the puppets!" It was a good opportunity to win Tatiana over. But Tatiana didn't have time for art that day. Some other time, she said. Mother was waiting for them; they had to go back that very minute. "Both of us!" she added, striving to catch Ania's talkative hands through the sleeve-tunnels of her red sweater. Ania's hands appeared at the other end of the sleeves and regained their loquacity. "Please, Tatiana, it'll only be for a minute, you won't be sorry!" So Tatiana made a rapid visit upstairs, marveling at everything with exaggerated ardor and finding her way around much too easily for someone who was a stranger to the old house and the world of puppets.

The rain had washed the garden, stirred up the strangest

smells in the beds of blue weeds. The pool in front of the veranda reflected the old house upside down, still shivering after the storm. Jean Paul shook the tree for green walnuts while they stood under it, shrieking when water ran down their neck and inside their dress. "They are almost ripe," Tatiana said, inspecting the walnuts, but nobody thought that this was going to mean a change in the season. Wasn't that summer going to be eternal?

But then—how did it ever happen that without any warning summer slipped back, joining what was called the past? Until the day before it had been called the present. A corridor of reverberating amber light, a corridor of amber, that was what the summer had been. Did fall come exceptionally early that year? Did it sneak in during the last part of August when the season lies like a dry, open fruit from which all the seeds have blown away? In your sleep you felt a chill running through the room, the curtains blown by an unfriendly breeze, and the tall lamps shivered, like storks stuck on one leg in the prairie of the rug. You groped for the blanket folded at the end of the bed and pulled it up without awakening. Yet the following morning was still a summer morning—except that a melancholy truth was discernible: the morning glories were pregnant with seeds. And Tatiana had started to mend the elbows of her green woolen jersey, the one she wore in winter.

THE END OF WHAT?" Mother was saying into the telephone when Ania opened the living room door. Then she laughed, glanced at Ania and added, "Yes, I know, but you are spoiling her! . . . No, don't cook a special meal. She eats canary food. . . . One of us will come for her after dinner. Don't make it too late, please."

"Do you want to have dinner over at Jean Paul's tonight, Ania?" she asked, putting the receiver down.

"All of us?"

"No, just you. He said"—Mother fought a smile but lost the fight; the smile flooded her eyes, their blue water oscillated—"you're invited to watch the end of the summer. Father will come for you at eight."

"Eight thirty, Mother!"

Mother didn't answer. "The end of the summer," she said in a wondering voice. "The things he thinks of!" And from her tone Ania knew that this was one of Jean Paul's great victories. Of course she knew this was a game but it was a challenge, a walk on a tightrope. "And would you know the very minute? The very last one?" she had asked him when they talked about it with the yellow clown between them. Jean Paul had nodded confidently. "The very last minute." But she thought he had forgotten all that.

She was ready to go, her hair specially brushed by Mother since Tatiana was busy with the fruit tarts. "Can you carry them all by yourself?" Mother asked.

"They'll be safe if she remembers not to skip or run," said Tatiana, standing in the doorway, holding a plate covered with a white napkin. "Some are with sour cherries and some are with apricots—will you remember? And hold it this way, Miss Ania," she advised, "or the syrup'll be all over your dress."

Jean Paul received her at the back door, wearing a white

66

apron and a huge cook's bonnet he had made out of tissue paper. "Here's one for you!" he said, handing Ania a smaller one. "First we're the cook and helper and then we're going to be the lord and lady of the mansion. It's easy for puppets to change behind the scenes." The white of his bonnet made him look tanned, and his ears stood out on both sides of it and gave him a very busy air. He unpacked the tarts with respectful hands. "Oh, Tatiana-Tatiana, you won-der-ful girl," he sang, moving them to a cake plate. The kitchen was hot, the great black heart of the stove was pounding loudly, and as he opened the oven door and looked inside it with one eye narrowed, the roast breathed into his face a complicated aroma of wine and garlic and herbs which floated past Ania and made her weak with hunger. "The soup is calling me," he said, inspecting the tureen on top of the stove, and with the refined wrist motions of a conductor he dropped liquid ribbons of batter into the pot. "Aaahhh," he approved with noisy satisfaction, blowing into the spoon and tasting from it.

But they couldn't sit down to dinner just yet. They heard steps running across the garden and then along the veranda. Sonica's checkered dress showed in and out of all the windows; then Sonica herself jumped down the two steps into the kitchen, brown and shiny, her hair longer, her smile gleaming. "Sonica! When did you come back?" "Just now!" Fräulein Cuna was unpacking. "Couldn't you stay for dinner? Look! Look at the roast Jean Paul has made!" Oh no, it was impossible. She had just told Fräulein Cuna she would run over to Ania to tell her she was back. She nibbled a slice of meat and the top cherry of a tart and was ready to leave, the talkative, inviting glitter at the corner of her eyes. "You look beautiful, Sonica," Jean Paul said, and Sonica turned around, forgot she was leaving, basked in his look. He took her cheeks in his hands, felt without wanting to acknowledge it the throbbing color of her cinnamon skin, lifted her head, and mirrored himself in turn in each of her lacquered eyes. "Your eyes look longer," he said, and then lowered her head gently, as if putting everything back in place. "Let me see," Ania said, standing on her chair. "Yes, they do, Sonica!"

Sonica left, and they sat down to dinner at the kitchen table, which Jean Paul had covered with a piece of green velvet. "We eat on velvet?" Ania asked, amazed and at the same time alarmed. "Sure. I eat every day on velvet," he said seriously. The door to the living room was wide open and they could see how, even before seven o'clock, the sun had collected all its spears—the one stuck in the draperies, the one planted in the plump back of the armchair, and the long one, the last, in the middle of the carpet—and had gone home. "The days are shorter now, aren't they? I hate winter," he said. Then they ate in silence, smiling at each other from time to time. But a premonition went through the house, made you feel that somebody upstairs somewhere was standing on tiptoe, prepared, ready to take off.

It happened suddenly, shortly after Jean Paul had changed the plates for dessert, just as he was about to lift a tart on his fork. The cuckoo inside the big clock in the dining room put its head out and slammed the shutters back seven times, and its cry had an urgency that made Ania shiver. The noise went up the stairs and through the house and the silence that followed was unbearable.

"Is it now?" she whispered.

"Sssshsh," he said, nodding, lifting his head and swallowing hard, his Adam's apple moving inside his open collar. A door closed in the attic all by itself and a muffled sound—hurried steps?—ran all over the house as if the place was being emptied in a hurry by an invisible tenant. And then, with a shock, she felt the earth had stopped turning for an instant— had hesitated—had resumed its motion. It was what the apples must have felt jumping from the tree, the apples in the poem—I-heard-the-apples-jumping-to-their-death-their-suicide-was-fragrant. Was this their death, good-bye to the rains and to the stars, the foliage brushing their cheek while they fell deeper and deeper into—?

How long did it last? They were facing each other in silence, fork in hand, eyebrows raised, eyes enlarged. Jean Paul stirred, turned to the blue kitchen clock, consulted it with an expert look and said, "It's over. Let's go outside and see what the world looks like now."

He opened the front door and stood on the steps under the ivy in the dusk. Oh, you could see right away that summer had ended. You could see how the garden had saddened. And how much farther away the stars were! The Milky Way looked foggy and the thought of riding on it now in fall, of crossing a cold, dark sky, made you shiver. At the end of the street, far away on the boulevard, a trolley passed. The long, familiar sound it made had a sharp melancholy to it. Fall was in the city. The evening was touched with a blight which was soon going to spread, to eat into the vigor of summer.

"Just as I thought," Jean Paul said, looking up. "That was it. Come, let's finish the tarts."

AT eight o'clock Father's white coat came out of the blue of the garden. "It suddenly felt chilly a while ago," he said seriously. "Now that the summer's over I need my coat." And the three of them smiled, a short, quick smile with an edge of conspiracy on it.

Father stayed a while, seated on the front steps next to Jean Paul, and Ania leaned against his leg, full of sleep. "No, I am not," she protested when Father wanted to know if she was sleepy. Jean Paul put out the entrance light to send away the mosquitoes, and a new wind, a silky, thin wind, rose from the dark corners of the garden. The scent of the linden trees, which until the other day had burned white incense, was suddenly missing, and a long, sad, damp smell of wilted calyxes had replaced it.

She woke up with a start and heard Jean Paul saying, "It was not my idea, this end of summer, it was hers, I only suggested——" "Yes, I know," Father answered, "but you staged it." "The way she went along with it, that was something to see. She is very talented, I have told you that before," Jean Paul said. "Ah," Father answered after a hesitation, "I don't know if that makes me happy or not." "Come now, there are some artists who dare to be truly happy, you know. Puppeteers are, anyway." "Are they?" Father asked hopefully. "Of course they are. They're children. They play."

She looked up from under Father's sleeve. Father seemed sad, the sockets of his eyes were full of shadow. "You always thought you could have her around to carry in your pocket. True?" "Yes," Father said, "at least until she is ready for the world." "Like a kangaroo!" "Pretty much so!" and Father laughed helplessly.

"But you won't have to leave immediately," said Father, continuing a conversation they must have started while she was asleep. "No," Jean Paul said, and his voice sounded as if his neck were arched back. (He was looking up at the stars.) "No, I don't think so. I'll have to try and sell the house first." But she wasn't sure she had really heard the last words, her head was full of sleep.

"Do let us know if there's anything we can do," Father said, trying to lift Ania off his leg. "Get up, sleepy, we have to go home." "You have both been wonderful to me. You must send this puppeteer to me one day when she is 'ready for the world.'" But Father waved his hand, chasing away the thought, got up and rubbed his leg. "I'm not asleep," Ania protested when Father asked her if she could walk in her sleep. But she wasn't sure she had really heard their talk.

The street was empty when they left, and the darkness so transparent that they seemed to make two moving shadows on the blue of the curb. Jean Paul leaned on his gate, humming.

"Won't you miss such nights?" Father asked as they walked away, and his answer came back with his great laugh, "Not only the nights," and Father waved.

"Miss Ania, not in bed yet?" asked Mr. Totis, suddenly stirring in the darkness of his open door. He was out in his chair, taking the air before going to sleep; a whiff of stale room and cinnamon came out of the shadowy house, his old mother groaned and moved in the rocking chair behind him. And at the end of the street the darkness released Picu's tasseled silhouette, and then his padded staccato step sounded on the warm stones. He came closer to inspect them and his tired tail signaled absolute friendship.

"Is Jean Paul going to leave?" she suddenly asked, as Father started to unlock the garden gate.

Father looked down at her sleepy head, saw the white part in the middle of her hair, the tender skin inside her creased collar, and one pigtail undone, the tiny ribbon trailing desolately on her shoulder. "Not right away," he said. And then he added, "But aren't you a puppeteer in your own right now? You could always manage by yourself, couldn't you? Aren't you going to give a show in school when it starts?"

She laughed, full of sleep, confidently holding onto the iron gate with both hands. Father was huge in the darkness next to her. She laughed again. "Why did he call you a kan-

garoo?" "He is like that," Father said, laughing (the lock had
to be changed, it was starting to rust), "he gets ideas like
that—you know him, don't you?" She nodded her head, yes,
she knew him. The garden was talkative, the crowns of the
trees chatty, and their own shadows walked them along the
wall when the lock opened at last. Far away, in the illuminated rectangle of the kitchen door, they could see Tatiana in
her brocade shoes drying the dishes in a hurry.

IT MUST HAVE BEEN THE COOKING of the plum povidla that
rushed everything, brought the end closer. One morning Ion
was at the back door, his baskets full of small juicy plums.
They cooked them the same afternnon.

Ania had invited Jean Paul to assist them. It was a complicated operation. First they pitted the fruit and left it open,
bleeding and flabby in the blue pail while Tatiana made a fire
outdoors under the big kettle. And then, obviously embarrassed by the presence of a guest, yet betraying a certain
secret satisfaction, she squeezed the plums in the kettle with a
huge wooden spoon. Walking softly over the gravel path,
stopping, hesitating, and then approaching again, Sonica
came too as soon as she heard Jean Paul's voice outside. She
had been very moody during the past week and had refused
to go over to Jean Paul's when Ania called her. She had blue
shadows under her burning eyes and walked cautiously, as if
her head were too heavy for her neck and she had to tilt it a
bit on the flat white collar. She stopped at the other side of
the boiling kettle and looked at Jean Paul through the steam.

"Watch it! Watch it now!" Tatiana kept shouting. The
plums were bubbling, whispering mysteriously, giving up the
ghost in a divine aroma, splashing black stars over the spec-
tators, who jumped back with shrieks of laughter. Jean Paul
put on one of Tatiana's aprons and, seizing the wooden
spoon, danced around the fire like a cannibal, shouting words

backwards. They were magic words, and he was going to change them all into povidla jars! Tatiana's blouse was stained under the arms with two half-moons of sweat, and damp pearls were shining on her upper lip. Roused from his siesta, Picu barked furiously. The noise spread over the bushes and reached Mother's ear through the open windows. Twice she appeared at the door to supervise the proceedings, her right eyebrow slightly raised in disapproval. They were driving Tatiana crazy! But by this time her authority intimidated only Picu, who was persuaded to retire to his own yard.

The preserve was made, and the jars filled up, covered with paper bonnets and lined up on the kitchen table. They sampled it sitting outside at the garden table, spread it, still warm, on big slices of dark bread. A chilly wind rose from nowhere, made them button up their sweaters. "Fall," Ania announced, looking up. And like a stone thrown into water, the word made rings that got larger and softer, and what remained of that eternal summer was gone with the last of them.

What happened after that, not only to the season but to all of them, was really strange. Things that had been familiar and light and easy yesterday now became halting and difficult. Wrapped in a mysterious silence, Sonica seemed to avoid Ania. She went to visit Jean Paul all by herself. Her pauses when the three of them were together were longer and ambiguous now. Sometimes Jean Paul looked solemn, seemed to surround Sonica with special attentions as if she were recovering from some illness. Impatient, the season moved on. One morning when he was shaving, half his face furred with white, he saw in the mirror that the ivy flag at the bathroom window had turned the color of cinnamon.

THE DOOR OF ANIA'S BEDROOM had been left ajar. She liked to have it that way. In the dark she could see from her bed a string of light around the door and a tiny star stuck in the keyhole.

"I wish I knew why he is leaving." Mother was talking to Father in the dining room.

"We saw it coming, didn't we?" Father said. A pause followed. Ania heard the scratching of a match against a box, then the pk-pk-pk of his pipe lighting up. The smell of tobacco curled and uncurled in the room. Tatiana's step hesitated between the cupboard and the table.

"What's the matter, Tatiana? Are you dizzy again?"

"I . . . don't know, Madam."

"I am going to take you to the doctor. You don't look well."

"I'm all right. Nothing wrong with me."

A door closed.

"What were you saying about Jean Paul?"

"I am sorry he is leaving us." Father's voice smiled. "I have invested in this friendship and I was counting on it for the long winter."

"Something wasn't quite right," Mother said again. "From the very beginning he didn't seem too eager to start working here. He talked about giving shows but I don't think he really wanted to."

"He had a difficult time. He didn't know if he was going to settle here and kept postponing the decision. How can you work under such conditions?"

"No, it isn't only that—"

"I know," Father interrupted her, "I know, but puppetry is not like writing."

"That's no excuse!" The rubbing sound must have been Mother's hand smoothing the tablecloth.

"What excuse?"

"That one kind of art is more difficult than another. Everyone has to solve his particular set of problems—"

"Yes, but it doen't work that way. You have to—"

Lying in her bed in the dark, Ania forgot to listen to what they said. The words came in through the door, but she let them float around softly hooded in darkness. They didn't know what had happened. Nobody knew what had happened. She moved her cheek on the pillow and a tear slipped into the corner of her mouth. She caught it on the tip of her tongue, it tasted salty. She kicked the quilt with her foot. She wasn't going to tell anyone what had happened. The quilt fell on the floor with a silky sigh. Nobody knew. . . .

Jean Paul had returned home for dinner late that evening; he had shopped for groceries at Totis' and stepped out again into the fall night. Shivering, he shrank into himself, like a migrating bird with its feathers ruffled by the early cold. He knew just how the garden would look in winter, the trees bald, icicles at the front door, the water freezing inside the old pipes, the house hostile, impossible to heat. He hated the cold. What was he doing here anyway? Ania and Sonica would come to see him on Sundays, wearing heavy coats and fur hats. Sonica would be wearing her school uniform with black cotton stockings. She was only a schoolgirl. Funny, she looked so much older. Suddenly he felt sobered. He made his way through the weeds outside the back door, stumbled over a stone, cursed, remembered he had intended to put a new bulb in the outside light, and then stepped down into the kitchen. The kitchen lamp squinted a timid light over the sinkful of dirty dishes. At the kitchen table, elbow propped on the stained tablecloth, cheek in hand, Sonica was waiting for him.

"Hey, good evening, late guest," he said, somewhat startled. "What are you doing here?" He shed his parcels on the table and only then, coming closer, he saw that Sonica had been crying. Her eyes were dry now but the eyelids were swollen and her face was burning. "What has happened, Sonica?"

Sonica didn't answer at first. There was a long pause and in the silence he suddenly heard the garden through the open kitchen door. The three-legged blue clock on the shelf ticked like a restless heart.

"I've run away from home," she said finally.

Jean Paul's smile narrowed and went out. It occurred to him that if Fräulein Cuna was looking for Sonica on the street she could see her through the illuminated kitchen window. "Come into the living room," he said, "they can see you from the street." Remembering that the living room didn't have any curtains, he left the lights out and the door to the kitchen open. It was cold. Sonica stood under the Chinese tapestry, hugging herself with her arms. He looked for his pipe and went to sit at the other end of the room.

"Why did you run away?"

Sonica opened her mouth, closed it again. In the dark he heard the dry sound of her lips parting, the air drawn in quickly. She said, "Fräulein Cuna—hit me!"

Oh, so that was what it was. All right then. "Is this the first time it has happened?"

Sonica hesitated. "No. But now—I can't stand it any more."

For a second his mind jumped to the garden outside, to a footstep; was someone running? No one. How very few crickets there were left. What did she say? "Can't stand it any more!" Poor Sonica! Poor Sonica in love. With that milky laugh of hers, that sweet and voluptuous laugh! She had never complained before. He did not know about her life at home and at what price she kept coming to see him. Now she'd run away to him. A ticklish laugh was growing slowly inside him, and he had to bite on the end of his pipe. "Come now," he admonished himself, "you put this idea into her head!" and crossed the room to Sonica. He couldn't see her eyes in the dark; taking her by the hand, he brought her gently into the patch of light from the open door.

"Listen to me, Sonica," he said seriously, and she looked at him in hope. "Listen, Sonica," he repeated. "You have to go back." There was a pause, and something changed within her tense immobility. She was listening now not to his words but to his presence close to her. He dismissed the idea, went on, "It's good that you came to talk to me, but you can't stay here. You have to go back." He hesitated. "Simply tell Fräulein Cuna she is not to touch you any more. You are grown-up now." He said "now," and all the possible, shadowy implications the word contained exploded like fireworks. Her eyelids went up; her eyes adored him, questioned him, closed again. "You've got to tell her that." But she wasn't listening to what he was saying. Resigned, rocked by his voice, Sonica sighed deeply. The air coming out of her nostrils was cool and fragrant.

"She is like that inside," he thought suddenly. "All new and fresh inside." She was very close, and shivering in her light dress. And it was then that it happened. Sonica's head came closer, again he heard her dry lips close then part pleadingly, a whiff of her father's after-shaving lotion danced between them. And was nothing going to come of that summer? Wasn't it going to bring anything? Wasn't he allowed to give her something to wear in her heart for the long year at school, like a locket on a chain to lie in that little hollow blue shadow where he put his hand to lift her chin—and it must have been then that it happened and they kissed.

They were still in the fog, groping their way back, when Ania moved at the kitchen door. They both saw her clearly, from her stiff face with the pigtails curled up as if magnetized to her sweater buttoned wrong and her antlike legs in heavy socks. She was panting after the long run and had stopped short, bewildered by what she saw. But they didn't look like Ion and Tatiana, no, not like the monster with two heads, dancing on one spot, tortured. Jean Paul had lifted Sonica's chin, had bent his head just a bit—when did Sonica grow so tall? They stood there quietly, facing each other, they let the night run through them, the cold night coming from all the secret corners of the house, the night without crickets, motionless, as if in a dark tapestry. . . .

Then she said, "Fräulein Cuna came to look for Sonica at our house. She was crying and she said she was going to call the police." And turning around, she disappeared into the garden. Motionless, they listened to the sound of her sandals along the fence, on the street.

"Run now, Sonica. Tell Fräulein Cuna you felt sick and you were out in the garden." Holding her by the arm, Jean Paul rushed her out of the house. "She'll be very glad to see you by now. Now is the time to tell her what I said! Come on, chin up! Run!" And in front of the gate, before the hurried parting, he took her hand and for the first time paid her the homage due to a grownup: "Good night, Miss Sonica," he said, bending to kiss her hand.

Dizzy, her head thrown back, Sonica ran home along the empty street. "Lord, how many stars!" she thought aloud, stopping to catch her breath at the front door.

So NOW JEAN PAUL WAS LEAVING. Ania learned the news with a stiff face, without saying anything. No, she didn't want to go visit there, she said. She blinked repeatedly and then left the room. She didn't want to think of them again, how they faced each other, how the cold night went through them, the cold night from all the corners of the house, of that house without secrets, without crickets. She wouldn't go there again. Mother sent Tatiana to help Jean Paul pack his boxes. Tatiana's face looked pale these days, her red hair seemed bleached by the sun, and she tired very quickly. When Tatiana came back Ania approached her. What had Tatiana done there? Had the puppets been packed? She wanted to find out if Tatiana knew something. Had she too seen them in the dark living room? Their shadows must have still been there, on the cold floor. She didn't tell Tatiana anything; she stood in the kitchen doorway, watching her feed the kitchen stove with wood. She didn't want to see Sonica either and Sonica didn't come to look for her. And then one day Fräulein Cuna was at their back door, speaking to Mother anxiously in a low voice. What was she saying? Had she found out about Sonica? What was she going to do to her now? Mother came back into the house, worried. "Sonica has scarlet fever! Don't go there any more!" Then Mother called their doctor on the phone. "What is the incubation period?" Ania heard her ask. "What does incubation mean?" she asked Mother. "It's Latin," Mother answered absently. She was in a hurry. "Can you really talk Latin, Mother?"

Sonica was very sick. The window of her room was closed and her curtain didn't even move. One could see the doctor cross the garden every day, holding his leather bag high to protect it from Picu's bold curiosity. Baba, her eyes red from crying, told Tatiana at the kitchen window, "She's a bit better today; she sat up in bed and had some soup; she's better now." And fall advanced very quickly that year. A curtain of drizzle hung over the city for days on end.

Jean Paul came to their house for the last time. They were giving him a dinner party. School had started and Ania had to go to bed early. She had eaten alone, served in the dining room by an absent-minded Tatiana. "You'll get dessert later," she said. "We can't start the cake before the party." Tatiana had on her blue dress and glossy, starched, white apron and over these her heavy, green sweater. A fire had been lit in the dining room, and the stove was restless, made strange surprised noises at being alive again after the long summer. A soft sound of tinkling jars and crystal stoppers came from the next room, where Mother was dressing for the party. "This is going to be a Farewell party," said Ania. Did Tatiana remember that night with the night moths; the cage of light in the garden; how Jean Paul had suddenly appeared out of the darkness? "Come, finish your dinner, Miss Ania," Tatiana urged, and her face was twisted by a hidden pain stirred by the memories of summer. "Hurry up; I've got to clean here and set the table for the party." Ania went to her room without asking Mother if she could stay up and greet the guests. "What is the matter with her?" Mother wondered, holding the powder puff still on the tip of her nose. "What has happened to her and Jean Paul?"

Later in the evening Jean Paul knocked at Ania's door and asked if he could come in and say good-bye. He looked strange as he opened the door; he had a coat on and Ania hadn't seen him dressed up like this before. He looked very small, as if he had shrunk, like a slim cricket in its dark, tailored shell, and was holding something wrapped in a piece of blue cloth. He sat down at the end of her bed, and they were silent for a moment, avoiding looking at each other. Then he said, "You don't want to talk to me?"

She didn't answer and looked away stubbornly.

"All right then. Don't talk. I'll do the talking."

There was silence. They heard the noise of the plates being changed next door and then Mother's laugh as she said, "Don't misunderstand me now, all I wanted to—"

"Listen to me, Ania. It wasn't anything bad. It wasn't anything serious. Do you understand that?"

They stood there facing each other, and the cold night went through them, the cold night of that house without secrets, without crickets. . . . She looked at him and finally dragged words out of her silence and threw at him: "It wasn't? Can I tell Mother then?"

Jean Paul returned her unsmiling look. "My opinion is that you shouldn't tell her. When two people kiss"—Ania looked away, blinking with embarrassment—"it's their own business and nobody else's."

"Please," whispered Ania, "please let's not talk about this any more. Sonica is sick," she added.

Jean Paul moved closer on the bed and took her hand. Did she connect Sonica's kiss with her illness? Helpless, unhappy, he held her tiny puppeteer's hand in his warm one, kneaded the frail fingers, the tender joints. A small, agitated sparrow hid under the breast pocket of her flowered pajamas. She had a naïve smell of unscented soap. (Tatiana had been in a hurry tonight and had rubbed her in the tub without rinsing the bath glove.)

"Listen, Ania, listen to me now, listen to what I am telling you. It wasn't anything bad. Grownups kiss. They kiss out of joy, you see, when it is . . . beautiful outside or . . ." He felt ridiculous. "Did you find us ugly? Were we ugly?"

They stood there and the night without secrets, without crickets, went through them. . . .

He lifted her chin to see her face, the tears in her eyes swelled and trembled. She moved her head, meaning "No."

"Well, then?"

"Yes—but—" Her chin started to quiver. She struggled to bring the words out. "But Sonica—was—my friend!" And now she was alone, abandoned on the lapel of his coat, sobbing, not wanting to look at him.

He smiled over her hot hair and after a while laid her head back on the pillow, then said, while Ania continued to look

79

up at the ceiling absently, like a convalescent, "Let's say good-bye now. Let's not write. I don't like writing letters anyway. Only the puppets. Remember only the puppets, will you? I've brought you something." He reached for the blue bundle he had carried in and opened it on the blanket. Crouching in her big skirts, Martine looked out at Ania with her suspicious button eyes. And in a pang, there was the sweet, putrid smell of papier-mâché in the old house. Ania didn't move.

This is how she saw Jean Paul for the last time: a plum-colored tweedy insect, leaving, moving away quickly, his head slightly cocked. He didn't turn to look at her, not even as he closed the door behind him.

THE END OF THAT TIME was wrapped in fog. The season had left behind a long train of tears, of damp and frowning days, of embarrassed silences. Something had happened to Tatiana too. One morning she was suddenly very sick in the kitchen and went back to her room. She couldn't get up. The dining room was empty, the table not set; the milk had burned on the kitchen stove and the smell filled the house. Mother went to Tatiana's room; she came out in a panic, wrenching the belt of her housecoat tight, and rushed to the telephone. Father had left home very early that morning.

Tatiana lay in bed, her face turned to the wall. There was a big bloodstain on the sheet. Baba was there too and talked to Mother in whispers behind the kitchen door. But what kind of illness was it if Mother, who was so sweet when Tatiana had the flu, shouted at her, "Have you gone mad? How could you do this, you stupid, ignorant—" "Why did you call her that?" Ania asked, on the point of tears, buttoning her school uniform in the living room doorway. (But nobody bothered to take her to school that morning.) "Don't you dare come out of your room until I call you!" Mother said.

Baba helped Tatiana get dressed. "She could have killed herself!" Mother cried. "Why didn't she come and tell me?"

A carriage pulled up in the street. They had to haul open the big, chained iron gate so it could enter. Tatiana, as white as linen, her hair bun disheveled, her head drooping on one shoulder, was hoisted into the carriage by Mother and Baba; Mother climbed in next to her and held her head. Ania was left alone in the empty house smelling of burned milk. The fires weren't lit and it was cold. Sonica was convalescing.

She never asked about the significance of that terrible event of groaning and blood. After a week Tatiana came home, white and thin, her face drawn. Soon after she left them and went back to her village. On taking leave she cried a bit in the kitchen and then kissed Mother's hand and Miss Ania's. But for a while, whenever she remembered Tatiana, Mother would grow angry again. "Such a stupid woman! She could have died!" And the tiny coffee cup would shudder in her hand.

JEAN Paul never wrote. They didn't know when the old house was sold, but it was clear this had happened when workmen started to tear it down. Ania stood at the curb every day, watching. A tall wooden fence had been erected around the place as if to hide what was happening inside. The day they cut the trees down Father came out and watched too. Speechless, they both looked at the old shivering branches, listened to the long wail of the saw advancing into the heart of the wood, followed with their eyes the desperate curve the trees drew on the clear day as they fell to the earth. "They are being murdered," he said.

PART II *

Es war Sommer und die Bäume flogen zu ihren Vögeln. (It was summer and the trees flew after their birds.)

—PAUL CELAN, *Gegenlicht*

* * * *

MONSIEUR JACQUES, director of the children's summer camp at Callian, Maritime Alps, was having breakfast on his little porch, a tray on his knees. The door to the bedroom was open. By turning a bit, he would have seen in the wardrobe mirror the plump reflection of his wife, her fat elbows raised, rolling her hair into a bun. But he didn't want to turn. In fact, he wanted to be left alone to enjoy this half-hour of peace before the camp woke up, and as long as conversation with his wife could be postponed, he would postpone it, taking his coffee in small sips, watching the exuberant sparrows in the tree in front of him. Last night he had worked late in the office again, paying bills and making schedules (pleased with the memory, he smiled and his eyes narrowed). He had returned late, and the key he dropped in the hallway made a terrifying noise on the stone floor. Had she heard him? Had she noticed the time? But Madame Jacques seemed to have other worries that morning.

"What time is she coming?" she asked in the mirror. Her ample flowered nightgown made her look like a toy bear, but the arms and neck emerging from it had the pleasant rosy color of a skin still young.

"Who?"

"The new counselor."

"Today? She said Thursday."

"It *is* Thursday," Madame said resentfully into the mirror. Where was his mind wandering?

Of course it is, he reprimanded himself quietly. Last night— he pushed the thought away, cleared his throat, and sighed wearily. "Where has the week gone?" Then he searched the pocket of his leather jacket and brought out a letter. "She doesn't mention a time," he said, putting the letter down on the tray.

Madame Jacques removed the big amber hairpin from her mouth, unplugging the way for a burst of acrid satisfaction. "I see! Someone who can't even give precise information about her arrival!"

This was the pattern of their morning talks. Her mood darkened, her irritation slowly began simmering like a kettle, and you had to step out of her way before it reached boiling point. But little puffs of steam shot toward you all day and occasionally the lid jumped. Cautiously, Monsieur buttered a slice of bread and hurried through his breakfast.

"Does she speak decent French at least?"

"Of course. They told me she does."

Madame sent a shrug at the authority invoked. She despised the Foreign Students' Bureau.

"Where did you say she comes from?"

"Bucharest."

"Hungarian?"

"No, Rumanian. Not Budapest, Bucharest."

"What's the difference, anyway?" she asked. "It's all the Balkans. Didn't they have that queen who went to bed with everybody?"

"I am sure she's not related to the queen," he said appeasingly, and his mustache moved up and down as if he were going to sneeze, but he was only smiling.

Madame's image in the mirror vanished, and her voice came now from the corner of the room. She was panting, probably trying to get into her new girdle.

"Why did you have to take on a foreigner again? Didn't we have enough of it last summer? How long has she been in France?"

"I don't know. Not too long. Only a few weeks, I think."

"Is she a refugee?"

Monsieur moved restlessly in his chair.

"I don't know. What's the difference? How many foreign students know if they'll be going back home or not? She came to study. She's going to Paris in the fall and I thought if she could travel back with us we'd have the advantage of—"

Madame saw no advantage. "What is she going to study?" she asked, cutting him short.

Monsieur Jacques hesitated as if he wanted to delay the answer. He licked his spoon carefully. "Art," he said at last, and then added casually, "She is a puppeteer."

Quick steps crossed the bedroom, and Madame herself stood in the doorway fully dressed, her belly wrapped in black silk, her bosom thrust out into the morning sun. Her short arms were folded high on the platform of her breasts in consternation. "That's the last straw," she said. "What on earth do you expect me to do with a puppeteer?"

"She's a very fine girl. They told me so. A bit shy."

"Shy! She won't be too shy to leave us in the middle of it all if the work doesn't suit her!"

"She'll be all right," Monsieur said, getting up and preparing to leave. "Just don't nag her."

"But why didn't you ask to talk to her first? Aren't there any French students left for summer jobs?"

"For the money we pay?" Monsieur went down the veranda steps.

"They have to come here and study puppets!" she complained to the back of his leather jacket. "Hasn't the war taught them anything? Puppets!" The leather jacket disappeared around the corner. "Send Mark to meet her at the bus!" she shouted after him.

Something stirred in the middle of the large bed and pushed aside the blanket. A Siamese cat emerged from the bed covers, disturbed by the noise. Georgette opened her pale eyes, twitched a lofty ear and gave her mistress a reproachful look shimmering with sequins. "She might not know enough French to ask her way up here," Madame explained to the cat.

BUT SHE SPOKE FRENCH FLUENTLY, Madame had to admit that evening, with an accent of course. The girl's raw, Slavic way of rolling her *r*'s made a curious contrast with her soft, almost timid manner. "Ah, she must be English," decided the village women sitting on the bench in the market square, who greedily witnessed Ania's arrival in Callian at four in the afternoon. (This was a temporary decision, because soon Madame Marchand, who ran the post office in the back room of her general store and who read everybody's mail, announced that the girl's letters did not come from England. A conference with the mailman threw little light on the problem. "But she is a very well-mannered girl," Madame Marchand concluded generously.)

Two little yellow buses, an afternoon and an evening one, connected the village with civilization—Nice. There was no other way to travel from place to place in that part of Provence. Knowing this, the little buses put on airs, were often behind schedule, puffed and coughed dramatically climbing the winding road through the olive groves. The evening bus, the more modest one, always arrived in the dark at nine o'clock, quietly carrying a few passengers nodding with sleep inside its dimly lit belly. But in summer, after the opening of the children's camp, the four o'clock bus became insufferably self-important. The mailbag it brought every day grew fat and heavy; the conductor, his shiny meridional locks parted in the middle, was loaded with messages, which he solemnly wrote down in a notebook; there was a sprinkling of summer tourists. The local passengers, dry, somber farmers scorched by the sun, sat in silent hostility to this summer traffic.

Four o'clock marked the end of the daily siesta. The village stirred; the mailman crossed the empty market square to wait for the mailbag inside the bistro in the coolness smelling of damp barrels; black-skirted and swathed in black scarves, the old women of the village took their places on the warm stone bench in front of the bistro to knit and wait for the bus. Their knitting needles jerked on the wool nervously, and in the baskets anchored between their black-stockinged legs the balls of wool jumped like startled animals. From time to time they threw impatient looks to their left, where the sputtering of the bus would soon be climbing the hill. The trees, too, bent to look around the corner, the impatience grew sharper, the village patriarch, an old eucalyptus that shaded the market fountain, made nervous little motions with its pointed leaves, like a pianist warming up with finger exercises. A complicated embroidery of shadows danced over the water in the fountain's bowl. And just before the bell in the tower struck four, in the suspense of that instant, sharp and pure, the sound of water-sprays becoming water-pearls and falling back into the fountain rolled over the square like the gurgling of pigeons.

Then at last the sputtering noise sounded away to the left; the bus was heard coming closer and closer, hiccuping smoke, climbing, diligently swallowing the ribbon of road, and in a whirl of dust it made its entrance into the square and stopped determinedly in front of the bistro. The doors opened; busy, noisy travelers stepped off, milled about, called for their bags, dragged them over the cobblestones. A young, blue calico dress appeared, the crowd thinned, the blue dress became a tall slim girl with a straw hat dangling from her arm. She looked forlorn and apologetic when with a groan the bus conductor deposited an old bulging valise at her feet. There was some loud conversation at the door of the bistro, the mailbag was dragged down from the bus roof, the mailman acknowledged it lazily, buttoning his coat; glass tinkled hurriedly on the counter; the driver came out, climbed astride his seat, and the bus departed in a fit of coughing. Ania was left alone with the foreign village.

The girl looked twice across the way at the knitting women, a little intimidated, then took a few steps around her valise and reached out to fish a floating leaf from the fountain. Her long arm and its blue puffed sleeve mirrored in the water, she crushed the leaf in her fingers and sniffed at it; surprised at the eucalyptus scent, oblivious of the village watching her, she gave a short, frank laugh. Across the way the knitting women nudged each other. "She must be English. And look at the size of her valise. This one means to stay." The news was transmitted with a jerk to the knitting baskets, where the balls of wool jumped higher. At the window over the bakery a cautious hand opened the shutters and an inquisitive eye peered down at the visitor.

Then the bead curtain in the bistro doorway was pushed aside and Monsieur Jacques himself rushed out to meet the girl, his straw hat under his arm, sucking his mustache dry.

He put out a rough, warm bear's paw and shook her hand vigorously. He was awfully sorry to have kept her waiting. He was just having a drink. And it was so much cooler inside. Did she have a good trip? His round gray eyes inspected her while she answered (yes, she did speak French fluently) and he nodded. "I hope you will enjoy yourself here, mademoiselle." But when he tried to lift her luggage his neck stiffened like a bull's, a dark vein stood out in it. "Mark," he called into the bistro. "Mark?" And the knitting women saw Monsieur Mark, the Jacques' nephew, come out in his overalls and his huge, blue espadrilles. "This is Mark," Monsieur said to the girl. "Mademoiselle is our new counselor." ("There, what did I tell you. She's from the camp. They've brought over an English girl for the children!") The girl put out her hand, but Mark had lifted her valise onto his shoulder and his hands were occupied. He acknowledged the introduction with a nod, his head bent sideways under the load.

"Where does it go?"

"Children's cottage. But you aren't going to carry it, are you? Where is the truck?"

"Reine said to leave it in front of the kitchen for Babette to load the empty crates."

"But didn't she know we had gone for—"

"It isn't that heavy, I can carry it."

"And it's hot, too," Monsieur Jacques said, pulling out an enormous handkerchief. Wiping his brow under the brim of his hat, he turned toward the girl. She was looking over her shoulder at the market square. The four o'clock excitement had dissipated, the market was empty again, and in the approaching evening lavender and gold dust rose in the calm air. The girl put her straw hat on, steadying it with one hand, and said in her curious high voice, which rang limpidly across the square, "Your village is so pretty." Mark looked at her quickly and smiled, protected by the shadow of the valise. But Monsieur wiped his forehead again uneasily. "This way, mademoiselle," he said soothingly, the way grownups talk to excited children.

THEY walked in silence behind Mark, their eyes on his noise-less steps in the big espadrilles, until he suddenly took a right turn and disappeared among the bushes. "He's taking a short cut to the cottage," Monsieur explained. "But we'll go the easier way."

"What sort of work does Mark do here?" She couldn't decide if she had to give him a tip or not. "This is Mark," he had said. But was he a workman? A village boy? She didn't have much change left and tipping was always a blistering moment for her.

"Oh, he drives the truck and does the marketing and fetches the doctor and—everything, I guess. He's always with us in summer, we really depend on him, we're very short of help. Well"—he regretted the last sentence—"it isn't that bad, the village teacher gives us a hand and she'll take over for your time off." She listened absently, still tortured by indecision about the tip. "It isn't really bad, but we were impatient to get you here." A tremor went through his mustache, and Ania guessed he was smiling. "Here we are," he said, as they passed a row of cypresses, "the children's cottage. Your room is upstairs. It's nice and quiet now, Mademoiselle Amèlie has taken them down for a swim. It doesn't always look like this!" Then he pulled his big hand-kerchief out and wiped his forehead, preparing for a difficult task. "Come meet my wife," he said, inspecting her once more out of the corner of his eye. "See that door across the lawn? That's her kitchen. She'll be there. Come as soon as you're ready, she's waiting for you."

HE was coming down the stairs, blue espadrilles first, then his overalls, and his head last, his face half hidden by sunglasses. "It's up there," he said, pointing to the landing. And as it seemed to her he had purposely stopped for a second in front of her, she brusquely took the decision and reached out awkwardly. For a startled moment he thought she was shaking hands, but then he understood, quickly turned his palm up; the two coins were hot from having been squeezed in her hand all the way up the hill. "Thank you very much," she said, looking miserably embarrassed. But was it all right? A smile had flashed across his face below the dark sunglasses and had been called back instantly. "Very kind of you," he answered, and the hand holding the coins touched his temple lightly in a casual, friendly salute. She rushed up the stairs, blushing with relief.

Her luggage was waiting in the middle of her room, and there were two large, dusty footprints on the red stone floor. The empty cottage smelled of chlorine and damp sneakers. A lazy afternoon torpor filled the rooms; the shutters were closed at an angle, and strips of sun and shadow moved on the floor when a shutter rocked in its hinges. Through the open doors of the toilets came a whiff of ammonia and fresh paint. Pipes gargled. But below her window the quiet, tame landscape of Provence unrolled hill after hill into valleys of olive trees. The village was out of sight, and the ruin of a medieval castle watched in the distance. The afternoon sun had just reached it, and the keep, still partly standing, was now wet with a pearly light that brought out a rose hue one would have thought the old gray stone had long forgotten. In the middle of the road one of the black charred-looking old village women walked in somber silence, leading home an indifferent cow.

The camp grounds were on the other side of the cottage, and from the window of her shower stall she could see part of the old mansion where she had to report, a severe building half covered with wild rose bushes climbing angrily up to the weatherbeaten shutters. From the open door of what she now knew was the camp kitchen a striking-looking dark woman in red skirts, one sleeve of her blouse rolled up, came out to shake the salad in a wire net. She did it with zest, in a teasing way, putting her left hand on her hip like a dancer, looking all the while at somebody who was coming toward her and whose steps Ania could hear on the gravel path: Monsieur Jacques. His presence reminded Ania she had to hurry, but the sight of the red skirts had cheered her up and she whistled all through her shower.

When Ania entered the kitchen, dressed in her best, she discovered with surprise that the dark woman who had shaken the salad outside the door wasn't Madame Jacques, after all. She was now rolling dough on the kitchen table, an apron over her red skirts. The real Madame Jacques, small and plump, thrust inside a black silk dress and propped on small shoes, stood in the middle of the room, a skimmer in her hand, watching the stove. She looked like a bad-tempered, big-bosomed puppet holding an oversized spoon, and her eyes, puppet eyes made out of old-fashioned shoe buttons, took a rapid inventory of the new counselor. The girl was standing there awkwardly, hands clasped in front of her with the painfully imposed relaxation of shyness. The inventory seemed to disappoint Madame; still holding the skimmer, she folded her plump arm high on the platform of her bosom, a gesture which, Ania was to learn later, meant annoyance.

"Did you have a good journey, mademoiselle?"

"Yes, thank you, madame."

Yes, she spoke fair French—but her accent, her accent!

"Has Monsieur explained the work to you?"

"No, not yet, madame."

"We have twenty children this year. Eleven girls and nine boys. You will have complete charge of them." She looked at Ania again, this time clearly doubtful about what she saw. "Unfortunately, we're too short of help this summer to be able to give you a definite plan of your time off—"

"It'll be all right, madame—"

"But you can arrange here and there for an hour or two's rest," Madame went on, blinking with irritation (she disliked interruptions). "I shall take the children too, the village teacher comes in to help. We have three meals daily and a *goûter* at four o'clock. There's a siesta hour in the afternoon, and I don't care how you keep them indoors, just do so! Dinner is at seven and they have to be in bed by nine." She hesitated. "In general they're quite manageable. How old are you, mademoiselle?"

"Twenty."

"You look a lot younger."

Ania smiled apologetically, the smile relaxed her face, her air of austerity faded.

At last Madame unfastened her eyes from the girl and moved them over to the woman in red skirts. "This is Babette, our cook. Mademoiselle will eat with us tonight. Amélie has the children until bedtime." Babette turned her face to Ania, still kneading, and smiled at her. The smile curled her upper lip in a delightful manner. "I think you should take time off now to settle down. Better make good use of it while you can."

"Oh, I don't need much time to unpack, madame. Do you—shall I help with the dinner?"

"We have enough help in the kitchen," Madame said, and turned to the kettle. "This is boiling over, Babette," she accused the soup. Ania felt dismissed.

"Mademoiselle," Babette called after her, "here is your *goûter*. Dinner is a long way off." She put a large slice of white bread and a bar of chocolate on the corner of the table.

Ania munched at them absently walking slowly across the grass. A truck came by, and when the cloud of dust had whirled down the hill she realized that the driver who had waved at her was Mark, the owner of the oversized espadrilles. She took a few undecided steps in the direction of the dust cloud, but turned back.

SHE DIDN'T MEET THE CHILDREN until bedtime. But she knew when they returned from the river; the evening was suddenly full of a strange restlessness, the bushes around the dignified old mansion shook with giggles, steps churned the gravel, and a secret army hid behind the trees surrounding the dining table.

The grownups' dinner was served on the lawn in front of the kitchen. People came slowly out of the darkness and gathered around the long table; a short greeting like a grunt accompanied the sound of chairs being pulled away from the table. It was an uneventful meal, the even silence interrupted only by the tinkling of spoons working diligently inside the soup bowls and Madame's call, "Babette, Babette," darting like an angry bird toward the light inside the kitchen door. Babette did not appear personally; she led the dinner efficiently from her kitchen, like a captain steering his boat from the bridge, and delegated the serving to her helpers, two charred village women who went in and out with trays and tureens. She came out only at crucial moments, and then, even when carrying a plate or helping to clear the table, she kept a hand on her hip, preserving her air of soft but indisputable authority. But that night she wasn't only supervising the meal; she was alert, ready to smooth over any accident that might expose the asperities of camp life and scare the new mademoiselle away. ("That little English girl is terribly thin," she informed her kitchen crew.) Twice during the meal Babette came out of her captain's bridge and ran to the end of the lawn to slap the darkness with her dish towel, the way you chase away flies. *Mais allez-vous-en! Laissez-la manger, la demoiselle! Qu'est-ce qu'elle va penser?* *La demoiselle* was sitting between Monsieur Jacques and Père Barthe, the old man in charge of the vineyards, and sipping her soup noiselessly, her elbows close to her sides. ("She looks too refined to be any use," Madame thought, her little button-eyes darting at the girl over the tureen.)

"What is going on, Babette? Isn't Amélie with them? Who was there?"

"Albert and Siona, madame! Who else? They're worried," she added with humor, "they want to know what the new mademoiselle looks like."

"Ah, *they* are worried!" Père Barthe said, and his rough hand patted Ania's wrist gently. *"J'espère que vous avez le courage et la foi, mademoiselle!* It's war around here!"

"Oh, leave her alone now, Père Barthe, why are you trying to scare her?" Babette said. "They're not that bad, mademoiselle. They're just kids."

But under shriveled eyelids the old man's eyes were bright with playfulness.

"Sure they are! Have you noticed Georgette's tail?" Madame's cat had jumped on her shoulder and was tasting the lobe of her mistress' ear. "Have you seen her tail is missing?" Unable to wait for his joke to take effect, the old man was shaken instantly by an explosion inside his chest; the laughter mounted to his throat, convulsed his mustache, and escaped through the black space of his missing front teeth. He was like the trunk of an olive tree, twisted and knotty, shaken by the storm of his merriment.

"She was born that way," Madame fondled the cat, *"pas vrai, choupette?"*

"The children'll be just fine," the old man said, wiping his eyes and patting Ania's wrist again while a smell of foul tobacco and rotten wood came out of his sleeve. "They only need a good whipping in the morning and another at bedtime."

"Oh, you," Babette said, flapping her dish towel at him. She was still behind Madame's chair. "I told them, 'It's all right, she seems nice, far too nice for you!'" She lifted her tray high, and in the light of the wall lamp you could see she did not wear a brassiere and her nipples stood up under her blouse when she laughed.

"Babette," Monsieur asked, "where is Mark?"

Babette lowered her tray. "He won't be in before nine, monsieur, he went to Draguignan for the tires. I'm keeping his food warm."

"Did it have to be today?" Monsieur ventured to ask his wife.

Madame, who had spread her napkin in front of her to check the hemming, folded it slowly without taking her little eyes off him, clearly wishing she could fold him up too and store him away out of her sight. A few smiles flashed around the table.

"It had to be today. Tomorrow is market day. We're not a summer resort here."

"But he's been out on the road since seven this morning."

"It's good for him, takes him away from his books."

"Is Mark your bookkeeper?" Ania asked anxiously with her fork in mid-air.

"Mark? Of course not! That would certainly bore a doctor of mathematics."

"Oh, is he—?"

"He is going to be," Monsieur said proudly. "He has just won a fellowship abroad. He'll finish his master's at the university at Marseilles this year."

"How are we going to manage without him next summer?" Père Barthe asked.

"But he'll be here next summer. He won't leave till the fall."

"Does he know yet where he's going to go?"

Madame shrugged, irritated again. "Who listens to his aunt? If Philippe tells him to choose the North Pole, that's where he'll go. He doesn't want to be an engineer and make a good living. He's got to teach mathematics."

"Is Mark your—nephew?" Ania asked.

"Of course he is!" What was the matter with the girl? She had seized her glass and taken two hasty gulps, as if the food had burned her. "Eh? What do you think of it?" Père Barthe asked her, clicking his tongue. But he wasn't referring to the tip she had given the Jacques' nephew, he was motioning to her glass. "It's ours," he said, "from up the hill. We make it. Doesn't it taste just like velvet?"

But then Babette came out again bringing with her own hands a huge cherry pie on a copper tray and put it down in front of Monsieur for him to slice. Her long twisted curls kept getting inside her blouse; she fished them out time and again and threw them back over her shoulder. A warm seductive smell, half pastry and half hot skin, spread out of her skirts whenever she passed Ania's chair. "I have another pie for you and Mark, Père Barthe. Come take it before you go up to the mill." "That's right," Madame grumbled, "spoil him, Babette." "Someone's got to spoil him around here," Babette said happily. And then the meal was over. Madame folded her napkins, this time conclusively, and Monsieur offered to take Ania to the cottage. "You might not find it alone in the dark." They walked along in silence; leaving her on the steps, he added with that soft reserve in his voice, "Mademoiselle Amélie will show you around before she leaves." In the light coming from the cottage she looked thin and helpless to him. Oh well, she'd manage—and he took his leave.

SHE'S COMING! SHE'S COMING! Siona! She's coming!" Excitement rolled through the cottage when her step was heard crossing the playroom downstairs. Naked feet ran up and down the stairs, a heavy object was dropped on the floor, and toilets were flushed in a desperate rush. Then a formidable salute was given to the new counselor by a blown-up paper bag banged behind the door of the linen closet. Ania flinched it was a success. "I scared you, didn't I?" A little boy in plaid flannel pajamas came out of the closet; his hair was sticky with hair lotion. "Will you please go to bed this minute, Albert!" Mademoiselle Amélie, the village teacher, appeared at the end of the corridor, gray-haired and bony, and pointed at the boys' bedroom. The door opened, a head appeared. "Mademoiselle Amélie, Simon has just wet his bed!" "Liar! Liar!" a voice cried passionately inside the room. "He didn't. He's just gone to the toilet." "So why is this blanket wet?" "Because I had some water in a balloon and it burst!" Mademoiselle Amélie looked hurt.

But as they stepped inside the boys' room there was a sudden silence, everyone in bed, covers pulled high under the chin in an exemplary manner. The blankets rippled with giggles when Mademoiselle Amélie ceremoniously introduced the new counselor. The introduction made everyone shy. Then the door was thrown open and a small boy rushed in. Blinded by surprise at finding the ceremony started and himself on stage, he scurried to his bed and fled under the blankets. "This is Simon," Mademoiselle Amélie said, "the one who wets his bed." It was a terrible moment; Ania didn't know what to say. She sent an undecided, embarrassed smile at the stigmatized bed. But Simon was ignoring his social obligations; he had pulled the blankets over his head and disappeared in mortification.

The uncomfortable silence that had spread through the cottage was coming from the girls' room. But when their door was opened it proved to be a false silence, ready to burst at the seams as soon as you turned your back. "What is it, Siona?" Mademoiselle Amélie asked the dark-haired, olive-skinned girl in the bed under the window, who was holding a blanket coyly around her breasts.

"Mademoiselle," the girl said to Ania, bent on making use of her services right away, "I feel feverish."

"Go to sleep, Siona, and quit being silly, will you," said Mademoiselle Amélie. But Ania had already advanced toward the bed looking solicitous and had to finish the movement in some way. With her most professional air—her ears started to burn—she took Siona's hand as it lay on the blanket and then felt her forehead. Siona closed her eyes with a martyred look as giggles broke out in the four corners of the bedroom. "You're all right," Ania said, and tucked a corner of the blanket in.

"I'd better warn you," Mademoiselle Amélie said as they crossed the playroom on their way to the cottage door, "to keep an eye on Siona." Through the open door the rustling night was cool and restless. "Then there is this boy Albert—" She paused and looked embarrassed. The wind ruffled her woolly bangs and gave her a mysterious air. She sighed and left the sentence unfinished. "You'll find out about them by yourself. I'm awfully glad you're here. This is my first night off in two weeks. And I am only supposed to help part time. Good night, mademoiselle." Her checkered dress plunged into the night and dissolved a few steps away. "Put a chair in front of the door," someone upstairs was preparing a barricade. "If she comes in this way. . ."

Arms crossed, hands tucked in her armpits, Ania lingered in the doorway. She looked up at the freckled sky. Yes, it was a summer sky and September was far away. But she was closer to Paris than she had been last year. And then a shutter opened with a bang over her head, a pajama sleeve signaled into the night, and a voice still girlish and clear said in rapture, *"Oh, les enfants, il y a tant d'étoiles!"*

"MADEMOISELLE! Mademoiselle!" Someone was calling up the stairs through the cottony silence of the cottage gone to sleep at long last. What time was it? She felt for her housecoat in the dark, found it in the pool of moonlight at the end of her bed, and came out on the stairs dizzy with sleep. The little boy who wet his bed was standing at the foot of the stairway clutching the waist of his pajama pants. "What is the matter, Simon?" "Somebody's walking outside!"

She came down to him; he looked old and gray in the blue night-light on the stairs. "Is it the Countess?" "What countess?" "The Countess going to the vault—" He struggled to explain. "Did you have a bad dream?" "No, I didn't go to sleep at all, I can't sleep. I can't sleep after he tells us stories. He said the Countess is Death and she goes to the vault at night—" "Who said that?" "Albert." "Who is Albert?" "The tall one." Simon put his hands up to show Ania how tall Albert was and his unattended pants fell down, uncovering skinny legs with unwashed knees. He grabbed at them in panic. "The elastic has come out," he explained. Ania searched her pocket for a safety pin and fastened his pajamas. "Come to the door and look," she said, "there's no countess, it's the wind."

They stood in the doorway at the edge of the bottomless, frightening night and listened to the wind coming from somewhere up the hill, fingering branches and leaves. "See, there's no one there." "But sometimes I have dreams," he said unhappily, "it's better to stay awake." "What dreams?" "Things with teeth," and he rubbed his forehead. He looked small and old and wrinkled again. "Come in now, you'll sleep well if you know there's no one outside."

But there was a vague echo of a footstep on the gravel far away and she heard it again while she watched Simon crawl into his bed and disappear under the blankets with a sigh. Then she climbed the stairs to her room slowly, holding hands with her shadow on the wall.

STRANGE THINGS HAPPENED IN CALLIAN on summer nights. Sleep came late, reluctantly; people tossed under the covers for a long time, as if they couldn't resign themselves to wasting such beauty, to putting it to such silly use. Maybe Callian summer nights weren't really nights. The darkness could never decide to take on its deepest shade of black. And for a long time the horizon retained its lavender sheerness, reminding you of the day that had just dissolved there. And then the moon rose, that unbelievable, cold green moon that poured its waters on your bed until you couldn't remember very well what you had dreamed and what you had lived through. Such nights were unconnected with the day that followed. They left behind a vague momentary happiness which was completely wiped out by an army of bright roosters re-establishing order. Whatever happened during those nights happened outside time and place, outside convention, under the light of the watching green moon. The fruit ripened in such nights. The apples turned sweet without haste. More than the sunshine, Callian apples seemed to need the liquid light of the green moon to give them their special taste of honey and dew.

AFTER making love with Babette, Monsieur Jacques lay on his back, one arm still under his head, and studied the dim pattern of the rug hanging on the wall over their bed. It made his naked shoulder itch when he brushed against it. He was a shy lover, and would not touch her where she wanted most to be caressed. But in the end he loved her well, vigorously. His mustache choked her as he pressed it against her mouth.

The window was open, the Callian night invaded Babette's room, a clock sleepily struck four. "I think you'd better go now," Babette said, and he rose regretfully, leaving the woman behind him, like a fragrant lizard, on the hot, disheveled beach of the bed. He stood in front of the open window waiting for her to put a skirt on over her billowing white chemise and listened to her bare feet grip the floor, firm and warm, as she went into the kitchen to make coffee. He was grateful that she never walked around naked. Her wide red skirt balanced on her hips like a stiff lampshade. He followed her into the kitchen. Her back gleamed, her dark hair hung from an amber comb, a shoulder blade moved, a satin ripple rose under her skin, and he wanted to hold her again. Putting his coffee bowl down, he brought her close, circling her with both arms, and after a second's hesitation he took her breasts under the chemise. Surprised, the soft nipples stood up but she quietly finished her coffee. The comb fell out; her hair hit his face, hot, dark, and broke into little waterfalls. Their breath climbed a blind night and reached to the top with a groan. He searched in her mouth under her tongue and found the fresh taste of coffee melting in the slippery limpidity of her saliva.

"You really have to go now," Babette said later, bending for her comb in the dark. He finished dressing, she helped him into his leather jacket, and he left without a word, suddenly embarrassed by his daring desire to love her standing up in front of the open window. She leaned against the doorway, the smell of sweat and coffee around her. But they had both already started to forget. By the time he was passing the children's cottage, careful not to crush the gravel, Babette was reaching a naked arm into the night to close the shutters, and she yawned.

And then the navy-blue sky faded in the east and soon grew red. Roosters came out of their stuffy houses, their lilac nightcaps hanging depressed over one ear, and told Callian something was burning on the eastern side of the sky. The first trucks carrying baskets of cool, wet, sleepy vegetables drove up the hill to the camp kitchen; their motors purred under the windows. A fresh, naïve morning was there, unrelated to the night of love. Fat sparrows gossiped in the trees.

SIONA WAS THE CAPTAIN OF THE GIRLS. The title was honorary and did not carry responsibilities. It brought only favors. It was tacitly understood that she would always take first place uncontested, take the lead at games, have the bed under the dormitory window (an envied strategical position), and strike silently and vengefully at whoever doubted her authority. She had already had her first period, and it was this above all that gave her prestige. When that mysterious thing happened she had to lie in bed, and Madame herself came upstairs carrying a box from the infirmary room. That whole morning two girls kept watch at Siona's bed and bent over her giggling. The guards wouldn't let the boys in. Simon asked through the door if it was contagious, but Albert, well-informed about the event, climbed the tree outside the dormitory window to peek in, only to find to his disappointment that she looked like the everyday Siona, maybe a bit more uncombed and with blue shadows under her eyes.

She was also the only girl in camp who wore a brassiere, and this delightful item had been handed around the dormitory and tried on by all the flat-chested, penguin-fat girls. The owner of that envied piece of rose-trimmed cotton wrapped herself in mystery and cool superiority. Her breasts with pale-violet nipples untouched by the sun kept her company inside her bra, while the other girls, no matter how hard they tried to swell their pectoral muscles in the shower, still displayed that desolate landscape, a frail-looking chest like a boy's, divided longitudinally by the pearly channel of the sternum.

The prestige of owning this emblem of femininity was overpowering, and her admirers in the girls' group started to wear their socks in a new fashion: rolled up in two small balls and tucked inside their blouses. Unfortunately, they were constantly losing one breast, if not both, and suddenly quitting games to retire behind a bush and fish the sock out from around their waist.

Siona exerted her authority over the boys too. Barefoot messengers in pajamas too long for them continually carried orders from dormitory to dormitory, and at bedtime the noise of bare feet tapping on cement stairs would go on relentlessly until Mademoiselle appeared at the door, her loose hair hanging over her housecoat and a look of reproach on her face. The children scurried away to their rooms like rats surprised by a sudden light. But as soon as she had gone back upstairs the excitement would rise again, swell, run through the house and break into another earthquake.

Nobody knew how Madame Jacques came to appear in the cottage in the middle of Ania's first bedtime bedlam. But there she was suddenly standing on the landing in her black silk dress, green wrap around her shoulders, her tightly corseted bosom heaving with the effort of climbing. "I could hear you screaming from the porch. Where do you think you are?" All activity stopped instantly; boxes of games were shoved under beds with a kick. The news spread quickly to the toilets where Jeanine had locked herself in, announcing she wasn't ready yet. (Later Ania found her still sitting on the toilet, the pants of her pajamas rolled around her legs. "Is she gone?" she asked, whispering in terror.)

It was after that first inspection that Ania discovered she had a protector among the boys; he was the one who ran upstairs the following evening to warn her Madame was walking toward the cottage. Some semblance of discipline could be maintained when the black silk and green wrap appeared at the top of the stairs. It was a bit humiliating to be patronized by him, but Ania was too tired at the beginning of that first week in camp to do without his help. She decided to accept the protection, and in front of the linen closet where they met—he was waiting with his short arms extended to receive a pile of fresh towels—she said, "Thank you, Albert."

"I am Armand," he said nicely, "the tall one is Albert." He propped the towels on his chest. A key hung on a chain over his striped jersey. He waited, disposed to continue his conversation.

"And what is that key for, Armand?"

He looked at her seriously before answering. "For my valise. I don't want the kids to open it."

All the available keys in the cottage were periodically tried on Armand's luggage yet the lock, though half pulled out, was unconquered. Ania remembered she had seen him at bedtime lying flat on his belly under the bed checking the lock. "She's been at it again, the bitch!" He meant Siona. "But what do you have in there?" "Nothing." He was peculiar. He wanted his privacy respected. No one was allowed to sit on his bed unless invited.

He appeared later that morning in the infirmary to talk to her again.

"Do you like to look at things?" he asked her.

"I do," she answered seriously, and waited.

But he decided to close the conversation and turned away, his hands in the pockets of his shorts, leaving her there. At siesta time, when everybody had to lie down for an afternoon nap, Armand was missing. Ania waited for him outside on the hot stone entrance steps, and after a while his panting striped jersey appeared out of the bushes. He was startled to find her waiting.

"Why aren't you in bed?" she asked him as severely as she could. But she didn't sound convincing.

"I had to have a look at the coach."

"What coach?"

"The Countess' coach."

The Countess again! She raised her voice.

"Look here, Armand, I don't want you to make up stories. You've got to be here for siesta like everybody else." But this implied that he was not like everybody else. Why was she favoring him? "And I don't want to have to tell you twice."

"It isn't a story," he said reproachfully, "it's a real coach. Want to see it?"

"Where is it?"

"In the barn."

"Which barn?"

"Behind the office building." He had already turned around hopefully.

She didn't want to be seen by Madame walking Armand around the grounds during siesta time, but she was curious about his story.

"We can't go now," she said. He turned a disappointed face toward her.

"But now is the best time—that's why I've just been there. It's the only time you can be alone."

Of course she knew what he meant. The best time, the only time when you could be alone in camp was when the others were asleep, the day drowsy with the noon heat, and the shadow of the shutters rippling on the floor. She looked at him conspiratorially.

"Do you want me to wake you up before the others and run to the coach with you?"

He hesitated.

"Fifteen minutes," he said, "if you mean it."

When she went to his bed later she found him lying on the blanket fully dressed, his sandals full of sand. She touched him, and he sat up immediately and smiled sleepily, and only then remembered why he'd felt he had to rush through his sleep. They tiptoed out of the dormitory into the blazing sun.

The barn was hot, the dry silence crackled as their feet crushed the hay, and a smell of warm earth pricked their nostrils. "I can't see a thing," Ania said, and he took her hand, gently piloting her in the dark. Small sparks like firecrackers seemed to cling to her eyelashes. "Here," Armand said. The black shape of a coach raised its back against the barn wall like a strange animal chained there. "It's a very old one," he ventured, encouraged by her admiring silence. "Do you like it?"

"Oh, Armand!" she said, moving her hand slowly over the cool lacquered side of the slightly curved door, expecting the strange animal to quiver. "How did you ever discover it?" He smiled mysteriously, and for the first time she saw the little black space between his front teeth, a dark notch that divided his smile in two. "It was here," he said modestly. "Want to get inside?"

The coach was a romantic coupé wearing carriage lamps ornamented with silver hats on both sides. The high coachman's seat still had its fancy tassels, tarnished by weather, and the shafts were awkwardly propped up in front like desperate imploring arms.

Armand reached up to the high doorknob, fought with it and opened the door with a flourish. A breath of heat and mold came out of the blue silk upholstery. "It's a bit spoiled," he said apologetically, "they should have put moth balls in. The springs are still good." He tried them with one hand. "Come sit down." She climbed in. They sat there for a long while, speechless, listening to the silence rustling. "What happened to the Countess. Where is she now?" "She's mad," Armand said, and grinned. "What do you mean, 'mad'?" "Yes, mad! Haven't you seen her down in the village, an old lady with a flowered hat? She looks like a beggar. She hangs around the vault all the time." "Where is this vault?" "On the way to the mill, up the hill. We saw her there once, before you came. She was shaking the door, like this. She is mad. She talks to herself." "Where does she live now?" He shrugged. "This was her house. It isn't any more."

Was this the sadness that recurred every evening in the Callian sunsets? The old woman shaking the door of the vault, shaking Time, calling back her ghosts? Or was it just summer, the season growing ripe? Through the window beside her Ania could see the open barn door, and beyond it, far away, as if through the other end of a telescope trained on a strange world, the drowsy summer: half a tree, Babette crossing the lawn in her red skirts, calling softly for Georgette, vanishing from the picture again. Armand sat in rapture, his hands between his bare knees. "Isn't it beautiful?" he asked the darkness through his window. "Siona never comes in here. I told her there are bats hanging upside down from the ceiling." He chuckled.

"I would be afraid of bats too," Ania said, turning her face to him. He was touched by that confidence and by her being so helpless and vulnerable as to fear bats. "No, there aren't any really. I just don't want her in here."

When the bell rang for *goûter* they jumped and looked at each other. "We have to go, Armand." But they stayed on just for another minute, a full, rich minute; they breathed in the hay smell and the silence. "Come, we'd better go now." The *goûter* procession passed the barn door, moving across the lawn from the kitchen to the cottage; Babette walked ahead like a grave prelate, hugging the blue milk pail; her helpers followed carrying the tray of bread and marmalade.

They were late and the cottage was awake. Siona leaned out of the girls' dormitory window and squinted at them, full of sleep. "Hey, Fortunée, come and look! He took her to the coach!" Instantly the window filled with grinning heads. "Just watch them scratch now! That thing is full of fleas!"

SHE DIDN'T HAVE A SINGLE CHANCE TO EXPLAIN to Mark about the tip, as she had decided to do. She did see him around during the day, crossing the lawn, carrying parcels in and out of the office. He had waved at her from his truck, his face half covered by sunglasses, but he never stopped to talk. She was relieved. The only time she met him she had been sitting on a small chair in the window of the village cobbler's shop, waiting for her shoes. The shop was in an old cellar and the window at street level. She had seen a pair of huge blue espadrilles step slowly along the cobblestones past the window. From where she sat they looked like a giant's shoes. Gulliver has landed in the village, she thought with a smile. His boots have been soaked by a storm and he is bringing them to be mended, so he has to wear his espadrilles. The espadrilles vanished and the door opened. It wasn't Gulliver, it was Mark. When he discovered her in the window he came over to ask if she wanted a ride back to the camp. The truck was in the marketplace. She thanked him, but she wanted to walk. Climbing the hill to the camp alone in the heat of the afternoon, she was furious with herself—she should have explained about the tip. She tried to relieve her embarrassment by rubbing her nose on her parcel. When he wasn't wearing glasses (they were in the breast pocket of his shirt and they had left a white bridge on his nose), his eyes were soft and undecided, the way nearsighted people look when they take their glasses off; his brown irises were circled with a warm yellow ring.

She spoke to him for the first time the night she went up to the mill, with the children, the night of Madame's birthday. They learned about the birthday from Babette, who had asked Ania if she couldn't arrange a little celebration. But there wasn't enough time to set up a puppet show, and after consultation with Mademoiselle Amélie the program was reduced to an evening procession to Madame's porch with pumpkin lanterns, where Siona would recite a birthday poem. The poem was contributed by the village teacher ("Wewishyou-longandhappy-days." "Slower, Siona, slower, and with feeling."), and the pumpkins were delivered to the cottage that afternoon in a basket mysteriously covered with a sheet.

For two days they carved the lanterns outside under the oak tree. The work had to be kept secret and Simon, who couldn't carve and who was in everybody's way, was asked to keep watch in the middle of the lawn in case Madame should come along. This gave him little to do; then he *thought* he saw her and gave the alarm, slapping his sides with his arms like a skinny plucked rooster, and they hastily covered the table with the sheet. But Madame didn't appear after all. Simon was fired, but later rehired to carry the pumpkin scraps to the rubbish can at the end of the lawn.

Saturday was too long. Because they had been waiting for it the evening came late, the red dusk took a long time to extinguish itself in the pale premonition of night. Locked up in the shower room for the sake of concentration and the only full-length mirror in the house, Siona said the poem over and over, one hand on her heart like a prima donna. "It's getting blue," Armand announced, stretching out his arm to test the color of the evening. Yes, at long last. Under the oak tree, Ania walked around the table with a match in her hand and gently touched the candles inside the pumpkins. "Wake up, pumpkin, wake up and smile," Armand said every time the match touched the wick of a candle, and a shy, flickering smile spread on the pumpkin faces. A commotion followed as they formed a marching line. The prima donna, called at last on stage, darted down the stairs to take her place at the head of the line with Armand. "I'll walk with you, mademoiselle," Armand said, his face twitching with annoyance. Fortunée nudged Annette significantly; Siona saw her, and the birthday bouquet—tenderly stored all day in a bucket in the toilet to keep cool and trimmed with a ribbon from Adèle's night-gown—flew at Fortunée, scattering green feathers of fern. A lantern went out in the draft and the desperate owner started to howl. The match returned to bring the pumpkin smile back, and then they were on their way.

"Oh, the little angels," Babette admired them from her kitchen door. Calling the procession to a halt, she wiped Simon's cheek clean with a corner of her apron and set him free again. Madame was on her porch, waiting for them to come and let her go to bed (it was she who had given Père Barthe permission to deliver the pumpkins). She invited them in. The stately dining room intimidated the children; they lined up along the china cupboard and put all their hopes on Siona. She was magnificent! She stepped forward and recited her poem flawlessly—except for one short pause at the end of the first stanza when everybody's heart stood still. But she was only taking time out to lick her upper lip and then she took the poem by its handles again, rolling it back and forth mechanically, like a lawn mower, until she was through. The festivities were over. Then Monsieur Jacques handed around a dish of candies and everybody stored one candy in his cheek and, at Monsieur's invitation—the solemnity made even Albert shy—a second in his pocket.

"Who wants to take a walk up to the mill and bring Père Barthe his medicine?" Madame asked. "You could show him the lanterns." Père Barthe had been sick. His cough medicine had just arrived from Nice by bus. Now? At night? But you had to pass the vault! "Mademoiselle Annie will take you."

Armand raised his hand cheerfully. They would go and see the coach first. But a whispered consultation between Siona and Fortunée brought forward a second volunteer. Anyone else? Jeanine was last. "Hey, look who's going," mocked Albert. "You'll wet your pants when you pass the vault, Jeanine." But Jeanine preferred to walk past the vault at night holding tightly onto Mademoiselle's hand rather than return to the cottage with Madame.

The blue not-yet-evening had become a dark, intent night. Their lanterns didn't make a very strong light; the little candle inside put only a timid glow into the pumpkins' cheeks. But it was a mission, and Armand walked ahead like a man, the medicine bottle half out of the back pocket of his shorts.

Jeanine did not wet her pants when they passed the vault, but she stood in the road holding onto Ania, her teeth chattering, and waited for Fortunée's story to end. Fortunée was meticulous in the way she handled the details of a horror story, just as she rolled her socks and put them in her shoes at her bedside ready to be put on in the morning. "There's the vault," Armand announced, pointing into the darkness, and they stopped and looked down into the valley. Out of the black foliage wet with moonlight rose a stone chapel. They could see the big cross on the roof. "That's where they are buried," said Fortunée. "Who are 'they'?" "The Villemorins, the Countess' family. They don't like us here and they come out at night. They owned this place before." "There aren't any ghosts," Jeanine said. "Siona has seen them." "She has, eh? What do they look like?" "They are white and have no faces." Then the wind rippled bushes and black treetops, came closer, brought a strange odor of dried-up life, a sad, sinister smell. Fortunée sniffed at it and her pointed face turned left and right like a cautious rat coming out of its hole. "Feel that? The coffins must be open." "Will you stop this silly talk now, Fortunée!" "But it isn't silly talk, mademoiselle. They opened the coffins." "Who are 'they'? The ghosts?" "The soldiers." "What soldiers!" "German soldiers, during the war. They slept here in the house and they threw a shell inside the vault to open the door. Babette told us. They looked in the coffins for jewelry." "But the door is still locked," Ania said, "you can't get in, it's only bent. This is very heavy iron." "I've tried," said Armand, "but I can't squeeze through, I'm too fat." "So how do you know the coffins are open?" "The smell, if you—" But Fortunée wasn't allowed to finish. Jeanine had started to cry, her eyes sealed, her mouth open, an unbelievable quantity of tears rolling down her face.

They had to rush her up the hill, and then they asked her to sing for them. She had a little trembling voice still wet with tears, like a lost goat looking for its way home.

> *Le bon roi Da-go-be-ert*
> *met-tait sa cu-lotte à l'en-ve—ers.*

She dried her eyes on the sleeve of her sweater and they all picked up the last lines and threw them provocatively at the night:

> *"C'est vrai," lui dit le roi,*
> *"je vais la remettre'à l'en-droit"*—

until the mill suddenly rose at the end of the road, black, the roof glistening with moonlight—and they were safe.

Tiens, mais c'est la petite demoiselle étrangère! What are you doing out at this hour?" Père Barthe was sitting on the mill steps. "I was wondering what the stars on the road could be."

"Official mission," Ania said, as they rehearsed it on the way, and they all lined up and saluted. "Your medicine from Nice." Someone laughed in the dark at the top of the stairs, "Didn't I tell you the army has started to use pumpkin lanterns," and a blue shoe moved on the middle step. "Mark," the children asked the darkness, "are you there?" "Yes, I am. Sit down with us. Let's see how the lanterns came out."

The stairs were still warm from the heat of the day, and the moon loitered on the water behind the mill. A silvery splash—what was it?—and a mocking frog choir rose, then fell again. "What a silence!" Ania said, sitting next to Mark, "and do you have crickets, too?" "Don't you have any at the cottage?" "They have run away, they couldn't take the noise any longer." "Aren't the nights there quiet?" "Yes, but they are too short and we made the crickets jumpy!" He laughed.

At the bottom of the stairs, Père Barthe was inspecting the lanterns. "Fair," he was saying, "quite a fair job. Next time stick a few seeds in here for teeth and don't cut the top so deeply, see? The draft can kill the candle." An odor of tanned leather and tobacco rose from him; Armand liked it, drew it deeply inside his chest, moved closer.

"Père Barthe," asked Fortunée, folding her skirt around her with an old lady's fussiness, "Isn't it true that the coffins have been opened? Mademoiselle doesn't believe us."

"That I don't know. The opening in the door is too small for anyone to get in. Except a ghost!" He chuckled happily, and that peculiar explosion of laughter shook his chest, went up to his mouth and convulsed his mustache.

"There aren't any ghosts," said Jeanine from the safety of the step close to his leg. "Mademoiselle said there aren't any."

"Yes there are. Siona has seen them."

Père Barthe took Jeanine's hand and tucked it under his arm. "Siona!" he chuckled. "If I were a ghost, I'd be scared to meet her all by myself on the road at night!" Jeanine laughed, comforted and disloyal; Fortunée laughed too, hugging her knees.

"But then where do we go," Armand asked, looking up at him, "where do we go after we die?"

Like a stone thrown into water, the question stilled the frogs' chorus and made ripples in the silence. Suddenly the night was changed. Père Barthe searched inside his pipe with a finger, stirred up a smell of tobacco dampened by old saliva. "You ask Monsieur Mark about that," he said; there were echoes of an old argument in his affectionate tone. "He's a philosopher, he goes to school."

Armand turned to the top of the stairs, and one of the espadrilles moved on the middle step, lifted a speculating tip.

"I don't think I know, Armand, we don't go anywhere. We simply—are no more."

The mill leaned toward them to listen, wrapped them in her giant shadow. And it seemed impossible, incredible, that under this moon, with your coach safely asleep down the hill in the barn and this cool grass under your hands, it seemed unbelievable that you could be no more.

"But—what is it like? How—I mean, why should we stop being?"

"I think it's like not having been born. Before we were born, we didn't exist at all. So that's where we return, I think."

Armand fidgeted, drew closer to the shoes on the step. "But it isn't the same thing at all! It's unfair!"

"Why, Armand? Why do you say that? Where are you?" Moved by his cry, Ania searched for his hand. His palm was tough, with little hard, warm islands of flesh.

"Because," he struggled to explain, "when one dies, one is different—"

"Maybe he means that we know what we have to leave behind."

"But it isn't as terrible as that. You're given plenty of time for everything if you think of it. One season and another and another, and children grow up and they have children and their children have children." It was good to listen to him, of course one was given plenty of time.

"I know that, but it should go on for ever and ever!" Stubbornly Armand pulled up blades of grass and threw them away.

"Children die too," Fortunée remembered.

"Sometimes they do."

"They grow wings and go to heaven."

"The good ones," Père Barthe said.

"All of them!"

"The others become ghosts."

"Yeah, ghosts! Children can't be ghosts!"

"How do you know? Ever asked one?"

"You've got to be twenty-one to be a ghost," Père Barthe said.

"Will you please stop that?" Ania asked. "Now they'll be afraid to go to the toilet alone. Let's go back."

"I am going to give everyone some apples," Mark announced, making his way carefully down the stairs. "Green, the green ones, Mark!" they shouted after him. "He knows you like them green," Père Barthe said, with great depths of meaning in his voice. "It wasn't us, it was Siona," said Armand. "Never mind! These apples here are legal! Mademoiselle, please tell Mark to get you the basket with the handles. You can take it down to the cottage. The cellar is on the other side."

Ania circled the mill through the high weeds, touching the wall with one hand. "Mark?" she called, and then she heard him move close by. "Are you there? Père Barthe said we should take a basket of apples down to the cottage. The one with the handles." Then she stopped, ready to go back. But he was standing at the door on a patch of moonlight, holding the apples against his chest. "Here," he said, "this one. Can you hold it? Let's fill it up."

She crouched in the sawdust on the cellar floor and worked in silence. Then, with sudden decisiveness, she looked up at him. "I am sorry," she said, "I didn't know you were—" Her eyes were asking for help, their corners glittered full of broken sequins. But she was standing against the light and he couldn't see if she was smiling. He knew what she wanted to say. "Oh, I earned that! The valise was very heavy. What do you keep in there? Books?" She hesitated. "Some, and—half my theatre too." "What theatre?" Again that momentary withdrawal. "I am a puppeteer." "A what?" "Puppeteer," she said, lifting her hands in the dark and moving her fingers. "Puppets!" "Oh, I see," he said, but she could tell he was surprised. "You make them yourself?" She nodded. "I make them, I dress them, I write the play, I put on the show," she smiled, "and I pass the hat." "That is quite"—he searched for the word—"unexpected." "Why?" "Oh, I don't know. I haven't met a puppeteer before," he laughed, "I don't know much about puppets. I haven't seen any, except for the Guignol in the park in Nice." "That's different!" "I hope so, it isn't too pretty." Thoughtfully he put more apples in the basket. "It was very kind of you to take the money," she said, and the sequins shimmered again in the corners of her eyes. "I didn't have any choice! You looked so uneasy I couldn't take a chance and explain." She laughed. "I had been trying all the way up to figure what to do. You didn't look like a farmer but you had those overalls on, and then they told me at dinner that you're going away to get a doctor's degree." He chuckled. "I am so clumsy," she said.

The basket was full but they were still squatting next to it. She bent forward, and one of her braids brushed past his hand into the basket; it was elastic and warm. He was suddenly tempted to wrap it around his wrist and let it go, and hear once more the little slap it made as it fell on the cold fruit. "Anything the matter?" she asked. "Nothing," he said, "nothing. Are you going back to England in the fall?" "To England?" "Aren't you English? That's what they say in the kitchen." She gave her short, frank laugh. "No, I'm from Rumania. Didn't Madame tell you?" "I didn't ask her," he shrugged. "And are you going back in the fall?" "I've just come. I'm going to Paris in the fall." "First time?" She nodded. "To work?" "To study, and to work too, I hope." "Puppets?" She nodded again. "How do you study puppets?" he asked. "You get your apprenticeship with one of the greatest." "Do we have anyone like that around here?" "Yes," she said, and for a second she looked stubborn gazing down at the basket in the half-light. She told him Jean Paul's name and looked at him hopefully. "No," Mark said, "I haven't heard of him, but I am not very well informed about puppeteers." The fervor in her voice surprised him. "I suppose he is good if people come to him from other countries." "Oh, yes, he really is!" "You came alone?" She nodded. "He was a friend of my family's in Bucharest," she said, after a short deliberation. "Ah, that changes everything." "No," she said, "it doesn't. The last time I saw him I was nine." "But he knows you're coming." She looked up at him and said with touching confidence, "I didn't let him know. We haven't heard from him since—"

"Mark, can I carry the basket?" Armand's black shape stood in the arch of the cellar door. They hadn't heard him coming.

"It's too heavy for you."

"For him?" Ania said teasingly. "Have you seen his muscles?"

"I have another job for him. Here, hold the lantern while I get the matches. I'm going to take you down to the cottage and make sure all the ghosts have gone to bed."

"In the truck, Mark?"

"The truck has gone to bed, too. We'll have to walk."

It felt good to have Mark and his lantern with them on the road. It was a real, serious, country-road lantern with a little flame inside a glass cage, agile as a kitten's tongue. It cast an island of light ahead. The light skidded from side to side of the road, jumped from a black bush to a knotty tree across the way, sweeping the road clean of fears. A small ball of fur rolled over in panic and disappeared into the darkness; the bottom of its white pants flashed under the leaves. "It was only a rabbit, Jeanine," Mark said, squeezing her hand, and they all laughed in relief.

The cottage was dripping with moonlight, and farther away they could see the village asleep, petrified under the magic white light as if it had been conjured out of the past and made to come floating into the present.

"Is that you, mademoiselle?" asked Madame's impatient voice through the shutters. A small shadow crossed the rectangle of the toilet window. "We've brought apples," the children shouted, rushing up the stairs, "and Père Barthe said—Siona, Siona, he said—"

Mark was still on the steps with the basket in his hand, a little reluctant to leave.

"Thank you, Mark, I'll take it in. There'll be no tip this time."

"Well, it wasn't too heavy." He laughed, then he asked seriously, "Do they often talk of death like that?"

"The children? Yes, they do. Most of it goes on after the lights are out. The things they think of!"

"But it isn't really death they mean, it's a fairy tale, with ghosts and vaults. They don't know what it is all about, absence and separation."

"Except for Armand, tonight."

"Yes, except that. How old is he?"

"Eleven, I think." Mark nodded. "It was good what you told him."

He shrugged. "What else can one tell him?"

"Yes," she said, "it is unfair, isn't it?"

"Mademoiselle Annie, would you please see what has happened to the toilet door?" Madame called from the window above. "I think Siona has locked Armand in. Someone is rattling the lock."

"Yes, madame."

"Is that your real name—Annie?"

"No, my real name is Ania, the children call me Annie. They can't put the accent on the first *a*. Armand says it's too slippery."

"Á-niá?" he tried, and a quick, warm wave ran through her when he said it. "He's right," he said, "but I could practice. Bring the children up to the mill. It's a good place to swim." She said, "Yes, I will," and tried to see his face, but he was holding the lantern very low and the light fell only on his chest and the rolled-up sleeve of his shirt. When she shook hands with him, the light moved up, reached his mouth, and his lower lip looked full and kind with a fan of thin curved lines in the middle of it.

ARMAND didn't go to sleep. He lay awake on his pillow, hands under his head, working at the poem he had started that afternoon:

> Wake up pumpkin, wake up and smile,
> rub your sleepy eyes, the night is here,
> be a star . . .

"Albert! Hey Albert!" Simon called from his bed in a timid whisper. Albert didn't move. He lay sound asleep on his left side, an elbow bent under his cheek. His hair, stiff with his famous hair lotion, had gathered on top of his head in greasy spikes like porcupine needles. That's what Annette called him at meal times, banging her spoon on her plate "Porcupine! Porcupine! Por . . ."

> Be a star on my night table for a while
> be my friend and my . . .

"Armand!" Simon was trying the other bed now.

"What do you want?"

"I've got to go to the bathroom."

"Then go. Do you have to tell me? Go. You have my permission to go."

There was a silence. Armand heard Simon swallow twice. His throat was dry.

"There's no light in there."

"Don't you know where the switch is?"

He knew; he knew, but in order to reach the boys' washroom you had to walk past the staircase through the pale-blue light that burned all night in the corridor. Your face and hands got blue too. "Like ghosts," Siona said. "Ghosts look that way. I'm sure the blue light attracts ghosts to this place." And the running water forever gurgling in the pipes, through the walls, until it sounded like a moan going through the whole skeleton of the house, from wall to wall, from window to window! And then your shadow, the shadow you left on the floor behind you, when you fumbled for the switch it might put its cold hands on the nape of your neck . . .

"Armand!"

"Oh, look now! Why don't you wake Albert up? He's your friend."

"He'd hit me!" Simon started to fidget under his blanket. He couldn't hold it any longer. If the shadow were at least in front of you so that you could watch it!

"Simon." Armand had changed his mind.

"What?"

"Go at the window."

"It's too high. I thought of it but it's too high."

"Come, I'll help you."

Simon threw his blanket off and rushed between the white beds along that narrow dark space from which the nightmares came. He stumbled in his big pajamas and finally reached the island of moonlight on which Armand's bed stood.

"Here. Put one foot here. On the table. On the table, I said."

Perched on the windowsill, Simon felt the cold wood under his feet and curled his toes. Below him the night was fresh and rustling. He hesitated for a second—"Come on, what are you waiting for?"—and then both listened in silence to the sound of a timid fountain spraying the leaves.

"Wait a minute now, I want to go too."

Armand climbed straight onto the windowsill. Standing high on the sill, he unbuttoned his pajamas, his pants slide down, the wind touched him tenderly. Dizziness filled him to the brim, he steadied himself and Simon's hands fastened on his ankles. A cold wave went through him; he took his pajama top off and threw it on the bed, as if getting ready to fly off into the night. His head thrown back, he received in his whole body the night, the night, the night, the rustle of the big oak tree, the mysteries flying around the house like velvet bats, the face of the cold, pearly moon hanging over the ruined castle.

He settled himself on his open legs, and the arched fountain spurted hot and triumphant with steam and glints of light in it. It whipped the bushes underneath the window. Simon listened in admiration. But it was a temporary victory and not the sort that Armand wanted. He sighed, let the window go, and jumped down, buttoning his pants. The jump shook the glass on the night table, a tinkle glanced off into the dark room, rolled away, disappeared. Albert stirred in his sleep.

"Simon."

"What?"

"Don't tell the others."

" 'Course I won't."

Simon covered himself up, patted his blanket with satisfaction, sighed, and was asleep.

SUMMER.

A torpor rose with the steam of the hay drying in the sun, and when you lay in the grass and looked up through your eyelashes, the world was white, incandescent, glowing in its own heat. "Mark is spending a lot of time with the children this year," Madame said in the mirror, spearing her bun with the amber pin. Monsieur didn't answer. "We'll have complications," she announced prophetically. He lifted his head from the newspaper. "What complications? He's young, he's enjoying himself. He's a responsible fellow." "That's what I am afraid of."

Too hot. The tassels on the weeds rocked drowsily, full of gold dust, and fat, lusty bumblebees visited them, sending a shiver of love down their stalks. A lazy wind came down from the vineyards, threw the ripe fruit onto the grass, blew out Ania's skirts while she crossed over to the kitchen reading her mail and steadying her dress with one hand. Father's letter talked about the same summer; the heat melted the asphalt under your heels and the shades were pulled down. And this year they had missed the very beginning of summer, they forgot to watch for it, he wrote. She laughed aloud and folded the letter again. Would Jean Paul still remember that?

"Oh, this heat!" Babette greeted her. "What did you get? A letter from your father? I bet he's lonesome for you." Her hands were clasped comfortably on the front of her apron. In the afternoon, before she started cooking dinner, Babette's kitchen was another world, a world of shadow and silence disturbed only by the flies dying on the flypaper. Her helpers had taken their shoes off and sat outside shelling peas into dishes anchored between their knees. "Aren't you going swimming today? Monsieur Mark just went by. He said he was going up to the mill to swim. It's just too hot to do anything else."

For quite a while, when Ania came into the kitchen for *goûter* on her afternoon off, Babette had been diplomatically steering the conversation toward a single subject. Appearing innocently engrossed in her preparations—cutting the bread, working the big knife inside the marmalade jar, pouring the coffee, waving her apron at an obnoxious fly—she would inevitably end up by talking about Mark. "How that boy works! Mark do this, Mark do that"—she imitated Madame's voice—"and he does everything! Then he goes up to the mill and reads. He's such a quiet boy. He doesn't have a girl." The pause that followed this announcement was long and effective. "And he is so good!" she added fervently, wiping the knife clean.

Ania had to smile. The children said that too. "Mark is good!" Simon said it tightening his lips, shaking his head, amazed that someone could be good as well as big. Mark was not Authority. Authority was terrifying and annihilating like Madame. Nor was he Mademoiselle's familiar, persistent, irritating supervision. He was something else. He was good and firm and you couldn't bargain with him. He did things for you too. When they met him on the road he would stop the truck and lean out and ask them what was new today. The famous watch on his wrist—the rumor went around he could swim with it—caught the glare of the sun.

The truck was never empty, but sometimes he would take Simon along on the seat next to him. "Why him?" Albert protested, clinging to the door, lusting to work the brakes, to touch the wheel. "Because he's small and can't climb in the heat." ("I think he's sick," Mark had several times said to Ania.) White with fatigue, Simon disappeared into the truck to be delivered five minutes later, half-asleep and dizzy, to the front of the cottage.

You didn't bargain with Mark. Even Albert had learned that. Yet Mark skinned a snake for him, skillfully peeling the skin away with his pocket knife. "D'you know his pocket knife has *eight blades?*" Simon asked Ania boastfully. "Gold blades!" He was still talking of it at bedtime. "Sure, gold blades! With diamonds!" mocked Armand. All this praise of Mark irritated him. "Yes!" Simon cried out passionately. "Ask him tomorrow at the river!"

Lately Mark had been stopping at the riverside every day.

He returned from the village along the back road, a bumpy, difficult one that went by their swimming place, and often in the afternoon you could hear his truck's short breath climbing the hill, then the great roar as it took the curve before coming into sight. It stopped near the woods, and Mark's straw cap with the green plastic brim appeared up on the bank, his blue overalls moved through the bushes, and his espadrilles came down to them, crushing the weeds. "Mark, hey Mark, Mark-Mark-Mark," the children waved to him from the water. "Here he comes again! Listen to them!" Armand gathered up the collection of stones he had been shining on Mademoiselle's towel and went off. "Simon, your nanny is coming," he called over the water. But Simon was unruffled by such comments. He came running out of the water, blue with cold, shivering, his wet swimming trunks sagging below a wilted green navel; hugging his arms over his skinny chest, he complained that he was c-c-cold. "Could I get warm next to Mark?" Ania sat him down on the towel between them and patiently patted him dry. A faint odor of ammonia rose from his skin. "Did you take a shower today, Simon?" Mark asked. Simon shrugged. He had, but Albert had taken his soap, and then he— The explanation was long and complicated. ("I do think he's sick," Mark said again, watching him as though from a distance.) Simon made a tent out of his soiled towel and settled down next to Mark's hip, like a frozen dog in search of a warm spot. Every so often the towel-tent shuddered and split open, and his fish eyes peered out. "What was it you just said, Mark?"

"Come on, you're not eating. You're getting skinny here! What are you dreaming of, eh?" Babette insisted, buttering a second slice of bread for Ania. "Ah, loneliness isn't very becoming to women," she sighed.

"Does his family live in Nice?" Ania asked, trying to evade the dangerous subject that was looming up. "Whose family?" Babette asked innocently, as if Ania were miles away from the target. "Oh, Monsieur Mark's? He's got no one—well, except for Madame and Monsieur, but he and Madame . . . well, they don't get on very well, you've noticed that," she added diplomatically. "His father died in the camp during the war." "Was Mark in the camp too?" "Well, they took his father on account of his Polish passport." "I thought Mark was French." "He is, of course he is, but his father wasn't. So instead of hiding, he went after him. The old man was sick, you see, and Mark wouldn't let him go alone. He was a child at the time, he was sixteen, just a boy, but already——" She shook her head admiringly. "Then Madame got him out of there before they left." "Where did he go?" "Monsieur Mark? He didn't go anywhere. Madame and Monsieur went. He stayed in Nice with his friend, Monsieur Philippe. Hasn't he told you about him? No?" Babette paused. So what did they talk about at the river in the afternoon? She had seen them sitting straight and solemn on the grass, talking away like two philosophers. What was it good for, so much talking? They certainly needed a little push, they were both so shy. "He's a doctor now, Monsieur Philippe, a head doctor." Babette touched her head lightly over her right ear. "They think a lot of him around here. He was here last summer, maybe he'll come again. It's a pity!" she said, shaking her pretty head with unexplained compassion; then she returned to her topic. "How come you don't know about him? I see you talking a lot at the river. What do you talk about? He really must like you, he isn't much of a talker, Monsieur Mark." She laughed in satisfaction, folding her arms over her breasts like a good cook watching her meal being devoured. "What do you talk about, come on, tell me," she cajoled.

Babette had the simple, straightforward approach of a village matchmaker. But how could you be angry? The day before yesterday they had caught a glimpse of her hurrying through the bushes, red skirts hitched high. A sound of tinkling jars came out of her pockets. She hadn't seen them. "She takes the old countess leftovers from the camp. Occasionally she raids the larder for her too. Whenever you see Babette running up the hill like this, with her pockets full, you know my aunt is asleep, or away." He had looked pleased.

Well, they talked about——what did they talk about? They talked about puppets. (What would Babette think of that?) He wanted to know what it was all about. "Who makes puppets, mademoiselle?" the towel-tent suddenly split open and Simon's grinning head appeared. "I make puppets, Simon." "Real puppets?" he asked excitedly, throwing off his towel. "Real ones." "But where are they?" "You'll see them

soon." Simon ran to the river to spread the news. Mark
wanted to know if she was going to give a show. She didn't
know, she had very little time for art these days, she laughed.
And had she written to her old teacher yet? But he isn't old,
she protested, and he looked at her curiously. Then they
figured out Jean Paul's age together. "Was he forty when you
were first his student?" "Yes. I think so, nobody ever knew
how old he was. It wasn't that important. He couldn't have
grown much older anyway." Mark looked at her sideways
again and smiled.

The previous Thursday he had come to her with a techni-
cal question: "What fingers do you use to work the puppets?" "This one, and this one goes in the puppet's neck and
moves the head, and the others are folded here, like this." He
thought the answer over for a while. What would Babette say
to that? And he wondered what there was for her to study;
he thought she knew so much about puppetry. "It's the
technique," she answered. "I think I have the same techni-
ques I acquired when I was nine. You have to study with
someone, like a musician studying with a virtuoso." "And he
is the one?" "Yes," she said, "who else? Of course he is the
one."

"Come on." Babette was persistent. "You must talk about
something down by the river." Ania got up and rinsed her
cup at the sink. "We talk about the children most of the
time. I really don't know him very well," she said, embarrassed. Babette's eyes narrowed. She was ready for action.
"If you go up to the mill," she said, whisking a little basket
down from a shelf, "take this for Mark. It's his dessert from
last night. He didn't have any, nor did the old man. They
couldn't make it for supper." She winked conspiratorially.
"I—won't be going up today," said Ania stiffly, and Babette's
lower lip pouted with disappointment. "I'm sorry, I have to
go down to the village." "Well, it's here if you change your
mind," Babette said, replacing the basket on the shelf, and
then she sighed wearily. Young people today! They must
have it hard, being so shy!

OF course they talked about death. They talked about it
in bed, after the lights were out. What was it? What was it
like? The old countess crossing the street, keeping close to

the wall like a sick dog, her face hidden by the organza-flowered hat? "She is Death, that's who she is," Albert said, and the boys crowded on his bed breathed heavily, wiggled their toes in the dark and scratched intently under their pajamas. "Yeah! How do you know? Death doesn't look like that! With a hat!" "What does it look like then, smarty?" "Like a skeleton." "Death can look any way it wants to. It could come in this minute and you wouldn't know." A breeze shook the top of the oak tree outside, shadows of leaves ran over the white wall, over the blankets. "Mademoiselle Annieee!" Someone was hanging out of the window of the boys' room, face lifted toward Ania's. "Simon has wet his bed again!" and shortly after that the lights went on and Simon crept miserably to the toilet, the bottom of his flannel pajamas hanging wet and heavy.

And where do we go after we die? Ah, but we couldn't die in a summer like this, close together in the hot lap of the fields with the bees and the grapes swelling with liquid sun. Why would all this exist, if not for us to touch, to feel?

Yet, often when they passed the vault coming back from the river, a lanky, gray silhouette stood there. As they came closer and passed the last cypresses, they could make out a wilted organza-flowered hat; a canvas bag, a beggar's bag, lay in the grass. The Countess! White hair blown by the wind, gray dress one color with the green-gray olive trees, she shook her head and talked to herself, shuffling around the vault. Sometimes she touched the lock. But as soon as she heard them singing she would snatch up her bag and disappear into the bushes, her gaunt shadow following her like a hound on an invisible leash. Yet lately she seemed trying to overcome her fear of people; she would stay, turn her back to them, raise her head defiantly—the flowered hat trembled—and stand there motionless, staring at the pink horizon. Recently Siona, who was always the last one in the line, had got into the habit of lagging behind; she would turn her head several times toward the Countess, and twice they had lost sight of her when she stopped to do up her shoelace. But she had caught up with them, panting, her cheeks burning, and had been mysteriously silent the whole evening.

At the same time a coolness developed between her and Fortunée. At meals they separated. Fortunée moved her chair to the other end of the table and declared with her thin lips pressed together, "If Siona doesn't tell me her secrets, I won't tell her mine either!" She started to watch Siona with an air of calculation. Cautious, since Fortunée had been told too much in the past, Siona avoided provocation and even stopped annoying Armand. She hadn't tried to get hold of his valise for a whole week or to steal the key from around his neck. In need of companionship and approval, she recognized Albert's adulation at long last. He had been trying to win her for quite a while, mainly by standing on his head in the corridor outside the girls' dormitory, the top of his pajamas falling back on his face. The girls crowded fascinated in the doorway and secretly hoped that the belt of his pajamas would give way. It never did, and they compensated themselves for the disappointment with shrieks and screams. Albert prolonged the performance until his face got blue and Ania, coming downstairs to put the light out, chased him to bed. But he was exultant to receive Siona's attention at last, and in the hot bed of weeds behind the barn he kissed her on the ear, as he didn't know where else to kiss her and they were both in a hurry to get back to the cottage. Fortunée managed to witness this event and released bits of information about it whenever she had the opportunity. The news of the kiss spread to both dormitories the same evening. Furious, Albert told Fortunée she smelled like a church—he meant incense—and Ania, putting iodine on his cheek in the infirmary, wondered how, with a man's intuition, he had already divined what Fortunée was going to be: a dry, sexless, bitter woman.

Then Monsieur Jacques' flashlight disappeared.

On the outside windowsill of the dining room, which was called "the office," stood a box of tools and next to it a large flashlight ready for emergencies. "That's not the proper place for it," Madame had said several times (she had seen Simon eying it on tiptoe). Yet the flashlight continued to lie there— until it disappeared.

"Has anybody seen Monsieur's flashlight?" Madame asked the children at breakfast. "You know very well you're not to play with it! Would the person who took it return it to its place without delay?" Ania searched the children's faces. Fortunée looked shocked: how could she have missed such an event! Albert stole a glance at Siona, then whistled softly, carelessly. So it must have been those two! "It's always me, me, me! Whatever happens in this damn place, I'm blamed for it," Siona screamed, when Ania interrogated her, and threw her hairbrush on the floor. The flashlight wasn't found, and the incident lay dormant within a new restlessness in the children.

Then they went fishing for crayfish.

It was Mark who arranged the expedition. He brought down the nets stored in the mill attic and asked Babette to cut up small pieces of raw meat for bait. "But isn't it too hot for that, Mark?" Madame asked, and then "You're with the children all the time this summer!" "It's shady down there," he said, "and I'll take them in the truck anyway." "And the groceries?" "Tomorrow. I've arranged it all with Mademoiselle, I can't disappoint the children now." Then he left the room hastily to avoid more questions, the front door banged, his voice was heard in the kitchen thanking Babette for the bait. He was loading the baskets. "Well," Madame said after him, folding her arms, "now they arrange the schedule together." Monsieur lifted his gaze from the newspaper and his mustache moved up and down, eloquently. But he had trained himself not to be spontaneous. "You didn't give the girl her time off this week." "It was a difficult week. We're not a summer resort here. She'll wait until Sunday. She gets paid for her work, doesn't she?"

Under the oak tree outside the cottage Mark explained to them how the bait was hooked inside the nets and the baskets set under the bushes. "But you have to be absolutely quiet! Not a peep! Not a single sound! And move quietly too or you'll scare the crayfish!" "Oh, crayfish always look worried anyway," Armand said mockingly, irritated that Mark was chief of the crayfish expedition. But when Mark entrusted him with the eight-bladed knife with instructions to cut the young bushes and set the nets, he worked with a will.

"I should thank you," Ania said, whispering because of the crayfish, as she walked ahead of Mark along the river inspecting the nets. "I've never had such a quiet time in Callian. I've forgotten what silence sounds like. Maybe we should start raising crayfish in the shower rooms."

She had her bathing suit on and a blue jacket over it, an

old, faded jersey with a sort of hood, which she pulled over her head after her hair had twice got caught in the branches. She looked like a very young, blue-eyed monk in this severe garb. He wouldn't look at her naked legs, and even after she had turned around and gone on walking he stared straight ahead at the tip of her hood. But the whispering among the thin, expectant, suspicious trees gave their words a special meaning. Later, when he remembered that afternoon, even though he wasn't good at remembering, he used to think it was there that he had told her something exceptionally important to him, which he had forgotten, or maybe that he had held her close. "No, oh no, it was much later than that," she would laugh, but he remembered the silent, tender call of the faded blue hood dancing in front of him.

The first two nets were full. The children jumped away from the dark-gray encrusted, sea-weed-smelling monster made out of entangled bodies kicking the strings with innumerable legs, dancing on its back and slapping its own pale belly with a multiple tail. Mark started to divide the hunters into groups of three and four, entrusting each with the supervision of a net, and it was then they realized Siona was missing. "Simon is gone too," Fortunée announced with satisfaction. "And Albert." How long had they been gone? "Here comes Siona." On the other side of the road, up the hill, behind the rocks, Siona's lilac blouse signaled in alarm. "Mademoiselle Annie," she called down, "please come quickly. Simon is sick!"

"Shall I go?" Mark set the pail down.

"No, you stay with them. I'll see what she is up to."

Ania ran panting up the hill. "Siona! Where have you been? Where is he?" But Siona ran ahead, climbing the rocks like a goat, deaf to all questions. The vault came in sight. Albert was kneeling in the grass in front of the gate, his hands fastened on it, looking intently at something inside on the ground and imploring, "Simon, get up! Get up, don't be stupid! D'you hear me?" Simon wouldn't listen. He lay on the other side of the gate, his knees bent.

Ania pushed down her panic and struggled to crawl as far as her waist through the opening in the bent gate. The gravel scratched her chin, she breathed a smell of cellar mold. Grabbing Simon's ankles, she straightened his legs, then pulled him out. His tightly clenched teeth suddenly parted, and under the half-closed eyelids the gray irises rolled sideways and then jumped back. The little ball of foam at the corner of his mouth slid down the front of his soiled shirt. He blinked, tried to lift his head and gave up. His shorts were wet between his legs. The pool behind the gate in which he had been lying smelled of warm urine.

But she couldn't find out what had happened. When Mark came up the hill, trailed by Fortunée, Simon was slowly coming to.

"What happened here, Siona? Why was he inside?"

Siona shrugged. She was still squatting at Simon's side, leaning forward on her hands as if to prevent him from talking.

"I don't know. We found him in there."

"What do you mean you *found* him? How did you know he was there? Why did you leave the group?"

"What happened?" Simon asked Ania.

"You fainted."

"*I* did?" Simon's brows went up, then he looked at Mark. "But I don't remember," he said.

"Do you remember what happened before you fainted? How did you get inside the vault?"

Siona sat back on her heels and waited tensely.

Gently, Ania pushed Simon's hair away from his forehead. The gesture was merely one of tenderness. Simon's hair couldn't be pushed back. It was cropped short, lifeless and wiry. It looked gray now. "Why did you go inside, Simon?"

"Me? I haven't been inside the vault." He eyed her, puzzled. "I haven't been inside," he repeated. He looked back at the dark mouth of the vault, at the tunnel of terror out of which came whiffs of cold, moldy smell, and shuddered. For a second he seemed lost; a dull, blank look came into his eyes; his tongue fought a word that seemed stuck to the roof of his mouth. "Why did I faint?"

"I don't know," Ania said. "How do you feel?"

He shrugged and grinned.

"Look at me, Simon," Mark knelt on the grass next to him. "You do remember everything else." Simon hesitated again. "You do know who I am."

"Of course I know," Simon answered with irritation. "Why ask me that?"

Mark looked relieved. "Because you didn't come and shake hands with me today," he said, and everybody laughed. "Get up now," Siona said, bending over Simon and tickling him, "get up and let's go back."

"Listen," Mark took Ania aside into the shade of a cypress tree. In his preoccupation he had forgotten his reserve and had taken her arm. "He might have had a convulsion."

"What sort of convulsion?"

"I don't know. He's sick. I've thought so for quite a while. I think we'd better tell Reine about it. He should see a doctor."

"But she'll want Siona to—"

"Yes. I'll take her down. Albert too."

"Don't, Mark! Madame—"

"No, I'll see to it that she won't."

"God, I think I'm afraid of Siona!" Ania said, biting her thumb.

"You go back to the crayfish. I'll take care of them."

There was a commotion when Siona learned she had to go to the office with Mark. "But I haven't done anything," she whined.

"Fine, I know that. Just come and tell Madame how you found Simon. We have to know. He might be very sick. Take Albert's hand and let's not fuss."

"Do you want to go back to the river, Simon, or would you rather go and rest in the cottage?"

Simon stood between them, beaming with pleasure at having fainted. Now he was consulted about things.

"Down to the river," he said, grinning.

"Well, let's go slowly."

Ania turned around to look for Fortunée, who had lingered at the door of the vault and now was hiding something inside her blouse.

"What's the matter with you? What have you got there?"

"Nothing," Fortunée said, "nothing." But her little pointed face looked like the face of a satisfied rat.

THE trial was held in the office, where Madame Jacques consulted with Babette, planned the menus, dispensed medicine, answered the rusty, half-deaf, half-dumb telephone, and straightened out moral problems—that is, deviations from camp discipline. The big, dark room was designed to play on the culprit's feelings of guilt and blow them up into panic even before faced with Authority. Once a dining room, it was still full of the original furniture, a long table on elephants' legs and twenty-four chairs decorated so elaborately that they looked like twenty-four guests attired for a gala dinner. As the child walked in, the stone floor transformed his footsteps into metallic clicks, as if he had suddenly acquired artificial limbs. A shiver ran through the china cupboards lining the walls. The shiver was contagious: it started with the cups and saucers on the upper shelves and quickly passed down to the lowest ones that housed strange tureens with peacocks painted on their lids. Across the room sat Madame Jacques, a silent black-silk Buddha. Behind her a window framed a safe, free world of summer light and buzzing bees crossed by swaying branches, a tantalizing Arcadia.

Judge and jury were assembled in the trial room in no time. Madame had been lying down in the bedroom with the shutters closed. Her blood pressure was high again. But when she heard Mark's account of the event she disengaged her feet from the bedcovers and squeezed them hurridly into her tight shoes. "How do you know it's a seizure?" she asked Mark. She felt insulted, as if someone had accused her of sheltering an infectious disease in her camp. "I've seen it once before, at the hospital with Philippe. You'll have to have him examined. Come at once. Siona is so scared she may run away." "Let her dare!" "Threatening her won't help you find out what happened, and you've got to find out."

Even Monsieur, who never took part in disciplinary matters, was there this time, standing behind Madame's chair and regarding the accused with reproachful gray eyes. Babette had come in with a request for flour and remained there to listen, wiping her hands on her apron with an air of mild reproach, her way of soothing both parties on such occasions. "Ah, these kids!" she would say later in the kitchen. "How many of them have a decent meal at home!" The smell of vanilla she exhaled while rolling down the sleeves of her blouse heralded indulgence, though she was a bit alarmed

131

today. "But really! Breaking into the vault! That's no place for kids to play."

Siona told her story with Mediterranean volubility, punctuating it with dramatic grimaces and gesticulations, while Albert stood at her side, blinking with incredulity and admiration.

"What? The Countess spoke to you? When was that?" asked the black-silk Buddha in alarm.

Yes, she had. In front of the vault last week. She asked Siona to go in and see if her family coffins were covered. That was all she wanted. From her place Babette made a tk-tk-tk sound.

"And who told Simon to go inside?"

"*He* wanted to go."

(Albert blinked several times, his mouth half open, hardly believing she could lie so well. They had had to bribe Simon to come, he was the only one thin enough to squeeze through the gate. They had promised him Monsieur's flashlight. He longed to hold it. "It's not a toy, you'll break the battery. Well, all right, you can have it if you come with us to the vault." He wouldn't have to do anything inside, Siona had told him, only see if the coffins were open. She and Albert would stay right outside the gate and talk to him all the while. She really didn't think they were uncovered at all. "Don't call them 'they,'" Simon had said nervously. "What should I call them? The Villemorins?" "You don't call dead people by their name," Albert had said firmly.)

"Well, go on," Madame said.

The three of them sneaked away from the crayfish party. The vault was asleep in the heat of the day, lulled by the serrate songs of the crickets. Mark's voice reached them over the bushes; fuzzy dandelions shivered and swayed, gave the afternoon a tamed, lazy air devoid of mystery. Even the horrible smell that usually lay around the vault was gone, covered by the odor of freshly crushed wet grass.

Albert searched for the flashlight in the bush where they had hidden it the day before and put it into Simon's feverish hand. Without giving him any time to make up his mind, they squeezed him through the opening in the iron gate.

Feeling the damp earth through his jersey, his face tickled by weeds, Simon crawled inside on his belly, and the horrid smell hidden in the grass suddenly jumped at him. Then he was in and stood up on shaky feet, facing the darkness, feeling Siona's breath on the nape of his neck. "Don't be afraid, Simon, it's all right, we're here."

Albert straightened the flashlight in Simon's sweaty hand. Simon held it like a gun. He moved the spot of light around him, exploring the ground, the walls, making tunnels of light in the darkness. Patches of crumbling red bricks looked like raw flesh. Then he started to move, soft damp moss under his feet, putting only small distances at a time between him and the monotonous chant outside the gate: "We're here, Simon; we're here, Simon; still here, Simon——"

He took a few more steps and moved the light slowly from left to right along the shelves. His wet finger slipped and flicked the switch; the light went out. He pressed the switch again, panic-stricken; the light fell on an empty shelf, a dark, damp hollow from which the coffin had been removed. His heart jumped, the jump jerked the hand holding the flashlight, the spot of light darted to the floor, and there it was, a long, glittering box, the lid crooked, as if it had been put back in haste; there it was—the missing coffin. He didn't see it clearly but sensed that someone lay in there wrapped in a black cloth. A pair of black patent leather man's shoes stuck out of it, pointed, elegant, intact, a pair of shoes from another century. Panic blurred his eyes. The last thing he saw was another casket, broken, its white and gold baroque ornaments smashed, like a ruined wedding cake—and out of it a long strip of white lace trailed to the ground and across the floor—or was the long white ribbon only his own shattering cry for help? Siona and Albert heard the cry, then the thumping of his sandals, and Simon appeared in the sunlight, put his hand over his mouth and collapsed on the other side of the gate before they had time to grab him. They couldn't reach him through the gate—and then Mademoiselle came.

"What happened after he fell down?"

"He——"

"No, let Albert tell me."

Taken by surprise, Albert told the truth. "He shook like this," and he demonstrated with his arms bent, his elbows close to his chest.

"I told him not to come, Madame, I told him! He tagged after us."

Siona and Albert waited outside while the court deliberated. Babette lost interest and left too; all that trouble and they didn't even find out if the coffins were uncovered or not.

The conference flagged. "Couldn't you talk to the Countess, Reine?" "We couldn't get anything out of her. If supervision were only better we wouldn't have had any trouble." "But you know Siona," Mark said, irritated at Madame's implication. "Why don't you get a full-time supervisor just for her? How many times has she dragged Armand into the bushes?" "I don't need your advice to run this place."

But maybe more than this was said inside the dark dining room, because after a while Mark came out biting his lip, remembering just in time not to bang the door in front of the children. He was called back later and asked if Philippe would see Simon at the hospital in Nice. And then Madame had a long talk with Albert and Siona alone, the windows and door closed.

She was still in the middle of the room when a wonderfully polite knock sounded at the door. Fortunée stood there holding Monsieur's flashlight in two fastidious fingers: *"J'ai trouvé ça dans le pipi de Simon, Madame,"* she said smugly.

THEY REMEMBERED THE TRIP TO NICE like a holiday. The day seemed longer than it really was; and the talk they had there at the beach confirmed all the little guesses they had made about each other. They got back late and came straight to the grownups' dinner table after delivering Simon to the cottage; and they looked radiant, glowing from the sun, with a new air of closeness. Madame's eyebrows rose, and Babette waited on them with devotion, swinging in and out of the kitchen, sniffing the air for traces of romance: but there was no sign. They ate in silence and answered all the questions patiently. "And how is Monsieur Philippe?" Hearing that Philippe hadn't forgotten her or her tarts and had even sent personal greetings, Babette's eyes moistened. "Oh, Monsieur Mark, as long as there are people like him around, and like you——" and leaving the rhapsodic sentence unfinished, she retired to the kitchen to regain her composure.

In the uproar of their early-morning departure, they could hardly believe they were going to be alone for the rest of the day. It was difficult to get away, helped by an envious crowd constantly getting in the way. Simon discovered that to be a hero had its disadvantages. He was awakened early in the morning and escorted to the shower; Ania checked his ears and nails; Madame came to the cottage to inspect his underwear personally, and Babette rushed him through a big breakfast. "Come on, hurry up! Monsieur Philippe isn't going to wait all day for you! He's a busy man!" And then, his hair still damp, his best jersey on, solemn and a bit dizzy from all the attention showered on him, he climbed into the truck. The children surrounded the truck in their pajamas, patting it with envious hands. Albert offered to go with them to the hospital and describe exactly how Simon shook. Would he please quit being a nuisance and get out of the way, replied Madame, who was standing in front of the cottage supervising the departure. Babette handed Ania the lunch basket. As if drawn into his own happiness Simon disappeared between his two guardians, the door of the truck banged, and a cloud of dust was sent back at the rabble. The three of them looked at one another and smiled. They had the day to themselves.

The truck went bravely down the winding road through the vineyards, leaving behind in the blue hills the morning racket, the breakfast bell, the fights in the shower. It felt like a holiday. The villages were still asleep, and cows with marks of insomnia around their black eyes came to the fence to watch them drive by. The morning sun, still cool, touched the roofs of the stern stone houses. Dew clung to the ivy. They drove in silence. Simon had put on Mark's straw cap and for a while had looked eagerly left and right, afraid he might miss something. Then, rocked by the hum of the motor, he leaned on Ania's hip, knocking the cap askew, and went to sleep.

They let him sleep when they stopped in Grasse and got out to stretch their legs. On the promenade the shade was cool under the oleanders. They had the world to themselves. The houses crouched low among flowering bushes, and on the hills century plants raised a giant finger toward the sky.

The sea crept into the landscape shortly after they left Grasse. The light grew stronger and the smell of iodine teased them at the curves of the road. Simon woke up, put his arm on Ania's lap and waited for the sea to come. Without warning, it was there; it leaped at them around the last curve, turquoise and tamed, making short, glittery dashes between the rocks. Ania put her hand over Simon's and cried out, "The sea!" and Simon craned his neck happily to look.

"Can't we stop just for a tiny little bit of a minute, Mark?" "We can't, Simon. The doctor said we should try to be in before eleven. He'll have to give you a good checkup. We'll go swimming afterward, don't worry. Here's where we have to turn left, I think."

"There's the hospital." Mark pointed ahead with his chin, and the big, sad, dry garden and stone buildings came nearer. Simon started to fidget. "Will there be shots?" "For you? Shots? Are you trying to be funny?" Mark poked him cheerfully with his elbow. Simon grinned and poked him back. "I was only asking." "You're not afraid of a checkup, are you" "Me? Of course not." He rocked back and forth on the seat. "The doctor is a friend of mine," Mark said. "You'll like him very much." "I know. He's a head doctor," Simon said—Babette had briefed him too. Ania patted his arm. "And then we'll go to the beach and have lunch." Simon beamed and with both hands pulled Mark's cap firmly down on his head.

The sadness of large hospitals—pavilions in a big, dry garden, the smell of iodine and ether and cheap soup—fell heavy and reproachful in the middle of their holiday. A doorman stared at them with colorless eyes: "No trucks allowed, you park outside." They walked in, both holding Simon's hands. Three nuns like black birds cut across their path; the wind blew their veils aside and exposed, valiantly walking between them, a little boy with a peg leg. "Where did they put his other leg?" Simon asked, his head turned back in horrified fascination.

In the neurological department they were told to wait, the nurse would call their name. They sat down in the dark waiting room looking alert but lost, like the other patients. From time to time an angry old nurse appeared and barked out names. "She looks like the wolf in grandma's bonnet," Ania said to cheer Simon up. "What wolf?" he asked nervously; his teeth were chattering. "What's the matter with you? The Red Riding Hood wolf!" But he was livid and clutched Mark's hand as he stood between his knees.

They were watching the wrong door. Mark's name was called from the other end of the room where a group of people in white coats had been standing talking for some time. A sleeve waved, then a white coat advanced slowly toward them and became a very thin, very blond young man with a long, narrow, ascetic face. "Here is Philippe." They stood up and went to meet him.

He limped heavily; Mark had never mentioned it. Ania had to stand there and witness with her whole healthy body Philippe's struggle to walk: the deep curtsy to the left; the anguished pause; the silent order that his body gave to his right leg; the leg refused to listen, a blue vein throbbed angrily in his neck, the leg submitted, the short instant of rebellion was resolved; the leg was dragged along, the right foot lifted, and the elegant, narrow, creaseless shoe triumphantly set down in front of the left one. Then he stood before them, "Monsieur Philippe," his white coat open, a faint chemical smell coming out of the stiffly starched lapels. He leaned on his good leg, his right hand hidden in his pocket, and scrutinized her. The sternness with which he had watched his own walk still showed in his eyes. And then he smiled. Like a wave the smile invaded his blond skin, and she was immersed, engulfed in the blue of his look. "How are things, Mark?" There was a short agitation inside his pocket; the right hand wouldn't come out and the left had to go in and persuade it. Then the hand extended itself easily to the visitors, and its grasp was strong and reassuring. "How is the camp doing?"

"Come and see for yourself. I have an official invitation from Reine for you. We've fixed the room downstairs at the mill—no stairs to climb this time. And this is our new counselor." "I've heard of you," Ania said, fighting her reserve, flushed, feeling she was being produced for his inspection. "Monsieur Philippe, ah, he is a head doctor," and like Babette she touched her temple and looked awed. The smile flooded his face again; he smiled the way other people blush. "That must be Babette," he said, "I haven't forgotten her either, or the plum tarts." His eyes made a quick, shy tour of her face. So she was the one! "We'll take good care of you if you come," she said. That "we" in her invitation made Mark absurdly happy. "If you don't want to drive," he said, "I'll come for you Friday." Philippe's good hand rose to his lapel, felt for it—yes? Friday?—stayed there undecided. He looked from one to the other, cheered, and then seemed to relinquish something. His smile wore away, the gray returned to his eyes. "I wish I could," he said, and shrugged. "There's just too much work here right now."

He had been aware of Simon's presence all the while but had not looked at him. Sheltered between Ania's skirt and Mark's pants leg, Simon watched his doctor carefully. Suddenly Philippe looked down at him with a conspiratorial air and said, "I know your name." Simon beamed. "Do you want to see my office?" He extended his left hand, the strong one. "Did they tell you what a checkup is and that it doesn't hurt?" Simon nodded. "Ever had a spin in a swivel chair?" Simon grinned again, incredulously. "Come and try that first. Mademoiselle Ania"—he knew her name?—"will wait here and we'll send Mark to the front office to make out the papers."

"What's the matter with your leg?" Simon gave Philippe his hand, reassured and comfortable. "I was sick." "Does it hurt?" "No, it's all over now. Listen—" Philippe stopped and felt for something in his pocket, and then held out a big marble on his palm. "Have you ever seen such a beauty before?" "I've got two like that," boasted Simon, and extracted two marvels full of sleepy opaline lights from the back pocket of his shorts. "Mine are yellow." "Would you consider swapping one of them?" "I'll think about it," Simon said, and reached for the doorknob with a sudden feeling of power.

It was a long time before Mark came back into the waiting room, pushing ahead of him an exultant, exuberant

Simon who wore his jersey wrong side out and kept turning to wave at someone. "I thought that was the right side," he said while Ania dressed him properly. "I have been in the dark room, mademoiselle, but I am so ticklish! The doctor told me to say good-bye to you because he can't come out," and sensing her disappointment—why was Philippe avoiding her? didn't he like her?—Simon put his hand lightly on her cheek while she pulled the jersey over his shorts and explained, "because he can't."

"Look, Simon." Mark was waving a bottle at him. "These pink pills are for you. You've got to take one every day. You're getting so special they've even printed your name on the bottle. How do you like that? Can you read it?"

THE beach was deserted. It was close to two o'clock when they stopped there to eat. The town was taking a long summer siesta under the afternoon sun. The woman who rented umbrellas had gone to sleep in a deck chair, a straw hat on her face. Her straw slippers hung from her big toes for a while, then fell in the sand. They had tried not to wake her up, but the wind brought their laughter to her. She lifted her head and retrieved her slippers; full of sleep, she came over and planted an orange umbrella in the sand. They were left alone with the sea. The turquoise sea of that morning had become silvery and dull, and hungry seagulls swooped close and watched them sharply. Simon ran up and down leaving large footprints in the wet sand; a white-crested, foamy, playful wave came up, rinsed his toes, erased his footprints; he looked down at his feet with apprehension and delight, waiting for the sea to come to him again.

They had taken their shoes off and settled comfortably for the meal, but lunch was delayed—they started to talk of Jean Paul. Ania sat on Simon's towel, her feet buried in the sand, the lunch basket, forgotten, open in her lap. The brim of her straw hat made a pattern of shadows on her face and neck. And what was that summer like, Jean Paul's summer, Mark asked. What was so special about her childhood? He was stretched out on his back with his cap on his face watching her through a hole in its weave; the little shadow in the opening of her dress became bluer when she bent forward.

She must have very small and round breasts, set high, he thought, and he had to close his eyes to listen properly.

With both hands she built up the hot sand around her ankles, and when she wiggled her toes the sand fell off and the toes appeared, childish and pearled, and she looked at them amazed, as if she were seeing them for the first time. What was so special about that childhood? "Ah, it was like another planet!" He felt strangely jealous, and longed to have been with her and her people then, to learn more about the strong attachment they had for one another. They were the ones who had consented to this adventure. It was an adventure, he thought; she didn't even know if the old man was there, she hadn't written to him yet. "But he isn't old," she said, "why do you think he is old?"

"What have we got for lunch, mademoiselle?" Simon crawled up to them on hands and knees. The way his head popped up behind the lid of the basket, like a puppet, seemed to remind her of something. Her face rapt, she worked absorbed, feeling inside the basket, tying and untying the cotton dish towel Babette had wrapped around the bread, until a puppet suddenly stood behind the open lid. "Hey, look at that!" Simon punched Mark in the ribs, "Mark, look at that!" The puppet, a peasant woman with a tomato face and cotton skirts, ran along the lid, bent inside the basket, recited the menu, and took out in turn the bread, the cheese and the chicken, which she handed to an awestruck Simon. Then Ania announced the show had ended and licked her finger on which the tomato had bled. "Oh, make another one," Simon begged. "Now we eat; later on, for dessert."

But it must have required quite a lot of—well, courage, yes—to come like this, all alone to a foreign country, Mark said later. He was a bit dazzled by that stubborn force in her. Oh, she wasn't really alone, she said. She had traveled to France with two ladies; no, not quite close friends but the family knew them well. They were on their way to Nice, and so she went there too and not straight to Paris. It was helpful for the first move, the first days away from home. Then she got this summer job. And she had letters from home; Father wrote to her every other day. She wasn't really alone. Was she returning to Nice in the fall, he asked, sitting up hopefully. Oh no, of course not, she said firmly, she was leaving for

Paris with the Jacqueses and the children, so that she could get a half-price ticket. She had delayed long enough; she had to find a place to live, and——"But you still haven't written to Jean Paul," Mark said. "No, not yet. It isn't easy," and she smiled helplessly.

For a while Mark gazed inside his cap, closely interested in the red label at the bottom, "Fernand, Chapelier-Nice." Then he looked up at her and smiled with reserve. "I think that's wonderful."

But when they came out of the bathhouse in their bathing suits they were abruptly forced into a new intimacy, more real than words. There was a strange delight in it. The surf was wild, beating the shore with angry waves, and she was afraid to go into the water. "Come with me," he said, and took her by the hand; when the water became deeper, he took her other hand and was amazed, as he faced her, to discover that his happiness came from being in the same sea with her, from the thought that the very same water that bathed his hands licked her small breasts half out of the soaked bathing suit. He said abruptly, "I think the waves are too rough, better go back now," and suddenly turned and swam away in a whirl of glistening foam. She sat down next to Simon, squeezed the water out of her hair, and for a long time they watched Mark's head rolling far away on the waves. "I like Mark," said Simon, suddenly looking at her, and then he grinned.

They had to leave. The heat had bleached the landscape and the Promenade was deserted. At the edge of the beach Ania picked up a big silken shell for Armand. The truck was hot. Simon slept all the way back, a thread of saliva hanging from his open mouth. She held his head at the rough curves on the road while the century plants, the wild geraniums, the dangling jasmines, ran toward them. "Philippe is your family, isn't he?" she asked Mark and he nodded. And then they were silent all the way back except when Mark said suddenly, "Funny, why did I think you were returning to Nice in the fall?" "Oh no," she said, "it really wouldn't make sense, I've got to get started. That's the way it was planned."

As they entered Callian they found Armand alone on the road in the blue dusk, waving them to a stop. "Hey, Armand," Simon shouted through the window, holding up his bottle of pills. "See that? It's got my name on it!" But Ania was angry. "What are you doing on the road all by yourself? How did you get here?" "I walked!" The dark notch appeared in the middle of his smile. "They were playing and I got bored and I came to wait for you." "But who gave you permission to walk away? You can't do just what you please in a summer camp, you know that, don't you?" Mark said sternly. "You know Madame gets angry with Mademoiselle every time you break the rules."

The idea of hurting Mademoiselle hadn't occurred to Armand. He sat between them on the front seat with Simon on his knees and looked unhappy for the rest of the trip. In front of the cottage Ania gave him the shell. "I brought you a present but I'm still angry with you."

THE MILL HAD A DRY ODOR OF HEAT, of high summer. Mark knew it well from his previous summers in camp. He knew that the suffocating smell should be covered by that of seaweed and wet wood as soon as the night breeze touched the damp millwheel late in the evening. But this summer it hadn't rained enough; the grapes in the vineyards were dusty, the nights dry and stagnant, and he lay on his mattress on the floor, smoking, tossing, naked and hot. Once in a while he heard Père Barthe stirring downstairs, walking around barefoot, the boards creaking under his feet, his peculiar cough scraping his throat. The old man couldn't sleep either.

He couldn't read. He discovered, as he turned the page and started a new sentence, that he had been smiling without reason at something that wasn't in the book. Then he put the book down on his chest, rejoicing in the cool touch of the smooth pages on his skin, and openly admitted to himself he was thinking of her again.

That very morning, driving the truck up the hill, he had seen Ania standing behind the children's cottage waving to him. He had stopped and got out and walked toward her before he realized it wasn't Ania at all; it was only her blue dress hanging on the clothesline among the children's wet bathing suits and towels. Disappointed, he watched it dancing airily on the line, the little puffed sleeves pinched by the clothespins as if the dress were shrugging its shoulders as Ania did when she was embarrassed. He liked that blue dress, but he had never noticed the tiny red and blue flowers in the print until that day in Nice. She wore it most of the time whenever she wasn't in her old shorts and faded shirt, "my working uniform." And the day before yesterday—he steadied the book on his chest and lingered over the memory —she had come to him with Armand to borrow his pocket knife. (What word had she used for it? He could not remember now but he had corrected her. *"Canif,"* she repeated after him, and became slightly rosier under her straw hat.) She had her old shirt on over her shorts, the tails tied in front. Then she moved an arm and the shirt rode up, uncovered a bit of her secret skin. It looked childish and blond, untouched by the sun. But how could he remember it so well now when at the time his eyes had jumped aside in surprise and tried not to look at it? Yet the heat of that patch of skin, its blondness, had come to him through the air.

So it wasn't Ania, it was just her blue dress hung out to dry, and he had walked back to the truck regretfully, hands in pockets, and thought again of the end of the summer. She wasn't going to return to Nice, as he had hoped for a while; she was going to Paris, to this man, this teacher or whatever he was. She wasn't going to return to Nice and he hadn't told her yet. How was he going to tell her?

He looked for her in the office at noon without realizing that he was doing so until Babette told him, "It's her day off, she must be sleeping, the poor girl. She won't come to lunch. I'm keeping her food warm," and he went to set on the office steps and read his mail. Every so often he looked up across the lawn. At long last she came walking along with Armand. They were returning from the barn, Armand held her hand and swung her arm back and forth, laughing. He stopped short when he saw Mark.

Did she want to go to Draguignan that afternoon? No, not a very long ride, about half an hour away. He had to go there to see the garage man. Armand darkened. "What for? It looks just like Callian, there's nothing to see—another market, and another fountain! And you promised you'd come and watch the ball game!" But she'd be back for the ball game, she said. Armand let her hand go and kicked the grass. He was always moody on her days off.

Mark had waited for her in the truck in front of the kitchen. Her blue dress was freshly ironed, and a smell of clean sweat and linen dried in the sun came out of it when she moved on the seat hugging the basket happily.

But what did they talk about on the way there? That he could not remember now. He had been absorbed in her presence next to him and couldn't call to mind now how she looked or what she said.

The Draguignan shops were still closed; they had to wait for the end of the siesta, and they sat down at a bistro table out on the sidewalk. Mark took two coins out of his pocket and put them on the table. Did she recognize them? Of course she did, she said, laughing, he wasn't going to embarrass her again—She was too comfortable with him now. The incident of the tip was part of a forgotten time. Bliss shot through him as he realized that she divided time in two: there was the time before she knew him and the time with him, like two seasons. He made up his mind to tell her what he felt then and there, but the bistro owner, fat and short and oily-looking, came out to wipe their table dry. He inspected Ania sideways while he worked his rag on the table. Like Babette, he was fond of Mark ("Ah, Monsieur Mark! He's the salt of the earth!"), and he stood there concerned, hands on hips, determined to get all the news. "And is it true you're leaving us, Monsieur Mark?" "Yes, but not until next fall, Monsieur Aubanel." He took the order but was reluctant to leave. "They say you might even go to America to study." "Could be." "America is a long way away. Do you think you'll ever get used to the place?" "When you go to study, it isn't so hard." But Monsieur Aubanel was skeptical; his unbuttoned waistcoat hanging over his belly looked doubtful too. "Get yourself a pretty girl here before you leave, Monsieur Mark! I'd hate to see you coming back with one of those foreigners." Monsieur Aubanel flapped his rag to dry it like a patriotic flag; but then it occurred to him that Ania might be "one of those foreigners"; in fact, he had heard something of the sort from the Callian grocer's wife who had come up to Draguignan last week. Slightly embarrassed, he shuffled into the bistro and shouted, "*Deux filtres, en vitesse! Et essuyez les tasses! C'est pour Monsieur Mark.*"

They didn't talk. A dialogue of smiles went on between them as they watched the twig of water rising from the fountain in the marketplace. She took her straw hat off and put it in her lap. "Don't move now!" A dragonfly, curious about the silky shadows in her hair, landed on her head, walked on a hair like a green acrobat on a silken rope, and then was gone. The two filters arrived, the smell of coffee escaping through their tall tin hats. They still hadn't spoken.

He was going to talk to her seriously on the way back in the truck. Watching the road ahead, he wouldn't have to look at her. With a feeling of relief he let her go for a walk while he went to the garage. But he rushed the garage man and returned to the marketplace, stopped in the green shade of the awning over the butcher's shop and watched her on the sidewalk opposite. She was bare-headed (the heat had curled the little hairs at the nape of her neck), long-legged—like a flamingo wearing sandals—and was seriously examining the window of Les Grands Magasins. Then he watched her put the basket down and take off a sandal without her eyes leaving the object in the window, shake the gravel out of it standing on one leg like a child, then put it on again. Protected by the awning, which gave a deep, green secrecy to his thoughts, he suddenly felt that it was right to tell her now. He still didn't know yet how he was going to tell it, but it was right to tell her, because he knew that with all her reticence she was going to love him. Yes, that was what he was going to tell her, and then he would take her head between his hands and——

But at that very moment she turned and saw him standing there and called him over. What sort of candies were the black ones wrapped in red cellophane? Licorice? She wondered if this wasn't the sort Jean Paul kept in his kitchen drawer. His bread knife and even his bread smelled of them. She had never been able to find them at home. He must have brought them from France. She had gone away from him again, all wrapped in her past. "We can try them," he said, ready to go

145

in and buy some, but she protested, obviously wanting to tear herself away from that memory now. "No, really not, Mark," and her hand with the rough skin like a boy's took his arm above the elbow, drew him away, and they went back to the truck.

"But this isn't the way we came," she said, leaning out of the window, her hair blown across her face. "No, it's not," he said happily, "I want to show you something. It's a surprise." They were silent again until he stopped the truck in the shade and said, "We get out here." They had to put their heads far back to look up the steep bank across the road; high up, right at the top, was the ruin of the castle she could see from her bedroom window. "The castle!" she cried out, just as she said, "The sea!" the day they drove to Nice. "I knew you wanted to see it close. This is as close as the truck will go." Dazed by her presence so close to him, he felt he had to talk to her now, and then he would give her time, yes, and wait— He took her arm with authority: "Do you know—" But she knew, she knew what he was going to say, and quickly, feverishly, she started to talk about the castle, disengaging her arm to point at the portal and the coat of arms over it, half-eaten away. And he remembered what she had once said to him about the future, about the future desired and not yet consumed, the future about to happen, and looked at her trying to meet her eyes. But she was shading them with one hand, gazing intently at the castle, and he didn't have the courage to go on.

And when they went back to the truck she sat in the farthest corner of the seat, as far from him as possible, as if she knew about his green, secret thought under the awning in the marketplace. Her elbow on the open window, she sat upright on the hot upholstery, and the beginning of alarm or defensiveness showed in the way she looked straight ahead. But when he let her out in front of the children's cottage she thanked him, blue-eyed and rosy with the heat, holding her straw hat against her breasts, and said gravely how good, how soothing it had been to be with him that afternoon and away from the children. And this set his hopes ablaze again.

to let [?] easy[?] he[?] she protested, obviously resolved to tell herself. Why room that memory now. And no boy not Mark that everything [?] the moving story drew back away and drew near broken, he

So why didn't you go with them to Draguignan?"

"Because!"

"Yeah! Because! Because they don't want you along, that's why? Because they want to be by themselves! But you keep running after her like a puppy—"

The blood rose to Armand's head. He felt dizzy. Siona snaked out her arm, snatched the tennis ball he was holding and ran toward the cottage. "Give it back!" But she was in, running through the playroom and up the stairs to the girls' dormitory. The cottage was empty, the hot boring afternoon loafing in and out of the rooms.

"Give it back!" Armand shouted, drumming his fist on the door, rattling the doorknob, kicking the wood in a white-hot fury—*like a puppy!* From behind the door Siona's impudent laugh bubbled into his face. "Come and get it." She had to let the door go, Armand was stronger and the lock had no key. Twice he forced it open, and through the narrow slit saw Siona's face flushed with effort, a gleaming mocking eye, a flash of glistening smile, a long strip of lilac dress. She let the door go suddenly and Armand stumbled headlong into the empty room. It felt like falling into a pool of silence. The afternoon sun filled the air with powdered light.

Siona retreated between the beds, her little gurgling laugh punctuated by short infuriating squeals. Cautiously she held the tennis ball behind her back. She stopped between two beds, her back to the wall, watching him come, keeping her eyes on him like a lion tamer. Suddenly Armand jumped over a mattress and landed in front of her, cutting off her retreat.

"Give it back!" he said, exasperated by her hysterical laugh. But as he grabbed her wrist she swiftly dropped the ball inside her dress. It rolled down to her waist and stopped there, bulging the lilac cotton. Then she threw herself face down on the bed.

Hot and enraged, as if his life depended on that tennis ball, Armand fought to turn her over. Her neck wasn't clean and the lilac dress was stained with perspiration under the arms. He lifted one of her shoulders and innocently thrust his hand deep inside her dress. His arm froze with surprise at what it discovered; it detached itself from his body, went on a search of its own, groping into that strange damp landscape like an explorer entering a cave.

Between the brassiere hiding her breasts and the elastic top of her pants his tipsy hand traveled for a second on a soft, velvet valley which became hot and dangerous as he advanced. The ball was there, next to a deep dimple; it felt lifeless, dry, next to Siona's secret skin.

Siona stopped giggling and turned over on one side, soft and jointless like a rag doll; she closed her eyes. "Kiss me, Armand."

He regained possession of his arm and woke up in the sunny, empty silence of the dormitory. Children's voices rose outside on the lawn. "He did too, he stepped on the line, look at the foot-mark!" A shutter squeaked. He felt like kicking her in the stomach as she lay there spread on the bed, her neck unwashed. "You . . . idiot!" he said, getting up. "Idiot! Idiot!" and ran out and down the stairs rubbing the warm ball against his shorts, cleaning it of all contact with her naked skin.

THE MILL. THE SHREWD, HYPOCRITICAL OLD MILL. In daylight, seen from the river, it had always looked ffistrange, locked up in its steamy silence like an old animal lying in the noon heat. The stone molars which had been chewing for years were now at rest; they were still connected with the big wheel outside but the wheel stood still in the water, seaweed hung around the spokes. An old animal ruminating the cud of silence. What did it know, what was the secret it kept in its hot belly of rotten wood, in the smell of whitewashed walls and old beams? How they moved through the drowsy silence downstairs; how a somnolent cricket woke up; and how the shuttered darkness rustled when he touched her sleeve; and how the girl stood there in the middle of the room in her faded blue jersey, tamed, to be kissed?

UNDER the trees the children's voices sounded like bird calls. The air was hot and the noises hung low over the river in the burned grass and troubled the lazy water.

Mademoiselle Annie had agreed at long last to take them swimming up at the mill where the river deepened and made an elbow. They rushed through the mid-morning heat, their towels over their shoulders. Simon had already covered twice the distance to the mill; he would run ahead, but, finding himself alone with the crickets, return in panic to hurry them up.

The old mill looked unfamiliar in daylight, secretive, locked up in silence. The truck wasn't there. "They went to the market early in the morning," Fortunée told Ania. "I saw Mark in the—" "We haven't come to visit, we've come to swim!" Ania snapped. Fortunée licked her upper lip and thrust her head forward on her neck like a hurt hen. "Aren't you feeling well?" she asked Ania solicitously.

"Come on, everybody get ready. I'll count ten." The smell of wood, of hot earth and dry grass at the edge of the water slowed down the beat of her blood, infused her with a drunken desire to lie down in the weeds and go to sleep. But she had to stay awake and watch the children. This was the third day she had avoided Mark. And he had not come to look for them either. The indecision—but what about? what about?—made her depressed and irritable. Armand came to sit by her on the shaky little bridge; with his head bent deeply between his knees he watched the seaweed moving around his toes. "Go take a dip, Armand." But he shrugged, he liked sitting next to her better. "It's a short summer, isn't it?" he said all of a sudden, echoing her thoughts. "Why, Armand?" He shrugged again. "It feels short."

Getting ready to return for lunch was a long procedure devised by Siona and intended to try Mademoiselle's patience. Each leg had to be wiped dry very carefully with ostentatious care; toes were wiggled, then lifted high in the air to eliminate the slightest suspicion of dampness. Just when they were ready for dressing at last, Siona or Albert would throw somebody back into the water, and everything started all over again. "What can I do? I am wet! I can't dress like this, can I?"

Waiting for them to get ready, Ania walked round the mill in the shadow of the trees. The door was wide open and the dark interior sent out a long hot breath like a dry sigh. She advanced through the door on tiptoe, hesitated, and stopped to listen to the darkness inside. The mill was empty. The muffled echo of her bare feet crept about.

At first she saw nothing but darkness; then the darkness became thinner, navy blue, then lavender, and a light stain moved to her right. She started at the discovery—oh!—and the mill answered over her head, ". . . oh . . . oh. . . ." "Is it you, Mark? I—didn't know you were here—the door was open. Did I wake you up?"

He had been only half asleep and had heard them coming up the hill, her voice calling out, "Arrmand, Alberrt." He had listened to the odd way she had of rolling her *rs* and wished she would come in. When he saw her outside the door, her faded blue jersey over her bathing suit, her legs glistening with water, he had lifted himself on one elbow, ready to call; but with her braids tied high on her head she had looked so much like a shy deer with shivering ears peeking in, he was afraid he would scare her off. "I wasn't asleep," he said, still propped on his elbow. "I just wanted to—I haven't been inside the mill before." "Come in." But she stayed by the door. "Are there more rooms upstairs?" The whites of her eyes shone in the dark when she looked up. "The attic." "What a strange voice it has." "Who?" "The mill. Hear that? It repeats every word, no secrets" (". . . eats . . . ry . . . ords . . . o . . . e . . . ets" came from upstairs). "It's the shape of the ceiling." He got up and came toward her. "You can hear it best from this spot. She took two steps and stood facing him, but they couldn't find anything to say to the echo. Her mouth was slightly open, the lower lip pale and wet. And then the mill shut off the echo and refused to give away what it heard: the soft, pearly noise of drops falling from her wet bathing suit; the rustle of his hand leaving his side, touching the elbow of her faded jersey; a somnolent cricket woke up; the hand climbed up the arm; searched for her cheek cooled by water, the sweet enamel of her ear; and through the gauze of her breath, the kiss, like a fall head first into an empty well, shutting everything out except for the wonder—is this you? this mouth, unfamiliar hot island?

The noises outside faded, a strange concert of crickets filled her ears, the children's voices flared up again and she suddenly recognized the sound of the lunch bell. Hands climbed up, fingers made warm fences over her ears, held her head like a big bowl of voices, tried to bring it close to that strange mouth once more. But she slipped out of his hands, turned, and ran outside.

"They've rung for lunch," Siona said reproachfully. "Armand isn't here." Where was he now? "Armand! Armand!" The hot air hung heavily on their cooled skin. "Armaaand!" Her towel over her head, Siona shouted over the waters as if calling the soul of a drowned man. "Leave him alone, he'll come!" And they left in a hurry, the towels wet and heavy. "If Mark were here, he would have given us a ride down." "Don't you see his truck isn't here, stupid!" The mill raised its back in the middle of the landscape white with the noon heat and kept its secrets.

HALFWAY through the noon meal Armand's striped jersey appeared under the trees. He had been running, his shirt was wet and his face stained with tar. "Hey, look, drowned Armand is here," Siona announced with her mouth full, pointing over Ania's shoulder. He had been in the attic, he explained unwillingly, he was late. "I can see that," Ania said, and for a short second they measured each other over the soup tureen. Babette came out with a bowl of salad for him. "Eat now, you've kept me long enough." "And how did you get to the attic, anyway?" she asked him later thoughtfully. He shrugged darkly. "There's a stairway outside on the other side of the mill," Fortunée volunteered.

During siesta time Armand slept deeply, his fists under his chest—Ania had come to watch him from the door—showing even in his sleep a stubborn determination to be silent. He didn't ask her to the coach in the afternoon, or the next day; the day after when they were returning from the office with the mail, she proposed a quick run to the barn, and he nodded happily. But they sat together in the coach without speaking.

"Do you suppose he saw us kiss?" she asked Mark that night leaning against him under the big oak. "Maybe. Why? We're not the first people he has seen kiss. Why, did he tell you anything?" No, he didn't, but . . . Stars hung in the oak tree, huge summer stars, and when she put her head back they blinked at her sadly and, maybe, yes—reproachfully.

THEY BECAME LOVERS ON A SUNDAY NIGHT at the beginning of August, the Sunday of the fair. A country fair came to Callian toward the middle of the summer. Tents were put up in the marketplace. Stalls covered with colored paper were built around the eucalyptus tree which furled its fragrance like an umbrella and abandoned the square to the smell of cakes fried in oil, of cheap vanilla, of damp tent canvas and fresh paint. Paper flags shivered in the wind and the dust rose high. That year a wooden platform had been improvised for the dancers in front of the bistro, and a violin player in orange shirt and blue tie played from the doorway. Between songs he took off his hat and wiped his forehead with a big handkerchief. And when he sang, which he did quite suddenly, startling everyone, he opened his mouth very wide, and a gold tooth twinkled inside like a star.

Ania had an hour off in the afternoon. "You can take the evening too, if you want, Madame said. "There's going to be an awful racket. I'd better go over to the children's cottage. I won't be able to sleep anyway."

"Yes, it'll be murder," Babette said, shaking crumbs off her bright skirts—she had been dressed in her best since early that morning—"You'd be better off out there dancing!"

Mark was waiting for Ania in the lane leading to the ramparts. She came up the lane wearing a white blouse he didn't know with lantern sleeves and a ruffle gathered at the neck in a black ribbon—she looked unreal, as if coming out of a formal Renaissance landscape of trees and grottoes and paths receding infinitely into the distance. She hadn't braided her hair but had piled it up on her head in a soft nest. A small wisp had escaped the comb and quivered with her step like a jolly feather thrust behind her ear.

He put an arm around her waist and drew her inside a doorway, recognizing the warmth of her body through the starched linen blouse. "I don't know you today," he said in her ear. "Are you the lady of the manor?" "Yes, I am, my lord." "And where are you going, all dressed up like this, with no horse and no squire?" She laughed, and under his hands the laughter rippled inside her like a pigeon's call. "Hear how quiet it is? The village must be empty," she said later, emerging from his kiss. A faint hum came from the marketplace. An asthmatic accordion heaved a sigh over the valley whenever the guns stopped their noise in the shooting booths. "Everyone has gone to the fair."

The shops were closed. The grocer's cat, forsaken, was rolled up in the window on a box of sugar, an angry ball of fur, and when they reached the ramparts the valley beneath was deserted; the cows had gone home. In the light of sunset the big sleeves of her blouse were translucent and the ruffle at her neck shivered when she turned toward him. "I can't stay, Mark, I have to return to the cottage. I only came to tell you I'm taking the evening off. I don't have to be back"—she tried to smile—"before morning. Would you wait for me outside after dinner?" He took her head between his hands and kissed the serious frown between her eyes and then her eyelids. They answered with a flutter of eyelashes. "Let's go back to the fair now."

When the market came in sight he had to let go of her wrist; he kept one of her fingers, and then had to part with it too. Impatient, longing to hold her close, he could only walk next to her, walk in the light breeze she made as she moved, in the rustle of her skirt, in the soft breath of her blouse. She filled herself with his impatience, with the feeling of being desired and drawn out of her reserve. They stood together at the edge of the platform and watched the dancers, but were startled by the village mailman, who bowed to Ania abruptly and awkwardly asked her to dance. And while he held her respectfully in his big, perspiring hands and pushed his heavy shoes around the floor, she looked across at Mark, saw him watching her, amused, his head slightly bent, his arms folded over his chest, taller than anyone else in the crowd, and thought this was the last time she would see him like this, the last time when he was not her lover. They had talked about love before, sitting at night under the oak tree, like two solemn philosophers. He had understood that she needed time to part with all her complicated dreams; a bit drunk with her presence so close to him, he longed to release her patiently from the tangled line that moored her to the past. "But love is not like that," he had told her, "not what you think it is, this wait for the future, for the unconsumed future, this anticipation. Love is the present, don't you know that?" And she had listened with her face on his neck, breathing in the odor of the mill from his shirt, hearing the words inside him before they came out and hung hot in her hair, "Love is not like that."

She still had time to walk through the fair with Mark and win a blue glass cup at the wheel of fortune. But then she had to go back to the cottage, and she left him there and walked determinedly up the hill without turning her head, the blue cup dangling from her finger. The mailman's hand had left a damp stain on the back of her blouse.

She had dinner that night on the lawn outside the kitchen with the grownups. Mark was there too, sitting across the table from her, but they didn't talk. Babette served them in a hurry, still wearing her Sunday skirts, her face flushed by the dance. Ania and Mark tried not to look at each other, but he knew too well how the velvet ribbon throbbed at her neck and she could tell without looking where his blue espadrilles rested on the grass. The spoons worked in the bowls; night moths drunk with light invaded the table. Warm and fragrant, Babette stretched between Monsieur and Madame to reach for the plates.

"Is that horrible accordion going to scream all night long, Babette?" Madame said, putting her small fat hands to her ears.

THE children's cottage was ablaze that evening. Mademoiselle Amélie, called in to help for an hour, couldn't bear it, and soon Madame Jacques appeared at the door. In her pajamas, a boy's cap on her head, Siona was imitating the crooner on the dance platform. Her acid voice reached up to Ania's room. Ania sat on her bed, brush in hand, looking at her hair hanging in her lap. She got up suddenly, tied her hair back with a rubber band, changed her shoes and put out the light.

"Are you going to the fair, Mademoiselle?" Armand was sitting on the stairs in his pajamas. He had been waiting for her. "Is it your time off again?"

"I am not, Armand. Go to bed, please." She sounded as if she had been running.

"Where are you going?"

"I'm going for a walk. I have a headache. You are shouting too much tonight."

"Can I come with you?"

"You certainly cannot. Go to bed right this minute!"

"You have so much hair," Armand said, looking down at her over the banisters, but she had already closed the front door and was outside.

A dark form was floating back and forth under the trees, and a red star clung to it, the burning tip of a cigarette. At the sound of the cottage door the red star came to meet her. Mark held her in his arms for a long time, then tried to open her mouth with a kiss. But her feverishly chattering teeth resisted. "Don't be afraid," he said, and for a long time afterward he remembered her little brave laugh, "I'm not afraid." When they entered the barn the night stopped rustling and a soft, dry silence wrapped itself around them like a cloak. The coach came closer, restored to gallantry by this night of love, and for a second its lacquered side grew alive with the reflection of their two white forms. Mark opened the door and climbed inside. He lifted her in; her hair got caught in the handle and he undid it carefully while she watched him. The accordion complained at the distant fair, and she remembered that lament, and the dark tunnel, and also how for a long while, until he took her head between his hands again and talked to her, she hadn't been able to match a head, a familiar one, to that alien body lying next to hers on the seat of the coach.

smelling. Examination she was horrified. Yes, she was considerably older. And there was a face to be counted for—a face that had terrorized him. The closeted thing became—to him accustomed, become invariable. But that had brought her, she had never been ... there, her face; with a surprised thought, felt out for the fruitful.

THE RAINY DAYS CAME IN A ROW and they seemed endless. But after those heavy, sweet Callian summer nights, the cold, sharp air settled one's head. The past invaded the lazy, torpid present, and the desire to own it again sharpened and drove Ania back to her old obsession. Summer was drawing to an end.

The children grew impossible during the week of rain. The dormitories smelled of crowds; it was too cold to keep the windows open. Downstairs the playroom felt chilly and dark, and the racket, the cruel jokes, the perpetual bickering, became insufferable. The monotonous tap-tap of the rain lined the hours.

"I love the rain," Armand said, hanging by his hands from both door handles and rocking slowly with the door. The Provence landscape was wet, like a freshly painted watercolor. Ania expected the paints to run into one another at any moment, the dark green of the cypresses to spread into the gray-green of the olive trees, together to make dirty little rivers of color down the hills. "I love the rain," repeated Armand closing his eyes and ecstatically breathing in the odors stirred outside by the damp. He was only worried about the coach, and paid it a hurried visit with Ania, dashing back from the office with the mail. In tacit agreement they suddenly turned and ran to the barn under Madame's umbrella. Once inside they stopped to catch their breath. The rain drummed furiously on the roof, made a curtain of water over the doorway. An uncomfortable dampness had replaced the dry, soothing summer silence, and a new feeling of instability, of transience wrinkled the surface of the moment. They put the mail down in the dry hay, blew into their wet hands to warm them and caressed the coach.

"It's dry in here," Armand said. "She'll be all right." And they looked up at the ceiling, at the good, old, strong beams smelling of wet wood, sheltering silent white spiders. Yes, she was going to be all right. And they ran back to the cottage.

All the games had been played, all the tricks to bring peace tried; scratches had been bandaged, broken toys mended. A short attempt at creativity had ended with the boys throwing bullets of modeling clay at Siona; they aimed at her brassiere from behind a barricade of chairs. The peeling walls were sick with a sort of skin disease. The loot one army had taken from the other was scattered on the floor, abandoned. They had dressed up in sheets, but the ghost game ended with an accident. ("I can't run with that thing on me and Albert was chasing us.") They lived on a volcano due to erupt at any moment. "It's still raining," someone announced from time to time, sticking a head out of the front door. Yes, it was.

THE RAINY WEATHER had drawn Armand out. He was talkative now. Mornings, he stood in the door of the shower room waiting for his turn and talked. He would gesticulate with his toothbrush until the little white worm of toothpaste dropped from its perch. In the playroom he knelt next to Ania on the floor, pulled down the frayed cuffs of his big sweater, stuck his hands in his armpits and talked away. Had she ever been to Paris? No, she had not; she was going there in the fall. To stay? She hesitated. For the winter; to work. Puppets? She nodded. Yes, puppets. Going to school? Sort of, yes. He was quiet for a while, squinting, trying to imagine her returning home with books under her arm. Where would she be? Where was she going to stay? A students' hotel on the Rue des Écoles. Oh, but that was very close to his home. Was it? Sure. He looked away. Was she going to come to the park sometimes? What park was that? The Luxembourg. He lived across the street from the Luxembourg. He went there every day, he had to walk his dog, after school. But didn't it get dark too early for him in winter? He shrugged like a man loaded with responsibilities. He had to. They lived on the fourth floor, and the dog was old and had asthma, and their concierge was always angry with it. But doesn't your mother —? His mother didn't live with them, he said; his parents were divorced. They had a housekeeper. Ania sat back on her heels and saw him wrapped in a woolen cap and mittens and a muffler leading a tired, shivering dog along a damp street, coming to meet her in the fog. Would it snow? No, he said, it rarely snows in Paris.

Visiting Ania's room upstairs, he stood in front of her table and looked at the puppets in silence, his hands behind his back, pulling absently at his sweater. "What's her name?" he asked, lifting one cautiously. "Martine." "What happened to her face? It's all cracked." "It is a very old puppet. The paint is peeling." "You made them?" "Not this one." "Who made this one?" "My teacher. He gave it to me." "The one you're going to see in Paris?" She nodded.

She discovered it was much easier to talk about Jean Paul with Armand then it was with Mark." Armand listened with his eyes on Martine, and she felt he liked Jean Paul. But he wasn't really interested in puppets, and this disappointed her a bit. "Are there only two sorts of people," Mark said in the oak-tree night with his arms around her, "the ones who understand puppets and the ones who don't? Where would you put me?" "I think you understand puppeteers better than puppets."

To her surprise, Simon was much more impressed by the puppets than anyone else. He too came up to her room during that rainy week, pretending at first to be looking for Armand but staying on, his neck stiff, his eyes widened by the sight of the puppets on the table. The way Ania made Martine move her felt hands, then lift her apron to wipe her nose threw him into a fit of violent laughter. He bent and pressed his hands between his thighs. "Go to the toilet, don't postpone it," Armand ordered him, trying to prevent the disaster. But nothing of the sort happened, it was just Simon's way of expressing delight. Then he lifted limp and lifeless Martine, and intimidated by her look didn't dare revive her.

But they were interrupted. Downstairs the volcanic eruption finally took place, an earthquake followed, the cottage danced and creaked. Thunder? She rushed down in panic. The boys had loosened the screws on Albert's bed and it had collapsed. Somebody was fighting the blankets, trying to get out. Siona appeared among the pillows, her sweater unbuttoned. What was she doing in the boys' room? Playing, she said, getting up and tugging at her brassiere. The room was evacuated and locked.

"Still raining?" A messenger was sent to check the sky. "Yeah." There were wet footprints in the hallway. Annette's slip hung limp from a shutter at the girls' window; it wouldn't dry. The mailman came on his bicycle wearing a black oilcloth tent under which the mail kept snug and dry.

"Why are we without news?" Father wrote. "When do you leave for Paris? Was this interruption in Callian necessary? Have you written to Jean Paul? Has the winter coat arrived? For some reason known only to her special maternal antenna, Mother thinks you may be having a difficult time right now. Are you?"

It rained. In the village, the laundry was taken in, the windows and doors were closed; Callian looked wet and obstinate. The Countess crossed the marketplace stepping slowly along close to the walls like a waterbird in worn-out shoes, her organza hat dripping with rain. Was summer over? Was parting that close? No, Babette didn't think so. They hadn't gathered the olives yet, she said, with the assurance of one whose life is serenely ruled by such inevitable and important events. She turned the meat patties in the skillet with her big spoon and shook her head. No, she didn't think so.

Love was strange during the rainy days. Ania hoarded it; she was alone with it. The gap between meetings was too long, and faced again with the one she loved she felt shy, stole sideways glances at him, wondering what it was about him she had remembered differently. Growing straight and clumsy and frail and just recently unfurled, like the early fern before it acquires all the complicated, feathery summer shape, love needed time to spread and sun to chase the doubts away. But it rained. They couldn't see each other, or meet on the grounds during the day, or even wave from a distance. The grounds were deserted; the rain whipped the high grass, and the dandelions shook their fuzzy heads in amazement. They had never seen such rains before. And only one evening, huddled into her raincoat, her head tied in a big black scarf like a village woman, she was able to come and meet him in the barn. But it was cold. His hands were cold when he held her close, and the barn was full of curious padded noises like mice. In the coach they listened to the pattering of the rain on the roof, to each other's breath, to their heartbeats. But it was chilly. Sometimes streaks of white mist drifted from their mouths when they whispered. Her feet were frozen. Mark took off her shoes and rubbed her toes with meticulous care, then held her feet in his lap, wrapped them in his raincoat. "I wish you could come to the mill with me," he said unhappily. "But Père Barthe has insomnia. He'd hear us."

"Never mind," she said bravely. "I'll be warm in a second."

"Wouldn't it be good," he went on, hugging her feet against his chest like a valuable parcel, "to come up to the mill out of the rain and find you there cooking the soup like the miller's wife?" And then, "You'd have a bit of flour on your nose."

Her head was turned away from him, one cheek leaning against the back seat, and he couldn't see her face in the dark but felt she was smiling. "Have you noticed something?" he asked after a pause. "No. What?" "I think I've just proposed." And they laughed. But she moved her toes inside the raincoat and sat up. "I don't know how to cook soup," she said after a long silence. "I didn't expect you to know." "Why didn't you? Do I look so helpless?" "You don't look helpless, you look like—a puppeteer."

Their laughter muffled by the silk-lined walls of the coach echoed through the barn, but he never found out that night what the miller's wife really thought about his proposal. Between the long roaming of hands and mouths, the pauses, the repetitions—musicians touching their instruments and bending in concentration to hear the answer—there was too little time for talk. And when on leaving he tried to ask her again, her answer was far away from his thought. "This is what they must have done in Noah's Ark during the flood." "What did they do in the Ark?" he asked, tenderly amused and still dazzled by the wild flights of her imagination. "They made love, the lion with his lioness, and the ram with his ewe, and the gander with his goose"—he had put her shoes on her feet and was busy tying the laces—"and the donkey with—" She didn't know the French word for the donkey's wife.

"*Ânesse.*"

"*Avec son ânesse.*"

He tied her scarf around her head while she talked on, telling him what the nights were like in the Ark and how there was no real morning, ever; and they walked together through the tarry night, and by the cottage he kissed the taste of the rain on her lips again and again. It was the only night she could come out during the entire week.

When Ania saw him next it was in the kitchen, in daylight, and he seemed changed. He was darker, and when he took his glasses off to dry them, his eyelashes looked white, bleached by the sun. He was wearing an ugly raincoat, stiff and heavy like a tent, the one Père Barthe wore in the fields.

"Can you come out tonight after supper?" he whispered when Babette went out to the larder. "You can't? When am I going to see you? I've got to talk to you. The rain could go on like this for another week? It's been—" Babette came back with a basket of beets and he was silent.

"May I open the stove door for a second, Babette?"

"Go ahead. You poor dear, you must be soaked through. They ought to start heating the cottage!"

A world of crumbling corals appeared inside the stove, and Ania knelt on the floor holding her hands out to the fire as she talked. "Good fire, for boiling soup and keeping people company." But Mark stood over her impatiently, looking down at the back of her neck where the dampness had curled all the little strays of hair his fingers knew so well. "Are you going back to the cottage? I'll take you there. I'll borrow Babette's umbrella, is it all right, Babette?"

"*Mais oui, Monsieur Mark,*" Babette said, shaping her meat patties. Turning her back to them, showing them the green apron ribbons hugging her waist, Babette knew they were lovers. Ah, she knew that! Nobody could ever hide such things from Babette. She sprinkled flour on her board with a lusty hand.

"See that?" Ania said. "The Flood must have started like this, with fog and smoking hills, and then it rained for forty nights and forty days." She braced herself for what was coming; she knew what he wanted to ask her. "We'll grow fins and swim and learn to kiss like fishes." Under the big umbrella she had time to rub her face furtively on his sleeve before the children's cottage came in sight. She walked close to him, as close as his stiff raincoat would permit; his arm looked like a stovepipe and rubbed noisily against her sweater.

"Ania," he said suddenly, "camp will be over three weeks from now."

They stopped and faced each other. She looked up. The raindrops ran along the edge of the umbrella, chased each other to the tip of a spike, hung there in a bubble, fell onto Mark's sleeve. She blinked unhappily; her eyelashes dipped into the blue shadow she had under her eyes now. Her face looked thin and tortured. He lifted a finger, touched the blue shadow, said, "And what happens to us then?"

"Mark—I have to go to Paris first." She looked him bravely in the eyes. "You know I have to go."

"To see Jean Paul?"

"To—work, and see him, yes."

"Is it so important that you see him this fall? Can't you wait until next spring?"

"Next spring I'll be back here, Mark, and you'll be through with school, and then we—"

"What makes you so practical all of a sudden?"

She put her palm on the front of his raincoat, trying to feel the tender place underneath where she had hurt him. Like a cold, deft lizard her hand slide inside his coat, brought to his skin the rain from outside, stirred up memories of the nights in the coach. But he removed her hand and buttoned the coat. Rejected, her hand stretched out, broke a twig from the dark cypress behind him; the tree shed a thousand water-pearls. The twig tasted of rain and then of resin and rain. "It was all planned like this, Mark, and now—" Of course, he hadn't been included in her plans, he thought. But he knew she was going to love him in the end, he knew that, only when, in what end? He took her wrist, brought the twig she was holding close to his face, brushed it over his chin, back and forth. The resin breathed bitter between them.

"You haven't even written to him. It all seems so silly! What do you expect from this meeting? What do you want from him?"

"I am going to work with him, Mark! I'll be here next summer."

Next summer! A whole year away!

"Why don't you write to him first, for heaven's sake, Ania!"

"I wouldn't know what to say."

"But maybe he isn't there any more."

She looked up at him, astonished.

"Who? Jean Paul? Of course he's there!"

ARMAND DID NOT HAVE A VIOLENT DEATH. It was only a sudden one. Nothing, not the slightest premonition crossed that glorious morning, the first sunny one after the rain had gone. Summer had finally come back (yes, Babette knew best), a bit cooler and more dignified, like a friendship renewed after an estrangement. But you were lucid now; you could see that the treetops had turned brown, you could feel the season was suddenly ripe. Still, when thinking vaguely of parting, you thought of packing, of traveling again, not of death. Clear, polished, immaculate, that mid-August morning rose heralded by Callian roosters. How was one to know death was tucked inside it?

The boys were playing ball on the lawn in front of the cottage. The breakfast had been particularly noisy and Simon had cried into his cocoa, fishing out the floating pieces of milk skin with his fingers. "He makes me throw up!" Albert had complained, holding his nose. The morning air smelled of butter and fresh bread; bees circled the marmalade jar. Armand's sneakers dangled by their knotted laces, from the dormitory shutters, put there to dry. Last night Siona had poured a whole jar of glue inside them.

But at long last the boys started their ball game. "No girls in this game!" The girls brought out their knitting needles and skeins of tangled dusty wool, forgotten for weeks under beds and at the bottom of drawers; scornfully, decorously, displaying their feminine skills, they sat in a circle under the oak tree. Siona couldn't knit, but she was more dangerous with knitting needles than with a ball in her hand. At Albert's insistence she was accepted into the boys' game. "So you do take a girl in, do you!" "Because she's real good." "Nobody wants to be in your lousy game anyway," declared Fortunée, speaking for all the females in the world.

Bent over Annette's knitting, Ania was persuading the little wool loop to slide over the needle when Annette looked up and announced in a satisfied voice, "Armand has fallen down." She looked forward to a fight. A second before, Ania had lifted her eyes and seen Armand's red-striped jersey turn to catch the ball.

The ball had hit his chest with a harsh sound as if he had armor on under his jersey. He faltered for a second and put his hand to his forehead. The palm was dirty. He looked as though he were trying to remember something important. His knees softened, came forward, twisted, and he fell on his side. Ania rushed toward him, but before she could reach him Siona had already turned his face up and was shaking him. "Armand! Armand! Get up!" But he didn't wake up, not even when they carried him inside and put him on the infirmary cot. Someone ran to call Madame over and the children were sent out of the room. Ania didn't know he was dead. She soaked a corner of the towel in cold water and gently cleaned his cheek. The skin was still warm and elastic under her hand. But when she went to the sink again and looked at him in the mirror over it, she saw his eyelids go up suddenly with a strange noise and then he stared at the wall in front of him. But she didn't know he was dead. Madame Jacques burst into the room in slippers, her hair strewn with hairpins, pushing aside Siona, who was trying to look through the doorway. "What's happening in here? What's wrong?" She closed the door (the keyhole instantly became alive with a blinking eye) and ran to the bed. She stopped short; horror enlarged her shoe-button eyes; her fat hands went up to her neck to rub it, to make the air come into her throat. "But—God Almighty—he is dead!" She turned around for help, and the sight of Ania standing there, her hands clasped unsuspectingly, broke through the dam that all summer had held back her dislike for the girl. She grabbed her by the shoulders, her nails digging into the skin, and shook her, shook her empty, shook all the words out of her. "How did it happen? How did it happen?" A terrible smell of sweat came out of the black silk dress and her uncorseted bosom swayed violently. "What do you mean, dead?" Ania repeated numbly. "Why should he be dead?" Something was wrong inside her, a wave of nausea rose, spread up to her throat, her whole mouth was flooded with the smell of iodine. She thought she was going to vomit.

She did not. Madame wiped her face with the back of her hand like a worn-out washerwoman, her breathing calmed, her hands fell to her sides. The smell of iodine retreated. "God Almighty," she said again, and her small, fat person suddenly looked flabby. "I am losing my mind! Tell me what happened." With her hands over her cheeks she listened to the story, nodding. "In the chest? I don't understand that. I don't understand. Get the children out of here. Take them to the mill. If Mark is there send him down. I've got to get the doctor here!"

Ania moved toward the door but its flat surface seemed to undulate and elude her. The doorknob receded; she stretched for it but couldn't reach it. Madame's voice steadied her. "Hand me that sheet from the chair."

They stood facing each other across the cot and unfolded the white linen over Armand. The sheet descended slowly, bulging with air, then flattened as if it had been distended by an invisible sigh, and a smell of freshly washed linen breathed out of it, pure and childish, as if this was the last of Armand, the very essence of his soul.

"Is ARMAND DEAD?"

"No, he is very sick."

"It's not true! He's dead, isn't he?"

"He is sick."

"So why did his father come?"

"To take him to the hospital."

"Which hospital?"

"I don't know, Siona. Will you please let me go to bed now?"

"He's dead! He's dead!"

"Hey, Siona, what did she say?"

"She said he's dead."

"Did they put him in the vault?"

"Ask Simon. Go on, ask him."

"You're not supposed to talk to him about the vault. He'll wet his bed again!"

"Listen, they can't put him in there. Only the Villemorins go there."

"You mean they walk there?"

"They are carried there, stupid. They walk when they come out later to be ghosts."

"Siona, I'm coming over into your bed."

"Don't come, you've eaten onions."

"Then don't tell ghost stories."

"I haven't told any."

"You said they come out and walk."

"Well, they do! I've seen something moving in front of the window."

"When?"

"Now."

"Mademoiselle Anieee!"

Lights on. Steps.

"Siona, will you please leave Jeanine alone!"

166

"Leave all the lights on, Mademoiselle!"

"Mademoiselle—"

"Yes?"

"Please, is it true he's dead?"

ANIA would have liked to tell the children the truth about Armand. But Madame's orders were to use the illness and hospital version. "Why, Reine? Why go through all this? Nobody could know he had a heart condition. Not even his father ... It was nobody's fault," Monsieur said. "I don't like this sort of talk going around! I won't have children die in my camp!"

The complications that arose from trying to check the children's curiosity were endless. Babette would give them the same story but dress it in details that contradicted Ania's. Yet it was true Armand's father had come, only that nobody had seen him except the Jacques. The children went swimming with Mark the next day, when Armand was buried in the cemetery on the hill. The bell sounded once across the valley, and Babette put the egg beater down and crossed herself. Then she resumed the beating without dancing inside her blouse as she usually did when making pancakes.

"Mademoiselle Annie, here's the key to the boy's luggage. Madame said for you to pack his things; his father will take them away. *Pauvre petit!*" and she stretched up to unhook the key from her spice shelf. "*Pauvre chou!* He wore it on a string around his neck. The treasures they all keep in there."

In the empty dormitory Ania pulled Armand's valise out from under his bed, opened it, folded his pajamas, shook the sand out of his sandals and arranged them inside. She didn't feel well, her hands were shaking and the things around her seemed to swell before her eyes.

A copybook fell out when she lifted Armand's sweater. It had been hidden inside the folded sleeves. It was a copybook bought in Paris, the address of the bookshop was stamped on the cover, and under it Armand had printed his name in red. She put the sweater on the floor and opened the copybook.

Summerlanterns

Wake up, pumpkin, wake up and smile,
rub your sleepy eyes, the night is here;

> *be a star on my night table for a while,*
> *be a—*

"But where do we go after we die?" "We simply are no more." "I know, I know, but it should go on for ever and ever." "We have so much time between birth and death, Armand." A door banged downstairs in the empty cottage, the noise echoed through the whole house; a shutter closed in the wind, cast a square shadow over Armand's sweater spread on the floor. She read on.

> *With a red feather in my cap*
> *I drive my princess to the fair,*
> *We sway and swing and banners flap,*
> *The sun is laughing in her hair.*

Blind with tears, she buried her face in the bed; time and place were gone, there was nothing but the black tent of pain around her. She bit the blanket and moaned, rocking her head from side to side. In the darkness damp and salty with tears Armand looked at her, serious underneath a coach-man's hat with a red feather in it. Then she was violently sick and stumbled to the girls' lavatory. For a long time she vomited into the toilet bowl; the smell of chlorine added to her nausea, turned her stomach inside out like an empty glove. As she came back to herself, holding onto the wall, wiping the perspiration from her face, it suddenly dawned on her that she might be pregnant.

"LET'S SIT DOWN HERE, MARK."

"Are you dizzy again?"

"A little bit."

They sat on the wall and looked into the valley. The late afternoon made the light on the ramparts rose, then rose and red. Drying in blond heaps, the hay was sending up the hot, damp sadness that announces the end of summer. In a leftover patch of dark green, dignified cows were grazing. Death had hovered over the valley, circled high over olive trees, and was gone now. The village had returned to the calm routine of the seasons.

"We've talked about this every night, Mark."—Yes, every night late on the steps of the cottage, without being able to find comfort in each other's words, without a moon; as if Armand's death had put an end to the intoxication of that summer.

"I can't go with you to Marseilles. I can't do it now, this fall, Mark." She hesitated. "It wouldn't be honest."

He looked up at her. "Why do you say that?"

"Because it isn't even a whole summer since I started to love you."

"Isn't it?" He gave a short, hurt laugh. "It feels much longer."

"Yes, it does—time in Callian is upside down. But it's still only half a summer. I don't want to rush this sort of decision. You wouldn't want me to either. I have to go away from Callian first."

He bent for a stone and threw it into the valley. Well, she was like that—didn't he love her for that part of her too? Frowning like a serious child, and so clumsily, so desperately honest. That afternoon in the truck, hadn't she moved away from him when she knew he was going to tell her how he felt? "Yes, you told me that—"

"You know that it would be much easier to stay and give in than to leave. I am going away, but I'm not going back to the time without you—that time is finished—"

He gave the same short, hurt laugh. "You talk as if I were an imposition on your world."

She shook her head seriously. "In a way you are. Love simply numbs you at first. There isn't any strength left to attend to anything else. You have to go away, think things over—"

He looked up at her. Where did she get this strength, this stubbornness? Her face had grown thin, and the lips were parched as if by fever, the eyes red and swollen from crying. "She's like a child," Babette had said to him in the kitchen as she tried to feed her. "Look, she can't get her food down! Is it the death of the little one that has upset you so? But you've got to eat, *ma pauvre demoiselle,* you're melting away!"

"I don't want to upset you, I just hoped you might want to think it over again now."

"Because of the child, Mark?"

He nodded. "Because of the child."

The Black-eyed Susans at the foot of the wall frowned at her, rocked by the touch of her sandal.

"Would you have liked to have him so much?"

Little happy creases appeared at the corners of his eyes. "Very much," he said, and then he stopped, amazed. "I never realized that before, I've never thought about it—but I would." He turned his head to her, and the sunny rings that circled the soft brown of his eyes widened, the rings she had first seen in the cobbler's shop. "But it's for you to decide."

She looked at him, desperate. How he wanted the child! "I have decided, Mark."

Gently, his fingers moved over the soft skin inside her elbow. "Why don't you want him?"

"I can't do it, I can't have a child now, Mark!" she cried out and turned to him for help, pressing her head against his chest. "It was just an accident!"

"I know," he said, "but I thought, now that it's happened couldn't you just have it and forget about everything else for a while?"

"Oh, Mark," she pleaded into his shirt, into the smell of old wood, the smell of the mill where they first kissed, "not like that, not because it was an accident! To have children is something special—you prepare yourself for it, you have to want it with your whole self. But this happened before I could—" She sat up, panic in her eyes.

He put his arm around her; he wanted to hold her and put his ear against her throat, hear the secret voice of that terror inside her and reassure her; but he was afraid to hold her too tight, afraid he'd be clumsy. Her breast, a small, throbbing hill, was close, but he wouldn't touch it.

"Yes," he said, "yes, I didn't mean to start all this again. It's the last time we'll talk about it, I promise."

"No, we can talk about it whenever you want to—I want

170

you to understand. No one but you can understand this, Mark."

"I understand. I just wanted to make sure you know why you don't want the child before you go to Nice."

She shook her head, resolute.

Ah, it wasn't as easy as the old ride on the stars, this grown-up love. Treading on earth, looking for footholds, fearing a thousand times you might hurt the one you loved, hurting him. Down in the valley a shaggy red dog, come to lead the cows home, barked at them furiously until they placidly edged their way toward the fence. The sound of their bells marked the silence with vibrating copper stains.

"Here's where we walked the day of the fair, remember?"

She nodded. "Now I am two." She picked up a stone and threw it far into the green of the olive trees. There was no noise, no echo, as if all this were happening in a dream where things fell without end, where people couldn't hear their own cry.

"How does it feel to be two?"

"Not very pleasant. Rather sick most of the time. It's like food poisoning. And they seem to serve nothing else at meals but fried tomatoes. I can't stand the smell. It's up in my room and in my clothes, everything smells of fried tomatoes, my hair, the children's soap—What if the doctor can't see me next weekend? I won't be able to get any time off during the week."

"He will, don't worry about that. I'm going down to Nice tomorrow and I'll make all arrangements. Philippe knows him, he thinks he's very good. By the way, he's going to be there too."

She was terrified. "Philippe? In the room?"

"No, no, not in the room. He'll be there if you need him. I'll give you his number."

"God, I'm so afraid, Mark," she said suddenly, like a child, forgetting her determination. "I'm so afraid!"

"Of course you are," he said, rocking her to and fro. "Why don't you let me come with you?"

But she had dried her eyes and was brave and resolute again. "Please don't. They'll be suspicious here and—no, it would make me uncomfortable."

He looked away, bent for a stone, and rubbed it unhappily

on his knee. He would make her uncomfortable! So he wasn't yet someone she turned to when— But she would see, she would learn. To reassure himself he took her by the shoulders; the skin of his arm felt the sweetness of her neck. "There isn't much to be afraid of," he said, "he'll put you to sleep."

"Death has come so close. . . . I think of him every night. In the daytime it's better, but the nights, the nights, with his empty bed downstairs in the boys' room— Oh, the absurdity of it! What can it mean? We cheated him, you know? You told him we have so much time between birth and death, so much to live—"

"I know," he said, cradling her head on his chest, "I know, but why do you keep looking for a meaning?"

"I can't accept that."

"Why? It's beautiful just the same; with accidents, with limitations, but just as beautiful. We are always trying to put order into it, but how can you make a system out of a segment of infinity? It's our order and our system and then, when it doesn't work out, we are baffled."

> *With a red feather in my cap*
> *I drive my princess to the fair—*

"Feel the smell of the hay?" He nodded, his chin in her hair. "We'll have to go." But they lingered, tired and empty and weary of words. The sky was ablaze now behind the olive groves.

"Why didn't you let me talk to his father, Mark?"

"Because you have enough as it is. Because you are two."

"Did he know Armand was a poet?"

"No."

"When we used to cross the vineyards he would say, 'Mademoiselle Annie, I can't help it, the grapes are *calling* me,' and he said the frogs at the mill had a 'burping choir' and he—he was a poet, Mark, and he was going to explain the universe to us! Who is going to remember him now, with his jersey and his key on a string and his coach and all his poems?" She sat up and covered her face with her hands as if she were looking for Armand in the darkness inside her palms.

Mark moved his finger along her braid as it hung between them, felt the pattern, that point of confluence repeated again and again, the bit of cool shadow it contained.

"You're talking about Eternity again," he said. "Eternity is not our fate."

She lifted her face out of her hands. "We've got to go." The fingers had left red marks on her skin.

"Tell me his poem about the coach again."

> *"With a red feather in my cap*
> *I drive my princess to the fair,*
> *We sway and swing and—"*

Her voice thickened; she swallowed and dabbed at her nose with her handkerchief.

> *"... banners flap,*
> *The sun is laughing in her hair."*

"Did you know you were the princess he took to the fair? He must have had a wonderful summer."

THERE WAS NOTHING SORDID ABOUT IT, the way it was always described in novels. She didn't have the feeling of undertaking something forbidden, except by French law, and the whole business was simple and quick. Yes, he was an excellent doctor. She found the hotel where Mark had reserved a room for her, checked in and barely had time to look around. She changed, hung her housecoat in the empty closet among the dancing hangers, and at eleven thirty rang the bell of the doctor's office. She could never remember his face afterwards. He wore heavy glasses with gold frames and they flashed constantly, mirrored the window, the furniture, the white walls, so that she could really never see his eyes behind them. After it was over, coming out of the narcotic, she remembered him as eyeless and thought it must be a night-mare, but then she recalled the glasses.

Her heart pounding in her throat, she took off her skirt, folded it neatly on the chair, hid her pants under it, climbed onto the operating table, and realized that the doctor had started to strap her down. The shock nearly emptied her of consciousness. She wanted to ask him why he had to do this, she wasn't going to run away, but before she could move her white lips he had stretched her right arm, touched a vein with his finger and then with a needle, and sleep tumbled down like a black avalanche.

She awoke not on the table with iron claws clasping her heels but on a narrow couch near a wall. The shades were pulled down and one of them moved, tapped the window frame rhythmically. From the street came the repeated cry of a man selling something, and from the tone of his voice she knew it was still early in the day and sunny outside. She was not in pain and the fog in her head had started to retreat. The memory of what had happened came back. She lifted her head, retched into the little bowl carefully placed by her side and then lay back exhausted. The horrid sensation of food poisoning was gone. She wasn't two any more, she thought; it was over.

At the noise of the bowl being replaced on the table somebody came in, a maid bringing a smell of cooking in her dress. She wiped her hands dry on her apron and laid a package of cotton on the little table. The doctor had left, she told Ania. He had had to give her ether as well, she wouldn't lie still. That's what was making her vomit now. He wanted her to rest and then go home. The maid offered to call a taxi for her when she was ready and looked at her curiously, without compassion.

"What is the man in the street selling?" Ania asked.

"Oysters."

"Oh, that's what it is. I was wondering," the patient said, relieved, as if this were of exceptional significance to her, and turning her face to the wall, she went back to sleep.

She was awakened again in the afternoon by the little maid. "You'd better go home now." "Home?" Ania sat up on the couch trying to remember where home was. She discovered she was sitting on a little tough wet mountain of

174

cotton, and uncomfortably lifted herself to her feet, helped by the maid. She was curious about this patient's accent but had probably been trained to ask no questions. However, as she passed Ania her skirt she asked her how old she was. Oh, really? She looked much younger than that. And then, was she having "this" done for the first time?

The taxi left her at the hotel and she climbed the three floors slowly, pausing a bit at every landing to catch her breath in the musty darkness. She went straight to bed, groaning with tiredness, finding the chlorine-smelling sheets quite hospitable. She slept and then lay in bed a bit drowsy, trying to think of nothing, to empty herself of thoughts the way you clean an old bag. She was going to sort things afterwards. Her eyes followed the stain of sun moving with the hour around the room. When it reached the mirror it made a silvery blur on it. The toilet was outside, on the corridor; it had a dirty stained-glass window and pieces of newspaper scattered on the floor. She walked slowly back to her room along the empty corridor. A colored maid was singing behind an open door.

She stood in front of the window clutching the sill and wondered which way the turquoise sea was, with the beach and the fat woman who rented umbrellas. The sea was not in sight but from time to time a faint smell of salt and iodine drifted through the window. The shadows on the sidewalk across the street looked damp, and through a narrow space between two buildings like a notch between two teeth the swaying panache of a palm tree moved in and out of view. She went back to bed and played with the street noises; doors closed, shades were raised, children's voices soared, a ball bounced against the asphalt.

Late in the afternoon the phone near her bed grunted. Monsieur Philippe was there to see her. Should he come up? Yes, he should. She waited tensely, sitting up in bed, her sheet pulled up to her chin; why did he come if he disliked her? Mark had sent him, of course. He stood at the open door for a second, then carefully watched his leg cross the threshold, and walked in. The carpet absorbed the sound of his broken and mended walk. He pulled a chair to her bedside, took her hand and counted her pulse. He held her wrist in a professional manner, yet something hung in the air for a second. His best friend was her lover and love lined all the events that had led her to this place. No matter how childish and helpless she looked now in her dotted cotton pajamas a bit faded at the collar, the knees making two pointed islands under the covers were lover's knees. He laid her hand back on the blanket and said she didn't have any fever and looked quite well. And then he allowed himself to smile for the first time, and she was again enfolded in the blue limpidity of his eyes.

Philippe bought her dinner. He served it quite adroitly on a piece of paper on the bedside table, and only once his left hand had to come to the aid of his right. He had a pocket knife, like a schoolboy, and took it out of his pocket to cut the cheese for her. He watched her eat in silence.

Philippe gave her the hospital number and told her to call him if she needed anything. She thanked him, nodding. But she was not going to need anything. He thought her an intruder, didn't he? She was not going to call. Yet next afternoon he was there again, early—had Mark asked him to come every day?—and this time knocked at her door without having himself announced on the telephone. She had got up and walked around the room a bit, and he found her sitting in the chair next to the window brushing her hair. Visibly embarrassed, she hurried to pick up the rubber bands and hairpins in her lap and hide them in the pocket of her housecoat. But she went on braiding her hair, conscious of his interested look; wishing to look dignified, she put her hair up, glancing only once in the mirror behind his chair. The afternoon sun touched her shoulder, lit up her crown of hair, made her right ear pink and translucent.

Had Mark asked him to come again? He blushed slightly at her question. No, of course not. Mark asked if he could phone her and give her a message but he—he had about an hour off and it wasn't difficult to—he had the car— What was the message, she asked, rescuing him, and he looked at her gratefully. The message was how was she feeling. He couldn't call from Callian post office, Mark explained. No, he could not indeed, she laughed. Madame Marchand would be there. Who was Madame Marchand? She was in charge of the telephone, and of the gossip too! Would Mark call again tonight? Yes, he said he would; was there any message for him? She hesitated, and could not, under the clear, sharp blue of his watching eyes, send Mark a message of love. He felt the hesitation, and it touched him to see how new she was to love, still shy and secretive, and how she could not confide in him. No, no special message, she said, just that she was fine and would be back tomorrow.

He had brought a jar of coffee and lumps of sugar wrapped in a paper napkin—"Is the water in the faucet warm enough to make coffee?"—and pulled them out of the deep pockets of his summer coat. He had them at home, a bachelor is always better organized than women think, he said.

Yes, the water was fairly warm, and she made coffee in the two glasses from the shelf over the sink and then sat down in her chair facing him. Was this his day off? No, no, someone was covering for him (he had forgotten he had told her something else when he came in). He'd have to return soon, he didn't have too much sleep last night. Someone had been brought in for an emergency. He rubbed his face with one hand, the good one, the fingers made red marks on the blond skin, and he left the sentence unfinished. For a second his shoulders hunched and he looked emaciated, all life drained out of him. But he remembered something and smiled, and the smile flooding his face brought him to life. He put his coffee glass down and dried his hand on a paper napkin. "I've brought you something," he said, pulling a little book out of his pocket. "It was on sale at the corner bookstore," he added defensively.

"But however did you guess!" she cried out, putting her glass down. "Andersen! It's the same edition as I had at home! The same illustrations! Oh, look! The mice in tall hats and their wives in bloomers!" Flushed with pleasure, she opened the book at random on her knees, looked up and down the page, unable to settle on anything. "Did you ever see his picture?" he asked, leaning forward happily, his weak hand hidden in his pocket. "You'll have to see that! I have one at home. He curled his hair so carefully and had a big, sensitive nose and a sad mouth and a gorgeous white silk tie. He was the most vain man! You'll have to see that!" he repeated. Wondering how she was going to be able to see it, she looked up at him eagerly. And suddenly he saw his words mirrored in her look, and heard their implication, and he checked himself. His eyes made a quick tour of her face— yes, she was the one for Mark—and their blue darkened. He turned his head unwillingly; the strong hand warned his right knee he was going to stand up.

"I've got to go back," he said suddenly. "How long have you been up today? You should go back to bed if you want to leave tomorrow."

She said, "Yes, doctor," and rose obediently. She folded her robe on the chair, dropped her shoes at the bedside. For a second she appeared not like a woman but like a young boy, long-legged and narrow-hipped in her chaste pajamas. But he had turned away and limped to the sink, where he rinsed the coffee glasses. She pulled up the blanket, her naked toes showed at the edge of the cover, then retreated. He stood indecisively with both hands on the wooden footboard.

"I'll come tomorrow to see you off," he said finally. "Can you take the afternoon bus?"

"Yes, I can. But can you leave the hospital?"

"I'll see to that." And it sounded like a little conspiracy, and a treat.

But he didn't come. He phoned her while she waited for him, reading in the armchair, the valise at her feet. He said he couldn't find anybody to take his calls and she'd better go ahead. She didn't know she'd say good-bye by telephone and hadn't prepared her speech of thanks yet. It took her a while to search through her French. Not at all, it had been his privilege, he protested. It had been awfully nice to meet her again. How was she feeling? "Fine," she said, "except for a bit of—" "That will stop pretty soon," he said, before she could mention the word "blood" and she realized that the girl at the switchboard might be listening. Without the clear blue of his eyes and that smile flooding his face, his voice seemed formal again, professional, and a bit lifeless. Would she say hello to Mark for him? Yes, she would. But what did he say after that? What was the sentence that closed their conversation? She could not remember. She was tired and empty and the afternoon was hot. And when she put her straw hat on she looked at the girl in the mirror for a while. She hadn't changed. Her white sandals needed cleaning.

BUT THE SUMMER WAS OVER, she felt, on her return to Callian, and in a week the camp would close. Armand wasn't waiting for her at the bus stop, and his bed had been taken out of the boys' room. Mornings, the village women wore woolen shawls over their black frocks. The dew remained on the grass longer into the day and soaked balls and sandals. In the afternoon, when they went swimming up at the mill, Mark would take over for her while she stood still dressed on the little bridge, too tired to swim, throwing stones into the water, thinking again of Armand. Summer was over, everything stained with sadness. And would love ever be like this again, the nights ever again like these drowsy Callian nights? "But love is not like that, not the way you think it is. Love is the present—don't you know that?"

The last Wednesday, the children were allowed to build a fire on the front lawn after supper, and Monsieur Jacques himself came out to supervise it. They sat around in a large circle, feeling the cool night on their backs and shoulders, their faces burned with the glow of the fire, and they sang "Rio-Rio-Ra" while sparks flew high like firecrackers into the dark sky freckled with huge stars. Babette and her helpers, who had worked late in the kitchen, came out too. You could see their laughing faces through the dancing red light. The last one to come out was Madame; a folding chair was brought for her, and whenever the logs burst into fireflies she moved it nervously away from the fire. Simon pushed himself closer to Ania and put his thin, unwashed elbow across her knee. "Did you take your pill today?" He nodded with importance. "And will you remember at home to take it regularly?" He grinned. He must have gained weight during the last weeks; his face was rounder and his wiry hair, bleached by the sun behind the ears, looked almost pleasant. She looked at the other children and thought she could see what they were going to be like in a few years, as if their future had started to sprout under the light of the leaping fire. Except Armand's. Then she remembered the pumpkin lanterns. Kept under the beds in the dormitories they had shriveled and grown moldy, and the day before they were dumped into the rubbish can at the end of the lawn. All day long the pumpkin on top of the pile had grinned at them, half its devastated face turned toward the cottage. They had to clean house before leaving: stones too heavy to be carried home, a dead snake that had started to rot, a dried-out velvet butterfly with a missing wing. They had packed. Siona had washed her brassiere. It hung swaying from a shutter at the girls' window, the insignia of femininity that had stirred so much passion and envy. And summer had ended brusquely with the noise of a valise lock snapping shut and a key turning conclusively. The last walks made you impatient. Around the vault the mysteries of summer had wilted, the tassels on the weeds hung dry and empty, and the ferns when you lay down in them didn't yield that green coolness your skin recognized but whispered dryly and angrily.

"Can you believe we have to die, when there are open fires and September nights?" she asked Mark as she walked with him in front of the cottage, his coat around her shoulders, after the children had gone to bed and the fire had been put out. She didn't realize she was asking Armand's question. "Come, let's not worry about that again," Mark said. Her face looked thin when he lifted it to kiss her eyes. "And the mill, I am going to be lonesome for the mill." "You chose that! The miller's wife wouldn't have left." "Next summer, Mark." "If you still remember the mill by then." She rubbed her nose against his neck. "Mark, do you still miss the child?" "Yes." But he didn't want to talk about it, nor did he want to reproach her with anything now. "You've lost weight. Are you feeling all right?" "Yes, I am." They hadn't made love since she returned from Nice. He had tenderly avoided that, and only once, when he put his hands on her neck under her hair, she had felt he was aching for her, but he only bent and kissed her in her ear.

THEY closed the door of the barn on Thursday. She was surprised to find the dark arch where Armand's world began now obstructed by a wooden door she hadn't noticed before. A heavy chain hung from the middle plank. She put her eye to a slit in the wood but couldn't see the coach in the darkness inside. Only the silence was familiar, and the dry odor of summer still clinging to the wood.

But Friday was a dreadful day, with all the last-minute packing and supervising to be done. Mark drove his truck to the cottage early in the morning. Waiting for the luggage to be closed and strapped, he came up to Ania's room. He sat on her bed smoking, and watched her finish packing. She was barefoot, in a short green housecoat tied around her waist with a white belt. Her loose hair kept running down her neck and getting caught between the clothes she was folding away in a valise. She tugged at it nervously and threw it over her shoulder. Her blue calico dress lay on the bed next to him, one sleeve folded dramatically across its heart. That dress was always alive, even when she wasn't inside it; and he remembered the day he had stopped for it down the road, thinking it was Ania waving to him from behind the cottage. The memory angered him now; her absence had already started to ache. He stood up suddenly, and feeling his irritation, she looked up at him, questioned him silently, still kneeling on the floor. She was packing a puppet on top of the clothes. "Look," he said, "you'll have to make up your mind? What is the matter with you? Do you want me or don't you? And how long will it take you to decide?" She let the puppet go, pain and bewilderment in her face, and he thought at the same moment how ridiculous he was to bully her like this after all that had happened to her this summer, death and grownup love and the child—and she alone and brave in the middle of it all. "Look," he said again, more softly, reasoning with himself, and went to her and lifted her and held her close to him. But he hadn't meant that, the door wasn't even properly closed—the belt came undone, and through the open housecoat her sweetness of hot coral leaned on him, a shoulder strap slipped, a small breast looked out—he hadn't meant to do that—and he was lying on her shoulder with his mouth in her hair, their feet entangled in the blue calico dress. The puppets looked discreetly away toward the ceiling.

He was angry with himself; he must have hurt her, loving her like this, hurriedly—now he remembered that short, soft cry of protest—was this the way to persuade her to stay? He couldn't look at her. She turned, trying to free her hair from under his weight, and asked with that disarming sweet seriousness, "What were you going to say, Mark?" "Nothing," he said, and smiled into her hair. "But you started to say something." She was always like this after love, impatient, as if making love made her clearer, transparent, sharpened her mind. She wouldn't curl up, lean warm and heavy on him; she was still a girl and not yet a woman. But then they never had time. "Nothing," he said again, "I was angry. Do you know," he said, raising himself on one elbow, parting at last with the hot dampness of her skin, "that married life isn't going to be like this?" "Like what, Mark?" "Having to look after twenty brats and never having time for ourselves and making love in a coach." "I'll remember that," she said. "I'd better finish packing now."

"Mademoiselle! Mademoiselle Annieeee!" Albert called under the window, and instantly Babette's voice rose in indignation. "For heaven's sake leave her alone! She hasn't had a single minute for herself! She's got to pack her things too, hasn't she? No, you're not going upstairs. You wait right here! What luggage? Hers? Don't worry! Monsieur Mark is there, he'll take it down."

THERE was plum pie for dessert at noon, and they had lunch all together, children and grownups, under the oak tree. The camp was divided into two parties: the ones who were staying behind, wearing their working clothes, calmly chewing the plum pie, and relishing its blond, glazed complexion; and the other party, the ones who, like migratory birds dressed for the trip in their best feathers, were impatiently turning away from summer. Were those staying behind more fortunate, Ania asked herself, walking through the deserted dormitories, checking for forgotten things. She turned the pillows over, threw the blankets on the ends of the beds. A raincoat hung over Albert's bed, she put it over her arm, secured the shutter in its hook. A dreadful racket rose outside on the lawn where the children had gathered. Mark was standing in the truck and loading the children's luggage with two workers from the vineyards. He must have been to the barber's; Callian's barber wasn't exactly an artist, she thought, smiling with tenderness as she leaned on the windowsill. He had cut Mark's hair too short, and it gave him the helpless look newly shorn men sometimes have. There was a narrow strip of white skin at the nape of his neck untouched by the sun. "But love is not like this, it is much simpler! Don't you know that?" How simple if she could stay now. Down on the lawn Siona had succeeded in opening the door of the truck and was trying to start the motor. Albert was coming around to give her a hand. Ania rushed out to them.

The yellow bus that was to take them all to Nice to catch the Paris train stood in the marketplace at four o'clock. Everything else was there in this last picture of Callian. The old village women had taken their place on the stone bench an hour earlier for fear of missing the commotion that closed the summer and brought back domestic silence to the village.

Mark was everywhere. He helped the conductor, gathered Madame Jacques' parcels in a string bag, looked over Monsieur's shoulder at the long list of chores to do before closing the place. Dressed for the first time in a town suit, Monsieur Jacques looked anonymous and his authority dimmed. Madame had a pearl of sweat at the corner of her little mustache and wore a black felt hat with a battered brim anchored by a rubber band under her bun. "I'm glad it's over," she said, with a sigh that heaved her corseted bosom. A resentful meow came out of the basket she was carrying. "Georgette, be patient, *ma chouppette*," she called through a slit in the lid.

Babette was there, standing at one side in her red skirts, a smile of regret on her lips. The end of the summer always made her sad, although she had a winter lover too. He came to Callian from the fields in mid-October. But she was sad just the same.

And then came that little bustle of departure, that tiny bridge of present between past and future, so elaborately loaded with unnecessary gestures and words when all we really want is permanence, that things should last, that eyes should keep on meeting, hands go on holding, words hang in the air between us, forever and ever. The bus door opened, the children assaulted it, throwing themselves onto the seats, fighting for windows, opening them and sticking their heads out. The doors closed, the bus coughed, sneezed, spat smoke. Mark stepped back, looked up at her with a tender smile conscious of the presence of the others. He waved. "The key to the small kitchen ..." Madame shouted at Babette, who nodded in comprehension. Siona's head hanging out of the window with all her tumbling black hair got in the way, covered Mark's face and then the old eucalyptus in the marketplace gave a last salute, a long, slow, perfumed breath, as if it had been the real, the only host that Callian summer.

PART III *

* * * *

IT RAINED THE AFTERNOON SHE MET JEAN PAUL. The fall rain
went on and on. But it felt good, it felt right. In a small wet
world memory took over and the impossible seemed possible
again. All through the night the gutters sang their gurgling
chorus, and the neon sign on the café across the street
blinked through tears: LE CAR—LE CARROU—LE CAR-
ROUSEL spilled down Ania's windowpane. The Rue des
Écoles glittered; the street lights, elegant and sad, had
wrapped gauzy scarves around their heads.

She had telephoned him, at long last. She rehearsed the
conversation for a whole week, weighing every word, polish-
ing the adjectives, adjusting the tone. She had brushed a coat
of tenderness over it all, but hastily wiped it off in a fit of
shyness—it was not simple to transform all those past years
into words—and postponed the call again.

And it wasn't simple to telephone from the Hôtel Impérial either. There were two chief obstacles. One was the very
age of the installation. ("Ah, this switchboard wasn't put in
yesterday," Madame Blais, *la patronne*, would say in answer
to complaints, nodding behind the lobby counter in her
greasy black shawl.) The other obstacle was Tarzan, the
hotel cat.

Tarzan slept on the lobby counter next to the main telephone, his giant tiger-head bent, his paws tucked under his
chest, like an old lady dozing over her muff at the opera. But
he was a *farouche* male, formerly the local ladykiller; he had
lost his left eye in a street fight. Whenever the telephone rang
he opened one ferocious eye glinting with poisonous green
specks; the missing eye, a suppurating buttonhole, gathered
his face into a hairy human grimace. If you reached for the

187

receiver he would stir a bit and rearrange his paws in the muff, giving off a hot, sleepy animal smell.

The hotel residents shunned the sinister one-eyed presence in the lobby and tried to make their calls from the telephone on the landing (there were no telephones in the rooms). But this was an adventure requiring patience and courage in the face of a new set of obstructions. Downstairs in the lobby Madame Blais would fish the fringes of her shawl out of the switchboard panel and announce that you'd have to wait. If she had something simmering on the stove in the next room you had to wait longer. The connection successfully made, the conversation had a strange acoustic accompaniment; an orchestra of electric saws played far away, little explosions occurred inside the receiver. And all the while Madame Blais (who listened intently to every conversation) and the angry operator kept up a running exchange: "*Mais ne coupez pas, vous dis-je!*" It made your heart race, confused your thoughts and left you limp. The little round man who played the cello in the room across from Ania's—she later learned he was an Estonian refugee—refused to go through this agony. But because he was afraid of Tarzan, before he would come down he always inquired over the landing telephone, "*S'il vous plé, madame, est vot' chat au téléphone?*" His French was bewildering, but Madame Blais had neither the time nor the disposition to appreciate such linguistic lapses, which were a common occurrence in her establishment, a hotel for refugees and foreign students. "*Allez, descendez, Monsieur Arno,*" she would answer, annoyed, "*le chat n'est pas là.*" And then you heard the little man's cautious step as he crept down the stairs, afraid he might meet the beast in the dark.

Ania telephoned Jean Paul from the post office across the street. It seemed the best place. When she had rehearsed the call the day before, she noticed that the light in the telephone booth was out of order. The discovery pleased her. It was a relief to talk to him in the dark like this, as if out of the past. She put the receiver back and stored the scrap of paper with his telephone number in her pocket. She still had time.

But next morning, eating breakfast, Ania felt uneasy. What if it was too late? Too late for what? For class registration. She snatched up the little yellow pamphlet announcing the opening of Jean Paul's puppet classes; it gave her a few more days. Suddenly she made her decision. She got up and shook the crumbs from her lap into the wastebasket. Feeling for the sleeves of her raincoat, she rushed out of the room and down the stairs. But she had forgotten her purse, and ran back, furious, fearing the interruption might make her postpone the call again. Darting across the lobby at full speed, she collided with the mailman, who was sorting the mail under Tarzan's suspicious eye, filling the place with the smell of fog and damp leather.

Seven times the little black wheel on the telephone turned and spun back. Like a wheel of fortune, she thought, perspiring in the hot telephone booth. The wall in front of her was covered with scribbles. And then the phone rang in an empty space—in his home?—on his table?—at the bottom of a black well. There was no answer. "I'll let it ring three more times." She was already grateful for her defeat when a single word, like a calm, heavy seagull, soared out of the receiver:

"*Allo?*"

Petrified, she realized she did not remember his voice. She couldn't speak. The drumming of her heart deafened her; the blood rose to her head; the phone, the glass window, the scribbles on the wall all blurred. "Yes?" the receiver repeated, impatiently this time. She tried to reconnect her broken circuit and use words again. Was this Monsieur Jean Paul? That was right. Was it—would it be too late to register for his puppet classes? No, of course not. Was she a teacher? No, she—was not a teacher. Oh, he asked that because he had a lot of teachers this year and gave them special hours. Well, could he have her name? He took it down carefully. He did not remember her. Was she Polish, he asked. N-no, not Polish. There was smile in her voice but he didn't seem to notice, and she was glad now that she didn't have to make her explanations over the telephone. Would she like to come that afternoon to talk with him? It wasn't absolutely necessary, but if she had time to . . . Did she know how to reach his studio? This time she laughed, a short, clear laugh. She knew by heart his corner on the map of Paris and the pink dot for the square where he lived. She had looked at it over and over with Father, bending over the dining table under the big lamp, and with Armand in Callian, too. Yes, she said, she knew the way. He sounded slightly curious about what had made her laugh but asked no questions. He seemed in a hurry. "*À cet après-midi, mademoiselle.*"

It's done now, it's done, she thought, leaning against the wall of the booth, her hands, her neck, her whole back wet with perspiration. Maybe she should have made the appointment for the day after tomorrow. Today was too soon.

"Do you feel sick?" a muffled voice asked through the glass window, and a finger knocked on the pane. An old lady with a net shopping bag on her arm glared at her. "Then why do you keep people waiting?"

It was still raining in the afternoon. A foreign rain, a big-city rain, with no smell of earth and leaves, no message from the clouds, the winds. The dampness was quickly sucked in by the gray stones and returned from moldy stairways of old houses she passed by. Ania was reflected in the wet pavement, long-legged with an open umbrella. The rain danced on the black oilcloth covering the bookstalls on the Boulevard Saint-Michel. Behind the wet canopies of the cafés people were sitting huddled in coats and scarves over steaming coffee cups.

She got off at the end of the subway line. At the foot of the escalator she encountered one of her favorite Paris advertisements, *La Vache qui rit,* a smiling red cow with a box of cheese dangling like earrings on either side of her honest, genial face. Head cocked, Ania smiled at her in delighted recognition. "Care for a drink?" A sullen young man lounged up, hands in pockets. She walked quickly up the stairs.

But the wet square into which she emerged was not pink like the dot on the map of Paris, as she had always imagined it. She walked under the wet, bare trees to the corner house and stopped at the first door in the narrow, stone-paved yard. There was no going back now. Closing her umbrella, she drew in her breath and pressed a finger to the bell. Inside, the sound of a phonograph stopped and a shuffling step advanced toward the door. A lock turned. A bolt gnashed. An eternity passed. The door opened. A small white-haired man stood in the doorway. The room behind him was dark. As he looked up at her the whites of his eyes seemed yellow.

"*Monsieur Jean Paul, s'il vous plaît.*"

"*C'est moi.*"

Her eyes flicked up for a second at the house number. It was the right house. The sentence she had prepared disintegrated, the words rolled away from her. "I phoned this morning," she said, and forgot the rest.

"Of course, the little Polish girl!" She did not remember this formal joviality either. "Come in. I didn't think you were so tall." His look ran all the way down her then jumped to her face again. "Your voice is so much smaller! Please sit down. We are rehearsing the bear, he doesn't know how to walk yet. It'll only take a minute. No, better keep your coat on, I haven't made the fire today."

There was no light in the room except for what came from a puppet stage with velvet curtains fastened back by silver cords. She felt the wood of a bench as she propped her umbrella on it, guessed the cement floor by the cold sound it made under her heels, and sat down next to Jean Paul. Puppets hanging from wooden pegs covered the entire wall at her side and in the darkness she felt their lucid eyes resting on her suspiciously.

"Go on, Marcel," Jean Paul said to the empty stage. The curtain shivered. "Start him from the right this time, I think his left profile looks funnier." A blond bear came in, lolling his head, his fur coat, collar up, tightly buttoned across his belly. "It smells of spring," said the bear in a pleasant, sleepy baritone voice, stopping in the middle of the stage and facing the audience. And with a sudden shrug he shed his fur coat—but there was a little accident, an arm caught in the sleeve. "Hey, watch it!" Jean Paul said. And then the bear was revealed in his underwear, an old-fashioned striped jersey, looking like an athlete in an old photograph. The bear had the modest confidence of a great actor who knows he is the public's favorite. It was irresistibly funny. Jean Paul sent a quick glance at Ania out of the corner of his eye. But she was still stiff from the shock of their meeting. Her unsuccessful attempt to smile hurt the way it hurts when you want to cry and can't.

"Once more, a last time," Jean Paul said. "And watch that coat. Don't rush him. A bear wouldn't rush out of hibernation, would he? This is my son," he said to Ania, motioning with his chin at the stage.

"He doesn't look like you though," she said. His eyebrows shot up and he burst out into his great laugh. The laugh was exactly as she remembered it, strong and full from the very start. She wanted to lean forward and tell him, "Oh, but I know you, I remember you so well"; but he took a tired-looking handkerchief out of his pocket and wiped his eyes, giving little groans of pleasure, just like an old gentleman recovering from a fit of laughter.

The bear came out again, walked to the middle of the stage, shed his superb coat flawlessly. This time Jean Paul watched the performance without amusement, his eyes keen and cold. She looked at him furtively. Unfamiliar. The profile, the small nose, were unfamiliar; so was the small hand covered with brown spots. Her gaze went down to his old man's felt slippers; embarrassed, she rearranged her umbrella on the bench and looked up at the stage.

"I think that'll do." The bear collapsed, sank to his knees and disappeared. A young man came out from behind the curtain. "This is my son," Jean Paul said with a smile. And to the young man, "We have a new student. She is Polish." Ania shook hands and postponed the explanation.

"I've got to run now, *Papa*. Would you fix that nail for the fur coat. Whenever I touch it the plaster runs down and gets into my eyes. That's when the bear's arm got caught." Busily he got into a corduroy coat. "I'll be back at six."

"Tell Mother to get ready if you go upstairs. I'll be up in a moment," Jean Paul called after him. The door opened, the sound of the rain in the courtyard came in, the door closed, the pattering sound moved to the little corner window. "He could be an excellent puppeteer," Jean Paul said to fill the silence, "but his mother doesn't want two of the breed in the family." He laughed again, a soft, elderly laugh. But what was the matter with the girl? She stood there motionless, her hands clasped before her. "This is a little commercial we're doing for a movie. Wait, let me close this window now or I'll forget." His slippers shuffled to the corner and he tried to reach the window with a stick. "Last time when I—"

"I—I know you," Ania said suddenly unable to remember anything else of her prepared speech.

"I beg your pardon?" He turned his head stiffly at this passionate explosion and put his stick down. He hadn't managed to reach the window and forgot what he had been doing.

"We—have met before. In Rumania. I'm not Polish, I'm Rumanian."

"Oh, are you? Now I recognize your accent." He waited cautiously.

"You used to live across the street from us in the house with the sundial—and the garden. The year you came to Bucharest. And you came to my parents' house—"

"What was your name again?" he asked, bending his head a bit. He blinked repeatedly, his eyes grew smaller, embarrassment and surprise showed on his face. "Of course I remember you! Oh, why didn't you . . . But wasn't your name, wait—Sonica?"

"I am Ania," she said reproachfully. "Sonica was the girl you kissed."

"Did I do that?"

"You don't even remember?"

"I remember most of the girls I have kissed," he said apologetically, "but not all of them. Ania! Of course you are Ania!" He took both her hands and stretched out her arms. "The skinny one! The ant! How was I to know you were going to turn out so pretty? What are you doing in Paris?"

"What am I doing in Paris! How can *you* ask me that! Puppets! Since you left I've done nothing but wait for this." She gestured at the puppet stage as he stared in astonishment. "I went to art school, I have a diploma, but there's always been this"—she touched her forehead with one finger —"lunacy."

"Did you get it that badly?"

She nodded seriously.

"I didn't know that," he said, amused and touched. "The little sorcerer's apprentice. And"—he hesitated—"are your parents still there?"

She nodded and blinked. There was a blue shadow under her eyes, a sensuous shadow deepened by the slow descent of her eyelashes. He noticed it—surprising for such a slim, ascetic girl. "Yes, they are still there. We talk about you in every letter. They haven't forgotten you."

He said with his hands spread open, his shoulders a bit raised, "Ah, if only one could keep in touch with one's dear friends over the years!" The little show of affection wounded her; she didn't remember him like this. She turned to the puppet wall. "Nobody I know," she said.

"I have a few of the old ones upstairs in a trunk. Would you really be able to recognize them?" He took out the watch he wore on a chain in a pocket of his vest, and she turned to him smiling, expectant. Now he was going to ask her upstairs. "I have to go," he said. "No wait, I can still take you to the subway. We haven't even had time to talk about the course. We start Thursday evening. Come earlier. Come very early," he pleaded.

They walked through the drizzle and he held the umbrella very high for her. "You've grown such a lot!" he said reproachfully.

"Yes, there wasn't much else to do during the war."

"Ania! This is bringing back so much!" His short legs jumped a puddle, and he lifted the umbrella higher.

"What does it bring back?"

"Oh," he smiled, "things you don't even— Where was that sundial? Over the bedroom window."

"No, no! Over the cuckoo-clock window!"

"What cuckoo clock?"

"The window in your workshop. I called it that. You don't remember? You used to bang your pipe on the windowsill and chase the sparrows away."

"Is that so? I've given up smoking." He looked at her in amazement. "Are you sure you remember all this or are you making it up?"

Ah, what did he know about remembering! Could he too pick one memory among thousands, shine it on his sleeve, and hold it against the light, make all its rainbows gleam? "I am sure," she said closing her umbrella. "You can test me next time." She turned toward the subway steps.

"Tell me, what do you want to do? What do you want to be?"

"To be great." She shrugged. "To have my own show, to be famous, of course!"

"As simple as that! How long can you afford Paris?"

"Oh, that!" She laughed. "I can't afford it at all. I've

worked this summer in a children's camp and that'll do for a while. Father helps a bit. I'll see how things work out."

"It isn't easy for foreigners here, it never has been. The war wasn't kind to us either." He looked worried, as if he wanted to warn her of all the things he couldn't do for her.

"Yes, I know. I'll manage."

"Are you alone in town? No relatives? Not even a friend?" She wanted to say, "But I have you," and explain how small and wet the world had been since she had first talked to him that morning. She shook her umbrella as if shaking off an embarrassing thought. "No one in love with you?" She smiled and became a bit rosier but did not answer, and she seemed to him suddenly very pretty with her hair all wet. "What has that to do with puppets?" she finally said. "Love? It has a lot to do with puppets! Now I recognize you. You haven't changed much. Still the puritan ant."

"You have to go now, and so do I." She put her hand out. He took it, examined it on both sides, checked the ligaments of the fingers and let it go.

"It's a good hand," he said, "a strong one, a puppeteer's hand. Oh look, I've come out in my slippers!" He laughed, waved, and walked back, hands in pockets, head deeply buried in his collar, stepping carefully between the puddles.

So HE IS MARRIED and he did settle down after all," Father wrote. It sounded like a little victory over Mother. "What is she like?" And Mother: "I imagine her as an interesting and very patient woman—who else would put up with him for more than a summer? But at least you're no longer alone there. One decent meal a week at their house, I suppose. When you see her again, please give her our love. . . ."

They were living this meeting from a distance, passionately, answering their own questions, unable to wait for Ania; borrowing each other's theories, weaving them through their letters like musical leitmotivs; speculating, and then discarding the speculations, resolved to wait for her news. "And has he really changed? For some reason, I didn't expect him to."

"Really? Do they really talk of me that often?" Jean Paul asked her later on. "You know, I did love them, truly!" But he used the past tense, as if the episode was closed for him now and he was not going to revive the old friendship.

"When you see her again, give her our love."

The truth was that he hadn't asked Ania upstairs to his home at all, and for a while she avoided the topic in her letters. Mother had visions of cozy and very nourishing dinners enjoyed under soft lamplight, of Ania's timid charm slowly winning over Jean Paul's wife. But Jean Paul had never invited her upstairs. Except once, and that was only an accident.

He had forgotten to bring his *History of Puppetry* downstairs, he wanted her to read something in it. The workshop door had been locked behind them on their way out, and he couldn't let her wait in the yard. He walked ahead of her down the hall, visibly annoyed, and in the old-fashioned, wrought-iron-trimmed elevator cage they faced each other in silence, she apologetic, he fidgeting unhappily. The lights on the landings passed over them six times, until at last the elevator stopped.

The apartment was comfortable and surprisingly light and airy for Paris. Jean Paul's wife came in wearing a black cardigan and skirt, her hair dyed a bit too dark for her tired polite face. She acknowledged the introduction with distant courtesy, detached from his past, devoid of curiosity. She was preoccupied with something else. "There's another letter from Julien," she told Jean Paul, and there was reproach in her voice. "I left it on the dresser for you." "Julien is my wife's younger son. He's still in the army," he explained. Then his wife reappeared in a black raincoat and beret. She had to leave; she taught Latin in a girls' school. She wasn't at all curious bout this girl her husband had brought in and whom he said with a nostalgic smile he had known abroad years ago. She was a busy, serious, knowledgeable woman; she carried her umbrella in a competent grip; her nails were painted with a pale-pink polish but the hand was a working hand. Jean Paul didn't make any comment after his wife left. They paused and listened to the elevator going down, passing the sixth, the fifth, the fourth landing with a repeated metallic groan; then the noise faded and he took down the book and explained why he wanted her to read it.

Eventually Mother had to revise her dreams, but she would not give up. "Well, this is not exactly the kind of hospitality I expected. But then, he was always like this, his private life always a mystery. He kicked it out of sight like old slippers when unexpected visitors come in. . . . Has he changed? How does he look now?"

A small white-haired gentleman with a watch chain across his waistcoat stood in front of the puppet class leaning on the stove tongs. (They had a coal stove in the workshop called Natalie. Jean Paul had forgotten who named it so and on what occasion, but its generous shape was that of a buxom lady standing on tiptoe in tiny shoes.) His eyes were the same, the small dark jumping raisins she remembered darting across their garden table from Father to Mother and back, the eyelids a bit puffy now. Moisture clung to their corners, and when he laughed, he dabbed at it with his crumpled handkerchief. His laughter was the same, still surprising, still a size too big for such a small man. It made the stage curtain behind him shiver, just as it had startled the draperies and silver dishes at home. But sometimes, listening to someone very carefully, he raised his eyebrows, and he was suddenly older. ("He must be—what?—fifty-six, fifty-seven now?" Mark asked her at the beach at Nice.)

"He has white hair but it's becoming. Why do you think he has changed?" she answered Mother belligerently.

Jean Paul felt Ania's look on him during class. He felt he was being scrutinized, confronted with somebody or something unknown, and whenever he could remember he would push out his chest and feel for his tie, a black ribbon tie, a *lavallière*, the kind artists used to wear. He watched the effect on her of his lectures, searching for her approving eyes at the end of the bench where she liked to sit; until it became noticeable that between the teacher and that tall girl with a foreign accent, a mysterious, allusive smile was thrown, caught, and retrieved again.

It was unreal, that workshop. When she told him how appropriate it was that on Father's old map of Paris the place was marked with a pink dot, Jean Paul looked at her intrigued and then, with a refined sniff, like an old retriever (a gesture she did not remember), he lifted his chin in amusement and tried to guess why. Perhaps the dot should have been dark blue, she wrote in her letter home, a dark damp one, like a fresh ink-blot. The nights outside in the square were inky and wet, often trimmed with fog, and the students looked secretive, hiding their puppets inside their coats like conspirators to protect them from the drizzle.

Diverted from visions of intimate, hospitable dinners, Father's hopes flared up again. What sort of people came to the workshop? Artists, of course. And did a poet drift in once in a while?

"I rarely get interesting students, real puppeteers, like you," Jean Paul said. "This year is a particularly poor one. I only have schoolteachers. The schools send them in; they have put this recreational program on and the teachers get credit for the course. Oh well, I work for the schools, you know that. But genuine puppeteers don't need me for long. They know everything from the start, they search, they invent, they struggle alone. They learn all I can teach them in three and a half hours and then they disappear. You can't keep them on a leash, they have to be on their own. You'll do the same." "I am faithful," she said with a smile. "I started my lessons with you pretty early and look, I'm still here!" "Really?" He seemed pleased; that alert retriever's look was on his face again. They were standing in front of the stove after class; the workshop was empty, and she ready to leave but lingering. "Really? What could you have learned from me then? I had no method for teaching magic in those days. What sort of a teacher was I?" "Oh, you were—" She looked down at the tips of her shoes. "The whole world swelled when you talked about puppets!" For a second he thought there was regret—or reproach?—in her answer. "And now?" he asked, and bent to rake the coals, freeing her to speak as she chose. Now it was something else, she said wistfully. Something else. But what was it, he insisted. For one thing, she said cautiously, she hadn't known anything about the space before the curtain then; now it terrified her.

What was the matter with the space? Well, it had another climate, like the open space above the clouds. "It isn't properly heated," he said, and she smiled. No, it wasn't the temperature. It was the panic; that second before you brought your puppets on stage. The open space made her dizzy and the smell of dust heated by the stage lights burned her nose. "And then?" "Then, the next second, the audience has caught sight of the puppets and it's all right, you know it's all right, you feel their mouths opening in wonder; but the second before that is just awful." "And it wasn't like this at home?" "I didn't know about these complications. We never had a stage." "We didn't?" "No, you said you were going to put one up but you never had the time for it"—Jean Paul looked uncomfortable—"and we worked with a folding screen." "And?" "And it was easy. What was inside me came straight out—I mean, there was no effort needed to bring it alive." He shook the tongs and put them down at the side of the stove. "It's the same game," he said. "You take it too seriously and it exhausts you. Just remember it's the same old game."

But it wasn't that, it couldn't be only that, he thought, locking the door of the workshop after she had left, hearing her steps along the wall outside and then farther away in the empty square. At the beginning of that winter, whenever he looked at himself in the mirror through half-closed eyes, he considered replacing his old ribbon tie with a younger-looking one. But then he forgot about it.

C'est la reine d' Angleterre
qui est tombée par ter-re ...

VOICES ROSE AT FOUR IN THE AFTERNOON. School was out and children met to play on the sidewalk in front of the hotel. And it was fall now, a big-city fall. You felt that in their song, in the way it filled the chilly twilight. The end of the day came quickly, without warning. You went into the bakery, out of the blue dusk into the smell of freshly baked dough, and with the bread for supper under your arm you came out again into a dark Paris evening. And all the fancy streetlamps went on at once.

> *C'est la reine d' Angleter-re*
> *qui est tombée par ter-re*
> *Napoléon Pre-mier*
> *voulut la re-le-ver . . .*

Disdainful and gray, aloof, it was Jean Paul's city. "It wasn't put in yesterday," said Madame Blais, gathering her shawl around her, whenever you ventured to complain about the heat or the plumbing or the telephone. The city's great age gave Madame Blais the right to save on heat and warm water, and in a way also explained the yellow spots on the frayed towels, the rusty bidet in the corner of your room demurely covered with a piece of flowered oilcloth, the din of the heat mounting in the radiators at five in the afternoon like a truck going through the house—the wave of heat died shortly afterward, before it had thawed out the ends of the corridor. Brown wrapping paper cut methodically into small squares hung from a nail over the toilet bowl. But then, there were advantages too in the great age of the building. The toilet had wonderful acoustics. The grave-voiced cello relentlessly playing behind the door across from Ania's could be heard best from there. She could even hear the pages of the score being turned, the little nervous tap of the bow against—what?—and the player humming, and she hesitated to flood all this with the vulgar gurgle of the flush. A dowager city. And in their games the thin, high children's voices celebrated her glorious past:

> *Napoléon Premier*
> *voulut la relever*
> *mais son pantalon cra-qua*
> *et sa chemise se dé-chi-ra!*

"I thought you would call Jean Paul first and ask him for a

good place to stay," Mother wrote. "Do you always have to do things the hard way? What sort of hotel is this?"

It was a small hotel, right at the beginning of the Rue des Écoles, facing the new post office. The brass sign outside, *Hôtel Impérial*, was spectacularly polished. Madame Jacques had given Ania the address on the journey from Callian. "In a very good location," she told her. "A small hotel, not at all expensive, and near both subways. Of course, it's not exactly elegant, but. . . ." "It'll be quieter than the children's cottage," Monsieur contributed. He was unshaven and all of a sudden looked old when they parted in the station early in the morning, groggy from a sleepless night in a third-class car. The platform was swarming with people, parents had come to fetch their children, and the reunions were noisy. Simon stood next to an old woman with her hair in a bun and held onto her shopping bag with one hand. "*Et alors, tu fais toujours pipi dans ta culotte?*" she asked him sharply, and he turned to wave at Ania for the last time.

Yes, the hotel was quite well located; she could walk to both the Quai Conti and the Rue Bonaparte for the art libraries, and her room faced a little garden square with pigeons and a stone bust of Ronsard (Father was delighted). And she had a direct subway to Jean Paul. "And what about your meals?" Mother asked. "What do you eat?"

Cooking in the hotel was forbidden. The hotel regulations, two pages of them pasted on all the doors, were firm on this point. Yet it was still done. You only had to hide the camp stove in the closet between meals and erase any sign of culinary activity before the cleaning woman came in. Ignoring regulations, the cooking smells sifted triumphantly through the doors to meet on the stairs. Privacy was not included in the price of the rooms at the Hôtel Impérial. The acoustics of the corridor divulged some information about your neighbors. What was missing could easily be supplied by your nose. You could practically smell everybody's nationality as well as income as you panted up the stairs. You learned that steak was fried only in the most expensive rooms on the first floor, and as you went on climbing you could identify Polish cabbage dishes, then Hungarian stew, up to the last floor which smelled only of wet mop and dank carpet. The customers here could rarely afford a hot meal. And you did not need more than a week at the Impérial to notice that Tarzan (who paced the corridor at noontime rubbing his head against doors, his tail quivering with gluttony) never bothered to climb up to the poorer floors.

"I wish you would not attract this animal here," said Monsieur Arno, the cellist, talking to someone on the corridor outside Ania's room. (Monsieur Arno had a preference for subtle words with double meanings, and he balanced each sentence precariously, like an acrobat carrying a stack of chairs on his chin, until, the last word added, the sentence swayed and crashed into a terrible blunder. Monsieur Arno serenely ignored the crash.

"I wish you would not attract this animal here, Mademoiselle Elsa." "*I* attract the animal?" replied a deep, hoarse voice, a heavy smoker's voice, which seemed to belong to Ania's neighbor. "Yes, your cooking smells too delicately," Monsieur Arno said. He probably meant deliciously. "But can you prove he comes for my cooking?" and Mademoiselle Elsa released a new ribbon of laughter, velvet this time, with two curls at the end. "I think he comes to listen to your cello." The conversation moved along the corridor and was drowned in laughter.

Mademoiselle Elsa took her time making an appearance, but she left plenty of clues about. High-heeled slippers would tap along the corridor, and then a strong perfume would cling to the telephone landing for a long time afterward, and sometimes even to Tarzan's fur when Elsa had nudged him aside on the lobby counter: "Ach, Madame Blais, why don't you get rid of him? He's full of moths!" Tarzan never held this against her; she was a good cook and he liked to lie outside her door and enjoy the smell of her Hungarian meals.

The acoustics of the corridor informed Ania that Mademoiselle Elsa worked in a dress shop. One day Ania heard her call the shop and announce she had the flu and would not be in that day. But after the call a burst of Hungarian singing and the sound of water splashing mounted in her neighbor's room with a vigor quite unusual for a flu patient. Then a man's step sounded along the corridor and there was a knock on Elsa's door. Was it the doctor? Yet for a doctor the visit sounded strangely cheerful; they seemed to be moving furniture, and great fits of laughter alternated with strange silences. It was intriguing.

Late one rainy afternoon Elsa appeared in person, rising like a plump Hungarian Venus out of the moldy stairway. Ania had come in loaded with dripping parcels, her drawing pad under her arm, and was trying to open her door (the lock was rusty). Just as she got the key to turn and gave the door an angry push with her soaked shoe, the darkness at the end of the corridor was agitated by whispers and footsteps and the familiar perfume. Then Elsa appeared in a half-open housecoat and stocking feet. "Please, could you—just for a second—could you take my friend in? Someone is coming up and I—" Out of the dark behind her she pulled a big bewildered man, pushed him into Ania's room, stored him behind the door as if stacking him in a closet, and fled.

They faced each other, dumbfounded. The big man was in his shirt sleeves, tieless, with his hat on; his coat and overcoat had been thrown hurriedly over his right arm; and under them his left was holding his pants up. He looked stiff with misery and didn't even dare blink, as though the tiniest motion would have threatened his composure. He looked at her with the good eyes of an apologetic dog. Then footsteps came up the stairs—they listened to them petrified—the steps went directly to Elsa's room, and there was a knock on Elsa's door. They were safe. Ania did not know if she should be angry or if she should laugh. She moved to the table and took a long time to set her shopping down, keeping her back to the man. In grateful haste he buttoned himself safely, and when she turned around he dared at long last to move a hand and politely take his hat off. The cello started to play.

"He doesn't speak French," Elsa told Ania later. Bubbling with laughter, she had come back and taken her friend out by one sleeve, thanking Ania all the way. In the evening she was again at Ania's door behind a flowerpot which she held up in front of her face, covering it in a pantomime of embarrassment. But she sat on Ania's bed familiarly and discussed the whole episode, sending up smoke like a whale spouting water. (A week later the little shrub produced tiny red flowers, carnal and unashamed.)

"I *tried* the toilet," Elsa explained laughing, "but there was someone in there. I thought of Arno, but your door was open and it was less embarrassing to explain to a woman. Don't you think Arno looks just like a dumpling? But if you took a bite you'd find he's tangy and sweet inside, like an apricot dumpling." She was a good cook; even her metaphors were tasty.

"Why not find out?"

"Ach, he's not my type, and I think he likes you, not me. Haven't you noticed?"

No, Ania hadn't noticed. She had noticed only the elaborate respect with which he greeted her, lifting his hat stiffly and setting it back very straight on his round blond head— yes, he did look like a dumpling. And then he stepped aside, holding his coat against his knees, and flattened himself against the staircase wall while she went by. This deeply respectful gesture and the sadness of his clown eyes brought a line of poetry to her mind: "*Wie soll ich meine Seele halten*—" But what was it? "Rilke," Father answered in his letter, "and it goes, '*Wie soll ich meine Seele halten dass/Sie nicht an deine rührt?*'" How shall I hold back my soul so that it does not touch yours? Then he went down the stairs— sometimes she turned and watched him furtively—in his coat with the worn-out fur collar, a coat that must have braved many Estonian winters; he looked like a cellist out of a Russian novel. But his back seemed happier, he walked with more of a swing. And then of course there were more casual meetings on the way to and from the toilet or to the telephone: Monsieur Arno in a striped robe and a hairnet, with a folded newspaper under his arm. Ania's eyes would be irresistibly drawn to the milky shine of his calves between the hem of his robe and the top of his socks, but he bore himself with dignity, and gathering his robe over the blond fur on his chest he would say, "Excuse me, mademoiselle," and make a dash for his room. "*Wie soll ich meine Seele halten . . .*"

"You haven't noticed that he likes you? He's going to fall in love with you," Elsa predicted. "But there's no real danger. He's married to his cello."

For a while the city took its time with the season, indulged in prolonged and sensuous games with the light. Across the street the café tables were still out on the sidewalk but the chairs had been removed; a fall sadness rose out of the bushes in the little garden square; the pigeons looked worried.

Then the fall rains settled in, and suddenly the afternoon voices singing of Napoléon Premier vanished. Wet and sulky, the city took the last sidewalk tables in, rolled up heavy flapping canopies, and became disagreeable. It rained. The vegetable baskets at the corner grocery were soaked— *Mauvais temps, mademoiselle!*—the salads had big tears on their leaves, and the neighborhood cats sat behind windows looking bored and very Parisian. It was Jean Paul's city. And only the lovers, forgetting the closed umbrella they were carrying, kissed in the rain, walked, and stopped to kiss again, knowing no season.

IT WAS THE COLOR OF HER HAIR that surprised him. She was reading a magazine, when Jean Paul saw her through the window of the bookshop on the Boulevard Saint-Germain. He stopped and looked at her. Evenings, under the electric light in his workshop, her hair seemed almost fair. But now, in the gray, tapering-off afternoon, it was a soft, quiet brown, and she had piled it up on her head in an unsuccessful attempt at elegance. He'd have to tell her how to wear it. He watched how she put her hand up, still absorbed in her reading, and checked the elaborate architecture.

He walked in and touched her sleeve gently, and she spun around. She looked frozen; her nose was red. What was there so absorbing in that magazine?

"Nothing, really. I was only waiting for my left foot to thaw. They haven't heated the hotel today. It's abominably cold."

"Is the right foot all right?"

"Yes, I can move all my toes now."

"Hot coffee would help."

The café across the street had a glass enclosure on the sidewalk. Bundled in coats and scarves, people sat close to the stove; they looked frozen but wouldn't give up and go inside.

Her gloves were woolen gloves, schoolgirl gloves, and she sat fumbling with them, awkwardly.

"I didn't hear what you said," she apologized, bending over the table.

"I've meant to ask you for quite a while—have I changed very much?"

"Yes, you have."

He had expected her to be more diplomatic. "You have too," he said resentfully. "You used to look like an ant in your gray stockings in the old days. I remember you very well now, a lot of things have come back since we met. You had your hair parted in the middle." He looked up. "You still do; it isn't becoming, it's too strict. I'll have to show you how to do it."

"But I don't want to cut it."

"Who said anything about cutting it?"

She laughed. Did he remember how he had cut Sonica's hair upstairs in his workshop? No, he didn't; why had he done that? They were all petrified after it was done: they couldn't imagine what they were going to tell Fräulein Cuna. Did he remember Fräulein Cuna? No? Nor Sonica? Vaguely; she was very dark, wasn't she? She was beautiful! They paused for a while.

"And how have I changed?" he asked again.

This time she hesitated. "I—really don't know. Maybe I didn't remember you right."

"What do you mean, 'remember you right'? Different people see you in different ways; you are an infinity of persons. Which one of me did you remember?"

"I thought you were taller."

"I was. You were smaller."

"And you never wore coats and ties."

"Oh, coat and ties!" He waved them aside. "It was summer. Come, you have something else in mind."

The waiter sailed through the tables to their side. "*Deux filtres,*" Jean Paul said. The waiter nodded and departed, glowering at the dishes stacked on his arm. Her answer was slow in coming.

"I am sorry," he said, opening his scarf and unbuttoning

his coat, "but what can I do, my child? The time that was good to you, made your legs grow longer and your lovely hair too, the same time was less kind to me."

She forgot her discomfort and put her hand on his like a child.

"It isn't that," she said, and paused. He noticed that she avoided calling him by his first name yet wasn't able to call him Monsieur or Maître, as his other students did. This often made her stop in the middle of her sentence and make a clumsy detour: "It's that you were—"

"What?"

"Sort of—the miracle man." She gave him a quick, embarrassed smile.

He freed his hand and laid it over hers. The skin was rough, her hand felt like a boy's hand.

"Miracle man!" he repeated to himself wistfully. She nodded several times. "So that's what I was! You did have a strange face that afternoon when you first came in to see me. As if you expected me to—"

"What?"

But he didn't know what. "I never realized that," he said apologetically.

"Neither did I."

The *filtres* arrived, the cups wearing their tall tin helmets, and they were silent for a while.

"What exactly is a miracle man?" he asked gently.

"Somebody who— This is difficult." She tried again. "Somebody who can hold up the future for you, right in front of your eyes. A master of—of anticipation I think . . ."

"What sort of miracles did I perform? Were there others besides the puppets?"

She smiled the half-amused, half-sad smile that came whenever his memory had to be refreshed. "You knew when the seasons ended, you showed it to me before you left. You don't remember that either?"

As he listened his eyebrows lifted and again he looked like an elderly gentleman. "Really?" he said, "did I really do that? Are you sure it wasn't in a puppet play?"

"It was a puppet play but we were in it too. You owned the most beautiful velvet in the world. Do you remember what you told me about it?"

"No."

"You said it had belonged to the last king of France."

His laugh shook the helmets on the cups, and the man at the next table turned around and eyed them with curiosity.

"Did you believe me?"

"Of course I did." She smiled sadly with her lips closed.

"I wasn't prepared for that, for competition with a miracle man. You make it too hard for me."

She hesitated, that same little struggle she always had, unable to call him by his first name; then she avoided the matter altogether and rearranged her sentence. "Why—why did you leave that summer?"

"I was uncomfortable." He shrugged. "I needed money and I had to sell the old house."

"Did you know they cut down all the trees?"

"They did? There was a big walnut. . . ."

She nodded slowly, like an old lady acknowledging disaster. He felt apologetic. "Bucharest was too good to me. I was getting lazy. Your mother knew that." He tilted his head back and looked at her half amused and half scornful, the way he used to look at Mother when he was being scolded. "I think I'd better go," he said suddenly, "or I'll talk too much." He didn't like talking about himself. He signaled to the waiter. "But isn't it unbelievable that they sent you to me, that you're here!"

The change tinkled in the little tray. "This waiter would make a good puppet," he said as they got up and buttoned their coats. "What sort of a puppet?" "A penguin, I think." She turned around for another look. "He looks rather like the photographic negative of a penguin, the whites are where the blacks should be." And they laughed.

Then they were out in the smell of the city and she looked up at the sky. "Does it ever snow in Paris?"

"Rarely. And when it does it melts so quickly, it is so dirty and sad. What sort of miracle man am I now? I can't even promise you a little blizzard around Christmas, with a sleigh or two. How are you going to forgive me that?"

"I am trying hard to," she said, and for a second, brushing her hair away from her face with a glove, she looked sad. "Is there a direct bus to the Avenue Marceau?"

"Come, I'll take you to the bus stop."

Through the window of a grocery store they could see the grocery woman, bundled in heavy clothes and boots and swathed in a white apron, rub her hands, wipe them on her belly, and pat a ball of cheese on the counter. A customer tried the age of the cheese with a doubting finger; soundlessly, as though in a silent movie, the woman reprimanded him.

The bus came slowly out of the fog and drizzle; the line shuffled forward. "I like being with you," he said as he shook hands. The damp blue scarf covering her hair floated for a moment above the crowd on the bus platform. *"Jusqu'à l'Étoile,"* shouted the bus conductor. And then Jean Paul watched her gliding backward into the fog, still smiling, just as people come and go in absurd, tangled dreams.

You have a *pneumatique,* mademoiselle," Madame Blais told Ania late that evening over the house telephone. A little blue note was in her mail compartment and Tarzan eyed her ferociously while she opened it.

You see, I still have some of my powers. I can reach you in only two hours. To tell you that I just wanted to make sure you are really here and coming to class tomorrow evening. It seemed to me as the conductor shouted "l'Étoile" that you were off for a ride on the stars again and I expected the bus to rise slowly into the fog at the end of the street, higher and higher, pour les étoiles.—J. P.

Fog," said the cello across the corridor, and after a little pause the complaint was resumed and developed, "November fo-o-g."

Paris was buried in fog. The days were short and indistinguishable from the nights. In the evening the fog reduced the buildings to a fuzzy shape against a cotton sky, and it was still there the next day, trailing about until mid-morning. The lights stayed on most of the time. If you had only one coat it never had a chance to dry thoroughly at the shoulders and under the collar. You put it on still wet and your skin woke up with a shiver; you walked around in a smell of damp wool. But there was a comfortable intimacy in this half-night in which you moved for days on end. The city seemed smaller, it shrank in the night and the rain. The broad avenues were filled with darkness, the severe courtyards and the austere parks with a sparkling drizzle; a thousand golden needles danced in the light of a fancy streetlamp in the Place Dauphine.

When the endless twilight lifted for a moment, you could see under the thinning streaks of fog the blue bridges of the Seine riding over the oily, somnolent water, over the bare, wet trees of the *quais* below, one behind the other, bluer and bluer, until they dissolved in wet lavender. It was intimidating, the city's grandiloquent beauty, emerging from night and fog. All the silent, haughty courtyards, all the windows of the old mansions, looked at you critically through their aristocratic latticework.

IT SNOWED IN THE MIDDLE OF NOVEMBER.

In the bakery at the corner of the Rue des Écoles, where she went in the morning for bread, Ania found the baker's wife angry and shivering, her hands thrust inside the frayed sleeves of her sweater. "It's unheard of," she said. "Snow in November!" She eyed Ania, suspecting her of some collusion with the weather. But the snow ignored the baker's wife and went on falling in big soft white flakes out of the gray Paris sky. Madame Blais was speechless with surprise, and looking at the wet footprints on the stairway, she considered raising the rent. "You are wanted on the telephone," she told Ania resentfully over the telephone counter.

"I managed," Jean Paul said on the telephone, "but we'll have to act quickly or it won't last."

"What are you talking about?"

"The snow! I did it! We're going to have a walk in the

snow. But we haven't got much time, the snow is very light. We must hurry."

She laughed, hugging the warm bread, and leaned on the lobby counter. "Is it snowing in the square too?" Madame Blais glared at her. Was this the important news that was tying up her telephone? "How does it look?"

"White. All white. I've just been down for my newspaper. The sparrows are bewildered. I suppose they must be a new generation that hasn't seen snow yet. I am going to be in your neighborhood this morning. Would you like a walk in the snow?"

"Oh yes, but I'd hate to disturb it. It is so thin, it won't last."

"We'll walk very carefully," he said, and Madame Blais looked up again when she heard his laugh, worried it might burst her telephone receiver.

"Well, how do you like my little blizzard?" he said proudly. He was gay and vibrant, quite different from the old teacher in the workshop, and for a second, glancing quickly at the small man at her side tightly buttoned into his winter coat, and tugging at a battered snow-covered hat, she recognized him again. "I've put in everything I could remember, except for the sleighs. And as for them"—he lifted a gloved hand—"you can't ever get them here."

But it was not a genuine, lasting, serious snow, Ania said, squinting into the sky, her head thrown back, licking a snowflake from her lip. Soon the boulevard sidewalk was patched with yellow slush and the pavement showed through, but high above, the smell of the air, the dizzy dance of the snowflakes whirling around their heads could still feed the illusion of a serious winter.

"She doesn't like it!" he cried out in consternation, slapping his side with his glove. "What's wrong with my blizzard? For someone who hasn't tried his hand at a miracle in years it's quite a good piece of work. What's missing?"

"It's good," she said, "but it won't last."

"Oh, come now, it'll last the whole morning, it's quite a good one. What else would you like to order?"

"Could you try a night blizzard? A good, furry night blizzard with empty streets and the snow falling in the light of the streetlamps and piling up—up to here?"

"That'll stop the traffic."

"Yes, let's have that."

"Very well. You'll have a night blizzard, but give me some time."

In the Place Rostand the traffic cop had the hood of his cape up, a navy-blue Santa Claus; his white baton disintegrated into the snowflakes. Along the street the stern houses wore arches of snow on their windows like bushy white eyebrows, and across the way the fence enclosing the Luxembourg had been knitted into a complicated new white pattern.

They walked on, puffs of mist coming out of their lifted collars whenever they spoke. He took her arm to cross the boulevard to the garden of l'Observatoire and then he wouldn't let it go. "Would you tell me once more about the end of that summer? How did it happen? Did I really do all that?"

"No wonder," he said after she had finished her story and they had walked for a while in silence, "no wonder you felt you had to come all this way and find me. The miracle man! But I have to tell you—" He stopped and faced her. She moved a finger along the powdered hedge, the powder changed to water, she shook her hand and waited. "I have to tell you. I wanted to tell you this before I discovered I was the miracle man. I have been thinking about it. I saw you in class. This passion of yours, it's partly my fault." She nodded and he looked pleased, and taking her arm again resumed their walk. "It's a game," he said. "Don't make it a fever! Don't let it be so important."

"Why the warning?" she asked defensively.

"Don't get angry now. I know they've brought you up this way. I remember I used to argue with your father about it. Why do you have to take things so tragically, so seriously? It's a game!"

"What do you mean, so tragically, so seriously? You make it sound ridiculous!" Her voice rose, the blue scarf slipped off her hair inside her collar, and she tugged at it impatiently. "You sound cynical!"

"Shall we turn back here?" The end of the garden came in sight. Through the last bushes the Avenue de l'Observatoire looked dark and wet; the snow had melted away. "Look," he said slowly, "look, puppeteer, do you really want me to tell

you something profound, that life is more important than
art? That love is more important than art?" She gave him an
indignant glance, and then looked away. "Is that what you
want to hear?"

"Is this part of the course?"

"No! I am doing you a favor! You won't last very long if
you tackle work like this! 'Cynical'! Big words! All I am
saying is—"

She interrupted him, stopping short. "But how can you tell
me that I should give up the raid on the stars? Is this what
the expectancy was about? When we put our heads back
after dinner in the garden and looked at the Milky Way, I
thought—" She drew a big arch with her hand and her gray
glove came alive like a sparrow.

"I know," he said softly, and took her elbows and held her
in a distant embrace, "don't I know it? But I am trying to
prune a bit what I planted years ago. I thought it might be a
tiny tree and look—it's a jungle!" She laughed. "I am serious," he said, "don't laugh! You scare me. Oh, look! Hey,
look at that!" He suddenly pointed at the path they had made
in the snow. In places their footprints faced each other, "Like
lovers who have stopped to kiss!" But she wasn't listening,
she looked away, lost in thought.

"It feels as if we have been arguing," she said later,
stopping at the gate of the garden to look at him. "Have we
really? Shall we make up?"

"No, we haven't been arguing, but we can make up anyway. Come, I'll buy you some chestnuts across the street. I
should have bought some before we started, I forgot all
about chestnuts; I didn't stage this properly."

"But what shall I do to make up?" she asked.

The chestnut seller rubbed his fingers in their half-mittens
and handed them a bag. Jean Paul held it up at her. She
looked inside it like a curious squirrel, took a chestnut, peeled
it and bit into it. He watched her. He still hadn't told her
how she should wear her hair. The chestnut was too hot, and
she rolled it from one cheek to the other and jumped up and
down with her mouth open for relief. Ah, God, she was too
young! She was too young! And she didn't know a thing
about the slender ivory grace under that ugly coat—about
women—about love. . . . Entangled in dreams and timidity,

still in a girl's world, inflexible and austere and sweet and serious, who was going to love her and hurt her and teach her?

"And what shall I do to make up?" she asked again after she had safely swallowed the chestnut.

"You can call me Jean Paul," he said. "You used to, didn't you?"

THE PIGEONS KNEW WHAT WAS HAPPENING. Surely they must have noticed. The end-of-the-year fog had chased them away, and the little leafless garden on the Rue des Écoles was deserted now. The door of the café across the street opened, and a light shone obliquely across to the garden fence; it died suddenly when the door closed. Footsteps sounded on the gravel, and the small man came around the frozen bushes with the tall girl, holding her arm; their two wet shadows merged into one. Gossipy, stirred out of their winter somnolence, the pigeons appeared from nowhere and followed them down the garden, their coral boots caked with mud. From time to time the pigeons stopped to look at each other, their amber eyes twitched significantly: *"T'as vu ça? En voilà une histoire!"*

A few *pneumatiques* written on Jean Paul's blue notepaper landed in Ania's compartment during the month of November.

> *Do you want to see the Javanese puppets at the Musée de l'Homme? I have to be there tomorrow afternoon at three. Come to think of it, it's an assignment.* Votre maître, J. P.

He waited for her in front of the checkroom hat in hand, the old ribbon-tie blooming out of his coat. He was very serious, as if to stress the professional purpose of their date. "Look, Ania! Look at the way the head is carved," he said, putting his finger on a glass case. "How well balanced the hair bun and jaw are on the frail neck! Once in a while you feel you just need a puppet with long arms like this one, don't you?" "But when a puppet runs across the stage to meet another and spreads its hands out, the arms seem long enough, much longer than they really are. I mean, the space between the puppet's open arms feels so generous—it could hug the whole world!" "Oh, yes," he laughed, "that's perfectly true, but you also need long-armed witches once in a while, with big sleeves, to cast a spell." "Couldn't it be done by rods moving the arms from below the stage, like this one here?" "No, that's too crude." "Not if you have the rods hidden inside the sleeves." "You might have something there. Try that." They circled the glass case with such concentration and passion that the custodian moved closer on rubber soles to keep an eye on them.

They had little cakes and coffee in a pastry shop across the street and talked of home. It rained. No, he did not remember how the rain sounded on the glass roof of his attic in the old house. He listened to her talk, chin in hand. That fresh ardor and the imagination she had to rise to what he invented; and the—what was it?—obstinacy?—to live it through. But he too—and he pushed his cup out of the way in exhilaration—he too could do that again, fly the same kite with her, giving it more and more string. His coffee went cold.

The tone of his notes became a bit stiff after a while and much too explanatory. She needn't come if she couldn't. He was going to be there anyway.

I am going to be on Blvd. des Invalides tomorrow—my lawyer. Just to let you know Rodin is next door. I'll wait at the corner of Rue de Varennes at 2:45 for only ten minutes so that you won't feel bad if you can't make it.—J. P.

But she did come. She arrived breathless, fearing she might be late and he gone. A thin, timid rain had started to sift over the city but they still walked through the deserted garden under the desolate trees. "*Les Bourgeois de Calais*" were wet and glittering; water had gathered in the folds of their garments, trickled down their faces like the sweat of humiliation. She wore a dark-blue wool bonnet pulled over her ears, and which made her eyes wider, brought out a violet hue in them; and as she put her head sideways and looked seriously at the carving, the bonnet touched his face and surprised him with a fresh fragrance he hadn't smelled in years. What was it?

Would you like to help shop for saints? I need some brocade and holy tulle for the Christmas play. The saints' costumes are worn out. Where would you say saints shop for clothes but . . . Chez La Samaritaine? Four o'clock, main door. Don't freeze outside, go in.—J. P.

She laughed aloud in the middle of the hotel lobby reading his note, seeing both of them standing in a shopping line with a whole row of saints in robes and sandals and halos. He was late. "Have you done your shopping without me?" "Just this piece of silk. I needed it." "What's it going to be? It looks like the lining of a crocodile's mouth." "Close enough! But I won't tell you, it's a surprise." He needed cotton, and wooden buttons for eyes, and padding for wings, and silk, and silver. He sighed wearily when they sat down for coffee at long last.

"Listen," he said, suddenly putting his cup down. "Have you always had blue eyes?" "Always." "But I don't remember that shade of blue." "Oh, these aren't my real eyes," she said, smiling. "I don't wear them every day. Only on special occasions. These are the ones you gave me." "I did?" "Yes, out of that big box of buttons you kept for puppets' eyes. Remember that box?" "You are absolutely crazy," he said, and for a startled second she thought he was going to take her hand across the table. The fizzling, sniffling, fussy coffee machine sent out its aromatic breath, clouded the mirror on the wall, made the face of the clock above the counter perspire.

Forgetting his open coat, his flying scarf, exhilarated by the prickly drizzle, Jean Paul stepped out into the wet evening and held the door open for her.

"Paul, you old rascal." A hatless gentleman with white hair stopped to poke him in the ribs. "A student of mine," Jean

Paul introduced Ania, a bit coldly, as the gentleman eyed her. The look went down from her wet hair to the valise that held her puppets. What was going on? Where were they off to? And what he imagined made him smile with complicity. *"Très enchanté, mademoiselle."* And to Jean Paul, "Are you still playing with dolls?" His big-bellied laughter hung in the air after he left.

"Old goat!" Jean Paul said, buttoning his coat soberly. "He thinks I'm abducting you!"

MADEMOISELLE ANNIEEEE!" Someone was shouting her name with the urgency with which they called her at Callian to solve some matter of life and death. She looked around, startled. The Rue de l'Arbalète was full of busy people returning from the Friday morning market, carrying shopping bags full of newspaper-wrapped food, losing a salad leaf here and there on the wet paving stones. Then she looked down. A little boy in a lumber jacket too large for him and a red winter cap pulled over his ears was wildly signaling to her from across the street. The shout went through her heart; hope rose and darted out blindly like an absurd bird. "Armand!" she cried out, running to him. "Simon! What are you doing here?"

Simon beamed up at her from under the brim of the red cap. His front teeth were missing. "Where are your teeth?" Ania asked laughing, holding his waist with both her hands. "In the kitchen drawer, Grandmother saved them." They stood facing each other, happy, speechless, unconcerned over being pushed aside by the crowds. "Where is Mark?" Simon asked looking around, expecting him to come around the corner any minute. "Mark? Why, in Marseilles." "Ah," Simon said, and knitted his brows to consider this piece of news.

He was still small, floating inside his winter coat. His face was thin. And what was he doing here? Did he live nearby?

217

Oh no, he lived outside Paris, in Montreuil; they had come by train. His grandmother was in there (he gestured at a store), they had come to his aunt's, that was her grocery. Through the glass Ania saw the same dark old woman who had met Simon at the station (*"Alors, tu fais toujours pipi dans ta culotte?"*). She was wearing a black hat which made little dignified jumps on her bun as she talked to someone in the shadowy store.

"So how are you?" she asked, and Simon shrugged. Words! What were they good for? His smile widened. She could not part with him. Still squatting, she searched his gray eyes for the past summer, and the unforgettable fragrance of the night in the barn rose around her, the memory of Mark leaped to the sky, blazed and was consumed. Simon coughed several times, a heavy, winter cough, and his nose started to run. "Do you have a handkerchief, Simon?" He searched his pocket and drew out a piece of chocolate and two wrinkled pictures; with a deeper plunge and a grimace a huge red handkerchief was produced, and she took it and wiped his nose gently. Touched, and because he found her smaller and sadder than he remembered her from last summer, he said tenderly, *"Merci, mademoiselle,"* and stored the handkerchief away and beamed again.

And then they had to part.

IT IS NOT A VERY GOOD YEAR FOR PUPPETRY," she wrote home. "Not much to see this season." "What do you mean by that?" Father asked. "Is puppetry better some years than others, like the harvest? Does it depend on the weather?" "It certainly depends on something. Tell him research is under way on the subject," Jean Paul said. He continued to evade Ania's invitation to write to Father. ("I'd love to, but I can't write letters, I never could." He looked away over her shoulder. "We were all so young that summer.") "Then *you* make it a memorable year," Father wrote back. "You wrote that the workshop has a Christmas show every year. Are you going to be in it too? I suppose quite a few important people come to see Jean Paul's yearly crop."

But there wasn't anything to see that season except for André Berger's puppets. They talked about him in the workshop. "Oh, you have to see him," they told her. Ania took the subway home with an elderly teacher, a spinster who was afraid of the dark. "Oh, you have to see Berger," the teacher told her, and her salt-and-pepper eyebrows rose right over the rim of her pink glasses. "He mixes styles and he can do anything, marionettes as well as hand puppets. He is an acrobat too, and a dancer. Once he had a life-size puppet in his show; he half-wore it, like this." She suddenly stood up in the subway holding an invisible partner in an ecstatic embrace. A few smiles flashed around them. "He was dressed all in black with a black mask on and black gloves and manipulated the puppet like a real dancing partner and you couldn't see him behind it. Oh, you shouldn't miss that! He might not be back for years. He disappears just like that; no one hears of him, he might be traveling abroad or preparing another show. He's playing now in a cellar on the Rue Mouffetard."

"A player of tricks," Jean Paul said when Ania asked him about Berger, and after a while added reluctantly, "He was my student." But she wanted to see the show just the same. "You aren't going to spend money on him, are you? I'll take you there. I'll phone him for tickets."

The cellar was on the dark, damp side of the street. The Friday morning market had left the pavement wet and a few scattered lettuce leaves gleamed in the rainy evening; a slight odor of fish and wet canvas still hung in the air. They went down the steps into the cellar and on through an icy corridor to a little hall, gay and warm, with layers of colored curtains hanging across the stage. But they were stopped by an incident at the door. The usher did not know who Jean Paul was, nor had the man in the box office been notified about the two seats. "Ask him," Jean Paul said, and waited for them to investigate, trying to look careless, scarf open, hat in hand, the lights making his hair suddenly whiter. They were let in at last. Taking off her boyish coat, Ania emerged in a plum velvet dress with collar and cuffs of old lace, her only gala dress, and Jean Paul stopped in surprise to look at her. "I wouldn't have thought you'd every wear anything like that," he said. "Why?" She was alarmed; was something wrong with it? "It was Mother's dress," she added disarmingly, "she said I had to have something special for the evening." He looked her up and down appraisingly. "Isn't the color wonderful?" she asked. "Gorgeous! It looks like something out of Chekhov." "Sometimes I'm tempted to cut a piece out of it to dress a puppet. It's such a lovely color." "Don't you ever do that!" he threatened her, and then offered her his arm to go in. "Princess," he said, and the girl in the checkroom bent over the counter to watch him. He was freshly shaved and smelled of eau de cologne.

He watched her during the show, the way she sat leaning against the side of the chair, her legs crossed, the velvet catching the light on two round mounds where her knees were, her neck shooting white and straight out of the island of old lace. "But he is very good!" she whispered when she felt his look on her. "He is excellent!" "Oh, his tricks bore me," Jean Paul said, and she spread out her hand palm up as if to say, "So what? Good tricks," and the palm looked pink and strong, like coral, in the half-light.

He would take her backstage during the intermission, she thought, and looked furtively in the mirror of her purse; the mirror sent back an image flushed with trepidation. But he did not suggest it, and the intermission ended. The life-size puppet she had been told about, a white Pierrot dressed in silk, appeared in the second part of the show. "He *is* extraordinary," she whispered to Jean Paul, "even if I am not quite sure this is puppetry." "I told you he's a player of tricks!" Invisible, Berger was wearing the puppet like an apron, but you felt his presence there moving against the black backdrop, a black presence, the puppet's dark soul; a fantastic *pas de deux*, one dancer visible, the other guessed at.

At the checkroom, she asked Jean Paul if he would take her backstage so that she could have a look at the puppets. "Of course," he said, and with his coat over his arm, he walked reluctantly ahead of her along the corridor. She wiped her damp hands on her handkerchief when the noise rom the room at the end came closer. Then they stood at he open door, and she gave the crowd a few minutes to ecognize Jean Paul, Berger's *maître*, and come to him.

The little space backstage was swarming with people pressng forward, babbling loud congratulations. Then Berger himelf appeared, dressed like a dancer in black tights and black ersey, his left hand gloved in black, the other looking naked ınd rosy. His head was still hooded in black, and the black mask he had been wearing was hanging around his neck on a ubber band. He looked like a man from Mars. The little vindow of his face, creased by tiredness, had a big sharp 10se, a puppet nose, and pretty lips. Then he pulled the hood off, he was going to be photographed, and his hair could be seen, wiry and cropped short. Nobody had noticed Jean Paul's presence, and twice he was pushed aside by the photographers as he attempted to get close to the black man from Mars. "*Pardon, monsieur*, we're very crowded here." The ights flashed and died. They advanced and retreated with the tide, until they suddenly found themselves behind the black sweater and Jean Paul stretched out his arm and touched it. The black man delayed the response—yet Ania had the feeling he had noticed them a second ago, he waited for the light to flash a third time and then turned around. "Ah, Monsieur Jean Paul," he said without surprise. The exchange of amenities was quick and short. "A very good show!" "Thank you," and he was ready to turn around. "This is a new student of mine. You'll be hearing of her very soon." "Ah?" said the black man, his eyes on Ania for a second, and down through the air in a big formal arch came his hand, the naked one. "Splendid, splendid." But she couldn't find anything to say to the man from Mars. Her face was flushed, her lace collar turned under, and she looked lost and helpless. "We'll look around at your menagerie if we may," Jean Paul said. "*Je vous en prie*," and Berger turned away; the crowd closed in on him.

It didn't matter! She stood in front of Berger's puppets hanging in their neat gallows on the wall, hugged her coat against her, and told herself that it didn't matter. It was the fate of teachers to be ignored by their famous pupils, and surely this crowd did not know the Jean Paul who stood on the steps under the ivy with the velvet bedspread over his shoulder. Innocently, with no understanding of her silent struggle to defend him, Jean Paul came over and took her arm, absorbed in the puppets. "Look at that! He's great with lights, the bastard! See how he has lit it from the side? The beams cross in the middle and make a curtain of light. That's what keeps you from seeing him in the background!" The other puppets were there too, and they looked tired and empty after the show. Yes, they were extraordinary, Jean Paul agreed, with their big wooden heads and sharp, powerful noses ("They all have Berger's nose, noticed that?"); their eyes caught the light, played with it, stored it away so that it filled them with a liquid sadness. "There he is!" Pierrot the sleepwalker, who had danced across the stage fluid and white in tremulous sleeves, was now hanging from a hook attached at the back of his neck. She lifted one of his arms respectfully. The arm fell back in the empty sleeve, lifeless, inert. The motion went through the whole body, the silk rippled, the head nodded vaguely, yes, yes, yes, it was like this, my girl. . . . "Seen everything?" Jean Paul asked her, and she nodded and managed to turn and look at him. He stood before her, smiling.

THEY walked in silence down the wet street with the taste of the fog in their throat; they breathed it in like smokers, inhaling the night, intoxicating themselves with the sadness of the big city. "I am a classic, you see," Jean Paul said at last, and with a quick movement he shook off the evening's embarrassment. "I teach the basic illusion, the basic silliness— *la folie*"—the word sounded sweet in the night, and it touched her. "Yes," she said, "of course," and her breath made a small cloud in the cold air; with her hands deep in her pockets she suffered through his little talk. "I teach motion and patterns, then you take it from there. You should take it from there." But he was sad. "And I am an institution. That isn't greatly admired nowadays, but who takes shows to the schools? Not Berger, certainly." Did she want to have coffee with him here? No, she didn't want to have coffee, she'd rather go home. His face darkened. She would walk him to the subway though, it was around the corner from her hotel.

On the sidewalk in front of the subway entrance a man in

a trench coat was selling novelties, little figures with a key sticking out of their back between the tails of their lacquered tin coats. "Wait! Ania, wait a second!" Jean Paul stopped and looked at them. His eyes glittered. He pushed his hat back, squatted down, and slowly and methodically he picked them up one by one, turned their key and tenderly set them down again with a coaxing smile. The damp sidewalk became a roller-skating ring with little red-lacquered people running back and forth, bumping into each other, turning, and running again, as if in panic at discovering the mechanism they had inside them. He watched them intently, transfigured, younger, the same man who had made Martine for her out of a slice of rye bread and a napkin—and the whole past vibrated again, touched by a generous finger. "One is for you," he said, getting up, "and I'll have two."

She stood there speechless with the tin man in her hand; its mechanism was still going, shaking the red coat like little tin sobs, the grief of a tin man.

BUT THE CITY FELT GAY just before Christmas. The fog retreated; the dampness that in two short expert sniffs Parisians recognized as coming over from the Channel had disappeared. Frost blew a white powder over the city. It floated through the air, hung blue around the doors of bistros. When banged shut, the bistro doors sent out a warm blast, the smell of crowds that around the holidays replaces companionship in big cities.

In the Rue d'Amsterdam, across from the Gare Saint-Lazare, voices filled the evening. Holiday decorations sparkled on counters improvised in archways between buildings, and salesmen in berets and mufflers shouted to the moving crowds.

Electric mannequins crowded the shop windows, last year's smile freshly lacquered. After four in the afternoon, when

Ania came out of the library with her drawing pads under her arm, the whole city felt like a concert of mechanical gestures, all the lights were on; eyelids with wire eyelashes moved up and down, arms bent and stretched, heads lolled, smiles opened and closed under tinsel and tufts of cotton. In the delicatessen stores an orgy unfolded, swelling into Gargantuan fantasies in which little pigs, nude and tempting in their rosy skin, lay in a landscape of gelatine and parsley, and geese like matrons of honor with generous bosoms reclined in *pâté de foie gras* holding under their wings roses fashioned out of tender ham. A Santa Claus in full costume and a curly beard came out of the public urinal in front of the Magasins du Printemps, buttoning his fly with frozen fingers, and resumed his professional walk up and down in front of the store, a smile of satisfaction hanging in his silk mustache. *"Eh, 'faut bien qu'en pisse par ce froid-là,"* he said with an earthy wink and a sniff, catching Jean Paul's eye. Jean Paul looked at Ania. Had she heard him? She was holding the lapels of her coat together and inside her collar, like a turtle inside its shell, she was shaking with laughter, sending out a tiny streak of mist into the frosty night.

THE WEDNESDAY BEFORE THE CHRISTMAS SHOW a thick, heavy fog crept over the city. Cars groped through the streets; their lights, unable to pierce the gloom, remained suspended in the air, making dry stains of powdered light. Voices without their people came close: *"C'est la purèe de pois!"* *"En voilà un bien beau cadeau d'Angleterre!"* You didn't know if you were coming or going, if people passing by had their backs or faces to you. Brakes screeched. The bells on the bus platforms rang nervously. *"Mais ne poussez pas, Madame!"* cotton shapes protested in a cotton crowd suspended between no curb and no sky. The same strange landscape lay outside the windows for two days and a night, going from gray to blue and then to gray again.

"Ania!" Jean Paul cried out at the door of the workshop, poker in hand, ashes dripping on his slippers. "I heard your step but I didn't think it could be you! How did you get here?"

"The subways are running."

"Yes, but from the subway?"

"I walked. I didn't know where I was going, but I found the house. I can always tell where puppets are."

"That's what I call devotion. I've cancelled tonight's class and I was on the phone all afternoon trying to reach you. You were out."

"I was. I went to buy your tinsel and the ribbons. Then I thought since I was out anyway and I had a direct subway here—and you needed the stuff, I couldn't let you fix all this by yourself." He was preparing the workshop for the Christmas show.

"Oh, what a beautiful hat!" he exclaimed when she lifted her hands to take off her fur hat. "It isn't mine," she said in the disarming way she had of receiving his compliments, "my friend lent it to me." (She had met Elsa on the hotel stairs. "It's dreadful outside, Ania, don't go out without a hat. Want this one? Here, take my gloves too.") "Don't take it off yet," Jean Paul pleaded, "keep it on just a bit longer, please do. It gives you such a frivolous air. I never thought you could look so frivolous!" He examined her happily. "Frivolous?" she asked, dignified. "You're the frivolous one if you can believe that a hat can change a woman." "Oh, come now, puppeteer!" he exclaimed theatrically, "where on earth did you hear that? Who taught you that? Of course a hat can change a woman! Doesn't a wig change a puppet? Besides, it isn't just any hat! A puppeteer ought to know that. It's this glossy brown fur on you. She doesn't know a thing, this girl," he said in despair. "Wait, can I—may I set it just a bit more—?" His eyes narrowed, and with both hands, carefully finding the exact shadow he was looking for, he made the fur hat slide forward a bit over her left eyebrow. The blue of her eyes became suddenly darker and her right ear stood out burned by the frost. He was delighted with the result. "Let's

225

work," she said, uneasy under his look, and took the hat off brusquely and set it on the bench.

But he was in an extraordinary mood tonight, brilliant and restless. "How do you like it?" he asked confidentially, embracing her coat to his chest and forgetting to hang it up, "What?" "What! The fog I made for you!" "But I ordered snow! A blizzard!" "I know you did, but it came out fog. I must have mixed up the recipes." He went to hang up her coat. "And how will you stop it now?" "I can't stop it," he answered from the closet, "I don't know how, it'll never stop." But she wasn't joining in the game tonight, he complained, she was too serious. What was the matter? The Christmas show worried her; too much to prepare, and she was going to play for the first time before such a large group of— "Of what?" "Of professionals." "What professionals? Don't be silly. You'll see them and the little they're worth." She warmed her hands over the stove and then put her puppet case on the bench and snapped the lock open. "Here," she said, "I couldn't wait any longer to show them to you. The stars of the Christmas show, Jonah and the Whale!"

Jean Paul lifted old Jonah out of the box and looked at him for a long while. "Were prophets that elegant, do you think?" Elsa had stitched his overcoat and added a handsome yellow silk lining. "I have a weakness for him," she told Ania, "he looks like my poor grandfather," and she pinched his nose tenderly. "And did you want him with blue eyes?" Jean Paul asked, making Jonah's head bob on his index finger. "I thought all prophets had black eyes. Would you expect prophetic lightning and thunder to be produced by blue eyes?" "This one is a poet!" "Ah, that's what he is! He is—perfect," Jean Paul approved, holding him at arm's length. "And this is the Whale." Triumphantly she lifted out a blue silk whale under his incredulous eye. "It has a spring in here for the jaw," she said. "It snaps right back, see that?" And when he bent to look closer, the fog and the wet weather and a faint smell of smoke were in her hair.

"Hold it, hold it, charming, absolutely charming," he cried when she tried the puppets out behind the stage; he thought somewhere he had just the right music for the opening of the scene; he put on the record, approved of it with his head and his slipper. The Whale opened its mouth, showed the tender pink silk lining, and old Jonah waved his arms prophetically and walked right into the whale's jaws. One corner of his black coat hung out of it for a second; the Whale, looking satisfied and pregnant, made a turn, showed the public her left profile with the playful glass eye and sailed out of sight.

Could he perform just one more miracle for her tonight, Jean Paul asked, inspired. "Well, y-es," she hesitated, "only if you are sure you can stop it afterwards." He waved her reluctance aside. "This is my specialty," he said. He was going to provide real water for the Whale. Up on a chair, he groaned and busied himself with a screwdriver and coughed and hummed, and then told her to come and pull at a string that hung over her head. "Gently, gently." A curtain of blue gauze descended to the footlights. She went out in front to see the effect. "How do I look?" he asked from behind the gauze. "You look wet!" "Ah, you see?" and he made swimming motions with his short arms until he lost his balance and had to hold on to the side curtain. "It's real water, what did I tell you! Ah, they've never seen such a show in this place!"

Then she helped straighten the workshop and together they hung up the firm branches he had piled on the table. She sniffed noisily at each one as he passed it to her, scratched the bark to get a bit of the resin, while he patiently held the hammer and nails. Perched on the chair right under his eyes, her legs looked young and pretty, and when she reached up the hem of her skirt rode high and a mysterious blue shadow danced around her knees and hid her thighs. "No, don't sweep the floor, Ania. Stop that! The cleaning woman will do it in the morning." "But I used to do this for you, I was so good at it." And he remembered her carrying an oversized dustpan and a broom with a handle too long for her, her pigtails tied with wrinkled blue ribbons. "Ah, you were an apprentice then, now you're a star." She chuckled and emptied the dustpan into the stove. The fire crackled, spat out sparks; the pine needles exploded like firecrackers at a celebration; the workshop smelled of coal, nostalgic, like an old railway station.

They sat on the bench in front of the fire to rest. She had to leave, it was late. "Does my whale remind you of anything?" "N-no." "Do you remember the signs on the sundial?" "Yes, of course. I think they were animals." "I think they were animals," she mocked him. "Of course they were animals. Golden animals," she said, bending toward him. "That's what they were! You could feel the gold under your fingers!" Yes, now he remembered them. "I used to lean out and feel them. I thought I could touch Time with my hand. 'If you don't stop that,' you said, 'I'll have to put a net under the window!'" "I said that?" She nodded. "And what did Time feel like when you touched it?" "Warm. The tile was warm from the sun. The whale was blue. I've got to go," she said, shaking herself, looking at her watch. "How will you manage in this fog?" "I will, and don't feel guilty. Later on, you might still try for a blizzard." She went to the closet for her coat. "Sleep here," he said suddenly, "don't be silly." "Here?" She turned around. "What do you mean?" "Right here on that couch." There was a little leather couch next to the wall. She looked bewildered. For a second she had thought he was inviting her upstairs and imagined his wife dressed in a long housecoat handing her a cup of tea in the kitchen. "Oh," she said, "but I can't." "Why can't you? Don't be silly now. It's a horrible night. You'll leave early in the morning. No one ever comes in here except the cleaning woman and she won't be in till the afternoon. I have the only key. Wouldn't you like to be alone with the puppets a whole long night? It's part of the course." And he was the Jean Paul she knew, receiving guests in his big house, staging their visit, pulling out drawers, taking out a brown blanket, waving promises in front of your eyes. "Of course you'll stay, and I am going to see that this fire keeps going." She was dizzy with tiredness and suddenly realized how wet her shoes were. She sat on the couch tentatively, undecided, took them off and wiggled her toes. "I am soaked," she said apologetically, feeling that she had better go. He came from behind the stage. "Look, this is the only pillow I have here. Do you know what it is? We did *The Princess and the Pea* last year in schools. I can't find the other one." "Have you removed the pea?" "Yes, I hope I have."

"This is silly," she said later, scolding herself, "I could very well have managed to get to the subway. Lord, I am tired. And it feels so good to be here," and she yawned helplessly while she pulled the blanket up. Jean Paul checked the fire.

he raked the coals with the poker; behind him, he heard her settling herself on the couch, knew how her long, slender back like a boy's made a warm hollow in the leather upholstery, caught the woolen sigh of the blanket as it hugged her. He turned; his mouth was dry. "The key of—" But she was asleep! Her legs, too long for the small couch were folded, the knees pointing from under the blanket, and her big pile of hair had slipped and lay on her shoulder with a hairpin hanging out. He was disconcerted that she had retired behind her sleep without a word for him, cutting him out.

Then, standing and smiling to himself at the desk, he wrote something on a piece of paper and looked around for a good place to put it. He tried it in one of her shoes, considered the artistic effect; dissatisfied, he moved it into the Whale's mouth and set the Whale close to her.

I am locking you in but there's a second key hanging on the door. You fell asleep while I was trying to tell you this. Don't leave! I'll be down early and take you to the corner for coffee and croissants.

The Whale eyed him suspiciously with its glass eye. He put the light out, left one of the stage lamps on, and moved slowly to the door. He looked back once more hopefully, but she slept very deeply, young people's sleep, careless and sound, the sort of sleep that makes you grow or heal, or the sleep after love-making. On the floor the toes of her shoes met, like children's shoes.

BUT she was gone in the morning when, up early, freshly shaved and smelling of eau de cologne, his coat round his shoulders like an artist's cloak, he gingerly opened the door. The couch was empty, the blanket neatly folded with the puppet pillow on top of it. He looked around for signs of her presence. Had she really been there last night? The bathroom door was half open, the soap still wet—he touched it with one finger—and the towel wrinkled and damp in one corner. The Whale was in the same place, but the note had disappeared, and there was a guilty air on its face, as if it had swallowed the paper.

He went back to the open door and stood out in the

courtyard, disconcerted, looking up. The fog had started to thin away. What was it that he had hoped for?

MOTHER AND I WERE IN THE FIRST ROW of seats last night (not seats, benches, Mother has just corrected me!) attending your first show. I looked at my watch impatiently, and finally I could tell her, it's time, let's go, so we took our seats (reserved?), and sat quite still holding our breath as the blue velvet curtains parted."

The Christmas show brought nothing to quieten her trepidation. It came and went in a single rainy night, a Paris winter night, and left behind a tiredness, a discouragement she would not acknowledge. (Only much later could she look back at that evening with tenderness. The smell of fir branches in a hot room would remind her of her first professional show, of Elsa and her panther hat—Elsa was there too!—and of how, for the first time, as she walked to the subway exhausted and empty, Mark's absence had been shaped out of the wet night under the oblique silver threads of the rain.)

The workshop was crowded the evening of the show, and the puppets displayed on the wall eyed the unfamiliar public resentfully. The folding chairs stacked outside the entrance were brought in and there was only standing room for the performers. A smell of holiday hung in the air, the fir branches nailed over the stage and the door smelt fresh; the stove was too hot. In the audience children fidgeted between their parents' knees. A school crowd; none of the people you would find at Berger's shows—the whole evening felt like a school production. Madame l'Inspectrice des Écoles Maternelles was there ("Do use her whole title when you talk to her," Jean Paul asked Ania the day before), and she shed her coat like a queen's cloak, into Jean Paul's reverent arms. She kept on her wide-brimmed black hat, which blocked half the view of the stage, until Elsa bent forward and serenely asked her to please remove it. There were housewives, and relatives of the performers, and another Inspecteur de Écoles, a tall gentleman with a gray mustache. Ania stood among her classmates in the dress Elsa had lent her, rubbing her hands together, trying not to perspire or brush the wall with her collar, and watched her first audience. Jean Paul's wife had come down too. Her hair was freshly set and it made her look tired. Turning her back to Ania she complained to Madame l'Inspectrice that she hadn't finished packing and they were leaving next day for their country house. She was impatient with the show.

Elsa's entrance was spectacular. She had come in late when Jean Paul had already put the lights out, friendly and loud, and made her way to the best seat. Elsa was mistrustful of puppetry—what kind of career was this for a girl?—but had stitched puppet costumes for Ania late into the night and served as consultant on complicated patterns. She accepted Ania's invitation because she was curious and immediately took Ania's appearance into her own big hands. She "borrowed" a dress for her from the shop. The dress was a striking red wool creation with panther sleeves. "Hm? What do you say?" Elsa inquired, stroking the fur voluptuously. "I can't wear that, Elsa." "You will too! And you're going to put makeup on! Like a grownup!" "I can't work in such tight sleeves, Elsa. I've got to move." Elsa was adamant. She exchanged the dress for a black one, sleeveless, with a huge white collar. "You look like a nun," she shrugged, "but at least it's elegant." When Ania lifted her arms, rehearsing in front of the mirror, the big collar turned up around her face like a funnel. It got in the way. "You'll pin it here, like this," Elsa said, tucking it under with deft fingers. "But I am behind the stage. You only see the puppets!" "Never mind! You come out and bow and show your dress afterward. And take the pin out." It was a nuisance. The taffeta lining made scornful noises, reminding her she must be careful, the dress was only lent to her. Jean Paul was pleased. "You look so grown-up today, Ania? What happened? Let me look at you." He too was changed; he was wearing a narrow blue tie instead of his old-fashioned *lavallière*, and twice during the show he felt for it in the dark to check the knot.

Ania came last on the program, after all the other students

had exhibited their skills, little nursery plays with talking bunnies made out of white wool and green horses with raffia manes. A pleasant elephant looking very relaxed in a straw hat and flowered pants with suspenders introduced the artists, and the audience applauded good-heartedly. Then behind the stage Jean Paul pulled the blue gauze down. Ania took her shoes off and stood terrified in her stockings on the cold floor. "Ready?" Jean Paul asked, his hand on the switch, and ignoring the racing of her heart the record player delivered the music announcing the Whale's entrance.

"Delightful! Perfectly delightful!" the audience applauded loudly when the velvet curtain closed, and there were noisy requests for her to repeat the number. Then she came out from behind the stage to thank the public in her stockings, her hair ruffled. Her puppets were passed around for inspection. "No, it is not exactly a new style," she explained seriously to Monsieur l'Inspecteur, "pantomime with music has been done before. But it suits me best, I think. It means I don't have to make the puppets talk in my terrible accent." Ah, but she spoke quite well, said the gentleman gallantly. She must accept his congratulations: the whole scene looked as if it had been freshly painted in watercolors. And Jonah had such extraordinary eyes. "They are painted pebbles," Ania explained. "Ah, I see," Monsieur l'Inspecteur nodded. "How original!" "The world is full of puppet parts," Ania said. "Your pupil is quite charming." "I've known her since she was a little girl of ten," Jean Paul boasted. "Of nine," Ania corrected him. "Right! Of nine!" And because he could do it casually and openly under everybody's eye, he put his hand on the back of her collar under her ruffled hair, felt the hot skin through the crisp organza and tried to conceal how much and how long he had wanted to do this.

Elsa made her way through the audience, imposing in her panther hat, carefully holding in her generous shape. Jean Paul seemed rather pleased with Elsa when Ania introduced them, and he tilted his head back, amused, with that look of an old retriever sniffing at something intriguing. Elsa acknowledged his look with a quiet flutter of eyelashes, and with a maternal hand straightened Ania's collar.

"Why do you want to leave so early tonight?" Jean Paul asked Ania anxiously. "I won't see you for two weeks now, we're going to the country tomorrow." She was tired, she said. Was she going to be alone in town for the holidays? He looked concerned, displaying the solicitude he staged so well. It irritated her tonight. She'd take the puppets home, she said, she might try to do some work. "Ah, she is too serious," Jean Paul complained to Elsa, and Elsa laughed approvingly and touched her panther hat. "If you really want to leave now," she said, "I'll treat you to a taxi. My shoes are killing me."

A wet night with oblique silver threads of rain; under the streetlights everyone's hair looked white, as if the world had suddenly grown old with worry. "Maybe you should have stayed a bit longer. You've got to be more friendly if you're going to be in the theatre." "I am not going to be 'in the theatre,' Elsa. Puppets are not exactly that." The girl was wasting her time and her youth, Elsa thought, and she wasn't even enjoying herself! Elsa was impatient with the impatience of quick, practical people who can't bear to see waste, waste of energy, waste of time, and have no use for dreams. They have to intervene and advise. If only she knew the right man to pull this girl out of it! She wasn't going to make it in this world. She opened her elegant umbrella, and Ania took her arm and walked in the white, burning cloud of Elsa's perfume while Elsa lectured her. "And all these silly people look like puppets too!" "Yes, they do," Ania said amused, suddenly coming out of her thoughts. "The lady with that horrible big hat! She wouldn't take it off until I asked her to." "Elsa, you didn't!" "Yes, I did! Why not?" "But that was Madame l'Inspectrice des Écoles Maternelles!" "So what? The hat was horrible." "It could cost Jean Paul his position!" "The old man?" "What old man?" "Your teacher. He must be—what?—sixty?" "What are you talking about? He is only fifty-seven!" Elsa looked sideways at Ania's face raised indignantly under the umbrella and nodded, discouraged. "There isn't a single taxi in this damn neighborhood," she said, "my shoes are killing me."

At the corner, in front of the subway stairs, Ania asked suddenly, "Listen, do you think I can still make a long-distance call at this hour?" Elsa consulted her watch, holding her arm high in the light of the streetlamp. "There's a place behind the Bourse. It's open all night long. Do you want me to come with you? Wait, Ania, why are you running? The subway is right here."

THEY waited on a bench for the call to come through. "It'll be a half-hour wait," the operator announced sulkily, and Elsa leaned back against the wall, her eyes half closed, her feet out of her shoes, exercising her toes. "I'll have to buy another pair," she said philosophically, "I'll just have to." The post office was empty, the floor unswept and scattered with paper. And then the phone woke the place up, and Elsa grabbed her muff in fright. *"Mais ne coupez pas,"* the operator shouted into the phone, and signaled to Ania, *"Cabine numéro quatre."* Ania rushed across the room, pushed the door of the booth, shook it; the door resisted; "This way, this way!" Elsa scolded, half raising a buttock; the door opened, banged shut. "Monsieur Mark, please," Ania pleaded breathlessly into the phone. A sleepy, bad-tempered voice answered, "Monsieur Mark isn't here, he's out of town, he'll be back the day after tomorrow. Any message?" "No," she said, "no, but—maybe I could—no, no message, thank you."

SHE SLEPT LATE. Weariness had gathered in her bones, and her limbs ached when she tried to get up. There was a knock on her door at ten o'clock. Elsa must need change for the subway. She spat the toothpaste into the sink, and still holding her toothbrush went to open the door.

In the corridor stood Mark, unrecognizable at first, dark in

234

dark winter coat in the dark corridor; when he raised his hand a branch of mimosa appeared in it.

"But—why didn't you write you were coming? Why didn't you call? I phoned you last night and they told me you were away!" She blinked, blinded by surprise, and with one hand gathered the front of her old housecoat at her neck. "I was afraid you wouldn't let me come." "Why?" she asked unhappily. "Oh, Mark, why should you think I don't want to see you? I would have made myself pretty—of all days I had to sleep late today! I'm always up early but last night we had the Christm—" He wasn't listening; when he took her in his arms her words were lost, buried in his coat. The kiss tasted fresh and cold of toothpaste and winter, and it was only after a while that they recognized each other's taste, hot and clear and familiar. Forgotten, crushed between them, the mimosa shed powdery balls and breathed a damp, bitter protest.

It was strange to lie next to her in a real bed, to see her head buried in a pillow, the blanket pulled up to her chin vaguely imitating the long shape of her nakedness underneath. He thought she looked like a child with fever, her face red and burning after love. "Of course not, I feel fine," she laughed, and from her face his hand went down to her neck and up and down the sweet hill of her breast until, when it reached the girlish swelling of her belly, she turned on her side and lay heavily on his hand. He didn't know if she was calling him or asking for a delay. She was just the way he remembered her, the reserved girl of last summer, the line of her cheek shining white on the dark upholstery, her head turned away from him, alone in her world after he had loved her. He still didn't know what was going on behind the high white forehead, under the pile of hair out of which all the hairpins had fallen, one of them under his elbow on the billow. He waited patiently for her to warm to him again. Every time he brought her close to him, laying her against him, she drew imperceptibly away at first, although she applied herself seriously, naïvely to loving him, wanting to abandon herself. But in the way her palms slid along his naked back he felt how timid she still was, how amazed her happiness, and her thighs shunned the intrusion for a second until, persuaded, her secret world of hot coral opened and she loved him well, just the way he showed her to.

And it was strange to lie in a disheveled bed between coarse linen smelling of chlorine in daytime, and to sleep in tired contentment, your limbs abandoned, your foot possessively taken between two strange ankles, your arm asleep under somebody's hip, the movement of a finger waking up a satiny wave of well-being on your skin. A noise at the door made them stir; the cleaning woman was trying her key in the lock. She gave up and shuffled away, rhythmically banging her dustpan against her broom. The daily hotel noises rolled over their sleep. Someone was calling Tarzan on the first floor, the cello started its morning exercises, steps went along the corridor—"*Est le chat au téléphone, madame?*"— and half-asleep, Mark lifted his head, listened, and then laughed into the pillow and pulled the blanket up over her back.

They did not talk. There was not much time to talk. But he told her the reason for his visit to Paris. With her ear on his chest she listened to the words sounding inside his rib cage, "as if you are speaking from the cellar." "Are you listening or are you playing?" "I'm listening, go on!" "He had to return to Marseilles that evening. When had he come? Yesterday morning; there was an investigation about Armand's death; no, they would not call her. She sat up in bed, pulling the sheet around her, and that whole Callian summer, hot and dry, holding love and death, stood between them. And he had been a whole day and a whole night in the same city as she but he had thought she didn't want to see him. "Why, Mark? Why should you think that?" "What else should I think?" he asked her gravely. "We agreed not to write and not to call, but it seems so much easier for you to keep the agreement that it is for me—this undecided miller's wife," and he drew her gently back to him. The window went slowly gray, then lavender, and the glass started to sweat. It was raining.

"We'll have to have some food," she said late in the afternoon, stirring, shaking herself awake and slipping out of bed. She put on something white and silky, her arms up over her head, her belly and hips flashing silver in the neon light outside the window, unknown and mysterious to him; then she was recognizable again in skirt and blouse as the girl of last summer coming up the road to the mill. Sweeping the

arkness under the bed with one hand, she searched for her
tockings. No, she wouldn't put the light on, the room was so
gly. He watched her put the stockings on; she sat next to
im on the bed, rolled them in a ring then each leg filled in
urn their glassy emptiness. He listened to the little slap the
lastic garters made, and now that she was dressed he was
uddenly curious about that shadow above the top of her
tockings where her skin felt different, and softly searched for
he silver-bellied girl he had just seen in the light from the
window until she stopped protesting and lay gently back.

The second attempt at getting dressed was successful, and
soon she stood in her raincoat, lifted her collar and waved at
him. "But if the shops are closed here, I'll have to go all the
way up to Rue Cardinal Lemoine and it'll take a while." She
was going to lock him in. He slept. The noise of her key in
the lock woke him up, and two oranges rolling on the bed
shone like copper balls in the dark room. They listened to
Christmas Eve sweeping through the hotel. People were taking turns at the bath at the end of the corridor and returned
from there whistling cheerfully. The air was steamy and the
smell of a roast came from the lobby. They stood at the
window under the same housecoat and looked at the black
sky irrigated with lavender neon light. Down in the street
somebody had started celebrating early and was singing "La
Marseillaise" with all his might. His shape leaned against the
wall of the post office across the street; the song was interrupted respectfully while he urinated, then resumed with
renewed enthusiasm.

Was it sadness? No, not sadness. It was something unknown to her as yet. The rich, generous melancholy of
fulfillment, of standing with both your feet on a small island
of present with no past and no future. She noticed how Mark
put on his shoes, setting each foot on the chair in turn, a
knee against his chest. He did this at the beach, putting his
feet on a stone to lace his blue espadrilles, and at the mill
after a swim on the mill step. It made her smile. The room
looked sad and ugly with the light on, but just then the
late-afternoon wave of steam heat started to cross the hotel,
banging boisterously inside the radiators, and in a minute it
felt cozy. Her puppets appeared out of the dark on the top of
the dresser, and Mark stopped to look at them in silence.

"This is Jonah," she explained, "and this is his Whale. You missed the greatest puppet show of the year yesterday. If I'd known you were in town I'd have invited you." She took them out, made them work for him, showed him how old Jonah was swallowed by the Whale through the hidden pocket in its pink silk mouth. He watched them with the air of amusement and incredulity he had had looking at her puppets in Callian.

"And how is it going?" he asked at last, obviously meaning Jean Paul but not wanting to mention his name. He stretched out a hand and touched Jonah's nose with his finger. "Has it been a good meeting?" She didn't answer. She looked stubborn for a second, the old stubbornness of last summer, and then she put her head on his neck, shutting out truth, blind and deaf, and he hugged her, rocked her in the smell of his skin, of his coat, of his sweater. "Certainly," she said at last, "quite a good meeting." But he knew, rocking her, how rigid her loyalty was and how painful her effort to simulate. "Any message for me to bring the miller from the miller's wife?" he said into her hair, and instantly she drew back. "She hasn't learned how to cook the soup yet," she said. He didn't know what she meant but he lifted her face with both hands and her kiss was open and generous and new, a woman's kiss, and it enclosed all she knew about love.

She couldn't go with him to the station. The Jacques were going to drive him to the train. She could only go with him to the bus. They walked silently through the drizzle to the next bus stop, and then to the next one, and then to another corner. But it was late. They kissed a long time before the bus came, with the taste of rain and fog, with lips parched by the day of love, a smell of oranges floating around their mouths, and after the bus took him away she stood still on the curb, lonely.

"Allez, vous en faites pas, ma belle! He'll be back, I saw how he kissed you!" said someone next to her, and clicking its tongue encouragingly, a wet silhouette crossed the street mumbling to itself, unsteady on its feet, and disappeared through the door of the bistro.

WAS IT THE SEASON, a season adverse to affection, to intimacy, to miracles? Paris was having a raw winter that year. Vague blue silhouettes walked in the fog, a scarf tied over the collar, one long fringed end dangling. The smell of the subway was everywhere, and the damp stirred up the moldering air inside the old Paris houses. Sometimes the front of a cathedral shimmered out of the fog; the faces of the stone saints dripped with drizzle, their ascetic brows perspiring under holy pains.

The pigeons gave up their gossip and decided to hibernate high up along the roof gutters. But looking down into the street, they still could see the same elderly gentleman in his tight winter coat walking his girl to the garden square. They met every afternoon now. As he bent his head toward her his hat made a tender shadow on the girl's shoulder, and the pigeons, intrigued, watched it slowly advance toward her cheek. Ah, but it was too cold! It was too cold to go down into the square and walk behind them. They were not lovers, you could tell that. The pigeons gave up gossip and crouched motionless, bundled into gray knitted shawls, their lavender satin, the color of Paris spring sunsets, gone now.

One day the cold loosened its grip. A premonition of change was in the air at noon, when the neighborhood cats ventured to sit blinking in the anemic sun. The promise ended brusquely around three o'clock in the afternoon, when winter returned. But at Magasins Réunis the tables of cheap merchandise had been put outside and unhappy salesladies in heavy coats and boots stamped their feet on the sidewalk. Winter still lingered for a while around Les Halles. Truck drivers with clothes stained by raw meat and men with hands swollen by frost and hard work strode past open stalls covered with frozen fowls and chunks of lard and barrels full of fish with viscous eyes, making for the warm bistros. They came out with a toothpick stuck into the corner of their mouths, clearing their throats, looking up at the changing weather. Winter was ending.

ANIA felt it coming; she had a warning the last time she saw Jean Paul and they walked through a frozen, deserted Luxembourg; she feared it would happen. He stopped at the end of the empty pool, preoccupied with what he was going to say, took off his gloves, rolled them absently into a ball, and instead of putting them in his pocket, started to draw them on again. All of a sudden a pang of panic jolted her heart. Casually she put a hand over the spot, then noticed that she had forgotten to mend her glove again, and hid the hand in her pocket, secretly enduring the velvety throbbings that fear induced in her. "I have to go back now," she said finally, "I really do," and at the gate of the park she put her hand out. Jean Paul took it and held it, and seemed to search again for the beginning of that hovering sentence. Two nuns in white bonnets like the paper boats children make sailed past them through the gray afternoon, and what he had to tell her was postponed again. He only played for a second with her fingers, undecided, and discovering the torn place in her glove, felt for her fingertip; a teasing, tender smile came to his face. The smile reassured her.

But she didn't go to class next day. She felt tired and thought she was coming down with a cold. Early next morning the telephone rang. "What is the matter?" Jean Paul asked. "A big cold or a small one? Is the room warm enough? Can you make tea for yourself? This means we can't go for a walk today." He was his usual gay self, and yesterday's premonition vanished. But late in the afternoon there was a knock on the door and there he stood, a little embarrassed, holding a bag of oranges in both hands. Surprise prevented her from bothering about the room's disorder. She had just made tea, she explained, and took the camp stove off the only chair and put it on the floor. "So this is where you live," he said, and she looked around too. "It's a workshop. I can't keep it very tidy."

And then it happened right there in her own room, just

when she had stopped worrying about it. It happened as she picked up one of the oranges, pierced its skin with her nail and sniffed at its winter smell. "Isn't it ridiculous," he said before she could stop him, "I'll soon be sixty."

"You are fifty-seven," she said.

"What difference does it make? You are going to be twenty for a long time—"

"Jean Paul—" she pleaded, but he ignored her panic and swept on. She couldn't stop him. She looked up at him, at the scarf hanging around his neck, at the arm propped on the shabby tablecloth, at the hand on his knee. She hated to see him old and defeated. Turning to the window, she put the orange to her mouth, pushed her teeth into it. It yielded an acid, transparent blood, and for a second her mind ran into hiding, shut her eyes, blocked her ears. She came to herself to hear him say, ". . . I must have trapped myself in so many miracles—" She rubbed the wounded orange on her sweater. We both did that, she thought. He had come to stand behind her, and his desire, his begging eyes, were burning her back. She had to turn and face him. She put a perspiring, trembling hand on the windowpane and turned to him: "Jean Paul, we both—"

The kiss tasted of nothing, of hot dry undesired lips, and she waited with open eyes, listened to the storm rising in the stranger facing her. But nothing reached her, except maybe the faint sound of a door banging in a deserted house, a foggy silhouette walking on a garden path under a large umbrella, a dizziness like a concert of crickets. Down in the street, in the present, a woman's voice called, *"Henrrri, veux-tu rentrer!"* a child shouted, a car engine started. With authority, he laid her head on his shoulder. But he wasn't tall enough and she felt uncomfortable. His watch ticked in his vest pocket.

"You've got to go," she said, "you'll be late for class."

He discarded the class with a wave of his hand; the other took her shoulder, and his flushed face, his short white quivering eyelashes begged her again, very close. She stepped out of his hands, unable to bear his eyes. "You have to go."

And then the moment split and each of them held half of it; the halves were never going to match again. She had seen him before, hadn't she, leaving like this, tweedy and small, opening a door without turning, his head slightly cocked.

> *C'est la reine d'Angleterre*
> *qui est tombée par terre*

THEY WERE BACK. The afternoon voices were back. The earth had completed its cycle methodically, unrushed; the season had changed without the help of the miracle man. A playful sun bathed the stern houses, fondled their wrought-iron balconies, stole glances through open doors. The houses spilled out children and children's voices onto the sidewalk:

> *Na-po-lé-on Pre-mier*
> *vou-lut la re-le-ver*

Was it spring? "So soon?" the cello asked. "Ah, beware!" But everyone knew it was spring. "*Voilà le printemps, Madame!*" and as soon as Madame Blais heard this, she promptly cut the heat off. The rooms felt like vaults, and if Ania sat still for any length of time, she had to put her winter coat on.

"Ania!" Elsa had on a new red-and-white-checked spring suit and new patent-leather shoes. "Ania!" "Yes." "What are you doing here hugging that beast? He's full of moths!" Tarzan opened his eye and pierced Elsa with its green poison. Heavy and tamed, fitted into the scoop of Ania's lap, he closed his eye approvingly and turned on the motor he carried inside him, setting it on low. He liked this foreign girl, he really did, he liked her smell.

"What are you doing here?" "Nothing." "Let's go across the street for coffee. I want you to meet someone." "I am not going out today, Elsa." "What's the matter? Are you sick." "No, I just don't feel like going out." "You didn't go out yesterday either, and the day before it was the same story. Have you stopped going to the workshop too?" Classes have ended." "So soon?" "I'm tired, I cut a class or two. I haven't missed much." "But you're not sick or something?" "Oh, for heaven's sake Elsa, I am not sick! I am not sick!" "All right, what are you shouting for? I'll go on my own." The high heels clanked back from the door. Elsa had changed her mind. "Listen, Ania." "What now?" "Are you late? Every woman is late once in a while, you shouldn't start worrying before you know for sure!" Tarzan opened his eye, alarmed by the little earthquakes he felt under his belly. The foreign girl was laughing without noise; he liked that, he liked quiet people.

She wouldn't go out. The little garden in the square was suddenly full of young new mothers, chattering and arranging the sleepy contents of their baby carriages, and a sickening damp breeze stirred up an odor of baby food. The pigeons came close to look at her with twitchy amber eyes and told each other in staccato pecks like Morse code, "She's alone now, *en voilà une histoire!*"

She was still protected from spring while she stayed in her room. It would take a while for the new season to conquer the old house and make its way upstairs. The reek of the food fried surreptitiously during the winter, the sick-yellow stained-glass window in the corridor, the gray courtyard— they would oppose the change. The early-morning air, crisp and new and full of the unsettling future, was smuggled into the hotel inside the mailman's pouch. The letters he brought smelled good in your hand. "Spring is here too, having come furtively in the same old way," Father wrote. "We thought you were going to stay on and prepare a show for the fall. But maybe Jean Paul is going away for the summer—you didn't mention him in your last letter—and then of course you'd be better off in the south. What would a hot and empty Paris be like without him?"

> *C'est la reine d'Angleterre*
> *qui est tombée par terre*

Paris without him! Poor miracle man, she was leaving him. "Genuine puppeteers don't need me for long. They have to

243

be on their own. You'll do the same." "I am faithful"—and she was leaving him.

A correct, sober knock on her door made her stir. Carefully she put Tarzan down on the bed and went to open the door. In a spring coat and a new hat worn low over his ears, his round blond face shining with confidence, Monsieur Arno stood in the corridor. The air around him smelled sweet and tender of frail woodland green and fresh tears, and as he lifted his hat the other hand advanced toward her. "May I offer, Mademoiselle Annie?" "It's a French custom on May First." A little bunch of lilies of the valley shone in his hand. "Yes? Is it? Oh, how lovely, how lovely of you!" she said, embarrassed. "Do you have these flowers at home in the woods too?" Her high, clear voice enchanted him. She looked tired and vulnerable with her hair hanging down and her winter coat on her shoulders; maybe she had been crying—ah, who could make a girl like that cry! She put the flowers to her face. "They are still cold." Somebody flushed the toilet at the end of the corridor. Wasn't she going to invite him into her room? He cleared his throat. "I also wish to question you. Would you like to hear the concert tonight? I have two free chairs." Oh, she was sorry, she couldn't tonight. His face became less round and the glow dimmed. "Maybe some other time," he suggested hopefully. She was leaving next week, she said. Oh, was she? His hand pressed his new coat against his knees, effacing him from the corridor, from the world—"*Wie soll ich meine Seele halten.*"—So he was late. He was too late! He had hesitated a whole winter about asking her to a concert. But could you stop a girl like that in the corridor when you were wearing your bathrobe and say Mademoiselle Annie, I have two free chairs to the concert? And only today, *le jour du Muguet*, with his new spring coat and the lilies of the valley, he had at long last dared—and he was late. "Oh, so you are leaving us," and by "us" he meant the winter and its sadnesses, or maybe himself and his cello. He nodded sadly. But it was spring, after all, it was spring, and even his disappointment had a certain sweetness, because it was caused by her. His secret desire detached itself from him like a leaf, and floated away under their eyes. His sad clown eyes became a bit sadder as he put on his hat so that he could take it off again and solemnly take his leave.

IT CAME LIKE A GAY EXPLOSION. Driven by an extraordinary force the trees on the boulevard pushed out their leaves in a single night, a warm voluptuous one, a night of love. And next day the entire city demurely lowered its eyelids, let down the awnings over elegant shops and dignified hotels. Careless and light-headed, spring burst through the door of the Hôtel Impérial, swept past Madame Blais, ruffled her shawl, hurled itself up the stuffy staircase. On the lobby counter Tarzan opened his eye and sniffed at the air expertly. Yes, this was it!

Gayer, higher, the exuberant May breeze twirled up the stairs, knocked down a mop propped against a pail, banged shut the toilet door, and sent Elsa's laughter rolling down the stairs. Elsa was standing on the landing in a flowered housecoat saying into the telephone, "So are you coming this evening?" and then she laughed. Or maybe it was a pigeon gurgling on the roof. And only the cello tried to keep sober; out of the great sad belly the bow tore the same melancholy sound, "Ooom!" and all the incurable anguish of the world clung to it. But you had to understand the cello; its room looked out onto a courtyard piled high with rubbish, where a whiskered rat with worried, insomniac eyes swished through the empty boxes at dusk. It would take spring a long time to conquer that damp smelly patch; it would take Monsieur Arno a long time to find another girl. But on the street side of the hotel the winter was over.

SHE stood at the door of the workshop twisting a big mother-of-pearl button on her summer suit. The suit was a bit too big for her; she must have lost weight, and anyway she had never had an eye for clothes, except puppet clothes. But the suit had a honey color that made her look blonder and glowed in the dark studio when she paused in the doorway.

For a second Jean Paul raised his head in surprise. But the surprise melted and fondness invaded his eyes; he looked tired and older. "Come," he said gently, and took her arm, "come in. You're late, the course ended yesterday. Everybody asked about you." She nodded, yes, she knew. "I came to say good-bye. I am leaving." He ignored the news for a moment. "Ah," he said, waving his hand as if dismissing a trifle, "you graduated long ago. You really didn't need any of this stuff we hand out here, you knew that. Sit down if you can find a place. I was packing the puppets. I always have to store them away after classes." "Let me help you," she said.

She knelt on the floor and with knowledgeable hands folded costumes, stuffed sleeves with tissue paper, smoothed hair and buttoned collars, then passed the puppets to Jean Paul, who stored them in a trunk standing against the wall. It smelled of mothballs. They worked in silence. They had worked like this before, in his attic, moving through the aquarium light with the garden asleep under the windows. He was completely absorbed in what he was doing; he always worked like that. "Your Majesty," he said, lifting the big king and examining him in the light, "I am afraid I'll have to take off Your Majesty's pants. They need mending." He heard her laugh, and it made him happy. Her head came up, her hair ruffled. "Do you know that song the children sing on the street? I heard them again this morning. '*Na-po-lè-on Premier vou-lut la re-le-ver.*'" She sang in a high, child's voice. "Wouldn't it make a good number for puppets, with a court dance first?" Her reserve melted, and she put the fat king under her arm, took him to the drawer where Jean Paul kept the sewing box, and matched some thread with his velvet pants. Then she sat under the window at the far end of the bench and put a few stitches through the royal belly, while the king lay spread ecstatically on his back, his head hanging between her knees, his beard pointing at the ceiling. She bit off the thread busily; it made her look like a worried housewife loaded with responsibilities. Jean Paul smiled. Maybe it was the suit, or that old-fashioned knot at the neck of her white blouse, but today she looked older, grown-up,

vere and chaste, like the young woman who sometimes sits
pposite you on a train and covers her knees when she feels
our eyes on her and then leans back lost in her own
oughts. But you know from the look of her slim, nervous
nkle and from the soft curve of her thigh that if she were to
ove you she would love you well, her warm, fresh weight
eaped on you and smelling of— He chased the thought
way.

The king went into the trunk and they were through. Jean
Paul poured moth flakes on top of the puppets—he looked
ke a sorcerer making a little blizzard out of a paper bag—
nd then closed the lid. "There," he said, wiping his hands on
is handkerchief, "that's done now." And then, proving that
e had heard her and had been only turning the news over in
is mind, "When are you leaving?" "Tuesday." He nodded.
He sat with both hands on his knees, like an old gentleman
aking the air on a bench, and then put up a hand and
shrugged, a gesture of defeat. "*Eh bien, voilà,*" he said.
What else could he do for her now? All his tricks were used,
spent. Her heart went out to him. She put her hand on his
sleeve, and he took it but felt her reluctance to leave it in
his. With deliberate restraint he laid her hand palm up
between them and took his away. "Puppeteer," he said looking at her hand, "I can see your future. Your past *and* your
future. You have no secrets."

"What does the past say?" she asked gently.

"It's all here. You've been the sorcerer's apprentice."

"That is true. And the future?"

"You're getting married and you'll have twelve children."

"I don't know about getting married yet." She frowned at
her thoughts. He looked at her and said, "Ah," as if he were
fitting the pieces together. "And about the twelve children—
it's a slight error. You must mean twelve puppets."

"So you're not going to quit."

"But why should I quit?"

"I don't know. I thought you were. What are you going to
do then?"

"Try"—she looked up at him and smiled—"try it first in a
summer theatre, in a barn in a village. What do you think of
that?"

"It'll do you good! Where are you going?"

She hesitated. "To Marseilles first and then in June to the same children's camp I was at last summer. Callian."

"Is it—near Nice?" She nodded. "And who's going to travel all the way to the theatre to see your show?"

"I thought it would be just for the children at first, you know, a very modest sort of art, so beginning on my own won't scare me. And if I look after the children only part-time, I'll be able to change my show every week. And I'm sure the village would come, although I don't quite know how they'll take it, they're a bit, well, staid. And then I thought if I'm lucky I could move the show to a city in the fall. Oh, I don't know, I'm dreaming, it'll depend on—other things too."

He said, "I didn't know someone was waiting for you." She simply nodded "yes." He waited, but she made no attempt to explain and after a while his hand rose in the same defeated gesture. "*Eh voilà*," he said. There was a long silence. "Wait while I put my shoes on, I'll take you to the subway." She heard him drop a slipper behind the blue velvet curtain and knock the shoehorn against a chair. "I mustn't forget my whale," she said to the curtain, "it's going to be the star of the show," she unhooked it from its wooden peg. Holding it close with both hands she turned around and took a long look at the workshop. "It rained the day I first came," she said. "It did?" "And you didn't remember my name." "What? Who didn't remember your name?" "You!" She imitated their conversation: " 'What is your name again?' 'But I know you!' 'I beg your pardon!' " "Nobody could ever forget your name now," he said, reappearing. Holding the curtain open with one hand he bowed like a circus ringmaster: "Mademoiselle Ania, the greatest puppeteer of our times." Ah, he was like that, he had always been like that—and she laughed hadn't he paced up and down in front of the mirror in the old house, the velvet bedspread trailing on the floor? He felt she was only half in the game, and he let the curtain go. "Here is a box you can take for your whale. Is it warm outside?" he asked, filling his pockets with the keys and small change on the table. "I never know in this cellar what it's like outside." He unhooked the big key from the door. She watched him for the last time intently, to remember how he bent, how he turned the key in the lock, and how he stepped aside to let her go out first— "That suit is too big for you, it's got to be taken in at the sides," he said. "Yes, I know." "But the color is lovely!" "Isn't it, but Mother's old tailor isn't too familiar with Paris styles." He laughed, and after that she could smile too; the key was turned in the lock, and he bent to hide it under the doormat and straightened up with a little groan. Outside, they realized with surprise, it was summer.

Dusk was coming. Warm dusk, dusty and rosy, the city tipsy with the new season, tingling with the approach of the summer night. A thousand windows reflected the pink haze at the edge of the sky. Gold powder hung in the air, and a seductive warmth touched your skin, slipped away, came back. The lovers were out.

"Are we going to have another sad parting?" she asked when they stopped at the subway entrance and leaned on the railing. "The last time this happened you were trying to explain something to me and I was crying."

"Well, I notice some progress. I'm not trying to explain anything and you aren't crying—so far. What is there to cry about? Wasn't it beautiful that you came, and that I had you, half real and half imagined, and all this—" He didn't say what, but his hand drew a half-circle in the sky, a ribboned arch for an invisible puppet stage. Yes, she nodded, yes, like the old ride on the stars, but, "Ah, Jean Paul," she burst out.

"I know," he said gently, his hand on her elbow, "I know. Maybe I should explain after all. But listen, I am not repenting or trying to apologize. Understand that? I was a bit in love with you"—she looked away—"I'm a bit less in love already, even though I'll go on being in love with you until summer, perhaps until next winter. But we aren't going to worry about it, are we? I'm always a bit in love with every woman—if you don't understand that, it's because you're too young. But what I was going to say is that with you—"

A train passed below the ground, the noise drowned his words, the hem of her skirt danced, people came rushing up the stairs, the noise died.

". . . With you I thought it was going to be something

extraordinary. Only a certain kind of imagination, like yours and mine, deserves that. But we must have failed somewhere. Ah, you're too young and that makes you too serious and you don't believe that old people know how to love better than young ones. I thought I could teach you—" He felt he was making her uncomfortable. "There," he said, releasing her elbow, "go to Marseilles to your—I hope he isn't another puppeteer." Her frank laughter reassured him. "Of course not," and she laughed again.

"What does he do then?"

"He's a mathematician."

"That's quite right for you. I've noticed you can't count. And as deadly serious as you, I suppose. You'll look like a pair of deadly serious pigeons." A memory flickered through her smile, a memory that excluded him. "That's enough! I don't even want to consider his existence. And what will they think of him at home? I feel a bit responsible, you know."

His display of responsibility hurt for a second, but she pushed it away; he was like that, she knew he was like that.

"They'll like him," she said smiling, looking down at her shoes. But when she looked up again, her eyes shimmered as if their blue was about to spill over. "Please," she said seriously, "tell me something—something good, something great, a real parting word, something I can—"

"Something you can engrave on your memory forever so that next time we meet you can wave it at me and ask me how I could forget such a thing, and tell me it's my fault again?" She nodded violently, and the tear clinging to her eyelashes rolled down her cheek—but the tear wasn't blue. "Well," he said solemnly, "whatever happens to them, puppeteers have to stay generous—did you know that?"

She took his head between her hands and quickly and impetuously, like a woman, planted two hearty kisses on his cheeks. "*Au revoir, Jean Paul*," she said. And twice, as her head came close to his, the warm air vibrated with her presence; the smell of her hair and of her skin enfolded him; bliss shot through him. He reached out to hold her just for a moment, warm and fresh and serious, just for a single moment. But she had already stepped back to the top of the stairs and was now going down without turning back. He saw

her down to the waist, then to the shoulders, then he could
see only the top of her soft hair; he heard the door below
pulled open and swing shut.

ABOUT THE AUTHOR

MARGUERITE DORIAN was born in Bucharest, Roumania, and studied at the University of Bucharest and the Sorbonne before coming to America in 1952 to study at Brown University where she received a Master of Science degree. Her publications include a volume of Roumanian verse, a book for children in French, and two children's books which she wrote and illustrated in this country: *When the Snow is Blue* and *The Alligator's Toothache*. Her first work for adults was a *novella*, part of which appeared in *The New Yorker*. In 1965 she was a scholar at the Breadloaf Writers Conference, and won an associate scholarship to the Radcliffe Institute for the year 1966-67. She and her husband live in Providence, Rhode Island, where she is at work on a new novel.

The Politics of
Experience

R. D. Laing

Given the conditions of contemporary civilization how can one claim that the "normal" man is sane?

In this already famous book, a young British psychiatrist attacks the Establishment assumptions about "normality" with a radical and challenging view of the mental sickness built into our society . . .

"He has let us know. He has told us in such a way that we can not disregard it. . . . He speaks to no one but you and me."—Los Angeles Free Press

A BALLANTINE BOOK   **$.95**

To order by mail, send $1.00 (price of book plus 5¢ postage and handling) to: Dept. CS, Ballantine Books, 101 Fifth Avenue, New York, N.Y. 10003.

The great masterpieces of fantasy by
J. R. R. TOLKIEN

The Hobbit

and

The Lord of the Rings

Part I—The Fellowship of the Ring

Part II—The Two Towers

Part III—The Return of the King

plus

The Tolkien Reader